PENGUIN BOOKS

Crimes of Cupidity

Raven Kennedy is a California girl born and raised, whose love for books pushed her into creating her own worlds. The Plated Prisoner Series, a dark fantasy romance, has already sold in over a dozen countries and is a #1 international bestseller with over 1 million copies sold to date. It was inspired by the myth of King Midas and a woman's journey with finding her own strength. Her debut series was a romcom fantasy about a cupid looking for love of her own. She has since gone on to write in a range of genres. Whether she makes you laugh or cry, or whether the series is about a cupid or a gold-touched woman living in King Midas's gilded castle, she hopes to create characters that readers can root for. The Plated Prisoner series is being adapted for series by Peter Guber's Mandalay Television.

CRIMES OF CUPIDITY

HEART HASSLE BOOK THREE

RAVEN KENNEDY

PENGUIN BOOKS

PENGUIN BOOKS

UK | USA | Canada | Ireland | Australia
India | New Zealand | South Africa

Penguin Books is part of the Penguin Random House group of companies
whose addresses can be found at global.penguinrandomhouse.com

First published in the United States of America by Raven Kennedy 2019
First published in Great Britain by Penguin Books 2023
001

Edited by Polished Perfection
Printed and bound in Great Britain by Clays Ltd, Elcograf S.p.A.

The authorized representative in the EEA is Penguin Random House Ireland,
Morrison Chambers, 32 Nassau Street, Dublin D02 YH68

A CIP catalogue record for this book is available from the British Library

ISBN: 978–1–405–96085–4

www.greenpenguin.co.uk

MIX
Paper | Supporting
responsible forestry
FSC® C018179

Penguin Random House is committed to a
sustainable future for our business, our readers
and our planet. This book is made from Forest
Stewardship Council® certified paper.

To all the cupids, the matchmakers, the wallflowers, and the bridesmaids. It's your turn.

CHAPTER 1

Great. Just great.

It's my first mission as a super spy, and I'm already screwing it up by getting my ass yanked out of the realm. There's nothing I can do as my incorporeal self is transported to Veil headquarters, aka Cupidville.

After a nauseating little jaunt through space and time, I pop into Cupidville's waiting area. There are cupids everywhere, so it's a sea of pink hair and red wings. Most of them are awaiting judgment, just like me. Some of them will get promotions or better assignments. Some of them will get demotions or disciplined. And some of them...some of them will get terminated. Poof. Gone. Bye-bye, cupid.

And yeah, there's a pretty good chance that's what is about to happen to me.

Anxiety claws at me as I try to get my bearings. The reality of my situation slams into me when I look up and find myself directly in front of the glass reception area for the huge waiting room. It basically looks like a massive doctor's office with lovey-dovey heart paraphernalia everywhere.

Normally, when I get yanked to Cupidville's waiting room, I get plopped down at the seating area with the rest of the love schmucks. But being yanked directly in front of reception? Yeah, I don't think that's a good sign. I've been shirking my cupid duties and...yeah, they're probably not happy with me about that.

Fear grips me with the knowledge that I might actually be about to lose everything. My genfins. All three of them are so different, and all of them hold a special piece of my heart. Then there's my lamassu mate, Okot. The most gentle, adoring bull-man ever. It's a motley covey, but the four of them are mine, and just the thought of them being taken away from me makes me nauseated. I'd miss my new fae friends, too, like the earth sprite, Mossie, the cleaning hearth hob, Duru, and the Horned Hook, Belren. Not to mention the princess of the realm. I'm pretty sure we're friends, too.

If I get terminated...

No. I can't let that happen. I just *can't*. If I get terminated and never see my mates again...

Pain slices through me at the thought, deep in my immaterial gut.

"Cupid."

Startled out of my fearful thoughts, I blink and notice that the cupid behind the glass is glaring at me. She has an afro of curly pink hair and a mountain of paperwork beside her. She's dressed in a smart business suit and bright green retro glasses. Her no-nonsense expression makes me feel instantly chastised, like my mere presence is putting her behind schedule.

I take a tentative step back from her. "Sorry. I'll just wait over there…"

"Cupid one thousand fifty," she snaps. "Step forward."

Oh gods. They aren't even going to make me wait. Being popped right in front of the reception area and being called forward right away *can't* be good, right?

When I don't answer or move, she sighs. "Cupid number one thou—"

I jump forward quickly. "Right. Yeah, sorry."

"You are to report to room number one."

My mouth drops open in an O shape. "Umm. Number one?" I ask, holding up a single finger. "Like number one, as in the *first* room? The one where the boss of *all* bosses is? That room?" My voice grows higher and higher with each word.

She arches a penciled eyebrow at me. "Correct. Room number one. As I said."

I try to put my finger in my mouth to start biting my nail, only to remember I can't since I'm in my incorporeal state. I quickly drop it after my finger goes through my face. "Right. I guess I'll just go straight there, then?"

She levels me with an unimpressed look. Even her wrinkles seem to be glaring at me.

"Okay. I'll just go. To room number one. To meet with the big boss. Because he called me. Specifically."

"Have a cupidly good day," she drones, already moving on to call the next cupid forward.

I head to the doorway that leads to the offices as slowly as I can. Maybe I should make a break for it now? I have a bad feeling about being called to meet the highest of the higher-ups.

I enter the long corridor and stare at the door at the end with the huge number one on it. It's outlined in a heart, and there's an arrow going through it, as if that happy little emblem is somehow supposed to make me feel better about being called here. It doesn't.

As soon as I'm in front of the door, I hear a gruff voice telling me to enter. I float through and stop to take in my surroundings. Every surface inside the big boss's office is shiny. The floor is shiny red marble. The desk is shiny white wood. There's a shiny wall with shiny cupid numbers posted with some weird employee of the month mural. And, you guessed it, it shines.

I float past a bookshelf filled with cupidity books. There's the classic "From Courting to Sexting: A History in Love" proudly displayed, and "Stupid Cupids: What Not to Do While on the Job" is beside it. Yeah, I'm pretty sure I'm mentioned in that one. Then there's a real teaser called "Sixty-Nine: Why It's Not Just Another Number."

Three guys are waiting for me behind a long table. The one in the middle is the boss man. Red wings, pink hair, and a wicked frown on his middle-aged face.

As if he's not enough to freak me out, there are two more males sitting on either side of him, glaring at me. And they aren't cupids. One has white wings, and the other has black.

Gulp.

What do you get when you walk into a room with an angel, a cupid, and a demon?

Probably fucked. And not in the good way.

CHAPTER 2

Mr. Demon on the left has inky hair and black reptilian wings. There's a row of stiff black feathers poking out along the top edge of his wings and then thorns hooked at the ends.

The angel on the right has golden hair. Literally. It looks like each strand has been spun from gold threads. His wings are white and feathered, and he's so pretty that he's hard to look at.

"Sit," the cupid superior says.

They don't give me any greetings or smiles. Unease fills me as I float to a chair and hover above it. I have to play this cool. Maybe I can get myself out of this? It wouldn't be the first time I've had to talk my way out of being terminated.

So, I do what I do best. I slap a smile on my face and use my friendly charm. I nonchalantly lean my elbow on the armrest, but…yeah, my charm is insta-shattered when my arm goes through it, and my head jerks up awkwardly. The demon chuckles under his breath. Good thing I don't have a body, because I'm pretty sure I'd be blushing with embarrassment.

I clear my throat and sit up again, hovering properly over the chair. "So, what...um, what brings you guys here?" Gods, I sound like I'm trying to pick them up at a bar.

None of them answers me, and I really hate the silent-judgy look that they're all giving me. I turn to my cupid boss. "Nice office you got here. Really shiny. And big. Plenty of room to really stretch your wings, huh?" He doesn't answer. "Congrats on being the top corporate cupid. That's gotta be exciting stuff."

I spot something green on the other side of the room. "Oh, is that a golf putt-putt set?" I ask, craning my head to look past the angel. "I once watched these teenagers playing mini-golf, and it looked really fun! Well, it did until I accidentally blew too much Lust at them, and they started going at it in the windmill on hole thirteen. The police were called." I tilt my head in thought. "Actually, now that I think about it, I'm pretty sure it became a big scandal. It was in their local newspaper and everything. The boy might've lost his scholarship... Anyway, the point is, golf looks fun."

Hmm. Probably best not to bring up my stupid cupid moments to the head honcho.

The angel places his hands on the sides of his chair and looks me up and down with obvious derision. "*You* are cupid one thousand fifty?"

I narrow my eyes slightly at his tone. "I prefer to be called Emelle."

"Excuse me?"

I show him my wrist. "You know, ML? Emelle? It's easier to say than cupid one thousand fifty. Quicker. More

6

efficient. You guys look like you're all about efficiency, am I right?" I smile, trying to sell it. He frowns. I'm not selling it.

I steal a glance at boss man's wrist. Aside from his cupid number in the Roman numerals, CD, he also has an arrow-pierced heart marking below that, designating that he's the top cupid boss. "CD," I muse aloud. "Can I call you Seedy?"

"No."

"Listen, Seedy, sometimes it's nice to have a name, you know?" I look at him, but he looks back at me like he does not, in fact, know.

I look at the other two. "I bet you guys have names, right?"

Seedy looks like he wants to put me in a choke-hold, but the angel answers, "I am Raziel. Angel representative."

I nod in greeting and look over at the demon expectantly. Seedy motions to him. "This is the demon representative, Jerkahf."

A snort escapes me before I can stop it.

The demon narrows his black eyes at me, and literal smoke starts billowing off of him. "Is something funny?"

I shake my head adamantly. "Nope. No. Nothing funny at all." A little whimpered giggle crawls out of my mouth like a traitor.

His eyes flash with the fires of hell. It's super scary. "Are you laughing at my name? You think 'Jerkahf' holds some hilarity in it?"

I press my lips together as tightly as I can to keep from laughing, but it's *really* freaking hard. The way he's staring at me makes it even worse. It's a whole lot of added pressure. I don't do well under pressure. Kind of like those

7

uncontrollable laughing fits you get in the middle of a funeral.

"It's a family name," he defends. "There are many highly respected Jerkahfs."

Don't laugh, don't laugh, don't—

Laughter bubbles up my throat and strangles me on its way out. A half-laugh, half-choke comes gurgling out of me no matter how much I try to stop it. I only manage to cut my inappropriate laughter off with a noise that sounds suspiciously like a burp, and I try to clamp my incorporeal hands over my mouth to stop from embarrassing myself further.

The smoke dissipates as the demon sighs. "Did you get that out of your system?"

I nod vigorously because I don't trust myself to speak.

Seedy clears his throat. "Let's get back to the matter at hand. You have been summoned here in the presence of three Veil Majors."

I look between the three of them. "Wait, *cupids* are considered as important as angels and demons?"

The demon smirks at my question, but boss man looks affronted. "Of course we are. Life, love, and death," he says, motioning to each one of them in succession. "Life and death aren't much of anything without love," he finishes defensively.

I nod vigorously to appease him. "Yeah, obviously. We cupids are totally Major material."

"Moving on," he says, ignoring me. "We have received very disturbing reports about you."

I look at him innocently. "Oh?"

He pulls out a pink folder and starts slapping heart-shaped papers down in front of me. "This one says you failed to incite lust and desire on just over five-thousand available opportunities. This one says you failed to create any lasting Love Matches since being assigned in the fae realm. This one says you used Love Arrows multiple times on the same male, exceeding the three Love Arrow limit by…" He skims the paper. "By thirty-two arrows." He looks pissed. "That means you hit him with *thirty-five* arrows in a row."

I give him a sheepish look. "Whoops."

Seedy doesn't look like he appreciates my response.

"But," the angel cuts in, "what's even more disturbing is that you have been manipulating the Veil."

I squirm my intangible body under their glares. *Manipulating* feels like a strong word. "Umm…"

"Somehow, you have perverted your existence in the Veil and have been popping in and out of it," boss man says. "Not only is that against the laws of the Majors, but it can have very grave consequences, some of which we do not even understand ourselves," he says, gathering up the papers. His status gives him more corporeal-ness than a lowly front-line cupid. But even so, he has a difficult time lining up the heart papers so that they lie nicely on top of each other. Just another example of love being difficult.

I look between the three of them. I'm getting the impression that I won't be able to talk myself out of this one. I clear my throat nervously. "What…what are you saying?"

Seedy straightens the papers before looking back up at me. "I am saying that we'll have to decommission you."

I make a worried face. "Decommission sounds a lot like terminate."

"You broke Veil laws," the angel says sternly. "Plus, you're malfunctioning."

My wings fluff up behind me. "I'm perfectly fine," I say defensively.

He gives a pointed look at my mismatched feathers.

I follow his gaze to the black and white feathers marring my wings. "Oh. Those. That's just—"

"You can't lie to an angel, love dove," the demon cuts in with a laugh.

I promptly shut my mouth. "Okay, so maybe I'm malfunctioning a little."

Boss man shakes his head, deeply disappointed. "You have not only proven to be a failure as a cupid, but you've somehow disrupted the magic of the Veil enough that other powers are now infused into you."

I blink in surprise. "Excuse me?"

The angel points to my wings. "You've sprouted white and black feathers. Angel and demon traits."

The demon snorts and crosses his arms. "Yeah, just like it was a *demon trait* when she purged a soul."

Huh. So *that's* what I did to that fae when I sucked his essence out with my bare hands? Oh man. When Ronak finds out that I'm part demon, he's never going to let me live it down.

I give him a nervous smile. "Whoops."

"Whoops, again? Really?" the demon drawls.

"It's not like I meant to soul-suck someone. It just sort of happened."

The demon rolls his eyes. "Fucking cupids."

"I didn't do it on purpose," I say, thinking back to when I soul-sucked the soldier fae who attacked us in our genfin den.

"Regardless," the angel intervenes. "These other powers will continue to infuse with you, and you will continue to break Veil laws and pervert your own existence."

"I'm not a pervert," I defend.

"You are confusing the Veil with your ability to enter and exit at will. Only higher powers can do that. We cannot allow you to continue to take on powers of all the Majors."

"It probably won't just be the Majors," Jerkahf adds.

I frown. "What do you mean? I've never seen anything else in the Veil except for us and the ghosts."

Seedy answers. "There are the Minors, of course."

"The Minors?"

He looks at me impatiently. "Yes, the Minors in the Veil. The demon is right. You could very well pick up their powers as well."

"Like…"

He huffs. "Like…you could take on the powers of a sandman."

"Sand*man*? You mean only guys get that gig? That's a little sexist," I point out. "I could *totally* put people to sleep and give them awesome dreams. I'd do sex dreams," I say this part to the demon, because I feel like he'll understand. "Everyone loves sex dreams."

"Well, there's lady luck. No males for that. You gonna call that sexist, too?" Jerkahf says dryly.

"Well, yeah. I'm sure Razz would've been awesome at spreading luck around if he'd passed over the angel gig."

"My name is Raziel," the angel frowns. "Not *Razz*."

"There's also karma," the demon says, ignoring him. "They're also strictly female." He tilts his head. "Although, karma is always a shifter. Canines," he clarifies.

I blink at him. "Wait. Are you saying that karma is *literally* a bitch?"

11

Jerkahf smirks. "Yep."

I wave my hand around. "So all of these Minors, you're saying that I could get their powers, too, besides yours?"

"Yes, that is what we are saying," Raziel answers. "You are no longer just a cupid. You are something else entirely. In fact, I'd say your eyes look suspiciously like that of a lady luck."

Seedy nods gravely. "Exactly the problem. You have crossed lines that should never be crossed. You have committed heinous crimes against the Veil, and you have failed grievously at your cupidity duties. As your top superior, I cannot allow these crimes to go unpunished." He folds his hands in front of him. "So, cupid one thousand fifty, I hereby sentence you to be terminated."

Shit.

CHAPTER 3

*J*instantly jump up like my fight or flight instinct is about to kick in. It's silly since I'm pretty awful at both of those things.

I hold my hands out in front of me. "Let's not be hasty. Yes, I may suck at my job, but let's face it, this cupidity gig isn't all it's cracked up to be, and I'm not the only one who thinks so. Ask any of those cupids out there in the waiting room," I say, pointing toward the door. "Yeah, I screwed up. I suck, I get it. But I didn't intentionally break any laws. I was forced into a physical body. Did I take advantage of it? Yes," I admit. "I get to have a body now. A life. *Love.* Do you really want to take that away from me and my new mates? I just got to have sex for the first time ever. I'd like to do more of that. My mates are super good at it," I confide. "Their tails are not just for balance, if you catch my drift," I say, wagging my brows.

As soon as I mention love and mates and sex, Seedy's pupils dilate. Cupids just can't help but get jazzed up about that stuff.

"Seedy, don't terminate me. We can work something

13

out. Like a nine-to-five kind of gig. Or part-time, even? That way I'm doing my job, but I still can have a life, you know?" He doesn't look convinced. I raise my right hand, ready to take an oath. "I solemnly swear on cupid's bow that I will do my job. I'll smack lots of people with Flirt-Touches and blow a whole crap load of Lust into their faces. I'll make sure my Love Arrows are appropriately shot. Just...please don't terminate me. *Please*."

Seedy shakes his head, and my stomach plummets right down to my ghost-like toes. "I cannot allow this to go unpunished. I'm sorry."

His words echo in my head, and suddenly time is going far too fast.

He snaps his fingers, and the terminate button appears on the desk. It's big and round and red, shining with the word "TERMINATE" in bold letters. His hand moves automatically, reaching toward it, and I swear, my life flashes before my eyes.

This can't be happening.

I will *not* go poof.

I watch his fingers closing over the button, and in the blink of an eye, I turn corporeal and launch myself at him from across the table.

I plow into him, and a surprised shriek escapes both of us as I tackle him to the ground. We start to awkwardly wrestle, each of us trying to get control of the button, but he's just as terrible at physical altercation as I am. We fumble and even accidentally fondle each other as we try to gain the upper hand. By some lucky miracle, I manage to pin him down.

The angel and demon stand over us with matching frowns.

I look up, my pink hair in my face, my chest heaving,

one of my hands shoved against Seedy's nose and the other precariously close to his groin. Icky.

In our scuffle, the terminate button has landed beside us on the floor. We both notice it at the same time. Our eyes meet, and then we dive for it.

Our hands land on it at the same time, pressing down, and then...

Poof!

Pink smoke envelops me.

Oh shit. Oh shit, oh shit, *oh shit!*

"I've been poofed," I squeak out as terror and despair fills me. "I wanted to keep living!" I yell at the bubblegum smoke that is now my world. "I wanted more time with my mates. And more sex with them. And to eat, like, cartons of chocolates." Tears start dripping down my cheeks. "This isn't fair," I lament as I wrap my arms around my legs and drop my head to my knees. "I was gonna try anal, and maybe get a tattoo, and I would've even exercised if Ronak wanted me to. Probably. Maybe. At least for, like, five minutes," I cry to the termination universe of nothingness.

"Did she say anal?"

I shriek and flinch upright, nearly coming out of my skin. The pink smoke has dissipated, and I blink up through wet lashes to see Jerkahf and Raziel staring down at me. Raziel is frowning, but Jerkahf has a terrific grin on his face.

I stumble to my feet and look around the office wildly. "Oh my gods. I didn't get poofed!" I jump up and down excitedly.

"No, but it seems your superior did," Raziel says, still frowning.

I follow his gaze and look down at the strange pink

body outline on the floor where Seedy had been sprawled out just moments before.

I blink repeatedly at the space as realization pieces together. I must've hit the termination button before him. "Well, that was lucky."

Luck be a lady tonight, bitches.

"You just terminated the Head of Cupidity," Raziel points out dryly.

I grimace. "Whoops."

The demon cocks a brow. "You say that a lot."

I pick up the termination button from the floor and gingerly place it on the table. When I do, I notice that the heart and arrow symbol that marked Seedy is now on the inside of *my* wrist, right below my number. As I stare at it with bewilderment, I realize that I feel...strange. Like I just got a shot of cupid adrenaline or something.

I hear Raziel sigh exaggeratedly. "Great. I cannot believe that this imbecile is now in charge."

I swing my gaze over at him. I'm going to ignore the imbecile comment for now, but... "You mean *I'm* the cupid boss of all cupid bosses?"

"It would appear so," he says, giving a pointedly unhappy look at the marking on my wrist.

I feel bad about unintentionally poofing Seedy, but... holy heartcakes, I'm so *relieved*. I wasn't expecting to be the new boss, but...it's a hell of a lot better than being terminated. I fist pump a bit because I can't help myself. "Yeah! I'm the boss, bitches!"

The angel and demon look at me with matching expressions of "oh, for fuck's sake-ness."

"What are we supposed to do now?" Jerkahf asks the angel.

"The hell if I know," Raziel says.

Are angels allowed to say that? I'm not sure, but it doesn't seem like the best time to ask him.

"I guess this solves her little issue of Veil perversion," Raziel says.

"What do you mean?" I ask.

He shrugs a shoulder. "Veil Majors in top positions are permitted to enter and exit the Veil at will. The Veil shouldn't have a problem with you doing it now."

"Oh, so I'm not gonna pervert it anymore! That's good. Looks like all our problems are solved," I say, clapping my hands.

"For hellfire's sake. Her wings have changed," Jerkahf comments.

I look over my shoulder and realize that he's right. Instead of having random black and white feathers cropped up on me, now, my red feathers are gilded with black and white edges on the bottom of my wings. My lips tilt up with a smile. "Oh, come on, you have to admit that looks badass."

Raziel just shakes his head at me, but Jerkahf cocks his head and says, "Okay, you're right." Raziel huffs at him with frustration, but Jerkahf just shrugs. "What? It does look badass."

Raziel grinds his perfect teeth together. "In any case, it seems as though her malfunctioning has...solidified. Whatever powers she has now will probably be permanent."

A light catches my attention out of the corner of my eye, and when I look down, I notice that my new cupid boss tattoo is shining with neon pink light. "Aww. It's all pretty and glowy."

Jerkahf snorts. "You being Head of Cupidity ought to be good."

I narrow my eyes at him. "Don't be so negative."

"Can you turn that off?" Raziel says testily.

I rub at the mark, as if I can get the glow to magically wipe off. When that doesn't work, I shake my arm, because for some reason, that seems like the next thing to do in a situation like this, but it just starts glowing more brightly like it's some sort of weird light stick.

When I leave my arm still for a few moments, the pink slowly fades away. I smirk with satisfaction and then gesture to the chairs. I totally have a handle on this new boss stuff already.

"Boys, take a seat," I say with authority. They surprise me when they actually sit down. I try not to look smug as shit, but...yeah, a little bit of smugness slips out. It's kind of like Lust. Sometimes it's just hard to contain.

I take a moment to study the angel and demon. Since I'm no longer in danger of being poofed, I can relax a bit. Now, I'm a total wing-snob. I admit it. I've always been partial to my cupid wings, and now I'm even *more* of a wing snob because I have some badass angel-demon gilding going on, but even I have to admit that the angel's wings are *beautiful*.

"You have nice wings," I tell him seriously. "They look like they're shining. Are they shining?"

He preens. "Yes. They shine with the light of heaven."

"Wow, that's awesome. Really. Cupids and angels *totally* win in the wing department." I lean in conspiratorially. "I mean, at least we didn't get stuck with demon wings, am I right?" I whisper over to him and give him a little elbow action.

"I heard that," the demon says behind me.

I turn and smile at him innocently. "Hmm? Heard what?"

"Need I point out that your wings now have demonic traits?" he asks, giving my black feathers a pointed stare.

I cover my black feathers protectively. "They're still cupid wings. They're just...demonesque. My beautiful red feathers are outlined in a demon accent, if you will. And they have some angel flair, too," I point out. I turn back to Raziel with a thought. "Ooh, maybe mine will start shining, too!"

"Mine are heat-resistant," Jerkahf grumbles.

"Yeah, that's neat," I concede. "But they're all...bat-like and thorny. Also, they smell like burnt rotten eggs."

He narrows his eyes at me. "It's sulfur and smoke from the pits of hell," he defends.

I pat him on the shoulder. "Sure it is."

Jerkahf shrugs me off. "Can we move on and stop talking about our fucking wings?"

Raziel smirks at the grumpy demon. "Touchy, touchy. Are all you demons such p-p-p-wussies?"

I cock my head at him. "You can't say pussy?"

Raziel gives a terse shake of his head. "No, I can't. But that's exactly what the demon is."

Jerkahf glares like he's about to launch himself at the angel and scald him with hellfire. I press my hands against their chests so that they don't attack each other. Love is literally getting between life and death right now. I am Majoring the shit out of this Veil boss stuff. "Hold up. Jerky, I'm sorry. That was mean of me to criticize your wings." I tell him in a placating tone. "They're very... hellish looking. I'm sure they're super impressive in the pits where you're from."

He just rolls his eyes, but the fiery glow recedes somewhat.

"And Raziel," I say, turning to him. "Be nice. You're the angel. You're supposed to set a good example."

He gapes at me. "You expect me, an angel, to be nice to an entity that is *literally* evil? The very antithesis to my existence?"

I blink at him. "Yes."

He rubs his eyes. I'm pretty sure they're both completely exasperated with me, but hey, they no longer look like they're about to have a battle of good versus evil in my office, so mission accomplished. I drop my hands and lace them in front of me. "Anyway, since I'm the boss now, I am formally rescinding the order for my termination."

"Shocker," Jerkahf drawls.

"But as far as these other powers, umm, what should I do about those?"

"How about don't use them and just be a cupid like you're supposed to be?" the angel deadpans.

"Yeah, that isn't gonna work for me," I admit. "Not full time, at least, but I will stick some Love Arrows where they belong and Lust it up when I see fit. I'll also keep the soul-sucking to a minimum," I promise Jerkahf.

"No," Raziel says, pointing at me. "No soul-sucking of any kind. That's not your job."

"Sometimes it just happens," I insist.

"No, it doesn't."

"Well, it might."

"Demon," Raziel snaps. "You deal with her."

Jerkahf shakes his head with a chuckle, and a little bit of smoke escapes his mouth. "I don't believe there's any way of reversing the Veil powers now that she's been settled as a cupid boss."

Raziel laces his fingers together and props them on his

crossed knee. "No, I don't believe that there's any way to reverse it, either," he admits, sounding like I stole his favorite seraphic candy.

"So, I'm going to be some sort of boss cupid-angel-demon-sandman-lucklady-karma-other Veil entity…thing?"

"It would seem so."

I nod slowly. "Well, it's not ideal, but I think I can live with it."

Jerkahf snorts. "How noble of you."

"Can you guys just give me a crash course on angelology and demonology stuff? Preferably the short version? Because I'd like to get back home. I'm doing super important spy stuff. Plus, the sex with my mates. I'd like to get back to that."

Raziel glances at the demon. "Is she serious?"

The demon picks at his black nails. "It appears so."

"What's the big deal? Just tell me how to control the soul-sucking stuff and whatever the heck else I need to know about your powers, so that I know what to expect. I just need a little help," I tell them.

As soon as the word "help" escapes my lips, a puff of pink smoke erupts in front of me, and a cupid suddenly appears.

CHAPTER 4

Startled, I stare at her from across the table for several seconds without saying anything. She's young like me, her pink hair is pulled back in a tight, sleek ponytail, and she's wearing a frilly blouse with its buttons hooked together all the way to her high-collared throat. She's wearing a skirt that goes down to her knees and sensible black loafers. Her red wings are held firmly against her back as she smiles politely at me. Her frumpy clothing does nothing to deter how beautiful she is. Looking like a Catholic school teacher with pink hair, she's probably every guy's wet dream. I'm a little jealous of her boobs, to be honest. They're super perky. And round. At least two handfuls.

I realize that I've been staring far too long at her chest, so I quickly wrench my eyes up. Now I understand why guys do it so much. Some boobs just demand the attention. If she's bothered by my perusal of her jigglejoggers, she doesn't show it.

"Umm...can I help you?" I finally say.

She cocks her head. "You summoned me, Madame Cupid."

Madame? "No, I didn't."

"I believe you summoned her when you claimed to be in need of help," Raziel points out.

"Oh. Umm. Who are you?" I ask her.

She lifts up her wrist so I can clearly see the letters LXIX there. "I am cupid number sixty-nine."

"Of course you are," I mumble as the demon beside me snickers like a fourteen-year-old boy.

"Okay, well, I apologize for unintentionally summoning you...Lex," I call her. I'm totally not calling her sixty-nine. It's just not happening.

"Shall I go back to my cupid duties?"

"Yes. Wait, no." I quickly change my mind. "You're partly corporeal. Does that mean you're a higher up?"

She nods enthusiastically. "I'm Cupid of the Month. Have been for eight hundred and thirty-three months in a row. That's why I'm assigned the honor of being your assistant. May I ask what happened to cupid four hundred?"

I squirm in my chair. "Oh, umm, Seedy was terminated unexpectedly."

Jerkahf snorts, and I shoot him a glare to shut him up.

"Well, I am happy to serve you, Madame Cupid."

"You can call me Emelle."

She tilts her head. "As you wish."

"I didn't even know there was such a thing as Cupid of the Month," I admit.

"That's not surprising," Raziel mumbles beside me.

Without thinking, I kick him under the table, and he winces when I nail him in the shin. Am I allowed to kick angels? I look up at the ceiling, waiting for the wrath of

23

the heavens to rain down on me. I look back to the angel apologetically. "Sorry. My foot slipped."

He cocks a brow. "Angels can tell when you lie."

"Oh." Awkward. I turn back to the cupid in front of me. "So. Lex. How did you earn this prestigious title?"

"I have very clear cupid goals that I make sure to hit every day. For instance, I make sure that I make at least five Love Matches and no less than twenty sexual encounters each day. I also make sure to spread Flirt-Touches to at least one hundred different people."

My mouth drops open in surprise. I've never actually met a cupid who liked their job, let alone one who had, like…personal goals and stuff. "Good gods, you do all of that every single day?"

She nods enthusiastically. "I just *love* spreading love," she says, beaming. Her wings fluff up behind her, like just talking about it is really juicing her up. "We cupids have the best job in the Veil. Don't you just adore seeing someone fall in love because you helped them along?" she asks dreamily.

Wow. This girl has a really bad case of overactive cupidity.

"Umm. Sure."

She starts stroking the Love Arrows that are slung over her shoulder, and staring off into space like she just can't wait to get back to doing cupid stuff, so I snap my fingers at her.

"Focus, Lex."

"Sorry. I was thinking about all the possible Love Matches I can make once I get back."

Wow. Aside from this girl having super great boobs, she's also an overachiever. I don't know whether to be impressed or intimidated. I look down at my chest and push my arms together, seeing if I can make mine as buoyant as hers. "You know a lot about cupids and Veil stuff, I'm guessing?" Satisfied with my boobage, I drop my arms back down with a dignified nod.

She nods enthusiastically. "Oh, yes. Aside from being Cupid of the Month for over eight hundred months in a row, I also have acted as a Veil ambassador for...Seedy, as you called him, whenever he needed to meet with some of the other Veil Minor representatives. I have also studied extensively about cupid powers, duties, and our role in the Veil."

"Perfect," I say with a smile. "Let's talk hypotheticals for a moment, shall we?"

She flicks her eyes to the angel and demon before meeting my eyes again. "Alright."

"Hypothetically, let's say that a cupid was able to pop in and out of the Veil at will. And let's just say that she *accidentally* passed on some of her cupid traits to her mates."

"You did *what*?" Raziel snaps. I ignore him.

"Passed on traits?" Lex repeats.

"Yep. Like, say...cupid wings and a cupid number. Hypothetically, why would that be happening?"

She considers this for a moment. "Hmm. I cannot answer that, as I have never read of such a thing happening before. To my knowledge, a cupid has never taken a mate. We're far too busy to have mates of our own, because we are lucky enough to be able to give love to others. What a wonderful job it is to have!"

I start laughing at her joke, only to realize she's serious. I quickly cover it up with a cough. I'm really gonna have to get used to her go-getter cupidtude.

25

I turn back to the angel and demon. "Okay. So. Where were we?"

Jerkahf crosses his arms over his chest and leans back in his chair to give me a sardonic look. "You expected us to give you the CliffsNotes version of what it means to be two of the most powerful and influential entities in existence since the dawning of time," Jerkahf drawls.

"Yeah, that. Hit me with it."

The demon and angel give each other a long look... and then they promptly disappear in puffs of black smoke and white light.

"Dammit!" I say, slamming my hand against the table. "Veil Majors. More like Major pains in the ass."

I absently run a finger over my new cupid boss mark as I contemplate my next move. "Lex, can you find out information for me about all the Veil entities? Majors and Minors?" I guess I'll just have to figure out my possible powers on my own.

"Of course, Madame Cupid," she assures me.

"Lex, just call me Emelle."

"Of course, Madame Cupid Emelle."

"No, that's not—"

I get interrupted when two more cupids come floating through the room, their faces a mix of shock and rage as they stop to glare at me from across the table.

One of them is an old supervisor I remember getting disciplined by for the time I only gave out Lust when someone said the word "stroke" at midnight. Get it? Stroke of twelve? Yeah. I was bored. Anyway, he gave me a slap on the wrist in the shape of a hundred extra Love Matches. I don't like him much.

The other cupid is a wrinkled old lady with curlers in her hair. Poor thing must've died like that. I look down to see that she's wearing slippers and a zippered day robe. No wonder she looks so grumpy. Her death probably interrupted a nap.

"Where is cupid four hundred?" she demands.

I can't show weakness in the face of these cupids, or they'll pounce. I sit up straighter and look her dead-on. "He was terminated."

They both blanch. "Impossible. The Head of Cupidity cannot be terminated," she argues with the shake of her head.

I lean forward and scoop up the terminate button. "I don't know, it seemed pretty possible to me."

She takes a few hovered steps back, and they both take note of the boss mark on my wrist as they exchange nervous glances. "So that means..."

I prop my ankles up onto the table and put my hands behind my head for added drama as I lean back with a smirk. "That means I'm the new boss, and I'm gonna be making some changes around here."

They look at me with horror.

I beam. This is gonna be fun.

CHAPTER 5

"*Y*ou want to *what*?"

The old female cupid, whom I've lovingly dubbed Curlers, hasn't been able to blink for the past ten minutes. That's how badly her eyes have bugged out. I guess she really doesn't like the new direction I'm moving all of cupidity.

Seedy thought that I committed crimes against cupidity, but I disagree. I think the Head of Cupidity committed crimes against all the poor lowly cupids. And I intend to fix that.

We've been sitting here for *hours*. I've been going over old cupid boss notes, looking at stats and cupid requirements...and also doing my best to retain whatever information Lex can find about the other Veil entities.

The male cupid supervisor, number nineteen, has finally given up on arguing with me and is just hovering over the chair and tapping his finger against his semi-solid forehead. He also quietly sings nineties love songs under his breath whenever I give any kind of new rule or override an old one. As far as coping mechanisms go, I'm a fan of it.

"Cupids need more incentive," I explain to Curlers. "I bet the angels and demons have awesome employee incentives."

Lex is to my right, studiously taking notes. She looks up at my words and taps one of the books she's been furiously studying. "Demons have possession parties twice a year. In the human realm, it's once on Halloween and once on Tax Day."

"See?" I tell Curlers smugly. "Even Hell gives its employees incentives."

Curlers sniffs with clear disfavor. "Cupids don't need incentives. We get to spread love and desire. That's incentive enough."

Lex nods in agreement until I shoot her a look. She quickly jerks her head to a stop.

"What about the angels?" I ask Lex.

"Well…they get heaven."

Oh. Right.

"Okay, from now on, cupids get a yearly party. Maybe the day after Valentine's. We'll yank everyone to Cupidville and host a big shindig. We'll let them all have physical bodies, too."

Curlers gapes. "You can't do that!"

Lex slaps open a huge red book with pink pages and points to a line. "Actually, it states here that the Head of Cupidity has the ability to control any cupid's corporeal body. So, technically, she can do that."

I smile sweetly. "Physical bodies for all, for twenty-four hours. We'll reward all the top performers, have games, food, wine, and voluntary sexy times, of course."

I watch as whatever I say gets magically written into

the cupid law book, in pink glittery ink. Awesome. "And that's apart from the mandatory vacation time."

"Vacation time?" Curlers repeats shrilly. She looks over at Nineteen, but he's currently singing the boy band song "I Want It That Way" and completely ignoring us.

"Yep. Everyone gets two weeks each year. They can go to whichever realm they want and have physical bodies to do...whatever they want to do. When their vacation time is up, we'll pop them back into their designated realm, and I guarantee they will do their jobs more efficiently. And do you know why?" I ask, leaning forward.

Curlers grits her dentured teeth. "Why?"

"Because," I say with a sigh. "Maybe if I hadn't been so damn lonely and jealous, I would have been a better cupid," I explain honestly. "Happy cupids will spread better love. Trust me. I'm the cupid boss."

I think she might be imagining reaching across the table to throttle me.

"Oh, and no more terminating poor cupids unless they're doing something *really* terrible. Give them a break. They're lonely." I snap my fingers. "That reminds me. I want cupids to have partners."

"Partners," she repeats flatly.

"Yep. No more solo act. It'll help cut down on the loneliness. It will also bring a sense of camaraderie and friendly competition to see who can make the most Love Matches. It'll be good for business, I promise."

Curlers shakes her head. "In my day, cupids did their duty, and there was no talk of this loneliness."

"Well, it's high time we shake things up a bit. Let's make a cupid's life at least partially enjoyable instead of downright awful. No one likes to be stuck invisible in the

Veil, all alone, for years at a time, only to go crazy and finally get terminated."

I stand up, and Lex immediately leaps up to stand beside me. "I really do need to get back to my fae realm now. I have royals to spy on and mates to...mate with." I turn to Lex. "Will you be able to handle getting all of these changes enacted?"

"Of course," she says confidently. "I will see to everything."

Having an assistant is super helpful. "Curlers and Nineteen are to help you with all of the changes." I look at the grumpy cupids. "Unless, of course, you'd rather I demote you two and find someone else..."

Curlers quickly shakes her head, and even Nineteen stops singing Backstreet Boys long enough to say no. "Good. I'll be checking in. Oh, I almost forgot."

I walk over to my desk and pull up another magic button. I tap in number seven hundred twenty and watch as pink smoke appears, and then a familiar cupid is hovering in front of me.

He looks around in surprise. "What the fooking hell is this, then? I didn't do shite to get in trouble already!"

I smile at his tanned, pretty face and disheveled pink hair. "We meet again, Seven Hundred Twenty."

He stops looking around the office and swings his gaze on me. I watch as recognition flashes over his face, and his dark brows rise in surprise. "Well, I'll be fooking caught on a cock. Thousand fifty, that you?"

I beam. "It's me. But you can call me Boss Bitch Emelle because I'm running this lust show now."

His eyes widen. "You're fooking full of pink pig shite."

"Nope," I say, rolling back on my heels, practically giddy. "Totally true. And I'm making some changes." I

31

snap my fingers, and instantly he turns solid. Yep. Lex showed me that little trick. Being the cupid boss is badass.

He looks down at his now solid body and whistles. "Well, I guess you ain't gobbin' air after all. What a fooking trip this is."

He reaches down to his crotch and handles himself like he wants to make sure his dick is really there. When he catches Lex watching, he shoots her a wink. "You wanna be the first one to see it, luv?"

Lex blushes and sidles closer to me.

"No flirting with my assistant, Sev. You can get your stick wet *after* you've helped make the necessary changes around here, okay?"

He frowns and drops his hand. "What the fook you on about?"

"I'm making you top supervisor. Lex here will help you get settled in. I trust you to make sure the rest of these cupids get on board with my new laws. Can you do that?"

He grins at me impishly. "Luv, you just gave me my cock back. I'll do whatever the fook you want."

And they say the way to a man's heart is through his stomach. Nope. It's his dick.

CHAPTER 6

*L*ex gives me a thorough explanation on how to travel through the Veil, Cupidville, and the rest of the realms. It's pretty easy now that I'm the boss. So, with a clear visualization of the fae realm, I yank myself out of Cupidville. I know Sev and Lex will implement all of my changes in Cupidville while I'm gone. I've been gone for several hours by now, and I'm antsy to get back so I can look for Okot and the princess.

It's a bit weird yanking myself through the Veil and back to the realm, but I manage not to vomit all over my feet, so that's something at least.

I end up landing at the hunting shed on Ronak's land where I left my genfins. It's still dark, and I look around curiously. After a good thorough search, it's obvious that they aren't here. I stay invisible and make the flight back to our den to check there, just in case the guys doubled back.

Just a few hours ago, we were here, fighting for our lives because Princess Soora's soldiers had ambushed us.

As I float through the living room, a frown forms on

my face. Instead of the living room being completely destroyed, all signs of the battle have been wiped clean. The paintings are back on the walls, the bloodstains are gone, and there's even a new rug.

I pop myself into visibility and walk around the space, feeling that something is very *off*. When I go into the kitchen and look through the cupboards, my frown deepens. There's no food. Like, none.

Now, for a normal person, maybe this wouldn't seem like such a red flag. But my guys had this place stocked full of food. Not just because they eat like horses, either, but because, well, *I* eat like a horse. Just several hours ago, the cupboards were jam-packed.

I stare at the empty cupboards, trying to make sense of what I'm seeing. When I make another pass through the house, I finally figure out what else is bothering me. There are particles floating through the air. There's a mustiness to the house that definitely wasn't there before.

"Oh, shit."

Dread falls into the pit of my stomach, and before I know it, I'm invisible and flying through the walls and out of the den. I race through the genfin village, only stopping when I find a lone genfin walking on the street. I pop visible and land in front of him. I nearly scare the poor male right out of his tail, and he takes a swipe at me with his claws, but luckily, I dodge them.

"Sorry!" I say quickly, holding my hands up. I really should've rethought that whole "startling a predator" thing, but that's what panic does to me. "I just want to know what day it is."

He gapes at me, his claws still raised defensively, until he finally drops them and crosses his arms in front of his chest. "Who the hell are you?"

34

"I'm Emelle," I say impatiently. "I—"

He takes in my appearance, and his eyes widen. "You're the cupid."

I blink at him. I have no idea how he knows that. "Umm, yeah. Look, all I need to know is what day it is."

It takes him several seconds, but he finally snaps out of his surprised staring enough to answer me. "It's Summer Solstice."

"What?" I feel the blood drain from my face as I start shaking my head automatically. I don't even realize that I've grabbed his arms like a crazy person until he shrugs me off. "No. It can't be Summer Solstice," I argue. "That was…like four weeks away!" I say shrilly.

"I suggest you get out of here," he says, not bothering to address my issues with time. "It's not safe for the cupid to be out in the open. Not even here. The prince has eyes everywhere, and I don't want to be seen with you."

I can't even register his weirdly ominous words before he's already walked away. I'm still shaking my head and arguing when I'm left behind on the cobbled street. I'm ranting like a crazy person, with only closed doors and empty shops to hear me.

I was only gone a few hours. How can *weeks* have passed?

"Okay, Emelle," I tell myself as I spin around the empty street. "Think, think, think."

Ronak's words echo in my head. Three days. He gave me three days to go spy on the royals and figure out what the hell was happening. If I hadn't come back by then, my genfins were going to go to the palace themselves and figure out what was going on. Which would be bad. Really, really bad. I still don't even know if Princess Soora has betrayed us. And if the prince finds them…

Nope. No. Not going there.

When I hear the sound of a door opening and boisterous laughter, I go invisible again on instinct. A group of male genfins come staggering out of a pub and start swaying and stumbling home.

If I've been gone for weeks, then the guys are probably going out of their minds with worry. And they would definitely have gone to look for me by now. The question is, where should *I* look for them? Damn Cupidville and its stupid time warp.

Knowing Ronak, he would've gone balls to the wall and headed straight for the palace. But maybe Sylred, the more level-headed one, would've thought of a different approach that wouldn't get them killed?

I consider that for one-point-five seconds before I dismiss it. Genfins be crazy. And when it comes to me, even the calm one is crazy. I swear, if they got caught and kil—Nope. Not going there.

Knowing I need to go to the palace to search first, I launch into the sky and fly like hell in my invisible form. By the time I make it to the kingdom island, the sun has come closer, so I'm no longer bathed in darkness, but soaking in the purple hue of dawn.

One thing becomes very obvious as I get nearer— something has gone terribly wrong.

CHAPTER 7

There are soldiers everywhere. Doing sweeps in the air and on the ground, they're alert and all over the place. It looks like they're ready for a war. Trepidation fills me, and the urge to hurry takes over. Ignoring the magical barrier around the palace walls, I float straight through and into the palace.

If Princess Soora really did betray me and the guys, I want to know why. I head straight for her chambers, but the place is empty, and as I search through the rest of the castle, I realize that it's oddly quiet. I only see a couple of servants hurrying past, nothing like the usual bustle and activity. None of the lamps are lit on the walls; only the dawning light is coming through. Usually, at this hour, the servants would be busier than ever to get ready for the day. But everything is abnormally empty.

I turn and start floating toward the prison tower. If my guys are here, there's a good chance they'll be in a cell. If someone hurt my guys, I will use my new hybrid powers to rain down hell on them.

I float through the walls and straight into the ominous

prison tower. It's huge. I don't know if magic is in play, but I didn't expect the triple spiral staircases or for it to look like it's ten stories tall. It's going to take me a while to search all of it, but I start at the bottom and systematically start going through the cells.

The prison is exactly the way you'd expect. Dark, dank, and depressing. I search the cells and see decrepit fae inside each one. It seems like the prince has been busy. The prison is filled to capacity. Some cells even have two or three prisoners inside, and the squalor they're kept in hurts my heart. *Where the hell are my guys?*

After searching the lower levels, I go further up. I've searched nearly all of them, and there's still no sign of my guys. Frustrated, I'm about to turn around when I notice movement in the cell in front of me that I thought was empty, and I pop into visibility.

"Princess?"

My shocked question bounces off the prison walls and leaves an eerie echo to slither along the stones. I wince, but the purple-faced fae doesn't move. She has her back to me as she lies on a pathetic pile of straw, her body curled up to keep warm.

Checking to make sure there are no guards around, I step forward and grasp the iron bars. "Princess?"

At my whisper, the form rouses, and I watch in the weak lantern light as she turns over and sits up.

"Princess Soora," I breathe, covering my mouth with my hand.

She looks bad. Like, *really, really* bad.

Princess Soora has always been the epitome of grace and beauty. Never a strand of hair out of place, even when she was asleep. Never ruffled, never weak. But the fae in front of me looks broken.

Deep circles cling beneath her eyes, and her lavender hair is in dirty, matted knots. Her skin is covered in scrapes and bruises, and her once beautiful silk dress is now in stained tatters.

She blinks a few times and then stands, wincing as she gets to her feet. "Emelle?" she whispers, and her voice breaks, like she hasn't spoken or had water in days.

"It's me."

"Thank the gods," she breathes, and I see her eyes turn shiny with unshed tears. "I knew you'd come."

Aww. She had faith in my spy-ness.

Princess Soora begins to rush over to me, but when she starts to sway on her feet, I immediately pop invisible, fly through the bars, and go visible again, catching her just in time. I set her down carefully on the straw and sit beside her.

"Stay here. I'll be right back."

I go into the Veil and float straight through the walls and into the palace kitchens quick as lightning. I grab two loaves of bread and two jugs of water, and then go to her rooms, grab a new dress, coat, thick socks, a towel, and then rush back downstairs. Luckily, anything I'm holding comes in and out of the Veil with me, so I'm able to carry everything while staying invisible. It doesn't work on living things, though. I've tried. It did not end well for the butterfly.

When I turn visible back in her cell, the princess flinches in surprise at my return. I immediately set to work. I gently strip off her filthy gown and wash the grime off of her skin. We don't speak, but I methodically wipe her down, and she lets me, helping to lift an arm or shift a leg as I do so.

Once I've wiped away as much grime as possible, I

help her into her new clothes and get her shivering body bundled up in her thick fur coat. I carefully break pieces of bread and pass each bite to her, while giving her water to drink between each mouthful.

There's something to be said about the silence of camaraderie. It fills the space more than any amount of meaningless voices could. We're quiet as I tend to her, when she finally gestures that she's eaten and drunk as much as she can handle, I finally set everything down and speak. "What happened?"

She sighs, and it's a tired, defeated kind of sound. Not the sound I'm used to hearing from her.

"He outplayed me."

She means the prince, of course.

"He does like his games," I mumble, picking at my dress.

She nods and begins to clean out the dirt from under her fingernails. "He found out that I'd been working with the resistance. He brought me here..."

She trails off, dropping her gaze in shame.

"Soldiers were sent to ambush us. *Your* soldiers," I tell her.

Her eye ticks in irritation. "He's gotten to just about everyone."

Hating the defeated tone to her voice, I look around the dank cell. "I need to get you out of here."

She shakes her head. "You can't get me out."

"What about your power? Aren't you super good at glamouring? Maybe you can trick the guards into opening it."

She waves a hand at the surrounding bars. "The entire cell is fortified with iron. I'm completely drained of power."

40

I bite my nail in thought. "Okay. Maybe I can wait until one of the guards comes in and opens the cell? I'll turn visible and beat him over the head," I say hopefully.

But she just shakes her head. "They never open the door. Stay here with me," she says, grasping my hand. Her fingers are ice-cold. "Don't leave." Her purple eyes look desperate as she clings to me, and I feel another surge of pity.

"Don't worry. I'll find a way to get you out of here," I promise. "But me staying here isn't going to help," I say gently. "Maybe if I find my guys, they can help to bust you out. But then again, I really need someone who has a little more finesse…" Inspiration strikes, and I snap my fingers excitedly. "The Horned Hook! I'll get him to help."

She shakes her head. "No. I don't want to get him involved."

"Don't be silly. He totally warned us about the prince searching the island. I think we can trust him."

Princess Soora looks near panicking, so I quickly squeeze her hand in what I hope is a reassuring gesture. "Don't worry, he'll help, and then we can get you out of here. Now, do you have *any* idea where he'd be?"

"I can't ask him…" She trails off, her voice wavering. My cupid senses are suddenly tingling with some seriously intense love vibes.

I stop short, blinking at her.

Does she have a thing for Belren?

I remember the way she recommended him to the genfins when I was stuck in the Veil. I remember how he hates the prince. How he seems to know everything and is always in trouble with the monarchy. How he was banished. Maybe it's not just because of his thieving ways. Maybe the reason that he always seems to want to stick it to the prince is because the princess was stolen from *him*.

I thought that, when he showed up at the den right before I mated with the genfins, he'd been flirty with me, but maybe I'd read it all wrong? Maybe he came to warn me that day because he's the one Princess Soora has been in love with, and they've been working together all this time. But if that's the case, why hasn't he tried breaking her out already?

"If anyone can get you out of here, it's him. Now where can I find him?"

She lets out a shaky breath. "He'll have left the kingdom island and gone underground at the first talk of trouble. He'll go to the last place the prince will expect him to be."

"And where's that?"

"The island where he was banished. Arachno's island."

CHAPTER 8

Gods. Today is just not my day.

"Arachno? As in that super scary fae with the bazillion eyes, who likes to trap people in her web and has the creepy habit of being a freaking *cannibal*? That Arachno?"

Princess Soora nods, and my stomach drops.

"But how could he be at her island? He wouldn't be able to get past the barrier."

"I used my power to create a doorway into the barrier. He asked me to," she explains. "It's small, only large enough for a single body to fit through and very well hidden, but it's there."

I go over, in great detail, exactly where his hidden hideout is on the island. When I'm confident I can find it, I get ready to leave.

"Okay. I'll go find him for you. Don't worry, I can do this."

She gives me a strained smile.

"How did you find me?" she asks, eating some more of the bread.

43

"I was actually looking for my guys," I admit, feeling slightly guilty. "I don't know where my genfins are, and I haven't seen Okot since you sent him on that mission."

"About that—"

A noise sounds down the hall, and her explanation gets cut short.

"The guards are coming for their usual checks," she whispers hurriedly.

She grabs my hand again like she doesn't want me to leave her here, but I gently extract myself. "I'll find Belren, don't worry."

I give her a quick nod and then go invisible. I fly past the guard walking up the stairs and go back to the palace.

As I'm zooming through the walls of the palace, I pull up short when I fly through a particular room. Screeching to a halt, I double back and then stop dead at the scene in front of me.

Okot.

He's here.

He's here in a palace bedroom, sitting in a chair with his head hanging, his forearms draped over his thighs. I float closer, so surprised that I've found him that I nearly choke on joy. I've missed him so much it hurts.

As I get closer, his head jerks up, and I startle back in surprise and then notice that something is very, very wrong.

His bright red mohawk is unwashed and disheveled, nothing like his usual sleek locks that fall to one side. He leaps to his feet and starts pacing around the room like he's a bull in a pen, just waiting to rush someone, and oddly enough, he paces around *me*.

All the while, his expression changes back and forth between being utterly blank to becoming absolutely

44

enraged. His head ticks and he pulls at his bright red hair, clearly in distress.

As he paces, I'm able to take in the room. It's a mess. All the blankets from the bed are twisted, hanging half-off, and lanterns are knocked over with their glass in shattered pieces on the floor.

He keeps up his inexorable pacing, and I inadvertently float further away from him. I back myself into a table, but in one quick motion, he rushes forward, reaches down with both hands and sends the table flying across the room. I flinch as it goes through me, watching with wide eyes as it crashes against the wall and lands in splinters on the floor.

I look back at him, wide-eyed. Something is seriously wrong, and I can't wait another second to comfort him. I pop myself into the physical realm and take a tentative step forward.

"Okot?" I say quietly.

At first, he doesn't hear me. He's grumbling under his breath, although I can't make out what he's saying.

I take another careful step forward. "Okot?" I say again.

He stops dead in his tracks, and his head whips up. I suck in a breath at the sight of the deep purple circles under his eyes and his eyes themselves. His red irises aren't visible at all. His pupils have completely taken over, and the whites of his eyes are bloodshot. And the expression on his face…it doesn't look like him at all.

What happened to my gentle giant?

For a moment, we just stare at each other, neither of us moving. Seeing how awful he looks makes tears prick the back of my eyes. I so badly want to curl up in his big arms and breathe him in.

45

"Okot, are you okay?" I ask, my voice barely above a whisper. I smile at him, but my bottom lip shakes slightly. Why isn't he moving? Why isn't he saying anything?

But then it's like the spell breaks, and in the next instant, he's coming at me. My heart picks up the pace, desperate for this reunion. My smile widens as he makes his way across the room. He reaches for me and takes me by the arms.

But instead of pulling me into him and holding me against his chest, I find myself suddenly slammed against the wall.

A surprised shriek escapes me as my head smacks against the hard stone. I blink up at him, shock covering my face. His black eyes and the look of utter hatred on his face fills me with both shock and fear.

"Okot, what—"

My words cut off as he grips a hand around my neck. And not in the very adoring way that he usually does. No, this hold on my neck isn't tender. It's violent, and panic shoots through me as he puts pressure on my windpipe.

I keep waiting, though. Waiting for this nightmare to stop. Waiting for him to snap out of whatever madness this is. Because I don't understand what the fuck is happening.

But as my vision begins to dim, his thumb choking off my air supply, the sickening realization that I've been so utterly wrong about him finally sets in.

He said he had a mission for the princess. The princess was put in prison, but Okot is…here. In the palace. Trying to choke the life out of me.

I mouth "please" through my lips, since no sound can escape me except for a wheezed exhale. I plead with my

46

eyes as tears start to fall down my cheeks. He doesn't relent. If anything, his grip tightens.

Just as I start to black out, I finally concede that this is really happening, that's it not some sort of sick joke, and I pop back into the Veil.

His body falls against the wall where I was, and I fall to the floor, heaving out fake-breaths with my invisible lungs. I float out of range of him and hover on top of the four-poster bed at the very top of the banister before I reappear.

I take in a few gasping breaths despite my sore throat. "Okot," I croak. "It's me. Your mate."

I've never wanted to hear the words "my beloved" so much in my whole life.

Except he doesn't suddenly snap out of it and come to his senses. No, he just sneers at me in an expression I've never seen on his face before. At least, not directed at me. He comes forward and grips the banister that I'm straddling, and with the strength of his massive arms, he snaps it in half, sending me flying to the floor. I have about two seconds to react.

Unfortunately, I don't react by popping invisible, because I'm an idiot. Instead, I just shriek and crash to the floor, landing painfully on my shoulder. I barely have time to roll over before he's on me again. He hauls me to my feet, keeping a painful hold on my arm.

"Okot. Just talk to me," I beg. "Tell me why you're doing this!"

I don't understand. I'm a mess of confusion and emotions. Okot loves me. I could tell every time he looked at me. He couldn't have faked that…right?

He ignores me and pulls me toward the door, his

fingers digging painfully into my skin. "The cupid is the enemy."

I shake my head, wishing it would clear the nonsense he's spewing. "So you just lied the whole time?" I ask, my voice cracking.

I feel the hot tears trail down my cheeks, but I don't register that I'm crying. I'm too shocked. It's like my brain is still refusing to believe that he betrayed me. The Okot currently pulling me down the corridor, ready to haul me off to the prince, is not the same Okot who cradled me in his arms and petted my hair. I just can't reconcile the two, and yet my mate bond tells me without a shadow of a doubt, that this indeed my Okot.

He doesn't answer, just continues to pull me forward. "Okot, if the prince is threatening you or something, just tell me. Let me help—"

Instantly, a puff of pink smoke appears at my side, and then there's Lex, her face beaming with a ready smile... until she sees me, at which point that smile quickly falls from her face. "Madame Cupid Emelle?"

Okot whirls on her, and then it's her throat that he's gripping. "Okot, no!"

I try to claw at him to get him to release her, but of course, the freaking lamassu is way too strong. "Lex. Go invisible *now*," I order.

Just like that, she disappears, and Okot's fists clench around nothing.

He turns a livid face on me, but before he can get a grip on me again, I go invisible. Lex is there, hovering beside me with wide eyes. We both watch as Okot yells in frustration and punches his fist at the stone wall so hard that chunks of rock fall to the floor. When palace guards come running up, I turn to leave, floating through the walls and out of the palace as quickly as my intangible body will take me.

For decades, I have watched people's hearts break into a million pieces. It just comes with the job as a cupid. You don't get love without that risk of it going all wrong. For years, I struggled to put hearts back together again. Sometimes it worked. Sometimes it didn't. Sometimes, I had to watch the loveliest of people suffer in the worst of ways.

I would watch them cry or scream or shut down, and I would hate that I had played a part in their misery of broken love. But I never really knew what it actually *felt* like. Not until right now, at this moment.

It's ironic, really. I'm a cupid, and my heart has just broken.

CHAPTER 9

$\mathcal{I}$'m crying in a smoke tree.

Like, a literal smoke tree. As in, it's smoking. Instead of leaves, the branches just have wisps of curling, thick smoke that constantly change color. I'm not sure why I decided to land on one of its branches, enter my physical body, and start crying. It just seemed like if I was going to have a total breakdown, it was a good idea to do it with a bunch of rainbow smoke around.

I have snot and tears on my face, and my hair smells like smoke, but at least it's hiding me from any prying eyes. The colored smoke curls around me like it's giving me a little hug. Yeah, I know. That's weird, right? Right. But I'm wallowing right now, and I could really use a hug, so if that means that I have to pretend to get it from a weird magic smoking tree, then dammit, that's what I'll do.

I sit on the branch and have an emotional breakdown until I can't cry anymore, while Lex sits on a branch beside me in stoic silence. When my tears finally dry up, my eyes are painfully puffy and I feel perfectly miserable, but the flood that escaped me helped unleash the torrent inside, so I feel a little steadier. I still have a job to do.

I have to shove all thoughts of Okot out of my mind for now; otherwise, I'll just want to crawl into a ball and sleep for a hundred years so that I don't have to deal with the pain that I'm feeling. But I can't do that. The princess needs me. My genfins need me. I have to get Princess Soora out of the prison and find my mates.

After that...then I'll deal with the pain of Okot's betrayal. But not now. I had my cry, and that's all I'll allow myself for now.

"Better?"

I look over at Lex where she's perched on a branch, looking at me expectantly. She looks so prim and proper with her sleek pink hair and wrinkle-free clothes, while I...I have rainbow smoke stains on my dress, and my face is splotchy from my sob fest.

I'm also not positive that I don't have snot in my hair. What? I just had my heart broken. A girl is entitled to ugly cry.

Lex's question hangs between us. Am I better? No. Not at all. But I wipe my nose on my arm and nod at her anyway. "Yeah."

Lex does some crazy limber move and swings from her branch to mine, landing gracefully beside me. If I'd have tried that move, I would've for sure lost my balance and fallen to the ground in a clumsy heap.

"I've fixed over nine hundred thousand broken hearts," she tells me matter-of-factly. "My method is tried and true. You choose one or more acceptable replacements, and I will hit them with two Love Arrows in rapid succession and then add precisely three Flirt-Touches upon first glance. It's a guaranteed love-at-first-sight outcome that has a success rate of eighty-two per-cent."

I blink at her. "Umm...wow. That's really something."

"I take great pride in doing my job well."

I sniff. "Thanks for the offer, but no thanks."

She cocks her head and reaches behind her to her quiver full of arrows. "I could go to the mate in question and hit him with Love Arrows? Granted, it might not work on him. He seemed quite enraged."

"No thanks to that, either, Lex."

The last thing I want is for any of my guys to have their feelings pushed into love territory by force. Especially Okot. He betrayed me. Lied to me. Faked everything. I want to get love on my own without cupid intervention.

A thought occurs to me. "Wait. How are you here? I thought only I was able to cross in and out of the Veil."

She shakes her head. "As your assistant, I come automatically whenever you need aid. I suppose that goes for when you are in the physical realm as well."

I run a hand down my face. "You won't start malfunctioning, right?"

"No, I have travelled for Seedy to the physical realms in the past. The Veil understands it's part of my duties."

"Oh, okay. Good."

"Forgive me, but...are your hands dirty?" she says, staring at my palms.

I look down at them and realize that they *do* look dirty. Filthy, even. I rub them together, and brown particles fall to the ground.

"Is that dust?" she asks.

I glower at the pile that lands on my feet. "Nope. Not dust. Sand," I tell her. "Sandman powers. Sandwoman?

Sandlady? Sandperson? Whatever, you know what I mean."

Her brows shoot up in surprise. "Oh."

I try to dust off the...dust, but the movement just makes my cupid boss mark start glowing pink again. I sigh and give up.

"At least the pink glow can give off light whenever you're in the dark," she says hopefully. She's really a glass half-full of a fruity cocktail kind of girl. "And I'll bet you can find a way to use all your new powers in a way that will help all of lovekind."

I peer over at her curiously. "You really like being a cupid, don't you?"

She nods enthusiastically. "I do. Making Love Matches, watching people get so filled up with love that they nearly burst...it's fulfilling."

"No wonder you're always Cupid of the Month."

"Thank you," she beams.

I take a deep breath and get my bearings. "Okay, why don't you go back to Cupidville for now? It's not exactly safe where I'm going, and I know you're excited about getting in that Love-Surplus you were talking about."

She looks me up and down, no doubt noting that I look like I'm barely holding myself together, and shakes her head. "No, Madame Cupid Emelle. I'll stay with you."

"Lex..."

"Don't worry," she rushes in to say. "At the first sign of trouble, you can push me back into the Veil."

I can see by the look on her face that I'm not going to talk her out of it. Short of ordering her away, she's going to stick with me. And honestly? I'm glad for the company.

"Okay, then. From this moment on, we're in super spy mode. Let's go invisible. I need to fly to an island and see about a thief, and believe me, we don't wanna get caught."

She practically bubbles over with excitement. "Do you think we can shoot some Love Arrows on the way?"

"Have at it."

"Yay!" She claps.

We both go into the Veil and fly through the kingdom. It's clear that Okot alerted the soldiers of my presence, because guards are scouring the city, even more so than before. Lex shoots at least a dozen fae with arrows before I make her stop and we take to the sky. She follows beside me as I head straight for Arachno's banishment island. It's easy to find, since my genfins' banishment island is below the kingdom's, and then Arachno's isn't far off from that.

It doesn't take long for us to get there. Neither of us have to worry about the protective barrier, so we pass through it without a hitch. Following Princess Soora's directions, I start scouring for Belren's secret hideout. Luckily, it's on the other side of the creepy, rocky island where Arachno's cave is located.

I find the mountain at the edge of the island, and we float all the way to the top. "What are we looking for?" Lex asks.

"There should be a door," I say, looking around the rocks. I know we're in the right place. I just need to find...

"This door?"

I whip my head around and see Lex pointing to a flat slab of rock propped up against the mountainside. I fly over and immediately find an *H* carved into the side. It's tiny—barely an inch across.

I give her an impressed look. "You are super good at this assisting stuff."

She practically gleams. "Thank you!"

We float through the stone door and then pop into our physical bodies.

"Come on," I say, grabbing her arm and pulling her forward.

We make our way down the winding stone tunnel that was carved into the mountain. There are some sconces hanging on the wall every few feet that magically burst with light as we pass.

"What's that noise?"

I stop to listen, and my ears perk up. "I think it's... music? Go invisible, Lex. Just in case."

She nods and pops out of view, and I hurry toward the sound. When I get to the end of the tunnel, I find a fae slumped over, snoring soundly against the wall. Edging past him, I push open a crooked wooden door and walk into the huge room.

Sure enough, the music is coming from a quartet of fae collected on a makeshift stage, playing flute-like instruments. There are a dozen more fae gyrating to the music while in various stages of undress. The room is smoky and reeks of fairy wine.

In one corner, there's a group of fae getting it on while another group sits by to watch. Belren is right in the thick of it.

"That damned Horny Hooker," I mutter through clenched teeth. He's lying on his back, his gray horns curled over his silver mask as he sucks on a fairy pipe and blows smoke into the air in the shape of butterflies. Female and male fae alike are tittering around him, acting perfectly impressed.

I march over and stand over him with my arms crossed. "What the hell are you doing?"

His gray eyes snap up to mine in surprise. He takes a

moment to look at me, his eyes calculating through the slits in the mask. "I thought I made you promise never to come back to this island," he murmurs.

He takes a long, slow drag from the pipe before pursing his lips and blowing a stream of smoke up at me. A smoke butterfly forms and starts flapping its wings in front of my face.

"Yeah, well, that was before I had to track your thieving ass down." I wave my hand to dissipate it, which makes several of the other fae boo me. I frown at them. "You shouldn't boo people. It's not nice."

A slow smile spreads over his face. I can just barely see his flashing white teeth beneath the mask. "It really *is* you. You're back," he says, more to himself than to me, as the smoke curls around him. From the smell, I know that he's not just smoking bay leaves. This stuff seems…potent.

In one fluid movement, he rolls up to a standing position, grabs my arm, and then starts pulling me out of the room toward a wooden door at the back. When we're inside, he closes the door behind him, plunging the room into darkness. Total darkness.

You know, except for my glowing cupid boss mark.

CHAPTER 10

*A*midst the pink glow I'm giving off in his dark room, I see him remove his mask and then arch a white brow. "New trick?"

I look down at my arm. "Yeah."

With a flick of his wrist, he uses his telekinesis to strike a match and light the candles and sconces in the room one by one. Soon, the space lights up enough so that I can see that we're in a bedroom.

True to his Horned Hook style, he has jewelry, weapons, and all things glittery hanging up all over the place. "New stolen goods?" I say, poking a jeweled dagger at the wall behind me.

He grins. "It's a tough job, but someone has to do the thieving around here."

"How can you just be here, throwing a weird underground party on a banishment island? I thought you were supposed to be laying low?"

"This *is* laying low. I only have a few dozen fae here. It's a very humble hideout party."

I sigh and rub my brows. "Belren…"

He looks me up and down in a lascivious way, not ashamed in the slightest when his gaze gets stuck on my chest. "Have you come to your senses and left your mates for me? Is that why you're here?"

I narrow my eyes on him and put my hands on my hips. "How can you flirt with me when your lover is stuck in prison, all bruised up, frozen, and hungry? I can't believe you right now."

The amusement on his face disappears, and he looks at me, bewildered. "What in the realm are you talking about?"

"Princess Soora!" I say with a huff. "You're here partying, flirting, and smoking weird butterflies while fae get it on in your little party cave, when you should be trying to figure out a way to rescue the princess!"

He frowns and absently runs a hand through his long white hair, tucking it behind his gray horns on either side of his head. "The princess has been missing for weeks. Everyone believes her to be dead."

"She's not dead. I just saw her a couple of hours ago. She's being kept in the prison tower."

He turns and starts pacing around the room, his fingers pinching his lips in thought. "She's alive," he says under his breath, more to himself than to me. "You're sure?"

"Yes, and I don't think she'd appreciate you flirting with others," I say, pointing a finger at him accusingly. "And I should warn you—as a cupid, I don't take kindly to people breaking other people's hearts."

Especially hers, I think to myself. She's had enough heartache. If he hurts her, I will shove a Love Arrow so far up his ass, his heart will poop out sonnets and glitter for the rest of his life.

He stops to look at me with bewilderment. "Wait, you think that the princess and I..." His words trail off, and then he tilts his head back and lets out the most obnoxious laugh I've ever heard. It isn't a short bark, either. Nope. He just keeps going. And going. And going.

"What's so damn funny?"

Wiping tears from his eyes, he shakes his head, making his horns catch in the candlelight. "The princess and I aren't lovers."

My brow furrows. "You aren't?"

"No. Why did you think that?"

"Well...I mean, I just thought I was picking up some love vibes from her." A thought comes to me, and I groan. "Oh gods, it's not unrequited love, is it? She's in love with you, and you don't give her the time of day? How could you, Belren?" I demand.

He laughs. "Take a breath, Veil female. It's not me she loves. Needs, sure, but loves...no."

"Well...now I'm just confused."

"Let's just say we have a mutual acquaintance."

I tilt my head. "What does that mean?"

"We've both been searching for someone."

This piques my interest. "Who?"

He tosses me a smirk. "Sorry. I don't give away secrets for free. I'm a collector and a thief. It would be bad for business."

"I think you might have a hoarding problem."

I start walking around the room, touching the stolen items hanging up in his room while I think. If the princess was captured because Prince Elphar found out that she'd been helping lead the rebellion, why *didn't* he execute her? He must have some other agenda I don't know about yet. No matter what I do, he's always two steps ahead of me.

"Can you not do that?" Belren sighs.

Interrupted out of my thoughts, I shoot him a look over my shoulder. My hand is frozen on a scarf made of silk and diamonds. "I can't look at your stuff?"

"Not that," he clarifies. "Stop gliding around. It makes your ass look too good, and we've already established that you're going to stay with your harem of mates. So stop *swaying* around my damn bedroom."

Now it's my turn to laugh. "I'm not swaying, I'm *walking*. And what, you're not a sharer?" I tease.

He scoffs. "I'm a thief. I thrive on taking what belongs to others. Of course I don't share."

He starts striding toward me, his eyes locked onto me with a daring expression. He doesn't stop until we're toe to toe, and I have to crane my head up to look at him. The look in his eyes makes me gulp. And yet, as handsome as he is, Belren holds his cards too close to his chest for me ever to get a good read on him. I don't understand him, and I don't know what his motives are. I'm also sure as hell not going to abandon my guys for him.

"But as I said, I'm also a collector," he goes on, his voice low and husky as he takes a piece of my pink hair and rubs it between his fingers. "Which means that I am entranced with the rare. The special. The unique. And you, my dear female from beyond the Veil, are entirely singular."

I have to admit, his close proximity, and the way he's looking at me freaks me out a bit. I swear, if he moves even an inch closer, we'd be kissing. And I *can't* kiss him. He's not my mate, and he just made his stance about sharing quite clear. I'm not about to cross a line. I need a distraction and quick. So I do the first thing I can think of.

"Help," I squeak.

Lex pops up into existence beside me.

"Hi," she says brightly.

Belren drops my hair and flinches back in surprise. I see his gray eyes widen and dart between us. I press a hand against my hot cheeks from the intense moment between us and take the opportunity to duck past him and put some space between us. There's no doubt that Belren is attractive and exudes a particular sexy swagger, and it's difficult to think when he focuses all of that charisma straight-on.

I clear my throat and force my heart to calm down. "About all of that being special stuff..."

"There are two of you," he says, still staring at Lex.

"There are not *two* of us," I correct. "There's me and there's her."

"Two females from beyond the Veil. How is that possible? And why do you look similar? And where the hell did she come from?"

"We're cupids," Lex answers. "All cupids look like this." She looks over at me and tilts her head. "Well, Madame Cupid Emelle's appearance has...altered slightly. And I came from the Veil."

Belren's silver face turns to mine. "*You're* the cupid everyone is whispering about?"

I tense slightly, remembering how the genfin in the street called me that, too. "What have you heard?"

Belren taps a jewelry-clad finger against his chin. "That there is a cupid from another world. That she's wreaking havoc on the realm. Some whispers say you're a demon, here to punish all of faekind. Others say you're actually here to help us defeat the prince and end his tyranny. And then, even more say that you're just a

61

human-bird mutt who has grotesque wings and you're actually fighting alongside the prince, killing anyone who stands in your way."

I bristle. "I do *not* have grotesque wings."

He cocks a white brow. "That's what you took away from that?"

"I just don't like to be incorrectly depicted," I insist.

"You're serious about being cupids? You mean, love and sex and all of that?" he asks.

I gesture at the Love Arrows I currently have strapped to my back. "Yep."

Belren looks bewildered and immensely intrigued. "And she's your assistant?" he asks dubiously. "Who in the realms gave *you* an assistant?"

"Don't say it like that. And it's a long story. There was a bit of a scuffle in Cupidville."

"A *scuffle*?" he laughs.

I wave a hand at him. "I'm sort of in charge now. The old boss, well, like I said. There was a scuffle."

"I'm sure," he says, his head moving back to eye Lex.

He does a slow head-to-toe eye fucking, no doubt taking note of the whole hot, strict school teacher thing she has going on. His eyes light up with a predatory kind of challenge. I can practically taste the waves of desire wafting off of him. "You don't have a gaggle of mates snapping at *your* heels, do you?" he asks her.

Lex frowns. "What?"

I sigh at him. "Don't try to seduce my assistant."

He ignores me. "What's your name, Pinky?"

"I am cupid sixty-nine," she answers matter-of-factly. I groan and inwardly face-palm.

The widest smile spreads across his face. "A giver *and* a taker. What a treat you are."

"Lex. I've shortened her name to Lex," I say.

"Well, *Lex*," he begins as he saunters over to her. He's putting his charm on its highest setting, but rather than melt or bolt, Lex just continues to smile at him like she's the receptionist at a hotel, waiting to check him in and get him out of line. Even when Belren props a hand up on the wall behind her, essentially caging her in, she never loses her polite but aloof expression. "I'd love to become more acquainted with you."

I roll my eyes. "You were *just* flirting with me."

He shrugs and looks over his shoulder at me. "You're a beautiful, unique creature. I can't help myself. Like I said, I'm a collector. I know it when I see something valuable. It was only natural for me to be attracted to you. But like I said, I'm not the sharing type, and you're stubbornly sticking with your multiples, aren't you?"

"Yes, dammit! They're my mates."

He shrugs unapologetically. "Well, then. I know a lost cause when I see it." He looks back to Lex. "This one, however, doesn't seem to have a horde of mates tied to her yet. I intend to seduce you," he tells her, being perfectly serious.

Lex cocks her head. "Seduce me?"

Belren lets a slow grin crawl over his face. "Indeed. Tell me, have you ever done your namesake?" He slowly traces his finger down her arm. "I can assure you, I'm quite good at that number."

I snap my fingers to get his attention. "Would you please focus?"

He sighs and drops his hand. "You know, for a cupid, you're being quite the cockblock."

I open my mouth to tell him off, but Lex interrupts by saying, "Oh, I apologize sir Horny Hooker. I'm not available for romantic relationships. Not only am I a cupid, I am also Cupid of the Month as well as Madame Cupid Emelle's assistant. So you see, I cannot enter into any sort of liaisons, flings, or love affairs of any kind. Not only is it against cupid laws, but I simply don't have the time. I take my cupid duties very seriously. Apart from my other responsibilities, there are simply too many Love Matches and sexual interactions that I need to be spreading in the realms."

I snicker at the look on Belren's face. "First of all, it's the Horned Hook," he says, shooting me a dirty look. "And what is it with you cupids turning me down?" he grumbles.

I chuckle. "Not used to being turned down?"

"No, actually," he admits.

Yeah, I can see why. Belren is one hot fae wrapped up in pretty silver packaging.

"Can you just rein in the ego for a minute and help me figure out how we're gonna rescue the princess? You can try seducing Lex later."

"Fine," he sighs, like I'm really putting him out.

"Lex, why don't you go do some cupidy stuff and check in with me later?"

She tilts her head. "Thank you, Madame Cupid Emelle. I'm jonesing to get started on today's goal!" she says excitedly.

Belren watches her with an amused expression. "And what's today's goal, Sixty-Nine?

"I have a broken heart challenge. I'll be going to the human realm to work on fixing those who have been blocklisted."

"Blocklisted?" Belren questions. "Cupids blocklist people?"

"Oh, yes," she nods primly. "If a person has had more than three Love Matches but has then ruined said relationships through nefarious actions, they become blocklisted. At that point, only higher-up cupids, such as myself and Madame Cupid Emelle, are permitted to attempt another Love Match. But since those people have abused love, we must do quite a bit of work to ensure they deserve it and that the next Love Match is one that they do not abuse. It's a challenge, but when it works, the blocklisted people can often become the best lovers because they realize how lucky they truly are that love gave them another chance. Rehabilitating blocklisters isn't easy, but it is rewarding."

Belren looks over, and I hold my hands up. "Don't look at me. I never worked any of the blocklist people. I could barely get regular ol' school sweethearts to stay matched up."

"And yet you're in charge," he says sardonically.

He's got a point. Not that I'm going to tell him that. I turn to Lex. "Go ahead and get back, Lex. I'm good now."

In a puff of pink smoke, she disappears.

"Alright," Belren says, his voice and expression turning serious. "Tell me exactly where the princess is being held."

I do, and Belren takes notes as I talk. Not by actually writing with the quill, though. Nope, sir master thief uses his power to make the pen write on the paper for him, while he starts packing up supplies in a leather knapsack. He's great at multitasking.

"Not only does the prison tower have no windows or exterior doors, it also is protected by great magic. No one has ever escaped it before," he explains.

My heart drops. "Well, that sucks major meatwhistle."

His lips tilt up slightly. "But…" he goes on as he tucks

the pack over his shoulder. "That's because *I've* never tried it," he finishes with a cocky grin.

"So you can do it?"

He floats his mask back to his face, and I watch as it reattaches itself. "I'm the Horned Hook. I can steal anything or any*one*."

Relief spreads through me. "Good. I also…sorta lost my genfins," I say quickly.

He gives me an exasperated look. "You lost your mates *again*?"

"I didn't do it on purpose!"

He sighs at me and rubs a hand down his face. "Okay. We'll get the princess out, and then I'll help you find your genfins." He points at me. "But this is the last time. Stop. Losing. Your. Mates."

"Okay, okay," I promise. "Can we please go do your Horned Hook master thief stuff now?"

I can see his smile flash behind his mask. It's an excited, mischievous look that nearly makes his gray eyes glow. "Let's go steal us a princess."

CHAPTER 11

$\mathcal{J}$ have to help break up the orgies.

There are quite a few more going on since I first went into Belren's room. He sighs at the sight of all the fae still *thoroughly* enjoying themselves, with a look of wistfulness. "Okay, you get those ones, I'll get the beached kelpies over there."

I watch as he makes his way over to the pile of bodies with green seaweed-looking goo leaking out from their orifices. Eww.

I march over to the opposite corner where some other fae are getting it on. I feel a little bad about breaking it up, to be honest. I like to start orgies, not end them. The closer I get, the more my cupidy senses start tingling.

When I reach them, I clear my throat. I also try to avert my eyes since, you know, I'm mated and stuff. The orgy participants don't react at all. They just continue sucking and thrusting and making a lot of noise.

"Excuse me?" I say, my head pointed up to the dirt ceiling.

Nothing.

I clap my hands loudly, which makes them finally look over at me but also makes my cupid mark start glowing again.

The one with antlers looks me up and down and stops slurping at the dangling bits between another fae's legs. "You want to join us?" he asks.

He's currently on his knees, propped behind another fae who has four legs and a back pouch. Huh. I bet a back pouch really comes in handy when he's shopping. Oh. Wait. That's not a back pouch.

"Enjoying the view?"

I quickly snap my eyes back up to the ceiling. "Umm. No. Yes. I mean, it's interesting. But no, I would not like to join you. I have mates. Plural," I explain. "One of them has super strength. Another one does something weird when he whistles. I don't really know. But he's a super good whistler. The third one—"

"Oi! Break it up!"

I flinch at Belren's booming voice, since he somehow came up right behind me without me noticing. He also sort of shouted right into my ear. Probably on purpose, the jerk.

The other fae start scrambling to their feet. There's a lot of…squelching that goes on as they disentangle. Also, a lot of wet spots. I turn my back on them as they quickly dress and disappear out the door.

I turn to Belren. "Do they know how to get off?"

Belren opens his mouth to make a dirty joke, but I roll my eyes and cut him off. "I meant get off *the island*."

He grins but drops it. "Yes, of course they do. They'll go through the barrier doorway that the princess made. Ready to go?"

"Yep."

He looks me up and down. "You should change."

"I didn't exactly have time to pack a change of clothes," I say, looking down at my dirty dress.

"Darling, I'm a thief. I have everything you could ever need or want, and if I don't, I can sure as hell get it."

He flicks his wrist, and for a moment, nothing happens. But after a few seconds pass, something comes zooming out of Belren's bedroom and launches itself at me. I barely catch the clump of fabric with an oomph as it slaps into my chest.

"Put those on."

"You could say please," I grumble as I look through the bundle. There are thick brown pants, a white blouse, and a pair of sturdy leather boots. "Do you have any real arrows?" I ask.

He eyes the red and pink ones in my quiver. "And those are..."

"Love Arrows, obviously."

He grins. "Obviously."

Another moment passes, and then arrows come hurtling toward me. And they're going *fast*. When they're about to pierce my face, I squeak in surprise and hit the ground.

Belren laughs, and the sound bounces off the room's dirt walls. I glare up at him. "That wasn't nice."

The arrows are hovering inches above the spot where I was. "Sorry. Couldn't help myself."

I stand and pluck the arrows from the air, quickly stuffing them into the quiver.

"Now stop dawdling and go get changed."

He saunters off to the other side of the room before I can volley a string of curses at his face. I quickly go into Belren's bedroom to get dressed, leaving my dress and silk slippers in a pile. When I get back out to join Belren, the other fae are all gone, and he's waiting for me out in the tunnel and doing some fancy wristwork.

"What are you doing?" I ask, looking around.

"The last of the fae just left. I'm just opening the passageway for us. Ready?"

Am I ready to go break out the princess from an un-breakout-able prison? No. "Yep," I say. "I'm a super good spy. I can do this 'stealing people out of prison' thing, no problem."

His mouth twitches, and he turns to the direction of the stone door while I follow behind him. "How did you all stay here without Arachno finding you?"

"Magic. Princess Soora wasn't just able to make a door into the barrier. She also glamoured this part of the mountain with a cloak. Our old cannibalistic spider friend doesn't know anything is amiss on her island. Besides, the princess ensured she had a...delivery to keep her occupied."

I stop, horrified. "Princess Soora dropped fae off here to be eaten?"

"Nothing quite so dramatic," he says over his shoulder. "She dropped off a cart of serpentinal skins."

"What the heck is a serpentinal?"

He shakes his shoulders like he has the heebie-jeebies. "A particularly ugly fae who shed their skins once every few years. It's a gruesome process, but their skins are actually quite valuable. Once they're dried and set, you can use them for all sorts of things. Healing tonics, fabrics, even aphrodisiacs."

"Huh."

"Indeed. But to Arachno, there is power in the pieces of fae. Somehow, she's able to ingest power from it. She'll

70

be quite busy with her gift as she goes through the tedious process of drying it. It can go badly wrong if the temperatures aren't exactly right."

The thought of Arachno drying some fae's skin turns my stomach. I still remember when she took that banshee tongue and chewed it like a piece of gum. I gag a little just at the memory.

Belren hears me and chuckles. "With four mates, you'll have to work on that gag reflex."

"My gag reflex is perfectly fine," I defend. "In fact, Sylred told me that I exceeded his expectations," I say smugly.

"Well, he's the nice one, isn't he?"

I frown at his back. "Yeah, but…"

"Exactly."

My steps falter slightly. "My gag reflex is great. Just ask the other ones!"

He shrugs, like it's no matter to him. I mean, it *is* no matter to him, but I don't like being accused falsely.

"This discussion isn't over," I warn him.

He looks over and shoots me a grin. "By all means, please bring it up again when we find your missing mates."

"I will," I say, tilting my chin up obstinately. He just laughs like that's the funniest thing ever.

CHAPTER 12

$\mathcal{W}$e get to the stone door that Belren used his fancy magic on earlier to move the stone away, but instead of heading toward the barrier door, he starts heading down the mountain toward Arachno's side and pops his wings out of his back.

They look like moth wings. Slightly fuzzy but with beautiful hook-like shapes in the centers. "Horned Hook makes more and more sense," I tell him. "But what doesn't make sense is why we're walking *toward* the crazy cannibal spider fae who tried to eat us."

He continues making his way down the mountain, moving rocks out of his way as he goes, making it look like he's gliding down the damn thing. When he gets to some of the larger rocks, he simply jumps into the air and flaps his wings to speed his way over them. I, on the other hand, slip, slide, and scrape my way down until giving up trying to do things as gracefully as him. I fly the rest of the way down and land beside him huffing and puffing.

He looks over at me. "On second thought, maybe you should just…stay here. If you had that much trouble just getting down the mountain, I'm not sure how much help you'll be."

"Shut up," I whisper-yell. I seriously don't want Arachno to hear us. Even with the gross serpent-fae skin stuff, I'm not convinced she'll be distracted enough not to notice us now that we're no longer protected by his hideout's cloaking magic. "Will you please tell me what the heck we're doing over here? I thought we were going back to the kingdom island?"

"Well, we can't very well go there yet," he says, striding forward. He's still heading toward Arachno's caves.

"What? Why not?" I say, rushing over to catch up with him.

"Aren't you supposed to be Princess Soora's operative?"

"If you mean her super awesome spy, then yes."

"For a spy, you're not very…adept."

"And what the hell do you mean by that?" I snap. First the gag reflex, and now he's questioning my spy skills. I don't appreciate it.

"That prison tower is not just impenetrable from the exterior," he explains, never slowing his stride as we walk through the rocky, sparse ground. There are a few trees here and there, and a low, thick fog covers the entire island, making it look extra creepy. All of the trees resemble massive spiky skeletons rather than plants.

"I know," I tell him as I try not to pant to keep up with him. I miss my guys. They totally would've carried me. I fly for a bit to give my legs a break.

"But," he goes on, "it's also protected by magic. Magic that will tear apart any fae that attempts to escape its walls."

I picture Princess Soora walking out of the tower and

getting shredded into a thousand little pieces. I wince. "Well, that…isn't good."

"Indeed," he agrees. "Which means we need to find a way through that magic." He turns to look at me. "And how do you break into an impenetrable prison tower that will turn you into a thousand pieces should you try to escape?"

Is this a trick question? "Ummm…I don't know."

He smirks at me. "You don't."

He turns around again and hops over a huge rock before landing nimbly on the dirt about three feet away. When I try to recreate the move, I don't stick the landing. The landing sticks me.

"Ouch." I land on my butt in a pile of dead, sharp sticks and pull the twigs out of my rear end.

Belren takes my arm and pulls me to my feet. "So, if we can't get through the magic that's been put on the prison tower, how are we going to get the princess out?"

He starts pulling me forward again, and I do my best not to stumble over the rocks at his hurried pace.

"The prison tower's magic is being supplied through one source. The king. And do you remember what King Beluar's magic does?"

I think back to the culling when my genfins were forced to fight to the death. The scene of the trial where they were forced to wield swords that had minds of their own comes clearly into my mind. And so does the way Ronak went animalistic and cut down every last opposing fae. The thought makes chills break out over my body. "Yeah, umm, King Beluar's magic somehow controlled the swords so that they had a will of their own."

"That's right," Belren says, helping me past another

74

rocky area. Arachno's mountain is looming closer and closer.

My mind scrambles to keep up. "Wait. You're saying that he did the same thing to the tower? That he some-how...gave it a mind of its own?"

"Not a mind. A *will*. The walls of that prison tower have one purpose. To keep its prisoners inside. The prison will destroy any who try to escape."

My brow furrows in thought. Not only do we have to figure out a way to get Princess Soora's cell open and get her past the guards, but the entire prison itself will be fighting us. The odds don't sound good. Then a thought hits me. "Wait," I say, huffing and puffing. "The guards. They're able to go in and out, and the prison doesn't harm them."

"Very good," Belren says. "The guards have a magical stamp put on them, so to speak, that the king himself puts on them so that they can enter and exit freely."

"Well, since the king is a giant douchefunnel, I doubt he'll do that for us."

Belren pulls us to a stop behind a scraggly tree to peer behind it at the entrance to Arachno's caves. "No," he murmurs. "He won't. At least, not the real him."

I look at him like he's crazy. "What were you smoking in that pipe? Stop talking in riddles. And could you please tell me why we're going *toward* the crazy fae-eating spider villain's lair?"

After his gray eyes scan the surroundings for a beat longer, he continues to pull me forward, his grip firm on my arm. "Because, little Veil female," he begins as we start quickly climbing the mountain. "Arachno has a taste for parodworms. She always has a stash of them."

"Parodworms?"

"Yes, the writhing, wriggling worm-like creature that feasts on equal amounts of soil and animal dung."

I wrinkle my nose in disgust. "Eww."

"Yes, I'd rather feast on mutton and pie, myself," he says. "But, do you know what the parodworms are known for? Do you know *why* Arachno has such a taste for them?"

I've never heard of parodworms before, but... "Well, when she eats, she's also eating their power. So I'm guessing they're powerful in some weird wormy way?"

"Very," he says, pulling me up to the lip of the cave entrance. We crouch down, listening and scanning the surroundings for a beat. Nothing is moving anywhere that I can see through the fog and rocks, but every shadow cast on the ground gives me the creeps and makes me look twice.

"And what can the parodworms do?" I murmur.

He looks over at me. "Oh, the usual worm things," he says quietly. "They break down organic matter in the soil, for one."

Well, that doesn't sound that impressive. I open my mouth to say so, but he stops me when his lips curl into a smile and he says, "Oh, and they're imitators."

CHAPTER 13

*B*elren starts pulling us into Arachno's hidden entrance of the cave. Unlike Belren's, this tunnel is completely dark and has an ominous feeling in the stagnant air. "Can you give us a little light?" he asks.

I give my hand a shake. Immediately, my mark lights up. "I'm a glorified torch," I grumble.

"At least you come in handy in the dark," he says with a proud look on his face. "Get it? *Hand*y in the dark?"

I roll my eyes. "Can you please explain the imitating thing? I don't get what you mean," I whisper as we start making the dizzying journey through Arachno's tunnels.

Belren must have done some investigating beforehand, because he never hesitates at the turns to choose which direction to go. "I mean exactly that. They imitate. Biologically, they become stronger when they ingest soil from the healthiest magical roots. Same thing goes for feces. The more powerful the fae, the better the dung feast."

"Gross."

"In return, they take the magic and digest it, only to return it to the ground in new forms. They are responsible for keeping our lands healthy and vibrant with power. A fae's power comes from the lands, after all," he explains as we continue down the dark paths. "Unfortunately, the parodworms are often hunted and have become rare nowadays. They're not just a meal, after all. They're a power supply. Animals and fae alike often prey on them."

"So they imitate fae as a defense mechanism?"

"Exactly. And parodworms not only imitate a fae's appearance, but they can also imitate their powers. Only for a very short period of time, but that's all we need."

My heart picks up the pace at this new information. "You're saying that if we can get one of these things, it can imitate the king?"

He flashes me a grin. "That's exactly what I'm saying."

He stops and holds up a finger to his lips. I watch as he peers over the corner where I can see the glow of a fire casting light and shadows against the walls. "We're clear," he murmurs.

He pulls me into the room, and terrible flashbacks come to my mind as soon as I see the space. The huge pot brewing gods-know-what in the center, the spider web covering the wall, and the shelves filled with bits and pieces of fae at the back.

"What do the things look like?" I ask as Belren hurries to start looking around the space.

"The parodworms are thin but very long," he says quietly as he starts to make his way around the room. "One good thing about being held captive here was the view."

He stops in front of the web wall and looks back at me expectantly. "Can you do your Veil trick and pop behind the web?"

"Yeah, but I can't bring the worm back out with me that way. I can't bring living things in and out of the Veil," I explain as I hurry over to him.

"I'll get you back out," he assures me. "Now, when I saw them strung up back there," he says, gesturing behind the web wall, "they were suspended at the top. They have a slight blue glow to them."

I rub my sweaty palms against my pants and nod. "Okay."

"Arachno is probably busy drying her new skins, but that doesn't mean she can't walk back in here at any moment. Best to hurry."

He doesn't have to tell me twice. I slip into the Veil and walk past the web wall, then gasp at what I find there.

Going physical again, I whisper-shout, "A little warning would've been nice!"

"Sorry," he says, even though he *totally* doesn't sound sorry. "I figured it wouldn't do any good to tell you about the dehydrated corpses beforehand."

I grimace as I carefully step past the bones and body parts that litter the entire area. It's bigger back here than I had guessed. There are also more bones than I can count in here. The ground is at least two feet higher with the pile of them.

There are also dangling bits hanging from the ceiling by pieces of web. Some of them are animals, like rabbits and mice, but others are bigger, and from the smell, I can tell that there are definitely dead fae hanging all around me. It's a terrible way to go.

Debating for a half a second, I start searching the macabre web cocoons to see if I can find anyone alive. Everything is sticky and the webs are stronger than they look, but I manage to rip open a few of them, only to be

79

met with lifeless corpse after lifeless corpse. It's not a cheery sight.

"What's taking so long?"

Belren's hissed voice makes me nearly jump out of my skin. "Holy hearts. Don't do that!" I whisper-shout.

"What, talk?"

"Yes," I snap. "I don't want to hear voices when I'm looking at corpses."

He gives a long-suffering sigh. "Why are you looking at the corpses? Focus on the mission. Does Princess Soora know that your attention span is this bad?"

"My attention span is not that bad! I was being a good citizen by trying to free a captive!"

"Just get a damn parodworm!"

"Fine!"

I whirl around and trip on the bones at my feet. I throw my hands out to catch myself, and of course, I catch myself on the web wall and get promptly stuck.

"What was that noise?" he asks from behind the wall. I can see his shadow following me.

"Nothing," I quickly say.

I try to unstick myself, but it's impossible. "What the chuck is this stuff made of?" I grumble.

"You got stuck in the web, didn't you?"

"No," I say hastily.

"Do I need to come in there and get the damn parodworm myself?" he drawls.

"I got it."

I quickly go invisible, unstick myself, and then go physical again. I double up on my effort, looking everywhere for the damn worm thingies when I spot it about four feet away. It's a long, glowing blue worm with its top half tucked into the dirt ceiling above.

"I think I found it."

I kick together a pile of bones to use as a makeshift stepladder until I can reach the ceiling, and then I start digging through around the worm, trying to find the head. It's in deeper than I thought and just seems to keep going.

"How long are these things?" I grit out as dirt falls onto my face and into my mouth as I continue digging. My arms are killing me from keeping them above my head, but I don't stop, even when my nails break and my arms start shaking.

If Ronak were here, he'd tell me that I need to work on my upper arm strength. I'd argue, of course, but he'd be right. Gods, I miss him.

"Hurry up," Belren hisses from the other side of the wall.

"I'm trying!"

More clumps of dirt come tumbling down, landing in my hair. I have to wipe my eyes on my arm to clear it away enough to see. Just when I'm sure that my arms are about to fall off, I finally reach the worm's head and pull it free.

"Yes! I got it!"

"Don't let it lick you."

I make a face and hold it at arm's length as it wriggles and writhes against me. The faint blue color does nothing to make it look less gross. "It has a tongue?" I squeal.

"Yes, now get out here," Belren says, his voice sounding anxious. "Someone's coming."

I hurriedly start to roll up the worm like I'm putting away a garden hose, winding it around my elbow as I hold the end. It wriggles as I carefully remove nearly all my arrows except for two and then stick the worm into the quiver. I also pick up a few handfuls of soil and dump it in on top, just to make it a smidge homier and so that the worm is less pissed off about being rudely relocated.

Finished, I carry the quiver in my hand as I rush to the wall where Belren has sliced a single strip, allowing me to squeeze through it. Several strands of my hair get ripped out from the sticky web, and I nearly lose my bow, but Belren cuts away the clinging web strands that want to keep me hostage.

"I got it, let's go," I tell him.

Before we take a single step, a terrible cackling bounces off the walls, and we both spin around at her voice. "My, my. The little bird has come back to Arachno," she says, making my blood run cold.

Her gray, decrepit-looking skin hangs off her bones, which only seems to compliment the stringy hair that reaches her bony knees. Her beady black eyes are all blinking at different times, and there have to be at least a dozen of them. Her mouth though...it's turned up into a perfect white grin that doesn't match the rest of her. A grinning Arachno doesn't seem like a super good sign.

"The pretty little bird flew away and took the Horned One from Arachno," she says, creeping closer to us.

She's blocking the one and only exit, because I took way too long behind the web wall. I clench the strap of the quiver in my hands and hold it against my chest like a shield, wondering how the hell we're going to get out of this.

Belren sneers at her. "I don't belong to you."

With the flick of his wrist, he uses his telekinesis to send her huge cauldron full of boiling liquid lifting up off the fire and zooming straight for her. But just as it's about to tilt and pour all over her, she snaps her fingers and the cauldron is yanked backwards and slams back on to the fire while Belren hunches over and makes a pained grunt.

"Are you okay?" I ask, casting worried looks at him, while I also try not to let Arachno out of my vision for a single second.

His silver skin looks paler than usual, but he straightens back up, even though I can tell that he's not feeling so hot. "She did something. My power. She must've...tasted a part of me to have control like this." He moves his hands to try to use his power again, but nothing happens. "Dammit."

Arachno keeps grinning. "The Horned One was a gift to Arachno. That means he *does* belong to Arachno," she goes on. "And the little bird took him. Little bird didn't make a trade to take him. She *stole* from Arachno," she says, the grin finally wiping away and a terrible evil glare taking its place.

Well, shit. That's worse than the grin.

CHAPTER 14

"*U*mm...Arachno, I want to make a trade!" I blurt out desperately.

She doesn't even deign to give me a response to that. Not that I expected it to work, anyway.

Instead, she lifts a bony hand and snaps her fingers again. Immediately, a circle of fire appears around us like a lasso, yanking Belren and me together so that we're back to back. The sudden movement makes me drop the quiver from my hands, and the soil spills over the ground as the parodworm tumbles out. I let out a surprised yelp as the fire rope cinches around our waists. It's hot enough to make me instantly break out into a sweat, but it doesn't burn unless I move or try to strain against the bindings.

"Hold still," I tell Belren.

He does, and the smell of burnt clothing fills the air.

"Birds and horns," Arachno tsks as she comes forward. "Horns and birds. What a nice meal they'll be for Arachno. Arachno had just a taste before. Just a morsel. Arachno is hungry for more."

"Go invisible," Belren whispers over his shoulder to me. "Get out of here."

"I'm not leaving you," I argue. "Like any respectable spy would even do such a thing!"

I'm almost affronted that he would even suggest it. Except for the fact that, you know, he doesn't want me to die. That's nice of him.

"Then do you have any other ideas? Because I'd rather us not be eaten alive today."

"You and me both, buddy."

Arachno starts moving around her cavern, tossing spices and...pieces of fae into the cauldron. I have to breathe through my mouth so that I don't gag from the smell alone. She starts singing some song about a bird with a broken wing who can't fly home.

"That's not very nice," I mumble.

"What's the plan?" Belren says.

"Don't worry, Horny Hooker. I got you," I say.

As soon as Arachno's back turns, I go invisible, nock an arrow, and shoot as soon as I pop into my physical body again. The arrow hits her dead in the center of her back...and bounces off.

"What the heck?"

Arachno turns slowly around. Like, creepily slowly. I swallow the bile that wants to rise up my throat. She raises her arms up, and I flinch back violently.

With a strange motion, Arachno creates a huge bubble of water from nowhere and sends it crashing into me. It encases my body, stealing all of my air and making me flail around in the water. Water tries to invade my every orifice, burning my eyes, pressing against my nose and ears and closed lips.

Arachno steps right in front of me, and I can see traces

of the death and the rot on her disgustingly perfect teeth. There are tiny bits of bone and skin still stuck between them.

"Go invisible!" Belren shouts as he struggles against the fire ropes. I hear his distorted voice through the water, much fainter than it probably is.

I try, but I can't. I try again and again, but it isn't working, and panic sparks to life inside of me. Whatever magic she's using against me, it's keeping me from being able to go into the Veil.

When she snaps her fingers again, the water slowly starts to heat up. I can feel the temperature rising, rising, rising, right alongside with the tempo of my panic.

I try to punch my way through the magic bubble that's keeping the air from me, but it won't burst no matter what I do. I toss a panicked look at Belren. I know that if I open my mouth and let water into my lungs, then it's all over. Belren is being held by fire, while I'm being threatened by water.

"Little bird may fly, but little bird cannot swim," Arachno cackles. "Little bird will boil. And Arachno loves a good bird stew."

Being drowned and boiled is not a nice way to go. I feel my bonds writhing inside of me just as much as the worm is writhing on the ground behind me. And even though Okot may have betrayed me, I still have three mates that I love, and I feel that now more than I've ever felt it in my whole existence as a cupid. It's what people have always been after. It's what *I've* always been after. Tears prick my eyes as black dots appear in my vision. I love them, and I never got to tell them.

That one word seems to catch inside of me, deep behind my ribs. I suddenly light up with it, a thousand times brighter than that of the faint pink glow of my cupid mark.

One second, I'm suspended in the water bubble, staring into Arachno's excited face, and the next, white light is pouring out of me. I open my mouth in a soundless scream, and water rushes into me, just as more light rushes out.

In an explosion of sound and heat, light erupts out of every pore of my body, instantly bursting the magic bubble and making water crash to the ground. I don't breathe, because I don't need to. My eyes stare straight ahead at Arachno's panicked face, her countless eyes blinking in shock, the light coming from me so bright that she shields herself with her arms.

But it's no use. She can't fight the light, and it engulfs her immediately.

In the span of a heartbeat, the light disappears, and I fall to the ground on my knees as I cough up water and take in deep, shuddering breaths.

I feel Belren beside me in an instant, slapping me on the back. I'm not sure if that really helps to get the water out of my lungs, but it's the thought that counts, I guess.

When I'm done spluttering and hacking, I look up at where Arachno used to be. All that's left of her is a shiny outline of her footprints.

"What in the realms did you do to her?" Belren asks, shocked.

"I think I just...destroyed her with the light of the heavens."

He looks at me incredulously. "I'm sorry, what?"

I shrug a wet shoulder. "I kind of have angel and demon traits. And maybe a few others..." I mumble. "But that one felt…angel." I don't know how to explain it, but there it is.

I notice the damn parodworm trying to slither away and quickly move to scoop it up. Taking up my quiver, I replace the soil and worm, and pack it in.

Belren blinks at me for a moment and then shakes his head as we start making our way out of Arachno's cave. "You're just full of surprises, Veil female."

He has no idea.

CHAPTER 15

"*Y*ou didn't tell me my worm had to lick the king!" I whisper-shout to Belren.

He rolls his eyes at me. "How else is the thing going to imitate him?"

We're both hunkered down in a storage closet inside the palace. It's cramped with mops and brooms, but it smells like lemons, so I can't really complain, even though Belren and I are practically on top of each other. I changed into a servant's gown and hid my wings, but Belren is still wearing his expensive dark silk shirt and trousers.

I was able to get in by going through the Veil, while Belren snuck the worm in by doing...whatever tricky thief stuff he does to get into places like this. Now we're just biding our time and trying to come up with a plan.

"So everything depends on the super long worm that I have stuffed in my quiver." Belren chuckles, and I punch him in the arm. "Shut up. It was going to sound dirty no matter how I worded it."

He has his mask on again since we're in public. Well,

we'll be in public once we're out of the storage closet. I can still see his lips and eyes through the holes, but I prefer to see his whole face. It's disconcerting talking to an expressionless mask.

"The king should be in his private chambers by now," Belren says. "If he's not already asleep, he will be soon. We'll go and slip in."

"Can you get in there without being caught? I mean, I can go invisible, but you can't. What about the guards?" I ask.

He rolls his eyes. "The guards aren't going to see me," he says with an arrogant tilt to his chin.

"Belren..."

"I'm the Horned Hook," he says, pointing to his horns. "This is what I do." He leans in closer so that his mouth is right next to my ear. "And I'm good at *everything* I do."

"Except sharing," I fire back at him.

His lips tilt up, and he leans back again. "Yes, except that. Let's go."

The castle is quiet as Belren leads the way through the servant's quarters. I've never seen it so quiet before. Usually, there are at least a few servants after hours, hearth hob fae scrubbing or washing something during the quiet hours of night. But there's no one except guards making their rounds.

"Why is this place so empty? Where are all the servants?"

"Use your multicolored eyes," Belren breathes, his voice not even loud enough to be considered a whisper. "Does the palace look crisp and shiny like usual?"

Frowning, I take a better look at my surroundings and realize right away what he means. Normally, this place is dazzling. Glistening chandeliers, polished stone, scrubbed carpets, shiny fixtures, but right now, I can see everything has a layer of grime and dust that had never been there before. Even small things, like the corner of a rug being flipped up or the drapes not being pulled shut for the night or candle wax being allowed to drip down onto the floor in hardened puddles.

No way the hearth hobs would ever allow the place to look like this. Duru, Princess Soora's right-hand lady, would have a heart attack if she saw this place. And since hearth hobs get their magic from cleaning, she would be practically glowing after tidying this mess.

"The hearth hobs are gone?" I ask, shocked.

Belren grins evilly and says, "Hearth hobs are often looked down on by the high fae. At least, by the prince's high fae society. But hearth hobs, as you know, are pivotal for our kingdom. Not just because they keep everything clean, but their cleanliness in the realm also promotes health and reduces viruses and bacteria from spreading. But the hearth hobs went on strike the day the prince announced Princess Soora's execution. They all disappeared."

My eyes widen in shock. "All of them?"

Belren nods as we round another dark corner. "Yes. The hearth hobs are incredibly loyal to Princess Soora. Their absence is felt in ways the high fae never imagined. Now, all the high fae snobs are quite out of sorts," he says, with a little bounce in his step. "I heard the king and prince were furious."

I mull over everything he said, wondering where the hearth hobs could have gone. I hope Duru is safe.

As we're about to round another corner, Belren holds his hand up for me to stop. I wait behind him, nervous in the dark shadows, while he peers around the corner.

Staying still, barely breathing, all while my heart pounds nervously inside my chest makes me extra jumpy.

Of course, right then, a guard surprises the ever-loving heart out of me by coming up behind us.

"Hey!"

I jump and shriek in surprise, and Belren whirls. But the guard is already reaching for me. I push my hands out to ward him off, and...oops.

I watch as my hands suck a gray essence out from his face. The stuff floats around his head for a moment, and his eyes widen in shock. Then, he collapses on the floor.

Shaky, I turn to Belren. "Crap. I accidentally soul-sucked him."

Belren blinks from the guard to me. "Does that... happen often?"

"You'd be surprised," I mumble.

He kneels down to check the guard's pulse, confirming what I already know. "Dead."

I grimace. "I hope he was a bad guy. He was a bad guy, right?" I ask hopefully.

When Belren opens his mouth to answer, I shake my head quickly. "Actually, don't answer that. I'm just gonna pretend he was and go with it."

Belren shakes his head at me. "Now we have to hide the body."

I look around the dark hallway, but there aren't any nearby rooms we can drag him in, and besides, he looks heavy. Noticing the carpet runner on the floor, I pick up the corner of it and cover him with it. "There."

Belren cocks a brow at me. "*There*? You're just going to toss a rug over him, which by the way, does absolutely nothing to hide him, and continue to *go with it*?"

"You have a better idea?"

He lifts his hands in front of our faces and wriggles his fingers. "Did you forget that I'm telekinetic?"

"Umm...actually, yeah."

With a flick of his wrist, his magic picks up the body, a nearby window is opened, and he goes zooming out into the night, the rug flapping around him.

"That's a good plan, too," I tell him.

He rolls his eyes. "Next time you hear a noise, go invisible instead of accidentally doing...whatever it is you just did. I'd rather not have to dump bodies in the river all night long."

I salute him. "You got it."

Belren and I continue the rest of the way in silence. Every time there's so much as a whisper of a noise, I go immediately into the Veil, and I have to admit, Belren is impressive in the way he finds ways to hide and use shadows to his advantage. His steps are completely silent, and he moves with a grace that I've never seen on a male before. No wonder he's such a good thief. He goes nearly as invisible as I do.

When we reach the king's corridor, Belren shoos me to go invisible and slip into the room alone so that I can unlock the door. Meanwhile, he uses his telekinesis to make something go crashing to the ground down the corridor, startling the guards and causing them to look away from the king's doors. It's all he needs to slip into the room undetected.

"Nice," I whisper, impressed.

Belren gives a small bow. "Shall we?"

I look in the darkened room, lit up only by the moonlight coming in through the windows high on the wall. We're in the king's receiving room, which is empty, and there are three more doors to search.

We share a look before heading to two different doors. Mine ends up being a closet, and when I look over at Belren, he gives a small shake of his head. We meet in the middle of the room, in front of the last door. After a beat, Belren slowly turns the knob and pushes the door open silently. When I peer in, I see a lit fireplace casting light and shadows around the room, and right there in front of the warm fire, is King Beluar in all his naked glory.

"Bath time," I mutter under my breath.

Apparently, I mutter a bit too loudly, because Belren grimaces and then the king picks up his head from where he'd been leaning back. His back is to me, so I only see the side of his face and his white hair, but he lifts an arm out of the steaming water and waves me forward. "Finally," he says with irritation. "All of you non-hearth hob servants are practically useless. Get on with it, would you?" He holds up a bar of soap for me, and I send Belren a panicked look, but the thief just backs away until he's completely hidden in the shadows of the room.

I glare in his general direction.

"Servant!" the king barks, making me jump.

I rush forward and reach out to take the soap from him. My hands are kind of shaking, so instead of getting a good hold on it, my hand knocks into it, sending it plopping into the water.

I lift my panicked eyes up to him, but he just sighs and tips his head back. "Fine. You can start with my bottom half."

Did I just hear the shadows chuckle? I'm going to smother that thief in his sleep.

Gritting my teeth, I roll up my sleeves and dip my hand into the water, trying not to grimace as I graze his purple-colored thigh in my search for the soap bar. I swear, if the thing landed on his junk, I'm gonna blow my cover.

Luckily, I find the soap in the corner near his knobby knee and snatch it up. I thank whatever lady luck powers that might have been responsible for that.

I move to the end of the tub and start washing his feet, since it seems like a safe spot. I start soaping them up and, yeah, the guy needs a serious pedicure. Doesn't he have handlers for this sort of thing? His toenails are like yellowed, ridged claws stuffed with toe jam. I'm forced to swallow a gag. Aside from his general ancientness, he also looks a bit sickly, to be honest. He seems paler and thinner than he used to and just...drained.

I hear the king sigh as he kicks his other foot at me. "What are you doing?" he snaps, his head coming up so that he can glare at me.

"Umm, washing your feet?"

"You're terrible at this," he declares. "Massage them right, or I'll send you to work in the stables shoveling horseshit for the rest of your insignificant life."

"S-sorry," I sputter.

"This is what's wrong with the realm today. Fae don't know their place. My son and I are royalty. What we say is law, and it's time you all are reminded of that fact!" he says, smacking a hand down on a knobby knee and making water splash all over the room. "These uprisings from lesser fae, and these servants thinking they can just walk out..." He pauses, his face full of furious indignation. "We will make them pay. My son is a thinker. Plans everything ahead. He saw the writing on the wall, oh yes," he says, nodding to himself. "We will have order and devotion, or we will wipe them all out!"

I flinch at the vehemence of his voice.

"Control," he goes on. "It's all about control. My son knows. He understands the need for control. I made sure of it." The king stops his rant, like he's suddenly remembered that I'm in the room with him. I wish I weren't. I'm pretty sure I can see a purple pube floating in the water.

"Well?" he barks. "Get to it!"

Jumping into action, I quickly start massaging my thumbs into the arches of his feet. After a moment, he relaxes back again and closes his eyes with a disturbing moan when I massage up to his calf.

Oh man, please don't let this be a happy ending bath time scrub. I will be scarred for life.

Just when I'm about to curse Belren for all eternity for taking his sweet-ass time, he finally comes sauntering out of the shadows holding the parodworm. He has most of it wrapped around his forearm, while he holds the head up with his fingers. Its tongue is already out, purple and lolling from side to side, trying to make contact with something as it wriggles in his hold.

Belren brings the worm to the king's back, and I keep up my massage, rubbing the muscles in his legs without pause. I'm terrified that he'll open his eyes, notice Belren, and raise the alarm. I'm so vigorous in my attempt at distracting him, that I go up a little *too* far. The king makes another little moan of satisfaction.

I snatch my hands back in mortification and repulsion.

Oh my gods, I touched his porksword. It was hairy. Also, slightly chafed. I'm *this* close to going into the Veil and letting Belren deal with him on his own.

"Don't stop," King Beluar snaps.

Fucking. Ew. And also, nope. Not happening.

I make a face at Belren, but it's clear from the way he's

practically biting off his own lips that he's trying not to laugh at me and is no help whatsoever. Jerk.

Having gotten its required lick, the worm starts shimmering. Belren gives a quick jerk of his head to follow him, and then slips out of the room without a sound. I'm left gawking like an idiot, trying to figure out how to get out of giving the monarch of the realm a handy.

Cupid problems.

CHAPTER 16

J'm still gaping at the shadows where Belren disappeared and totally ditched me with the naked monarch, when I feel the king's hand snatch at mine.

I yelp, but fortunately, I'm soapy enough that my hand slips out of his hold. I flinch back, falling hard onto my butt on the stone floor.

"What the seven hells are you doing?" King Beluar snaps, looking enraged.

I try to get to my feet, but I get tangled up in the dress and stumble back to the floor. The king narrows his eyes at me. Now that I'm closer to the light from the fireplace, I can see the wheels turning behind his eyes as he looks at me. "You look familiar."

I manage to get to my feet and shove a piece of frizzy pink hair behind my shoulder. "M-me? I'm just a servant, Your Majesty."

I watch his eyes widen as recognition dawns on him. He jumps to his feet, making me blink in surprise. Every inch of his lavender skin is on display, including the half-hardy he has going on.

"*You*. I know you."

I shake my head, but he simply steps out of the tub and comes stalking toward me. Despite him looking feeble and unwell, there's no doubt in my mind that he could take me down right here and now. He might be old, but he's powerful.

Of course, that's when my panic kicks in, and when I panic, I sometimes do stupid cupid stuff.

When he reaches forward to grab me, I simultaneously toss the bar of soap at his head and blow a huge breath of Lust right into his face. It comes out in pink puffs, but I don't stick around to see it. I duck under his arms and dart around him, running for the other side of the room.

When I don't hear him immediately shout for the guards, I cast a hurried glance behind me and see that he's now holding the bar of soap up and looking at it with the strangest expression on his face.

I jerk to a stop. All traces of suspicion and anger are gone. He's looking at the bar of soap like...

Oh, okay. He's kissing it now.

I wince when I see his purple tongue dart out and his eyes close on a moan as he starts making out with the sudsy bar.

I let out an exasperated sigh. "Dammit."

I watch him, equal parts horrified and entranced, as he continues to mack on the soap like he's hoping it'll sprout a cooter hole so that he can put his rising rod inside of it.

I almost feel bad for him and my wayward Lust-Breath, but not enough to hang out while he's distracted. Besides, it'll wear off. Eventually.

I dart out of the room, only to nearly barrel into a guard...and the king.

I almost freak out, thinking he's somehow magicked himself ahead of me, but then I see that the guard is actually Belren, and calm down enough to remember the worm lick. Belren closes the king's closet door, which he must've been in to dress the worm-king while also finding the time to steal guard clothes. There's probably some unconscious, naked guard stuffed into a broom closet now.

"Come on," he says, urging us forward.

The door to the corridor is already open, and the guards are gone. I have no idea what Belren did with them this time, but I don't ask as I hurry along beside him. We don't stop hurrying as we go all the way down to the kitchens and start making our way to the underground passage that will take us to the prison tower entrance.

"Go invisible."

I do, and then Belren and the king are stepping into the guard room.

There are two guards on duty, both of whom I recognize. There's the water sprite, Blix, who my friend Mossie has a total crush on, sitting at the table, and then there's the fire fae jerk, Ferno, with his skin that glows like embers and his curling, smoking hair.

Both males jump to their feet in surprise at our arrival but then give hurried bows when they see the king. Well, the worm-king, anyway.

Now that I'm getting a good look at him, I have to admit, the imitating thing is spot on. But there are subtle differences. Like how his white hair has a slightly bluish tint to it, and his expression is blank, like zero thoughts are going on in his head. Which, I guess, makes sense.

"Your Majesty?"

The king jerks his head down, and a grunt escapes him.

The guards share a look.

"How can we help you?" Blix asks.

Instead of answering, the king's arm raises, and he flaps it in the direction of the door.

When he does it again, I realize that Belren is using his telekinesis powers to move the worm-king. He looks like a weird puppet without strings.

"Are you going to just stand there? Your king wants inside the prison!" Belren barks, making Blix jump for his keys.

"Of course. Right away."

Ferno frowns, but when Belren moves the king's head to look at him, the fire fae finally drops his gaze to the floor. "Shall we accompany you, Sire?"

The king's head shakes no, and as soon as Blix gets the doors open, he jolts ahead, his footsteps loud and uneven.

Belren follows behind and slams the door behind them. When we're alone in the tower, I go physical and follow along behind.

"Which way?"

I point up the stairs. "All the way up."

Belren grumbles a string of curses under his breath. Apparently, moving the worm-king that much is going to be a strain on his magic, but we start making the slow progress up the many stairs.

Each floor has a corridor of cells, and there are all sorts of putrid smells and miserable sounds coming from them. It makes my heart ache.

"We have to help them," I choke out.

Belren shakes his head. "Not now. We have enough on our plate as it is."

"Just because you're a thief doesn't mean you can't be a good guy," I argue. "I don't buy that whole pretense, anyway. You are a good guy. I can tell. Besides, you have telekinesis. You can just flip everyone's lock. It'll be a good distraction!" I whisper-yell.

"First of all, stop thinking I'm a good guy," he says, looking irritated at the thought. "I'm not. I lie, cheat, bribe, blackmail, and steal for a living, and I *like* it. Secondly, I don't know if our wormy monarch here has enough juice to mark all of these prisoners so that the power allows them to leave!"

I cross my arms, stepping in front of him so he has to stop. We're right beside a cell that reeks of urine, and in the shadow, I can see a girl, probably in her early twenties, huddled up in the corner. She has a filthy maid's uniform on and looks positively terrified.

I approach the bars. "Why were you imprisoned?" I ask her.

She flinches away from me at first, but she answers, "King said I stole the silver. But I swear I didn't!" She cries, tears tracking down her dirty cheeks.

I turn to Belren pleadingly. "We have to try. Please."

He watches me for a moment and then grudgingly looks at the girl in her cell. He lets out a long-suffering sigh. "Fine," he says. "But you owe me. A lot."

Excited, I throw my hands around his neck and squeeze. "Thank you!"

"Hmm," he says, pulling away. "We get the princess first. She's our priority."

"Of course," I quickly nod.

When he starts walking away again, I turn toward the girl. "We'll be back for you soon. I promise."

She doesn't look like she believes me, but that's okay. We're totally gonna save her and everyone else in this prison tower.

Catching up to Belren, I nudge him with my elbow. "You're totally a good guy."

He scoffs. "I am simply an opportunist. You will now be in my debt, as will all of these prisoners. It's a good investment."

I laugh under my breath. "Sure. Keep telling yourself that."

The corner of his lip twitches before he schools his face back into impassive annoyance. But I saw it. The renowned thief totally has a heart.

CHAPTER 17

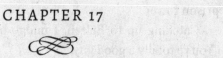

hen we reach Princess Soora's cell, Belren cocks his hand and clicks open the lock using his power. I rush inside to wake her.

"Princess," I whisper as I gently touch her shoulder. "We're here."

Her purple eyes fly open, and she quickly sits up. She looks to me and then Belren, but upon seeing the king, she stiffens.

"No, it's okay, it's not really him," I quickly explain.

Her mouth parts in surprise, but she doesn't waste time with questions, and we rush out. She leans in and gives Belren a chaste kiss on the cheek. "Thank you for coming, old friend."

Belren nods to her. "You've gotten me out of a few scrapes, now and then. It was the least I could do."

"I told you to get a different profession," she says as we start to make our way down the stairs.

"And if I had, I wouldn't be good enough to rescue you now," he points out with a smile.

Princess Soora's lip twitches in amusement.

"Okay, so what does worm-king here have to do to make sure the prison lets her leave?" I ask.

"A touch from the king," Belren explains simply.

Soora grasps the worm-king's forearm and then quickly drops it.

"That's it?" I ask.

"That's it," Belren answers.

"Okay. Quick. Let the others out."

"Fine. But remember. Many favors. A lot of debt."

I wave a hand at him. "Yeah, yeah. Move it, Horny Hooker. We got prisoners to rescue, and I didn't exactly leave the king on good terms…"

Belren narrows his eyes. "What did you do?"

"Nothing!" I say with a defensive shrug. "I just…accidentally made him fall in lust with a bar of soap…"

Belren and Soora blink at me incredulously.

"You…*what?*" Belren asks, exasperated.

"Okay, first of all, I don't like your tone. It could've happened to any cupid. Secondly, it was an accident. And thirdly, can we talk about this later? I don't know how long he'll be macking on that soap, but that thing's gotta melt down eventually. He was giving it a lot of tongue. Like, *a lot*," I stress.

Belren lets out a maddened sigh and then tugs the worm-king forward. "Let's go."

With every cell that we pass, Belren opens it, and I act like some peppy flight attendant to get them to follow directions.

"Please step this way. Don't push. Let's move in an orderly fashion. Yes, you sir. Touch the fake king. Don't worry, it's safe. Yes, that's right. Just give him a poke. Move along please."

Belren mutters under his breath about "difficult Veil

females," which is totally incorrect because I'm actually being super helpful. Which is the opposite of difficult. I point that out to him, but he just starts cursing instead.

We soon have at least a hundred prisoners in tow. Some of them are too weak to stand on their own, but the stronger prisoners help them out, sometimes carrying their entire weight.

I can see that Belren's strength is waning. The worm-king's movements become jerkier and even more unstable and unnatural than before. It seems our time is running out, and after having touched so many of the prisoners, the imitate power is draining away much quicker than we anticipated.

By the time we get to the bottom of the stairs, Belren has a sheen of sweat on his face and neck, and his face is drawn in discomfort and concentration.

"You okay?"

"Yes," he snaps. "We just need to get the hell out of here."

When we reach the corridor and start heading for the exit, Belren lets out a curse as the worm-king flops onto the floor.

Belren takes labored breaths as he braces his arms against the wall. He looks completely exhausted, and his eyes are bloodshot with the effort it's taking to move the worm-king.

"Here," I say, grabbing his arm and putting it over my shoulder to help support him. He doesn't even try to protest, so I know he's got to be seriously drained.

"We need to get out," he says in a tight voice. "I can't hold him much longer, and the magic is fading fast. He's about to be a worm again, and I'm pretty sure those guards out there aren't dumb enough to let that one go."

"We'll rush the guards," one of the stronger-looking fae prisoners offers. He's bulky, with blue skin and hair like moss. A few of the other prisoners offer to help, and they quickly form a plan.

"But you could get hurt," I protest.

The mossy-haired dude gives me a level look. "That is a chance we are willing to take. You released us from our cells. We can do our part now."

My mind runs through ideas, but the princess beats me to it. "Right. You two, take the imposter king so that he no longer has to be held up by magic," she orders, indicating two fae. "You four will rush the door first, once we get the guards to open it. The rest of us will follow. The weakened fae are to be put in the middle with stronger fae on the outside. No one hesitates. I'll lead the way once we get past the tunnel to the kitchens."

Everyone nods in understanding.

Belren gets some slight relief when the two fae pick up the worm-king. Swiping a hand over his sweaty brow, he takes a breath before slamming his fist against the entrance door. "Open up," he shouts to the guards on the other side to let us out. "The king is done."

As soon as the door swings open, the fae rush past like a wall of muscle and wrath. I hear the guards shout, and then power and fists go flying. The prisoners are the ones using brute strength, because the iron in the cells has sucked out their ability to use magic, but Ferno and Blix are flinging fire and water at the prisoners with a terrible frenzy.

Prisoners cry out as flames and walls of water pummel them, all while we scream for everyone to keep moving. But then the fire fae surrounds the entire room in a ring of fire, blocking the entrance, and the prisoners get bottlenecked from the doorway, and everyone else is stuck.

"Nobody move, or I'll fucking burn you all alive!" Ferno yells at the room. Everyone stops, the prisoners and Blix heaving with panted breath.

"Where's the king?" Ferno demands, his smoke-hair wafting around his scalp.

When no one answers him, his fiery eyes blaze brighter. "I said, where is the king?" he yells, holding a fireball in his hand, ready to launch it at us.

"There he is!" Blix calls out, pointing.

Ferno stomps forward, finding the floppy king being held by two of the prisoners. Even from a distance, I can see that the imitating magic is rapidly deteriorating. His skin is sagging and his body keeps spasming.

"Your Majesty?" Ferno asks. The worm-king's tongue lolls out of his mouth. It's not a good look. Ferno burns with rage. "You'll all be executed for this!" He spots the princess and stalks toward her. He wrenches her arms behind her back and pulls tight, making her flinch in pain. Even though she doesn't make a sound, I can tell that he's nearly pulling her arms out of her sockets, and my blood boils with anger.

"Well, well, well. If it isn't Princess Rebel Leader." He laughs at her. Then, turning to Blix he says, "Sound the alarm."

And that's when my feet start moving. Belren is nearly depleted of power. All the prisoners are too weak to fight back. We're surrounded by flame and a stupid asshole fire fae who is seriously pissing me off.

It's up to me to save us.

CHAPTER 18

I march forward, pretending that I'm not scared or intimidated in the slightest, even though I could just pee myself I'm so nervous.

Ferno narrows his eyes when he spots me pushing through the crowd. "*You*," he spits. "You're the cupid. I remember you posing as a servant."

"I remember you being a flaming douche," I reply tartly.

His hold on the princess tightens, making her wince, and my hands curl into fists. "Let her go."

He laughs at me. "Yeah, I don't think so. I think I'll take you and the princess here myself. I'll be considered a hero."

"If you hurt her, I'll claw your eyes out, ruin every romantic relationship you'll ever have for the rest of your life, and make you have insta-lust with something much worse than a bar of soap," I tell him conversationally. I tap my chin in thought. "I'm thinking a cactus. It makes sense since, you know, you're a prick."

In his fury, he releases the princess and lunges for me. Just like I wanted.

Before he can get to me, I pop into the Veil, sweep around him, and then turn visible again, Love Arrow in hand. I plunge that sucker into his back as hard as I can. A billowing puff of red smoke erupts on contact.

Now, I've never hit someone with a Love Arrow in the flesh. I've always done it in the Veil. So I'm not expecting it when the thing stays lodged in his back instead of disappearing in a cloud of colored smoke. I'm also not expecting blood to start seeping through his uniform.

He cries out and his arms go swinging, but I quickly dodge out of the way. The flame wall he erupted flickers out from his distracted pain, and I scream at the prisoners to run. Princess Soora leads the way.

"You…" Ferno says, whirling around to face me.

One second, his face is filled with rage, and the next, a dopey look crosses his face, and I feel a hum under my ribs.

Crap.

He lunges at me, but this time, I'm having to fend off his puckered lips.

I put my hand out against his face, smooshing his cheek and lips. "No," I tell him sternly.

"I love you," he says behind my palm.

I sigh and continue to watch the prisoners file out of the room.

"First the bar of soap, and now this. What a cupid day."

Blix, who was being held back and pummeled by a couple of fae, is dropped to the ground. He spits out blood onto the floor, and looks over at us, confusion crossing his face when he sees Ferno trying to feel me up and declare his undying love for me.

"What…"

"He's in love with me," I quickly explain.

I curse under my breath as Ferno continues to try to get to me. I move my hand to pinch his lips together with my fingers, while I bring my other hand to his crotch and squeeze his sensitive balls. He freezes his advance, his fiery eyes going wide.

"That hurts, doesn't it?" I say in a polite tone. "If I squeeze any harder, it'll probably *really* hurt. And we don't want to cause you any lasting damage, do we?"

He shakes his head so quickly I lose the hold on his lips.

"Good. I'm glad you're being so agreeable. Now. I'm going to let you go. And you're going to stay here. Okay?"

He looks at me with puppy-dog eyes. "But…I love you."

"Sure you do. But if you *really* love me, I need you to stay here and pretend you didn't see me. Or else someone is gonna hurt me, okay?"

A worried look crosses his face. "I won't let anyone hurt you."

"That's really sweet, Ferno," I praise, patting him on the head as I release my punishing hold on his balls. He relaxes a bit, but I want to make sure he's paying attention still, so I snap my fingers in front of his face. "Listen up, peenfork. You and your water friend here need to keep quiet about what you saw today. Tell anyone who asks that someone snuck up on you and knocked you out. And when you woke up, all the prisoners were gone. Can you do that for me?"

"Anything for you," he says dreamily.

"Great," I beam at him. "I'm gonna go now, okay?" I say, inching away. The rest of the prisoners have gone.

Ferno's eyes widen, and he takes a step toward me before stopping himself. When he sees my eyes narrow, he stops in his tracks. "But…when will I see you again?"

Never. "Soon," I tell him. "Super soon."

He nods. "Okay. Soon. Good."

"Remember. Not a word. But if I were you, I'd get out of here. How do you think they'll punish you for letting all the prisoners escape?"

Blix's face pales.

I blow them a kiss and dart away through the door, and then I run like hell.

CHAPTER 19

*W*hen I catch up to the prisoners, Princess Soora is in the process of letting a handful of them leave at a time. We're hiding out in the kitchens at the doorway to the outside, and she's carefully directing them where to escape without being detected by the other guards.

Belren looks nearly ready to pass out, since he apparently made something huge move on the east side to draw the patrolling guards away.

It takes forever.

I bite my nails the whole time, anxiety clawing at me. Slowly, painfully slowly, the number of prisoners dwindles until it's the very last group. When Soora gives them the go ahead, they sprint out, the servant girl with them. "Thank you!" she says to me and Belren. "Thank you so much!"

She squeezes my hand and gives Belren a kiss on the cheek before nodding and rushing out into the night.

I elbow him. "See? You know that felt nice to help an innocent prisoner escape."

He rolls his eyes, managing to look impertinent even though he seems like he's about to lose his lunch. "I felt nothing."

"Sure you didn't."

"Alright. The guards just passed over the wall," Princess Soora says. "It's our turn. Ready? You'll need to make the imposter king walk, Belren. Can you do it?"

He gives a terse nod.

Princess Soora leads the way outside, and we quickly cross the grounds to the stables, where everything is bathed in shadow. I can hear guards talking from above on the wall, and my heart pounds in my ears as I beg the fates that they don't spot us.

Darkness is quickly leaving with the coming dawn, and I know we have to get as far away from the palace as possible. When we don't come upon any guards in the stables, we stop near the end where she shows us a hidden door in the floor, behind some moved hay bales.

"You can let him go now, Belren," Princess Soora says softly.

He takes a shaky breath, and the worm-king's body falls to the ground at our feet, among the hay and dirt. He starts full-body wriggling like...well, a worm.

Belren reels on his feet, nearly falling to the ground, too, but I quickly shove my shoulder against his chest to catch his weight. "No you don't," I grit out, barely managing to keep him upright.

In a flash of shimmering blue magic, the king disappears, and all that's left on the ground is a writhing, glowing blue parodworm. "Thanks, little fella," I tell it, because that worm *was* super impressive after all.

"She's thanking the worm," Belren huffs under his breath.

I pinch him on the side, making him jump. "Do you mind?" he snaps. "I'm magically depleted here."

"It's no excuse to be a butthead. That worm kicked major ass. It saved, like, a hundred prisoners!"

"I saved a hundred prisoners," he pants.

"Sure. Take all the credit. I helped too. I totally defeated the fire fae back there. You're welcome."

Belren just rolls his eyes, and the princess starts climbing down the ladder to get to the cellar below.

The trip from the cellar passage to the palace walls on the west side is agonizingly slow, but we finally get to the concealed door in the wall and manage to slip out into the outside grounds. Belren grunts something and manages to point a heavy finger in the direction of the forest, so the princess and I turn in that direction and make our way over. But as soon as we hit the tree line, Belren collapses, taking me with him to the ground.

I squeak in surprise as he lands on top of me, crushed into the grass by his dead weight. "Oof. This guy is heavier than he looks."

Between Princess Soora and me, we manage to yank him off of me, and I sit up on my elbows and blow out a breath. "That was...exhausting."

Princess Soora checks over Belren and then sits down with her back against a tree to rest. The three of us look haggard, tired, and dirty.

"You think the prisoners all got out okay?"

"Let's hope so," the princess says.

She leans her head against the tree and closes her eyes. "We'll rest for a few minutes, then we'll have to get out of here. They patrol this area heavily, and we aren't far enough away from the castle walls."

I look over at the passed-out Belren dubiously. "How are we gonna move with him?"

The princess picks up her head and looks around. "Belren wanted us to come this way for a reason. I wonder…"

Her words cut off when a fae suddenly appears out of a portal in front of us.

I jump to my feet in front of the princess to block her from view, my heart racing. "Umm…who are you?"

The fae has antlers on his head and hair in dreadlocks all the way down to his groin. He whips his head in my direction and sniffs the air. When he spots Belren on the floor, he gives a nod. "I'm here to portal for Horned Hook," he says in a heavily accented voice.

"Oh," I say, brightening up. The fae bends down and picks up Belren, putting him over his shoulder and grunting back to his feet. He mumbles something in a different language as he makes his way back to the portal but stops when he sees that we haven't followed him. "Come," he says gruffly. "Horned Hook."

The princess is on her feet now, but I bite my lip, still unsure if we can trust him. Am I being a super bad spy by just assuming he's a good guy? What if he's kidnapping Belren right now, and I'm letting him?

"Who are you?"

"Me owe Horned Hook favor. This it."

Hmm. Well, the thief *does* like to earn favors. The princess and I exchange a look. "He's our best shot at getting out of here," she murmurs.

"Okay, but let me go first or something. Since I'm your spy and stuff, it only seems right."

The corner of her mouth turns up. "Very well."

All business, I stalk forward to antler-guy and give him

an intimidating look. At least, I think it's intimidating, but then he just wipes a calloused finger over my nose and shows me where dirt was smudged on me. "You dirty."

I frown at him. "That's not nice to say to someone. Unless it's in a sexual way," I inform him primly.

He just turns and stalks through the portal without so much as a how do you do. Taking a breath, I stand in front of the portal and prepare myself to go through. It'll either lead us to safety or this is some fucked up trick.

Regardless of the outcome, I have to go before the princess, since, you know, I'm supposed to be saving her life and stuff.

So after giving the princess a fake, plastered-on smile, I walk through.

CHAPTER 20

$\mathcal{I}$ remember immediately why I hate going through portals. They make me feel like I'm falling up and then down, and my stomach doesn't know which way to settle for gravity.

I land on all fours, the breath stolen from my chest as I gasp for air.

"Wow, you just went right down on your knees. This must be my lucky day."

At the mention of luck, my eyes burn slightly and then a handful of coins drop down from nowhere, landing at his feet.

I lift my head up and sit back on my ankles, looking around at all the shiny coins now mocking me from the floor. Pushing the hair away from my face, I meet the eyes of an orange-skinned high fae standing over me. His hair looks like marigolds, and his eyes are the same bright hue. "Throwing money at me?" he says with a teasing lilt to his voice.

"Lucky pennies," I say lamely and then move to scramble to my feet. Before I can straighten up, Princess

Soora comes through the portal, bumping into me in the process.

I was halfway up, so the movement makes me stumble face-first into the orange guy's crotch. He catches me by the elbows while my nose gets acquainted with his orangesicle.

"Sorry," I mumble against his crotch.

He chuckles and helps pull me all the way up to a respectable distance from his groin. His orange eyes twinkle with amusement, but then his gaze locks onto the princess, and he moves over to her, instantly wrapping her into a hug.

"Soora!"

I straighten my dress as I get my bearings, while the princess and orange slice have their moment. We're in some sort of luxurious sitting room, with five different seating areas, a harp, and windows from floor to ceiling that make white tiles sparkle.

When I make my way over to the window, I look out and see a gorgeous view of quaint cottages winding around a dirt road and wooden bridges set over a rushing river. The land looks lush and untouched, except for in the far distance, I can see an area that's been cleared of trees and looks like there are dots of temporary housing.

When I turn back to the princess to ask where we are, I catch her wiping the corner of her eye as he kisses the top of her head. A huge smile spreads over my face.

"So you're the lost lover!" I say excitedly as I rush over to them.

The two of them break apart from their hug to stare at me.

I clasp my hands together in front of my chest as I

beam up at them. "I can totally feel the love between you two," I say with a sigh.

Princess Soora gives me an indiscernible look. Is it embarrassment? I quickly rush in to reassure her. "Oh, don't worry, princess. I'm a cupid. Love is *totally* my thing. There's absolutely nothing to be embarrassed about. You guys look super cute together. I bet you could make some really cute fae babies." I squeal a little just picturing it. "Oh, with your purple and his orange, your babies would look like a sunset!"

The guy snorts but tries to cover it up with a well-placed cough. Princess Soora smiles lightly and says, "Emelle, let me introduce you to my brother, Zalit."

My eyes dart between them. "Oh." This just got awkward.

Princess Soora obviously picks up on my train of thought from the expression on my face, because she quickly shakes her head. "Not lovers," she clarifies. "Just siblings."

"Oh. Okay, good. Because that actually would be something to be embarrassed about, and then I would've been made a liar since I said there was *nothing* to be embarrassed about," I tell her seriously. "Glad we got that cleared up."

Zalit lets out a laugh. "But you can feel the love, eh?"

I narrow my eyes at his teasing tone. "I can't always tell what kind of love it is. Just that it's there," I defend.

He laughs again before turning back to his sister. Now that I know they're related, I can see some similarities in the shape of their faces. "Thank the gods you're free. We thought you'd—"

His words cut off, and his orange throat bobs.

Princess Soora puts a gentle hand on his arm. "I know. It's alright, Zalit."

A fiercely protective look comes over his face. "Now that you're home, he can't touch you. We'll take the asshole down."

"Then we have a lot of work to do," she replies. "I need to get caught up on what the rebellion is doing. Where is Belren?"

"Belren was in a bad way. I had him taken up to the infirmary so a healer can tend to him. He was quite drained."

"Thank you. I'm sure he just needs some rest," she says. "Which Emelle and I should get some for ourselves."

He nods. "I'll see that she's taken care of."

Princess Soora leans over to peck a kiss on his cheek. "She has four mates, brother, so don't take *too* good care of her."

He just laughs, but a pang of sorrow slices right through me, my mind immediately going to Okot. The way that he looked at me, like he *hated* me. I swallow down the sob that wants to come up and shake my head to clear it.

Princess Soora seems to catch what she said, and a regretful look crosses her face as she makes her way over to me. "I take it you saw him?" she asks quietly.

I nod miserably. The last thing I want to do is cry in front of her and her brother, so I take a moment to compose myself before answering. "Yeah," I answer. "How did you know?"

"He's the one who escorted me to the cell."

I shake my head in shock. "How could he have tricked both of us? I just don't get it. His...loyalty felt so real." I want to say love, but if I do, then I really will lose it.

Princess Soora rubs a finger over her tense brow. "Loyalties can change. People can be tricked."

I look down at my feet. She may have been tricked, but I was *gutted*.

The princess surprises me when she puts her hands on my shoulders and kisses me on the cheek. "Thank you for helping to rescue me, Emelle. You're far too good for this realm. More than you realize."

I try to give her a smile. "I'm your spy. I got your back," I promise her.

"I'm sorry about Okot."

"Me too," I say thickly.

She drops her hands, and with a nod goodbye, she sweeps out of the room. I take a shaky breath before I turn expectantly to Zalit. "So where exactly are we?"

"This island is our home. It's been in our family for generations. It's about thirty islands north of Highvale, the kingdom island."

"Hmm."

He crooks his arm and holds it out to me. "Allow me to escort you to your rooms? The manor can be a bit of a maze if you're not used to it."

"A maze? Just how big is this place?" I ask as I take his arm and start following him out.

He doesn't answer me, because he doesn't really have to. As soon as we walk out of the room, we're in an open hall on the ground floor, where I can see another three stories above. The corridors on each floor are open, showing off beautiful archways made of glass, with suspended flowers inside of them. Everywhere I look, there are embellishments of Princess Soora's family crest —the violet.

I whistle under my breath. "Wowzers. This place is super nice."

"Our family home has been here for centuries. We take great pride in it, along with the rest of our island and our people."

As I look around at all the purple and gray accents, I can't help but be impressed. "A manor," I snort. "Why don't you just call it like it is? This place is a freaking ginormous palace."

He makes a sound of amusement beside me as he leads me out of the huge open hall and starts taking me up the marble staircase. There are glass chandeliers hanging above and servants bustling around, the gossip probably already spreading that the lost princess has come back to life and returned home.

Zalit drops me off at a door at the end of the third-floor corridor. The balcony is only about waist high, so I can look out and see the entire hall below. "Here you are. If you need anything, call for a maid, and she will be more than happy to serve you."

"Thanks."

Zalit leaves me with a little tilt of his head, and I disappear behind the door, closing it behind me.

The inside is just as expensive and purpled out as the rest of the manor. A nice-sized bed with periwinkle blankets is calling to me, but I don't answer its siren's song. Not yet.

Instead, I walk over to the exterior balcony, turn invisible, and fly due north.

I get back to Highvale and into the castle in record time. I already have the rooms memorized, so I don't hesitate to find him.

It's still early, so when I get to his room, I find him

passed out on his back. Asleep like this, he looks like my Okot again. My loving, gentle, adoring Okot. Longing that I've never felt before fills me, and I swear, my heart hurts so much that it feels like it's fatal.

Still invisible, I creep up onto the bed and then carefully settle myself above him. It takes extra concentration to hover just right, but when I'm settled on the crook of his shoulder, I look up at his sleeping face, watching his even breaths and wishing I could bury my face into his neck and feel him pull me close.

I pretend to graze his cheek with my fingers, lightly tracing over his septum piercing and his troubled brow. I want to kiss it away, to hear him call me his beloved, and for everything to go back the way it was.

"Why don't you love me?" I whisper miserably.

Even in my incorporeal form, I swear, I can feel the heat of tears sting my eyes.

"I love you, Okot," I say with a shaky breath.

I bring my intangible lips to his and gently press a kiss against them. I close my eyes, pouring all the love and heartbreak into that one kiss that I can. Maybe like the stories, he'll wake up from his sleep and a curse will have broken. He'll be the Okot who loves me again.

But he doesn't wake up, and there is no curse. Only me, a broken-hearted cupid trying to stay with him the only way I can.

I don't know how long I lie with him, but I stay curled up against his side, watching him sleep, realizing just how awful it really is to have a broken heart. No wonder those humans were always so miserable. I don't blame them a bit for cursing my efforts at love. I'm quite sure this is the worst I've ever felt in all my lonely existence.

When Okot starts to stir and the sunlight grows

brighter, I know I need to get back. I give him one last lingering kiss on his lips. Just as I sit up to leave, I see him bring his hand up and run a thumb over his lip.

I freeze and a choked sob noise escapes me. "You can still feel me?" I breathe. "How can you, of all my mates, feel me, when you were just faking it?"

It isn't fair.

Feeling worse than before, I jump out of the bed and rush for the wall, floating straight through it and outside. I fly all the way back to Princess Soora's family's island and back to my room. As soon as I go visible and collapse on the purple sheets, tears take over my body, and I drown in them.

Only when I'm neck-deep and gasping do the tears let up just enough for me to fall into a wretched sleep.

CHAPTER 21

I wake up hours later with hair stuck to my face and my mouth open wide enough to let out a snore so loud that it startles me awake. I jolt upright and wipe the corner of my mouth. With a quick look out the windows, I can see that it's dawn again. I slept an entire day and night away.

I get up and stretch and use the pull-chain by the bed to summon a maid. One appears within minutes with a soft tapping at my door. She has chrysanthemums growing out her vined head, immediately making me think of my friend, Mossie. "Good morning," she greets me with a curtsy.

"Hey, I'm Emelle," I say, ushering her inside.

"I am Primmy, and it's lovely to serve the one who rescued our princess."

I blush at the earnestness in her voice and pick at my dirty nails. "Oh. I didn't do much. It was mostly the Horned Hook." I stop and point at her. "But don't tell him I said that. That guy already has a big enough head as it is."

She smiles and nods. "Your secret is safe with me."

I blow out a breath. "So, I'm not really sure what Princess Soora is doing or what I should be doing…"

Primmy gives me a kind smile. "If you're ready to bathe and dress, I can help you with that. Then everyone will be gathered downstairs for breakfast in the dining room in about an hour."

My stomach growls loudly, making the girl's eyes shine with amusement. "Let's get you all sorted, shall we?"

"Yes, please. Breakfast sounds heavenly."

As soon as I say that last word, a puff of white glitter explodes in my room, and Primmy and I both let out matching shrieks at the angel that appears before us.

When the glitter dust clears, I huff and stomp my foot. "What the Veil hole? First Lex, and now I have angels popping up in front of me, too?"

Raziel crosses his arms and glowers down at me. "You."

"Yes, me. What are you doing here?"

His frown deepens. "You summoned me somehow. How did you do that?"

I raise my hands in exasperation. "The hell if I know!"

Yep. That does it.

Black smoke billows up from the floor, and then there's Jerkahf, dusting himself off as he whirls around in surprise. When he notices Raziel and me, he grinds his teeth. "What the seven layers of hellfire am I doing here?"

"She has the ability to summon us, apparently," Raziel explains.

Poor Primmy looks like she's about to faint, so I pat her on the back in a show of comfort. At least, I hope it's comforting. I'm not really sure how you comfort someone when a pissed off angel and smoking demon suddenly appear in front of you. Is she always that pale green? Hmm. I wonder if she's a fainter? I hope not.

The angel and demon both turn to scowl at me, and I hold my hands up in surrender. "Don't get all scary-glarey on me. I didn't summon you! I just said *heaven* and *hell*. I didn't know that would do anything. I already have to be careful saying the word *help*—"

Yeah. Okay. I walked right into that one.

Pink smoke and a puff later, there's Lex beaming happily at me. "Hello, Madame Cupid Emelle."

That's when Primmy hits the floor.

Dammit. She *is* a fainter.

"This is getting ridiculous," I mumble as I lean over Primmy and try to wake her up. When that doesn't work, I grab a pillow from the bed and prop it under her head.

"Don't summon us," Raziel snaps.

"Okay, okay. Like I said, it was an accident."

"I was right in the middle of fighting for the righteous souls of Earth," he pouts.

I pat him on his arm. "I'm sure you were doing a super good job, too."

His wings pulse with their shining light a bit at the compliment. "I was. We were winning," he brags.

Jerkahf snorts. "Keep telling yourself that, dick dove."

Raziel curls his hands into fists like he's about to deck him, so I quickly let my wings pop out at my back, separating them. "Alright, you two. That's enough. I'm sorry for accidentally summoning you."

Raziel drops his gaze to me. "Don't do it again."

"It just happened."

"How can it *just happen*?"

"It's actually your fault," I tell him seriously. "Maybe this would've been covered in my CliffsNotes that you guys *didn't* give me because you were too busy being a pair of hairy dicks?"

"She's got a point," Jerkahf mumbles from behind my wings.

"See?" I say triumphantly. "I have a point."

"Do. Not. Summon. Me."

Raziel's gone a second later, leaving only his white glitter and a shining white feather behind. "I think he's starting to like me."

Jerkahf laughs as I turn to face him. "Keep telling yourself that. And don't tell the fucker, but he's right. Don't go summoning us on accident anymore."

I nod. "I promise to only summon you intentionally from now on."

He sighs at me, and smoke seeps out from between his lips. We both look over at Primmy as she comes to, her eyes wide as she blinks up at the demon and cupid still in my room.

"Don't worry, he's leaving," I reassure her.

"Yeah, yeah. Back to the pit-fires of misery and ash."

He disappears, leaving only Lex behind, and she's…

"Are you meditating?"

She pops open her eyes from her spot where she's sitting cross-legged on the floor. "Yes. I've found that if I visualize love and all of its many wonders, I can better remind myself why love is so important, even when it is difficult."

A smile creeps over my face. "The blocklisters giving you trouble?"

A slight blush creeps over her cheeks. "It's nothing I can't handle, I assure you."

"Aww, you are such an adorable overachiever."

"Thank you," she says seriously.

"How's Sev doing back at Cupidville?"

Lex gets to her feet and pulls out a heart-shaped notepad. "He has ensured all of your changes are being carried out, and I have been assisting him. He did have a few questions that I jotted down so that I could ask you."

"Ask away."

"One, he wants to know if cupid superiors can have four weeks of vacation instead of the standard two."

I roll my eyes. "He means can *he* have four weeks," I correct. "And sure."

She writes that down with her quill. "Excellent. Question two, he would like to know if he is permitted to hire a secretary."

I roll my eyes. "He just wants to play out the whole boss-secretary fantasy. Tell him no and to stop thinking with his dipstick."

She writes it down word for word, and I snicker under my breath.

"I'll refrain from asking you the rest, since they are, in fact, about his dipstick."

"Of course they are. Has he propositioned you?"

"Several times," she replies pragmatically. "But I have informed him that I have no wish to enter into a romantic relationship."

"You really mean that? I thought you were just saying that to get the Horny Hooker off your back."

"Oh, no. I'm quite serious. I much prefer to make Love Matches between others."

"Huh."

She puts away her notebook. "Alright, is there anything else that I can do for you, Madame Cupid Emelle?"

"Nope. Thanks, Lex."

She disappears, and I turn my attention back to Primmy. "Sorry about that. I'll try not to summon any more Veil Majors until after breakfast, I promise."

She just stares at me in shock.

"Primmy?"

She shakes her head to clear it. "Right. Bath. Shall we?"

Considering my back is covered with worm dirt, my hair is a matted rat's nest, and my outfit is most definitely ruined, I nod. "Sorry for sleeping in the clean bed like this. I was wiped out."

"No apologies necessary, Madame," she says, leading me to the bathroom where a huge silver tub waits. She's a little shaky, but overall, I think she handled the whole thing pretty well, considering.

She pulls a cord at the wall, and warm water starts gushing inside. After peeling off my clothes, I get in and let Primmy wash and comb my hair as I soak and scrub my skin. The tub is big enough to swim laps in, but I settle for just spreading out as far as my limbs allow.

When I'm done, she plaits my hair in fancy braids and curls, and I pull my wings into my back so that she can put me in a dress. It's lavender, just like nearly everything else, but soft as silk. The neckline is high, reaching just above my collarbone in a straight line across, but it gathers at the top of my shoulders with violet brooches, and then the fabric drapes down loosely, leaving my back totally exposed, right down to the top of my butt. It makes me look way more glamorous than I really am.

When I get down to the dining room, I'm the last one to arrive. The table is already laid out with heaps of food, and the princess, Zalit, Belren, along with three other high fae I haven't met are deep into their plates and conversations. I'm surprised to see that Belren isn't wearing his mask here and seems to be perfectly at home.

"Oh, Emelle, I'm so happy to see that you're awake and well," Princess Soora greets me as I take a seat beside Belren.

"Thanks, I must've been tired. How are you feeling?"

"Perfect, now that I'm home." She smiles. "Let me introduce you to my father, Sal, and my other sisters, Rilla and Reet."

The girls are young, maybe only around ten or so, with the same purple skin tone as Soora, while their father has the same orange as Zalit.

The girls giggle and whisper to each other until one of them blurts, "Is it true you're a cupid?"

Surprised, I look over to Soora, who grimaces slightly. "Your status has been exposed, I'm afraid. Somehow, the prince learned what you are," she explains.

I don't need to guess how he knows, and by the look on her face, she doesn't either. Okot had to have been the one to tell him. This information just twists the dagger that's already been stabbed into my heart.

Across from me, one of the sisters passes over a folded up Wanted page with my face plastered on it. I frown down at it. "This picture makes my wings look terrible."

The girls gasp in unison. "Do you really have bird wings?"

Smiling to myself at the good luck of my backless dress, I *push* out my wings, and the girls gasp again and jump to their feet. They rush over to me and start admiring and petting them, giggling excitedly. "I've never seen wings like these before!"

"They're even *better* than bird wings!"

"Girls, that's enough ogling our guest. Take a seat and eat," their father says.

I give them a wink and fold my wings up behind my back as they make their way to their chairs.

"I guess there's no sense in hiding them anymore," I say.

Princess Soora shakes her head. "Quite right. You've become quite famous in the resistance, actually."

My brows rise. "Really?"

Zalit answers. "Indeed. I'm fairly certain your wanted poster is being displayed in nearly every outhouse on the island."

I blink at him, confused for a second, until realization dawns on me. "Oh. Well, that's…flattering."

Zalit and Belren share a chuckle.

I start to load up my plate with the honeyed rolls and purple berries, but when I reach for the pitcher of drink, Belren flicks a finger and makes it float to my cup and fills it for me.

"If I had telekinesis, I'd be super lazy," I admit, watching the pitcher set back down.

Belren watches me with amusement as I start stuffing my face with food. I try to eat slowly though, since I'm at Princess Soora's table and everything, but damn, those rolls are yummy.

Conversation continues around me, and when I've cleared my plate, Belren finally leans over to me. "Do you always eat that fast?"

I look down at my empty plate with a shrug. "I was hungry." I wipe my mouth on the napkin and then take a big gulp of the fizzy orange drink before turning to him. "Sorry, I should've asked how you're feeling. Last I saw you, you were passed out with your tongue hanging out of your mouth."

"I'm sure it wasn't," he insists.

I shrug. "You were unconscious. It's my word against yours."

He rolls his gray eyes as he takes a steaming drink out of his mug. "If you're quite done talking about inconsequential things, I happen to have information on your genfins."

I nearly drop the cup in my hand, only barely managing to set it on the table before I clasp his arm desperately. "Where are they?"

"Calm yourself, Veil female. Besides, can't you use your mate bonds to find them?"

"I've tried," I snap, more in anger with myself than him. "Every time I try, it just wants to pull me back to..." My throat closes up, refusing to say Okot's name out loud. Belren doesn't notice the pained expression on my face, so I clear my throat and finish by saying, "I've tried. I can't track my genfins."

"Alright, I'll tell you where they are. On one condition."

"Are you seriously trying to make a deal right now?" I growl.

He shrugs, unperturbed. "I'm a thief, darling. I always make sure to come out on top. What did you expect?"

"Fine," I say through clenched teeth. "What do you want?"

"Your delectable assistant. I'd like to spend time with her."

My brows rise in surprise. "You want me to bargain Lex off to you?"

"Don't be so dramatic. She can always say no." He leans

in close so that his lips nearly touch my ear. "But I think we both know that she won't be able to say no."

I shove him in the chest, and he laughs and leans back. "Fine. I'll ask her. But if she doesn't want to, she doesn't have to."

He offers me his silver hand and a cocky smile. "Deal."

As soon as we shake on it, he says, "Word is that they're here."

"What do you mean, *here*?" I ask, my heart beating quickly.

He flicks his wrist and sends a pitcher soaring toward him. He plucks it out of the air and refills his mug, taking his sweet-ass time. "Belren," I snap.

He takes a sip, his eyes twinkling. The prick is totally enjoying this.

"Apparently, my sources say that a contingent of genfins amassed with some of the other rebels weeks ago, right after the rumor of Princess Soora's execution started spreading around."

"And the rebels are here, on this island?"

"Indeed."

"Where?"

Belren opens his mouth to answer, but Princess Soora beats him to it. "You saw the temporary housing from the window?" she asks, and I nod. "That's the rebel base. If they're here, that's where they'll be."

"The rebel base is right out in the open like that?" I ask, surprised.

Princess Soora's father shakes his head. "My Soora is very talented at glamouring. She glamoured this entire island before she departed. Only those on our side are able to see what's truly here."

"Huh," I say, impressed. "Neat trick." I jump to my feet. "If you'll excuse me?"

She waves me off. "Of course, go. Find your mates."

I can't help the smile that takes over my face. "Thanks!"

I rush out of the dining hall, not even bothering to walk out like a normal person. I go full invisible and zoom toward the rebel base as fast as I can.

Let's hope that my genfin mates don't hate me, too.

CHAPTER 22

land in a dusty makeshift town square. There are white wooden cabins all over the place, in haphazard rows and all of them in utilitarian sizes. I go visible behind one of the buildings and then walk out, searching everybody I pass for a familiar face.

There are various fae everywhere. High fae, water fae, and tons of fae I don't even know the names of. When I spot a few genfins with their furry wings and animalistic movements, my excitement ratchets up.

Aside from the cabins, there is a huge training yard where rebels are going at each other, practicing battle with both weapons and magic. There's also a stable, an infirmary, and an outdoor mess hall of sorts where tables and benches are set up for the fae to eat, all around a roaring bonfire at the center.

I spin around in a circle, trying to take in as many fae faces as I can, but the crowd is actually quite thick, and it's difficult to see over everyone. I get a lot of looks from the rebels, most of them eyeing my red wings on display. I hear the word *cupid* being whispered over and over again.

It seems the princess was right. I am a bit of a celebrity among the resistance.

I fluff my wings up behind me and smile sweetly at the gawkers. Then I remember that rebels, especially awesome spy rebels are supposed to look badass, so I trade my smile for a tough, I'll-kick-your-ass look instead. I don't think it's coming across right though, because most of them just start frowning at me. Maybe it's the princess dress I'm wearing? Oh well. My cheeks hurt holding my face like that, anyway. I drop the rebel-expression and let my wings drag slightly behind me because, dammit, they're heavy.

I go over to the wooden fence that surrounds the eating area and climb up on the first rung so that I can have a better vantage point. I have to concentrate to look around and hold on at the same time, because I definitely don't want to face-plant in the dirt and embarrass myself.

I'm busy searching the training yard when I feel a hand on my arm.

"What are you doing?"

I look down and see a speckled-skinned fae looking up at me. He has metal prongs coming out of his eyebrows that look wicked sharp.

"Umm, hi?" I say.

"What are you doing up there?" He looks me up and down. "You don't look like a soldier."

I hop down and put my hands on my hips, disappointed that the one rebel fae who decided to approach me doesn't recognize me. "First of all, I could *totally* be a soldier. It doesn't matter what I look like," I tell him snippily.

He looks dubious. "So you *are* a soldier?"

"Well, no, but that's not the point," I tell him.

He glances around, like he's looking for the punchline to a joke. I don't think he finds it. "Who are you?"

"I happen to be a spy," I say defensively. "Like, a really good one. I rescued the princess and everything. Plus, I'm *the* cupid," I tell him, stressing the importance of that fact.

He looks at me blankly. "*Ohhh-kay*... Well, if you're looking for the copulation room, it's that way," he says, pointing over his shoulder.

I blink. "A...copulation room?"

"Yeah. You know. Fucking."

I wrinkle my nose. "Why do you have a room for that? Why don't you guys just use your cabins?"

He throws his hands up in exasperation. "Because the beds are too small, obviously."

"Geez, okay. I didn't know."

I start walking with him toward the copulation room when I catch myself. "Wait a minute, I don't need to go to the copulation room!"

"Then why did you say you did?"

I tap my foot. "I didn't! I was—"

A booming voice yells down the path, nearly making me jump out of my skin.

"EMELLE!"

I nearly clobber spiky brows when my arms and wings flail around. I'm pretty sure I accidentally hit him in the happy sacks, too, based on the pained grunt he lets out.

But I can't apologize to him, because I'm too busy staring wide-eyed at the seriously pissed off looking genfin who yelled my name and is currently staring me down across the path.

Evert.

Evert, who just called me *Emelle*. Not Scratch.

That can't be good.

CHAPTER 23

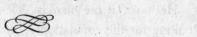

*E*vert is clear on the other end of the dirt path, standing in the middle of it like he owns the whole freaking rebel camp. His black hair is tousled, and sexy stubble lines his jaw. He looks freaking good in rebel wear with his leather pants and loose shirt. I'd smile, but the pissed off look on his face makes me wince instead.

All around us, I see that even the other rebels are giving Evert a wide berth. Eyes keep darting from him to me and back again, like they're waiting for us to either fight or fuck. Judging by the look on his face, I'm not sure which one it's going to be, if I'm being honest.

He lifts a hand and slowly crooks his finger at me.

"Dammit," I mutter.

I slowly start making my way toward him, nervous butterflies flying through my stomach. Before I can get to him, he turns on his heel and stalks toward the row of cabins. I follow behind him, stepping between the structures and out of the main pathway. He doesn't slow down at all, and I huff and puff as I try to keep up with him as he zigzags through the cabins. The further he goes, the quieter it gets, until I don't see a single other fae around.

Finally, he stops and turns around to lean against the cabin with his arms crossed and his foot crossed over his ankle. His blue eyes watch me intensely as I get nearer. I wring my hands nervously, but he doesn't say a word as I step in front of him.

I slowly lift my eyes to his and see the anger there. For a second, I flash back to the look on Okot's face. He seared me with such intense fury that my soul is still smoldering with it. Just the memory is enough to make me tremble.

I'm still seeing Okot's face when Evert raises his hands to touch me, and I instinctively flinch back. Evert freezes, and somehow, the anger on his face grows even darker.

"Are you...afraid of me?"

I blink up at him and then realize that I'm shaking all over. I swallow and try to bury my hands in my dress, but he just snatches them up.

"Y-you're mad," I whisper, embarrassed when I hear my voice shaking, too.

Keeping his hold on my hands, he slowly leans down so that we're eye to eye. The tension crackles between us, and my breath hitches. I want to look away. I don't want to see another one of my mates hate me, but his blue eyes hold me hostage.

"Mad?" he says quietly, making my skin break out into a cold sweat. He shakes his head. "No. I'm not mad. I'm fucking *livid*." He circles my wrists in one of his hands and then brings the other up to fist my hair. "But I would never *ever* fucking hurt you."

And then his lips crash down on mine.

In a single breath, the sickening tension turns into a

furious hunger. I feel the stress in his body as his hand moves to dig into my waist, and I wind my fingers through his hair. This isn't kissing. This is a desperate connection to assure him that I'm real. That I'm *his*.

And I *am* his. Just as much as he's mine. Which I promptly remind him by biting his bottom lip and scratching tracks down the back of his neck.

He groans, and the sound sends lightning down to my core, setting me on fire. A needy sound comes from my throat, and I grind my hips against his, feeling his hard cock straining against his leathers. I need him so badly it hurts.

Without warning, Evert lifts me up, shoves me against the wall of the cabin, and bunches my dress up at my hips. He hooks my right leg over his forearm, pulls away my panties, and before I can even anticipate it, he's pulling out his cock and slamming into me.

My head falls back with a thunk against the wood, and Evert's mouth moves down to kiss and suck the side of my neck as his tail wraps around my waist. I don't even care that we're out in the open or that anyone could walk by. Every time Evert pulls out and thrusts back into me, the delicious fire inside of me spreads deeper.

"Faster," I urge him as he continues to go harder and harder so that all I can hear is my body knocking against the wood.

"Look at me," he orders, and I let my head drop down to look him in the eye. "You are not allowed to leave me like that *ever* again."

I swallow hard. "I'm sorry."

"No apologies." He says with each thrust. "Just. Your. Promise."

I bite my lip from the delicious spot he's hitting so deep inside of me. "I won't leave you again," I breathe.

He pauses inside of me, and our panting breaths mingle together. When I notice the sheen in his eyes, my heart breaks. I hurt him. Badly. He asked me not to go, and I left anyway, thinking that it would be just fine—that it would be only a couple days. I ended up being gone nearly a month, and I can see by the look on his face that it damaged him in a way I never anticipated.

I lift my hand to his cheek and caress him, feeling the scruff on his jaw. "I'm here. I'm home," I say softly.

"I'm so fucking mad at you, Scratch," he confesses, his throat bobbing.

"I know. But I won't leave you again."

"You're fucking right about that."

He claims my mouth again, and I give him everything I have as he starts up his thrusts again. I need to come so badly, I'm aching and shaking all over.

"Evert," I plead.

He reaches down to my slit, but instead of touching me where I want, he just drags his finger over my wetness and then pops the finger in his mouth. "Mmm," he says with a curve of his lips.

I try to reach down to touch myself, but he takes my wrists and holds them over my head. I make a mewl of protest, but his thrusts become faster and harder, making me moan from the delicious pleasure. But before it can build to anything, I feel his release spurt inside of me. He gives one last thrust before he's pulling out of me and setting me back on my feet.

I stare at him as he starts fixing himself. "Umm…what the hell was that? You didn't make me come!"

143

Evert cocks a black brow. "Only good girls get to come, Scratch. You know that."

My mouth drops open in shock, and he just smirks as he finishes tying up his pants and then tosses me a handkerchief. I don't catch it, so it falls to the ground at my feet.

When he starts to turn around, I stomp my foot. "Evert, you get back here right now and make me come!"

Of course, this is the moment when a gaggle of rebels walk by. Four male heads immediately whip in my direction, and I squeak and step behind Evert so that I can die from embarrassment with a genfin shield blocking me from view. "Keep walking, fuckers," Evert growls.

When they're gone, I pinch Evert on the underside of his arm, hard enough to make him flinch. "Jerk," I hiss at him.

He turns to look down at me. "Mmm. I can smell your need," he says, leaning close. My entire body perks up again like a begging dog ready to get the bone. I already got the damn bone. What I need is the extra petting. "I can smell how much you're wanting me still."

I raise my chin obstinately. "I do not." I totally do.

Evert's eyes twinkle with mirth. He inhales and then blows a stream of his hot breath right into my face. And it's pink. *Pink!* His breath is freaking bona fide, one hundred percent bubblegum pink.

I gasp indignantly and try to duck away from it, but it's too late. Lightning strikes of lust shoot straight down to my core and instantly make me wetter. A freaking moan escapes me before I can stop myself, and my eyes widen in shock. "You have *Lust-Breath?*" I shriek.

He straightens back up and grins like he's the cat that got the freaking cream. Which he did, by the way.

"Yep," he says. "Payback's gonna be a real bastard for you, Scratch. All those times you Lusted the shit out of me? Yeah, you're gonna get it right back."

Great. The Lust-Breath war was only funny when he couldn't do it back to me. And holy honey pot, that Lust stuff is *no* joke. My peach pie is, like, ready to be stuffed in the oven, if you catch my drift.

I swallow thickly and try not to jump him. "That's... not nice," I tell him huskily.

Evert regards me. "What you're feeling right now, Scratch? How desperately you're wanting me? Yeah, that's how I felt every second you were gone." He leans in and teases me by running his nose beneath my ear.

When I feel his hot tongue make contact with my skin, I almost orgasm right there. I lean into him, hoping he'll forget about this stupid punishment, but before I think of a way to seduce him, he growls into my ear, saying, "You left me. So, no. You don't get to come this time."

He quickly backs away from me, and I almost face-plant on the ground from how far I was trying to lean into him. I steady myself, and an angry flush meets my neediness as I huff in annoyance.

I try to punch him, but he just dodges me with a chuckle. "Come on, let's go."

I angrily snatch up the handkerchief from the ground and start cleaning myself up as best I can, but...yeah, there are a lot of juices coming out. Besides that, I'm still hot and needy from all of that action and no release. I give up and roll up the cloth to act as a pantyliner.

"You're such a jackass," I grumble as I come up beside him.

He just chuckles again and throws his arm around my

shoulder as we start making our way back. "Yeah, but I bet you'll think twice before leaving me again, won't you?"

He has me there. It still doesn't fix the fact that my southern region is ready to combust.

"Maybe the polite one will take care of that for you," he teases.

"I'm positive that he will," I reply tersely. "Or Ronak."

Evert stiffens beside me and drops his arm. I stop, turning to look at him. "What? What's wrong?"

"Nothing," he says too quickly.

"Evert," I say warningly.

He sighs and runs his hands through his shaggy black hair. "Let's go find Sylred. Then we'll talk."

Well, hump on a heart. That doesn't sound good.

CHAPTER 24

*E*vert insists on taking me to get something to eat. We sit at a picnic table while I stuff my face. I just had breakfast not too long ago, and it's not the best, but I'm not one to turn down food. Even when it's something called a patty sack that resembles a, well…never mind. I'm kind of embarrassed that I ate it, to be honest. Also, Evert keeps making sack jokes now.

I'm about to ask Evert about what they've been doing while I've been gone, when, out of the corner of my eye, I see a flash of pink.

Pink hair, just like mine. "Is Lex here?" I mutter to myself as I get to my feet. "Hey," Evert calls at my back as I start to walk away. I don't heed him, and he curses and rushes to my side. "Where are you going?"

"I saw pink," I tell him distractedly, pushing away from him again in the busy food ring.

"What? Dammit, wait up!"

I veer around fae as I try to find that head of pink hair again. I know I saw it. It was just here! I dip under giant arms, elbow past obstinate bodies, and all but fight my way down the dirt path until finally, *finally* I spot the pink hair again.

The male is now leaning against the rail, watching the fighting yard, his pink hair slightly spiked up at the top of his head.

I stop dead in my tracks. That's not a cupid.

But I'd know him anywhere.

"Sylred?"

At the sound of my voice, he turns, and then his face goes slack with shock. We both stare at each other for a moment, and my eyes travel over every inch of his handsome face. But I'm nervous. So, so nervous. Is his face going to change? Morph into one of disgust and hate like Okot? Is he pissed at me like Evert?

One second, he's standing there, slack-jawed and frozen, and the next, he's bolting toward me.

I startle and back up a step, but Evert is suddenly at my back, and I'm stuck. In the span of a heartbeat, Sylred is in front of me. He reaches out and lifts me up by my waist and swings me around, an amazing grin spread across his face while his kind eyes are alive with relief and joy. I open my mouth in a surprised squeal, but he catches the noise in his mouth as he crashes my body against him and devours me with a kiss.

Heaven.

That's what it feels like. Not that I'm gonna say it out loud. I won't do that, because with my luck, Raziel would pop up and totally kill our romantical buzz that we have going on. Angels can be real downers for the libido.

But oh my gods, Sylred is here, and he's holding me and kissing me like he's been waiting to do it his whole life, and it feels *amazing*.

I hear whoops and catcalls around us, but I don't care.

My arms wind tightly around his neck, and I hold him as close as he's holding me. Our tongues dance together, and his hips grind against mine, making my neediness amp up. Evert left me wet and wanting, so I go from embers to a burning inferno in no time at all. When Sylred tries to pull away, I nip him on the lip and pull him back to me. He groans into my mouth, and I start to climb him.

Yeah. Climb.

Like, feet up his shins, arms scrambling over his shoulders, trying to hike him like a mountain trail. It's not sexy.

He grunts awkwardly but manages to grab hold of me and stop my awkward movements enough to pull away from the desperate face-sucking that I was forcing on him.

I know. It's embarrassing. But I'm really horny. Also, I missed him like pissing dudes miss the toilet bowl.

"Emelle," he breathes, putting his forehead against mine. His grip digs into my skin where he's holding me at the thighs like he's afraid to let me go. Which I'm glad for, since I'd totally fall on my ass if he did let me go.

"I'm here," I tell him. I realize that my face is wet with tears, and he brings one hand up to swipe them away.

"We couldn't feel you. Couldn't find you," he says, sounding horribly pained.

"I'm so, so sorry."

I press my cheek against his chest as he runs a hand up and down my back in that old familiar rhythm that he's so good at.

"Where'd you find her?" Sylred asks, looking behind me to Evert.

"In the road talking to some spiked asshole. Spotted her wings and hair through the crowd," he explains. "Just like she spotted you."

I look up to study Sylred's new look. "You have pink cupid hair," I muse, bringing a hand up to run it through his tresses. His brows and five o'clock shadow are still blond, but his full head of pink exactly matches mine. "My cupidity rubbed off on you, too. Are you mad?"

He takes my own hair between his fingers and rubs gently. "Don't you know by now? I'm partial to pink."

Gods, I missed him.

I snuggle into his chest again and just breathe him in. He smells like cedar and sweat and...

I lift my head up. "Are you carrying chocolate?"

He drops one of his arms down to reach in his pocket, and pulls out a small box. Taking it, I open the lid and see four little heart-shaped chocolates waiting inside.

I swallow the lump in my throat. "You...you've still been carrying chocolates in your pockets for me?"

He pops one in my mouth and gives me a peck. "Every day. Because I knew you'd come back to us."

Well, melt my heart. Am I crying over chocolates? Yes, yes I am. But it's not just about the chocolate. It's the fact that he never gave up on me.

"You're a good mate, Syl."

"You deserve it."

Gah. This guy. He always says the right things.

"Can I put you down now? You're kind of heavy with the wings."

Never mind.

"Oh," I sigh. "I guess so. Except I kind of missed you guys carrying me whenever I got tired. I had to walk *forever* during my mission to save the princess. Also, Evert was mad at me, so when we had hello sex, he wouldn't let me come. I'm kind of enjoying the friction, to be honest," I tell him plainly, rocking my hips a little. "Will you give me an orgasm?" I ask seriously.

Sylred blinks at me for a moment, and a blush spreads across his cheeks. "Umm…"

Rebel heads swing in my direction, and one fae with a sandy scalp raises his hand. "Hey, I'll give you an orgasm, sweetheart!"

Several of his buddies at the food table chuckle.

"I'll rip off your fucking head," Evert says evenly, one hand in his pocket. He looks super nonchalant when he threatens people.

At the expression on Evert's face, the fae and his friends quickly swallow their laughs and turn back around, looking really interested in their plates.

Evert looks over at me wryly. "Can you not request orgasms in a camp full of rebels?"

I sigh. "Fine."

Evert grabs hold of me and lifts me gently from Sylred, placing me back on my feet.

"Back to that other thing you mentioned," Sylred says. "It's believed that the princess was executed," Sylred tells me gently.

I shake my head. "Nuh-uh. That rumor isn't true. I totally rescued her," I say, rocking back on my heels proudly. "Well, the Horned Hook helped, but still."

Sylred opens and closes his mouth, at a loss. Evert looks around as if worried others might have overheard me. "Let's take this elsewhere," he says.

"Okay, sure. I want to see Ronak, anyway," I tell them as we start walking out of the food area and to the dirt roads.

Evert and Sylred share a look. "What?" I ask.

"Were you just over there?" Evert asks Sylred.

Sylred nods gravely. "Yeah. I wasn't supposed to return for a couple of days, but maybe we can get on the list again? Considering the circumstances..." His voice trails off as they look at me.

"It's worth a try," Evert says.

"What are you guys talking about?"

They continue on, pulling me along with them. The guys both tuck me between them so that I'm squished in the middle as we continue walking down the path. Our legs brush up against each other, and they both reach down and thread their fingers through mine. It seems like the three of us can't help but touch each other. I feel like I've only been gone for a couple of days, and I missed them a lot. I can only imagine how it's been for them to have me missing for a month.

We approach a group of cabins all set up within a few feet of each other, and I realize that I'm looking at the genfin part of the rebel camp. There are genfins all around, including some of them in a small fighting ring, practicing combat while in their genfin animal states.

"Is Ronak here?" I ask, straining my neck to try to see if he's in the ring.

I don't see him, but there are two genfins circling each other, along with two genfin spotters in the ring with them, making sure their animals don't go too far.

"Not exactly," Sylred says as they pull me toward a cabin. Evert reaches for my other hand, and then Sylred raises his arms to knock. Seconds later, the door swings open.

We're greeted by a genfin female with an ashy blonde head of hair and tail. Her furry wings are folded up behind her, and I can see two genfin males further inside the cabin. They're all wearing the leather rebel fatigues, and they pause what they're doing to stare out at us. She's pretty and has the muscles of a warrior.

Her brown eyes widen slightly as her gaze bounces between Evert and Sylred. "Covey Fircrown," she says, though I don't miss the slight tremble in her voice. My cupid senses pick up on something from her. Part of my cupid powers allows me to sense love or heartbreak, but sometimes, I can also sense other things. And right now, I'm sensing that this female is longing for *my* genfins— and it's *strong*.

Like…huge wafts of it are going up my nostrils and making my nose tickle with the need to sneeze. Her intense longing brings out an overwhelming sense of panic and possessiveness in me that I didn't even know I was capable of.

If I had a genfin tail, I'd totally wrap it around my guys right now in a public display of claiming. But I don't, so instead, my irrational emotions take over, and I watch in horror as I lift up Sylred's and Evert's hands in front of my face and then lick them.

Yeah. *Lick.*

Like a four-year-old who licks the toys she doesn't want to share.

And judging by their collective faces, I just made things awkward. Whoops.

CHAPTER 25

The four of us just stand there for a moment, staring at the hands that I still have in front of my face.

"You done?" Evert asks, the humor evident in his voice. He leans down to press his mouth against my ear. "Because if not, I have other places you can lick instead."

He backs away, his dimples showing, while my face burns with embarrassment. I quickly let go of their hands and shove mine under my arms. "Sorry... I...umm..."

Yeah, I don't have a good segue out of the licking incident. But I've staked my claim, so I can't be totally sorry about what I did. At least the female genfin isn't throwing out such intense longing anymore. They are *my* genfins, after all. See, now I'm defending the licking thing. Having mates is weird.

The female clears her throat. "What are you doing here?" she asks, her eyes flicking over me before returning to Evert.

"Hi, Viessa," he greets.

154

My brows scrunch together in concentration. Viessa… Viessa… Why does that name sound familiar?

"Evert," she replies, looking quickly away.

Then it hits me. Back on the banishment island with the guys, I remember Evert talking about her. About the one who got away. This was the female he chose to bond with before Ronak rejected her and decided it would be better to mate with high society Delsheen instead.

My heart gets stuck in my throat at the realization, and I inadvertently take a step back. Does Evert have the same longing that she does? I steal a look at him, wondering if I'll be able to pick anything up, but I find that he's looking right at me.

"Scratch, this is Viessa. We grew up together."

"And almost bonded to her," I mumble under my breath.

The corner of his lips twitch, and I feel his tail snake around my waist. "Viessa, this our mate, Emelle."

Her eyes flick to his tail that is now possessively wrapped around me. I see a flash of pain cross over her face before she covers it up. "Hello," she greets.

"Hi," I say back. I'm also tempted to lick them again. I stop myself because I'm an adult.

There's a pause between all of us, and it's more awkward than the time I accidentally made a guy jizz his pants at the supermarket. Poor guy. They had to announce a cleanup on aisle three. I didn't even mean to Lust-Breath him that much. I just thought it would be funny to make him launch a lap rocket while he was holding a particularly large cucumber. The memory makes me chuckle, but I quickly cover it up with a cough. Evert gives me the side-eye.

Sylred clears his throat. "Viessa, we're sorry to bother

you, but word is your covey is in charge of the portal today."

The two genfins inside the cabin come up behind Viessa, one of them putting a hand on her shoulder. She looks up and gives him a smile, but I can tell it's forced. They all have their wings, so they must be bonded, but I sense that it isn't a Love Match.

"That's right. We are," the male confirms. "How can we help you?"

"We need to get on that list today and travel through the portal."

The male frowns. "Didn't you just get back?" he asks Sylred. "Besides, the list is full today. You'll have to wait and try to get on it for next week. You know we have to limit it. If too many people go through at one time, the other high fae that work for the prince will feel the rift and be able to track it."

Evert tenses beside me. He goes to open his mouth, which I'm sure will just be a lot of swearing and threatening, but Sylred shoots him a look. The tic in Evert's jaw throbs, but luckily, he remains quiet.

"Look, we understand," Sylred says, his tone considerate. "But our mate just came back to us, and we need to go to Ronak. She's the only one who can help him."

My head whips in his direction, and although I see his tail twitch from my attention, he doesn't look at me.

"Now wait just a hot heart second. What's going on with Ronak?" I demand.

All five genfins do some twitchy, guilty movement that gives them all away. A darting look, fidgeting, shuffling their feet, or a twitch of their tails tells me something is very wrong.

I put my hands on my hips and stare down Sylred. He

can't help but look over at me and give a sheepish look. "What's going on?" I demand.

He doesn't answer me, but I see him and Evert exchange a look.

"If something is wrong with Ronak, you need to tell me," I persist, feeling the panic rise in me.

I hear Viessa gasp, and I follow her wide-eyed gaze to my hands. In my panic, I started wringing them a bit too enthusiastically, so of course my cupid boss mark is glowing again.

Evert and Sylred stare down at it, too, but I just snap my fingers in front of their face. "Ignore the glowing arrow through the heart. It's my boss mark and it likes to glow. It's just a thing. Now tell me what's wrong."

The three of us hold an intense stare-off, and I get angrier and more worried with every passing second that they don't say anything.

Finally, Viessa interrupts. "We'll take you."

Her male starts to argue, but she cuts him off. "No, it's fine. We can fit them in. This is important, and I'd want to go if it were me."

The male doesn't look happy, but he gives a terse nod. "Fine."

Viessa sighs. "We might as well get going now. The portal is due to open soon. You're lucky you caught us in time."

We make our way through the camp, but instead of walking between the guys, I stay a few steps ahead of them this time as I follow behind Viessa's covey. I'm upset that the guys are keeping something from me, and worry claws into my insides.

Viessa leads us all the way to a huge circus-style tent erected in the middle of camp. There are rebel guards standing around the perimeter, and a line of rebels is waiting at the entrance. Viessa and her covey speak to the guards at the door, and then with a nod, the guys and I are led straight through. Inside, there is a female high fae with yellow coloring, waiting with more guards in an otherwise empty space.

We wait off to the side, and I cross my arms in front of me. "I can't believe you guys won't tell me what's going on," I hiss at them.

Evert sighs and runs his hand through his black hair. "Scratch, it's complicated."

"I'm gonna complicate *you* in a second if you don't tell me what's wrong. He's my mate. I deserve to know."

"We think it's best if you just come with us and see with your own eyes," Sylred says gently.

I huff out a breath of frustration and turn my back on them again, instead opting to pay attention to Viessa, who is speaking with the high fae female. "How many portals can you open?" Viessa asks her.

"Four. I'll open each one for three minutes. You can have as many as you want go through, but I'm closing when that three minutes is up," the yellow high fae answers.

Viessa nods. "Very well."

She turns to one of the guards, and he passes her a list. She and her covey study it for a moment, speaking quietly. Coming to a decision, she then tells the high fae which four islands to open portals on, including the genfin island.

"Alright," the female says in understanding. "I'll open the portals in five. Get your people in here and ready to go. They have an hour until I reopen it."

Viessa nods and then walks back to the three of us,

where we are waiting in awkward silence. With Viessa and her covey overseeing all the fae, they start allowing people inside the huge tent, splitting them up depending on which island they need to visit.

When the islands are announced, and it's declared that only four portals will be opened, a lot of grumbling and complaining erupts. "I was told there would be a portal to Dalry today!" a particularly furious fae shouts from the line. "I've been signed up for two weeks!"

"We apologize," Viessa states calmly, looking over all the disgruntled fae. "But you all know that the islands we visit are not guaranteed until that day."

Several of the fae curse and complain, but Viessa's mates along with the guards keep them all back. "You will automatically be put on next week's list if your island was not chosen today," Viessa ensures them.

The discontented fae continue to give them a hard time, causing both of Viessa's genfin mates to growl. The other fae allowed inside the tent keep shooting nervous glances at the disgruntled fae, but it's not until one of the most vocal of the unhappy fae points at me that I start to feel nervous.

"Hey. That's the cupid," he says with a tilt of his head in my direction, his dark, bark-like skin dripping with sap. A few of his buddies, all of them with the same tree-like bodies, come closer.

I feel Evert and Sylred step up closer behind me, each of them pressing into my wings with their chests.

"The prince hates her," one of them says.

"Yeah, I heard she attacked the fucker," bark boy says, crossing his branchy arms in front of him. "Did you?"

All of the fae swing their heads to look in my direction, and all other voices die down in order to hear what I have to say. Nervous at the sudden attention from the hundred or so fae gathered inside the tent, I shuffle slightly on my feet. Of course, whenever I feel put on the spot, I tend to ramble.

"Oh, no. I mean, kinda. A little bit. I attacked him with some arrows. They were my pink arrows, though," I explain, motioning to the quiver full of Love Arrows at my back. "He totally overreacted in my opinion. He just made me mad, you know? He's really greedy. Also, a cheater. If you're going to have multiple romantic partners, there has to be an agreement, you know? That's just good manners."

No one agrees with me about the manners, so I just clear my throat and keep going. "Anyway, he attacked me right back. The whole thing could've been dropped right then and there. But *oh no*. He just had to keep going with it." I start ticking off my raised fingers. "He broke the princess's heart, hit me with magic, captured and had me beaten, threatened my males, oh, and the war. He's a total jerk for causing this whole thing to pop up," I say, motioning at all of the rebels as an example.

"Your rebel outfits are super rad looking, by the way, so you have that going for you. If I had to vote, I'd totally side with you guys based on looks alone. The leather really works with every skin tone," I say with a nod.

Crickets.

I look around curiously at everyone, but it seems I've struck them all silent. I hear a soft snort behind me and know that Evert is about two seconds away from laughing at me. I'd elbow him, but my wings are in the way.

Viessa clears her throat. "*Ohh-kay*. Let's get this started, shall we? Stand in your appropriate lines for each portal please. Everyone else *not* going through one of the four portals today, please make your way out of the tent."

The tree bark gang grumbles under their breath, but they turn to depart without giving her any more trouble.

Sylred grins. "Another one's been Emelle'd."

I look up at him. "What?"

"Emelle'd," Evert explains. "It's when someone gets struck silent from the crazy-ass words that come out of your mouth."

My brow furrows. "I don't say crazy-ass words."

Evert pats me on the head. "Keep telling yourself that."

I open my mouth to argue some more, but Viessa comes up, interrupting me. "You can go through first. Remember to be back at the same spot in an hour."

She shoots Evert one more look of longing before walking away, and I unintentionally bristle.

"What's wrong?" Sylred asks, picking up on my tenseness.

"I'll tell you later," I mumble before walking over to where the high fae is working her magic. Before my eyes, I see her wave her hands, and she creates the first portal. A swirling whirlpool hovering vertically in the air, it's plenty big for even the tallest of the fae in the room. No wonder they need such a huge space.

Immediately, Viessa's mates start ushering people through, while the high fae walks over to another part of the tent to open up the second portal. We wait patiently with a couple dozen other genfins until she makes her way over to us to make the fourth portal.

As soon as it appears, she gives me a nod, and I start walking forward with the guys right behind me. When I land on the other side, Sylred helps me to my feet immediately, and I thank him before dusting off my dress as I look around.

We're right in the center of town, not far from where I talked to the genfin male about what the date was when I first returned. The street is full of genfins working, shopping, talking, and walking around. Just like all the buildings on this island, everything is made of shiny, smoothed wood and shaped into domes that go deeper into the earth below.

The portal dropped us off in a small side street, and Sylred pulls me onto the main road as Evert comes out of the portal next.

I take a moment to just look around the bustling town, and it becomes immediately obvious that their race does in fact lack females. I don't see a single female as we begin making our way down the street, but genfin males of all ages turn to look at me as we pass. Evert keeps his black tail wrapped possessively around my waist, while Sylred threads his fingers through mine.

"Where are we going?"

"Just up ahead," Sylred says, pointing to the big egg-shaped wooden building.

I frown. "Isn't that where the genfin elders are?"

"Yes," Sylred says simply.

Uneasiness churns in my stomach, but I continue walking even as more and more genfins stop to look at us. It's a strange thing, to be stared at like this, and I'm not sure I like the attention. Sylred seems a bit nervous too, and he keeps running his hand over his pink hair, which the genfins are also eyeing.

"Achoo!"

I jump from Evert's sudden and super loud sneeze. A

big puff of Lust escapes his mouth when he sneezes a second time, making a giggle burst out of me.

He shakes a hand in front of his face. "Fucking Sex Breath," he grumbles.

This just makes me laugh harder. "Oh my gods, you're sneezing Lust!" I cackle.

"Like you can talk," he shoots back at me. "You leak this shit all the time."

"Hey, I haven't leaked a single time since I've been back. And for the record, I'm not even malfunctioning anymore, since I'm now the Head of all of Cupidity."

The guys both stop walking, yanking me to a stop as well.

"You're *what?*" Evert asks, looking down at me with bewilderment.

"There was a scuffle," I explain. "My boss tried to poof me. So I turned corporeal and poofed him first."

"That better not be a sex term."

I roll my eyes. "No, poofed as in terminated. I guess since I poofed him, the boss title passed directly onto me." I hold up my wrist where my ML mark is and show where the heart and arrow now accompanies it.

"So that's what happened to you?" Sylred asks, taking my wrist and running his thumb over the white tattooed mark.

"Yeah. As soon as I left to go spy on the princess and find out what was going on, I was yanked back to Cupidville. I got in trouble because they knew I was somehow going in and out of the Veil, and my cupid performance was somewhat below par."

Evert smirks. "Just somewhat?"

"Don't make fun of me. I can be a super good cupid sometimes."

He pats me on the head. "I'm sure."

"I want to hear more about what happened to you and why you were gone for so long, but for now, let's go inside so that you can see Ronak," Sylred says.

"Yeah, I'd just have to tell the story all over again to Ronak, anyway."

"Believe me, he's not in the mood for talking," Evert mumbles.

Before I can ask what the hell that's supposed to mean, Sylred starts pulling me toward the huge egg building.

CHAPTER 26

*I*nside, there's a fire pit at the center and a few curved desks around it. Aside from that warm glow, there's a circular skylight at the tip of the ceiling, letting in lots of natural light. A few male genfins look up from their desks as we walk in, and one of them gets up and starts walking over.

I recognize him immediately as the elder that brought Ronak the mating chalice for our ritual. He advised my guys not to mate with me since I'm not a genfin female. The elder takes me in as he approaches, with extra attention on my wings and hair.

"Back so soon?" he asks Sylred, to which he receives a nod. "Well, I see the resemblance," he states, tilting his head at Sylred's pink hair.

Evert tugs me closer to his side. "Yep. This is our mate."

"A cupid," the elder states doubtfully.

I liked it better when I was being called *the* cupid, but it doesn't feel like the right time to make that known.

"We're here to see Ronak."

The elder nods. "I assumed as much." He digs in the pocket of his robe and pulls out a key.

Sylred takes it with a respectful nod. "Thank you."

"I'm sorry about the vote," the elder says. "As much as I still believe your covey would've been admirable elders, I'm not surprised you were voted out."

Sylred gives him a tight smile. "We were expecting it, Elder."

"Yes, well. A non-genfin mate and a volatile alpha are not the stability that an elder council needs."

Evert's tail tightens around my waist, but I'm too focused on the echo of the elder's words to feel it.

"Volatile?" I ask.

The elder glances at me and then some sort of realization dawns on him. "You haven't told her?" he says incredulously to the guys.

"Thank you, Elder. We'll just go inside now, if that's alright," Sylred says in a strained voice.

Realizing his faux pas, the elder nods. "Good luck. I hope you can pull him out of it." He turns and strides away without another word.

I reach down and pinch Evert's black tail hard. He makes a surprised rumble. "What was that for?" he asks testily, rubbing the spot as they lead me toward the back of the room. There's a genfin guard there, who tips his head respectfully at the guys before opening the door for us to let us pass through.

"Why the hell are we here? And why did the elder just call Ronak 'volatile?' I'm done being left in the dark."

Of course, this is when the door closes behind us and we're *literally* left in the dark. It's like the universe is laughing at me.

I blink rapidly, trying to let my eyes adjust to the

sudden lack of light in the room. I stop dead in my tracks, refusing to take another step forward. I am officially freaked out. Is this some sort of trick? Are my guys... going to turn on me like Okot did? Was this all some elaborate scheme to trap me here?

I feel Sylred come up beside me, and see their shadows shift in the dark. When someone's hand moves to touch me, I slap it away. "Easy, there," Sylred croons. "Your heart is nearly beating out of your chest."

"What the ever-loving arrow is going on?" I ask, my chest heaving as I start backing away.

I hear Evert growl, and my panic spikes.

"She's panicking," Sylred says.

"I fucking know she's panicking!" Evert snaps. "The question is *why* is she panicking with us?"

My back hits the door, and my hand scrambles to find the handle, only to realize there isn't one. I'm about to start banging on the thing when a flame appears as Sylred lights a lantern.

"Sorry, I forget you can't see in the dark like us. We have to keep it dim in here," he explains as he holds up the lantern. "You're safe with us."

Sylred and Evert regard me curiously, and embarrassment floods into me. "I know," I say, dropping my arms from the door as I try to play it cool. "I'm just...afraid of the dark."

Evert snorts, clearly not believing me.

"Why do you have to keep it dim in here? I don't understand," I say on a sigh as I try to look around the wooden room.

In answer, Sylred takes my hand and pulls me forward until we get to a detached wooden room. No, not a room,

167

I realize as I see the fortified iron bars behind the decorative curtains. A cell.

Granted, it's the nicest cell I've ever seen. It's clean, large, and has a nice bed and toilet inside. There's even a soft looking rug on the floor. But a cell is a cell. And as I stop in front of it, I understand why they didn't want to tell me about Ronak.

My mouth drops open in shock as I stare inside at my mate. He's kneeling in the corner of the room, his genfin animal completely taken over. There is no Ronak in the form I'm seeing. He is completely animal. The way he's hunched and eyeing me with predatory eyes sets me immediately at edge. His canines are elongated and biting into his bottom lip, drawing blood that goes trickling down unchecked. His eyes are purely golden, flashing with animalistic intent. His claws are out, longer than I've ever seen them and curving down into wickedly sharp tips. His brown hair and beard are longer than when I last saw him, both of which are unkempt and wild around his already wild face. He's completely nude, and his brown, lion-like tail is twitching back and forth behind him in irritation, his wings tucked tightly at his back.

When I take a step toward the iron bars, he releases a terrifying growl, his lips pulling back into a sneer, his teeth flashing in the shadowed light.

Fear stops me and I swallow, not missing how Ronak's eyes track the movement of my throat. "What happened to him?" I breathe.

"Sometimes, when an alpha feels his mate's bond vanish, he goes feral," Sylred explains gently, his voice just a soft murmur. "When you left, we felt the bond disappear almost immediately. But when it didn't come back, we thought…" Sylred cuts off, and pain cuts into me.

"You thought I'd died," I whisper with dawning realization.

Sylred nods, and I feel Evert's tail snake around my waist again, as if his animal needs the reassurance that I'm here. "We hoped that you were just invisible, but we had no way of knowing for sure, and every day that you didn't return, each day that we couldn't sense you...Ronak fell further into his animal. It's rare for the mate-feralness to occur, but once it began, we couldn't stop it."

"So you locked him up?" I don't say it with accusation, but Sylred still winces.

"He locked himself up," Evert corrects, drawing my gaze. "He could feel his control slipping. After the seventh day that you were missing, he came to the elders and asked to be locked up. This is the only place that can hold him," he explains. "His strength power would've ripped apart anything else. Apart from the bars, the wooden walls are fortified with iron, as well as the floor. They even have to keep an extra supplement of iron in his food to keep him inside."

"What would've happened if you hadn't locked him up?" I ask.

"He would've gone on a killing rampage," Sylred explains. "We would've had to put him down. The only reason we didn't was because we weren't convinced you were really...dead," he says, struggling with the word. "We were searching all other avenues for you. I come here as often as I can and use my Sound Soothe power to try to keep him calm, but as you know, because of our covey link, it doesn't have much effect on him. I can't negatively affect him at all, and even when I simply try to soothe him, it barely does anything. I've gotten a few swipes for my efforts, though."

Surprised, I look at him. "You mean he'd even attack you?"

Sylred nods. "He has. Many times. Evert, too."

I shake my head in despair. Ronak's animal is incredibly protective of his covey. The fact that he's so far gone that he's even attacked them is not comforting.

Intense guilt cripples me, and I feel a tear fall down my cheek. "I'm here now, so he'll snap out of it, right?"

"We don't know. Alphas that go mate-feral have never been known to return to their senses."

CHAPTER 27

Sylred and Evert don't try to tell me it's okay. They don't give me false promises, either, and I'm glad for that. Ronak might not ever snap out of the feral state he's in, and it's all my fault.

"Okay," I say, taking a shaky breath. "What do I do?"

"Your presence here should help solidify the bond that's already present," Sylred tells me. "We were hoping if we brought you closer, that it might affect him." The three of us eye Ronak where he's still hunched in the shadows, watching us. He's sitting on a pile of fabric, but when I take a closer look, I realize that it's a bundle of my clothing.

My breath hitches, and Sylred notices the direction of my gaze. "It calms him," he explains with a tinge of sadness.

That...that kills me a little bit inside. My strong and steady Ronak was reduced to a mindless animal who sleeps on a pile of my clothing. I really messed up when I left them.

"The asshole is more aggressive toward me," Evert explains. "I'll let Sylred take the reins here."

Sylred purses his lips and begins to whistle a low, comforting tune. As soon as he does, the feral animal slowly rises to his feet. His knees are bent, his back hunched slightly, his lips still pulled back into a sneer. He begins to stalk to the left of the room, like a lion wanting to corner his kill.

"Maybe you should back up," Sylred mumbles, his whistle cutting off.

One second, the alpha is eyeing us with violent disdain, and then lightning-fast, he's at the bars and swiping his claws across Sylred's chest. Sylred lets out a painful grunt and jumps away from the bars before Ronak's second pass can make contact. My mouth drops open at the huge gashes cut into Sylred's skin, his shirt tattered and stained with the blood that now falls freely from the wounds.

"Fuck!" Evert curses as he comes forward. He places a hand on Sylred's injury, his power instantly stitching the skin back into place.

With the scent of blood now ripe in the air, the feral alpha starts growling and straining against the bars, gnashing his teeth and swiping his claws at air as he tries to attack Sylred and Evert.

"This isn't fucking working," Evert snaps as he jerks away from Ronak's claws.

"What should we do?" I ask anxiously, watching Evert finish up healing Sylred.

At the sound of my voice, the alpha's head whips around, and he catches me in his sight. Sylred and Evert forgotten, he moves in front of me. The guys freeze.

"Emelle," Sylred says, his hands out in a placating

gesture and his tone quiet and falsely calm. "Slowly back away from the bars."

I lift my foot to do just that, but as soon as the alpha sees the movement, he lets out a snarl so fierce that it makes my blood run cold.

Evert curses under his breath and moves to grab me, but Ronak roars in warning, and Sylred stops him. The alpha stares at me, his golden eyes dilated, and he purposely grabs the iron bars between us. I can tell that the iron weakens him, but even so, his fingers clench around the two bars and then he *pulls*.

With his incredible strength power, even muffled from the weeks in captivity surrounded by iron, the alpha wrenches the two bars of his cell apart large enough for him to grab hold of me and yank me into his cell.

I let out a shriek as I'm tossed against the wall, the back of my head knocking against the wood hard enough to make my teeth jar.

The guys shout and start rushing forward, and the alpha lets out a warning growl, his body poised in front of me, ready to strike.

"Stop!" I shout from behind him. The guys halt just outside of the bars, looking at me incredulously. "Don't come in here. He'll attack you."

"He attacked *you*," Evert snaps. "We're gonna have to put him down before he kills you!"

As if he can somehow still understand what's being said, the alpha roars again, the noise making the hairs rise on the back of my neck. I'm shaking all over, but I don't dare voice that fear, because the guys will try to protect me, and that will mean hurting Ronak. I can't let that happen.

Tentatively, I reach a hand out and touch Ronak's

shoulder, hoping I can comfort him. He whips around faster than I can anticipate and pins me to the wall with a forearm across my chest and flashing teeth bared at my throat.

I flinch, knowing he's about to rip out my throat, but then something else happens. His eyes flash black.

"Ronak," I breathe.

In a blink, his eyes return to being the animal gold, but I saw it. Ronak is still in there. I feel the alpha's hot breath on my skin as he drags his sharpened teeth over my neck, and his tail wraps around my arm in a possessive move.

When I flick my eyes over Ronak's shoulder, my stomach plummets when I see that Evert is holding a bow, an arrow already cocked and aimed at Ronak's back.

"Don't," I cry. "He won't hurt me."

"Are you fucking kidding me? He's about two second away from killing you!"

At Evert's raised voice, Ronak starts growling again, and he looks over his shoulder, baring his teeth at the enemy.

"Evert, you have to trust me. Back away. Both of you."

Evert's blue eyes bore into me, fury and fear warring in his expression. "I will *not* let him kill you. Don't make me choose him over you, because I'll choose you. Every fucking time."

Keeping my voice as calm as I can, I say, "I'm not asking you to choose. I'm telling you, Ronak is still in there, and his animal won't hurt me. Look at him, Evert. Really look. He's not trying to hurt me. He's trying to *keep* me."

At my words, I see that Evert's hold on the bow wavers. He takes in the scene with new eyes, looking at how Ronak is protectively poised in front of me, holding me and ready to defend me from what his animal views as the threat.

I hadn't even noticed that Sylred was trying to use his calming musical power this entire time, but he stops to say, "Evert, listen to her."

Evert grinds his teeth together. "Fine," he grits out. "But I'm keeping the fucking arrow trained on him. If he so much as breathes wrong, I'm putting him down and getting you out."

I nod and the two of them slowly back away, the alpha watching them out of the corner of his eye. When they're outside of the cell once again, the alpha spreads out his red wings, blocking me from view. Then he drops his arm from my chest and shoves his hips against mine.

"Oh," I exclaim in surprise.

The fact that he's totally nude becomes crudely obvious as his hard erection is shoved against my stomach.

CHAPTER 28

*M*aybe some people would be scared by the idea of mating with this feral genfin, but not me. He's still my Ronak, and as I look into his flashing eyes and see the strain in his body, it becomes completely obvious what he needs.

His animal needs to *claim* me, to feel me completely from the inside out so that he can know that I'm here. My heart swells, and all I want to do is comfort his animal, to reassure him that I'm back—and there's only one way to do that with a feral genfin who's only capable of animal-istic instincts.

"Ronak," I say softly.

At the sound of my voice, he brings his body flush with mine and grinds his hips against me. When I move my hand, he lets out a warning snarl, but slowly, so slowly, I let my hand drop down and curl around his erection.

A rumble erupts from his chest, and before I can blink, I'm being hauled off my feet and thrown onto the bed. I've barely landed face-first on the mattress before I feel his claws shredding the skirts of my dress, and then his hand is digging into my hip as he roughly moves me so that I'm ass up and head down.

I feel the air brush against my exposed bottom half and look over my shoulder at the alpha. His cock is swollen and dripping with pre-cum, so hard it almost looks painful. His golden eyes are riveted on my crudely displayed center, and he looks wild, yes, but he also looks hot as hell with his rippling muscles and shaggy beard.

He grips my hips, and in one brutal thrust, he slams his cock into me balls-deep, making me cry out in a mix of surprise, pain, and pleasure. Immediately, he starts fucking me with ruthless abandon, and it's so intense and *beastly* that a whimper escapes me.

"Emelle!"

I turn my head at the sound of Sylred's worried shout, but I hold out a hand. "It's fine. I'm fine," I assure him, even as I'm gritting my teeth and my face is being shoved against the mattress with each thrust.

In part, I'm grimacing because he's fucking me with violent and bestial intent, and yeah, it hurts a little. But his feralness is also unfurling a wild abandon inside of me that thoroughly enjoys this loss of control. Every pinch of pain seems to feed this wild pleasure, and it's so different from anything I've ever felt before. He's so rough, every movement so sharp and fierce, and I want *more*.

A thrill inside of me dances like electricity, crackling under my skin with every single punishing stroke. The way he's taking me is so different, even from when we went into heat together, because even then, Ronak was always right beside his animal's presence, allowing his animal to push me but never take it too far. This, though

177

—this level of intensity is something else entirely. It's one hundred percent animal. And I freaking *love* it.

His claws dig into my waist, but he never breaks the skin. His growls fill the air, and he continues to keep his harsh pace as his skin smacks against mine. When I accidentally let out another whimper, the guys mistake it for pain. Both of them move closer to the hole in the cell, Evert still holding the bow taut. When Ronak sees them encroaching, he pulls out of me to face them and lets out a ferocious roar, his claws lengthening in the offense and his body posed for attack.

Seeing that he's ready to strike at the guys, I quickly flip over onto my back and wrap my limbs around him. His arms automatically go around my waist and under my wings to hold me.

Gently but firmly, I bring my hands to his cheeks and turn his face back to mine. "It's alright," I tell him softly. "They won't try to take me away from you. Focus on me, Alpha," I tell him steadily, never once blinking as I look into his eyes. "That's right. It's just you and me." The hardness in his expression softens ever so slightly.

With his full attention on me, I bring a hand between us and slowly take his cock and line it up with my entrance. "I'm right here. Take me," I say huskily. That's all the encouragement he needs. With a growl, he pistons his hips and thrusts into me again, and my head falls back in a groan.

He holds me beneath my arms and wings like I weigh nothing, and his hips start working ferociously against mine. He soon becomes unsatisfied with our position and the tattered dress that still covers my chest, so he brings a clawed hand up and tears the rest of it away. And even though his razor-sharp claws scrape right against my skin, not once does he cut me.

Tossing the dress away, he hoists me up and sets me on the bed again, but this time, he doesn't try to take me from behind like an animal. He balances on his forearms and pistons into me from above, hitting my sweet spot when he reaches under my ass and tilts up my hips.

"Gods yes," I croon.

Like he's mimicking my declaration, the alpha roars again, but this time it's with his own release. With one last jerk of his hips, I feel hot ropes of cum shoot into me, and then his body finally stills. We're both panting, sweat mingling between our skin, and even though I didn't come, there was a different sort of satisfaction that I've earned in taming the beast.

After a moment, his muscled arms shift me on the mattress so that the wall is at my back and he's holding me at my front, his cock still buried inside of me.

When I'm securely cooped up in this position, safe from the other males in the room, the alpha flares out his wings and then curls them around us so that we're encased in a feathery cocoon. In the dim light, now filtered through his red-feathered wings, I watch him watching me.

"Did that take the edge off?" I tease him. He tilts his head in a purely animal way and then leans forward and licks my cheek. I giggle and grimace at the same time, using my shoulder to wipe off my cheek. "I at least hope you're house-trained."

He snaps his teeth playfully, making me laugh again. When I try to wriggle my hips away, he gives me a low growl in warning.

"Oh. Gotcha. You still want your beef bullet inside me. Can do."

He watches me with rapt interest, like I'm the most fascinating thing he's ever seen, and his tail gently strokes my leg. When he starts to purr, I reward him with a smile. "You are super good at purring. I knew you were a big kitty cat underneath all of that growly stuff. You just were cranky because you needed to get some cupid lovin', am I right?"

He nips my neck in response, his canines scraping against my tender skin.

"You know," I tell him softly as I bring a hand up to trace his feathers. "Ronak wasn't one for cuddling, so this is kind of nice," I tell him. When my fingers dance over the top curve of his wing, he shudders. "But I really would like to talk to him. I know he's an asshole, but he kinda grew on me, you know? Could you let him come out? Maybe tamp down on the whole feral thing you've got goin' on for a minute?"

He starts moving inside of me again, and I can feel his cock hardening. "Round two already? Wow, you're very… robust. Good for you."

His purr turns to a groan, sounding very Ronak-ish. Taking a chance, I lift my head and place my lips against his. He freezes, golden eyes wide as he stares at me like he doesn't understand. Undeterred, I gently coax him as my lips play with his, letting my tongue dart out to trace the seam of his lips and the edge of his canines.

"Come on, Ronak," I whisper against his mouth. "Come out here and kiss me back before this gets real awkward."

I pepper him with kisses, every part of his mouth mine to lavish attention on. Kissing is such a non-animal thing to do, and when I close my eyes, I can imagine that it's Ronak moving inside of me, cradling me with his arms and wings—that it's him kissing me back.

Wait.

I snap my eyes open and stare up at his eyes. His *black* eyes.

"Ronak!"

I squeal excitedly and throw my arms around his neck, tugging him against me in a hug. His arms tighten around me. "Little demon," he rasps against my throat.

A half-laugh, half-sob escapes me as I pull back to look at his handsome face. Gone is the wild, animal look about him. Gone are the tense and jerky movements of a feral beast. "You're back," I whisper in relief, feeling tears spill down my cheeks.

His voice is gravelly from disuse as he says, "So are you."

In a very tender gesture, he brings his forehead to rest against mine and sweeps his thumbs over my wet cheeks. Already, his claws and canines have receded. "You tamed my beast from his feralness. You brought me back from an impossible state. I don't know how the hell you did it."

I don't either, but I'm not about to admit that. I shrug a shoulder and look at him with all the confidence in the world. "You're mine."

The corner of his lip tilts up. "Yeah, little demon. And you're mine."

When I kiss him this time, Ronak's mouth moves with mine. Still buried inside of me, he moves his hips in a delicious rhythm that soon has me panting for more. "I need lots of orgasms," I gasp. "Evert wouldn't let me have one, and your animal didn't, either," I say with a small pout. "So I need at least three."

"Greedy little thing," I hear Evert say.

At the sound of his voice, Ronak shifts and folds back his wings. Rolling me on top of him, Ronak holds me smugly over his chest with his hands on my ass.

Evert and Sylred look down at us from where they stand beside the bed. Taking in Ronak's black eyes and receded fangs and claws, Sylred blows out a sigh of relief.

"Thank gods for that."

Evert shakes his head and finally drops his arms to hang at his sides. Ronak eyes the bow and arrow and cocks a brow. "Disappointed you couldn't shoot me?"

Evert shrugs. "A bit."

I smack Evert playfully on the leg, but his tail wraps around my wrist and traps it there, making my hand slide up to his very hard erection beneath his pants.

"Seriously? You're hard right now?"

Evert scoffs like I'm an idiot. "You're buck naked, lying on top of him with his dick still inside of you and your own cream sliding down your legs. Of course I'm hard."

"Well, I still didn't get to orgasm, so..." I start to move my hips, making Ronak groan and grip my waist.

"Don't give one to her," Evert says.

I sit up, bracing my hands on Ronak's chest so that I can glare at him. "What? Why not?"

He shrugs. "I'm not sure you've learned your lesson yet."

"You son of a butt chunk! I'm gonna tie your limp dick in a knot if someone doesn't give me a gods-damned orgasm!"

Ronak grimaces, stilling my movement on his cock with his hands. "Can you not talk about injuring penises while mine is inside of you?"

"I guess."

As soon as he lets me move again, I start gyrating my hips, because I'm not about to let a good cock go to waste. My pushin' cushion likes a nice prick.

Making my spine and hips move like a slow wave, I grind against him, and a groan comes out of both of us.

"Fucking hell," Evert grits out. "You're cheating."

"Not cheating," I tell him breathlessly, my head tipped back in ecstasy. "I totally tamed his beast. Plus, his cock is inside of me. Ronak is gonna do whatever I want right now," I say cockily. "Aren't you, Ronak?"

With his teeth clenched in desire, all he does is nod emphatically.

"See?" I say, pleased with myself.

Evert takes hold of my jaw and turns my face to him. "You are a naughty little thing."

"Yep," I tell him. "But you like it." I snatch his hand and stick his finger in my mouth so I can suck on it. When I pull it out with a pop, he growls.

"That's it. She wants orgasms?" he says, glancing over to Sylred as they share a loaded look. "Let's give them to her."

Inside I'm like, "Hell yeah!" But the look on his face also makes me pause a little. Just a little, though, because…well, I really don't see a downside to orgasms.

CHAPTER 29

*B*efore I can ask what Evert's look means, he moves behind me and grips my wings at the top, making my spine arch back. I pause, looking over my shoulder at him. My wings are super sensitive where he's gripping them, and it sends chills down my skin, my nipples pebbling painfully.

"Did anyone tell you to stop fucking him?" Evert asks me. "Keep moving those hips."

"I will, but not because you told me to," I tell him matter-of-factly. "I'm going to because it feels freaking awesome, and I want to."

When I hear his chuckle, I barely suppress the urge to toss my arm back and punch him in his creme puffs.

"Sure, Scratch."

"I have two other mates here who will be more than happy to scratch my itch," I taunt.

"Syl, I think she's done enough talking back," Evert says, ignoring me. "Why don't you take care of that mouth for me?"

I mean, that sounds good to me. Not that I'm going to

actually admit that out loud. I like to make them work for it. "Nope," I say primly. "I'm busy with Ronak."

Using my awesome cupid temptress moves, I start lifting up and down on Ronak's hard cock, making sure to put some extra bounce in my moves so that my tits look extra amazing. I know it's working, because I feel Ronak pulse inside of me, while the other guys quickly strip their pants. When Sylred puts a finger on my face to turn me to look at him, I pout out my bottom lip the way he likes.

His soft brown eyes are alive with hunger, which is apparent by the thick cock he's holding in front of me like an offering. Seeing a bead of pre-cum leak out from the tip, I lick my lips like I'm ready to suck down a smoothie. Like that movement is a trigger, Sylred pulls my face down and guides my mouth around his cock.

When my mouth is full of him and my tongue is busy swirling around, Evert reaches around and starts pinching and plucking at my nipples. "That's better, isn't it?" he taunts. "Our little mate gets testy when she doesn't have our dicks in her."

I moan at his dirty words, but because I know we both like a good fight, I flare up my wings, forcing his hands away from my breasts. An angry growl erupts from him when he's shoved away, and then two pairs of hands move me faster than I can track, and suddenly, I find myself on my hands and knees, and Evert's hand slaps against my ass.

"Don't test me, or you still won't get any orgasms," he warns.

I look up at him indignantly. You know...as indignant as I can look when I'm naked, on my hands and knees, and wetter than a leaky faucet.

"I'll just do it myself then," I challenge, bringing my

hand to my aching clit so I can start rubbing it just the way I like.

But before I can really get into it, Evert's tail winds around my wrist and holds it hostage behind my back.

"Good thing I have two arms and you only have one tail," I retort.

I bring my other hand around…only for Ronak's tail to come around and do the same thing. My eyes flash to him where he's sitting up on the bed in front of me. "Traitor."

"Be a good little demon and stop talking back," he orders.

Instead, I sit up on my knees in front of Sylred, slowly sliding my body up his chest. "You'll give me an orgasm, won't you? It would be totally *impolite* not to," I point out as I press my chest against him. Yeah, I'm playing dirty.

His mouth comes down to nip my earlobe. "I will…" he promises, making me grin. "But not until you listen to your alpha."

I reel back and narrow my eyes on him. Traitors. Traitors everywhere. But I'm so freaking horny right now that I think I might combust if I don't come. Or at least flood the whole island with my cupid love juices.

I sigh, sitting back on my ankles. "Fine. But just know, cupids have an *excellent* memory, and this is being filed away," I say, tapping my temple.

Ronak arches a brow. "Noted. Now get back on your hands and knees and arch that winged back," he says, their tails releasing me.

I pause, thinking of something sassy to retort, but Evert reaches around and pinches my nipple again. "Hey!"

"You heard the alpha."

With a sigh, I flip my hair over my shoulder and do as instructed. Outwardly, I'm putting on a super good front,

186

looking all annoyed and stuff. But Evert just smirks as he reaches down and strokes the curve of my ass. "Don't try to look at us like that. We can smell how wet you are from being bossed around."

Oh. Damn genfins with their superior sense of smell.

"There are three dicks in this room, and not one of them is fucking me. What's a cupid gotta do to get an orgasm around here?"

"She's still talking back," Evert muses.

"Yes, she is. I guess she's the one who needs to be tamed now," Ronak says with a dark chuckle.

I narrow my eyes. "I liked you better when you were feral."

He just laughs.

Then, like they always somehow manage to work in tandem, all of their movements effortless and coordinated, Ronak slides me up so that I'm on top of him again, and he pushes my head down on his cock. My lips part automatically, and I happily start licking and slurping around him. Behind me, Evert grips my hips and starts pushing the tip of his head into me, going excruciatingly slowly. I'm sure it's because he knows that I prefer it fast, and he's just furthering my punishment. Which, yeah, I get off on even more.

When he finally inches all the way in, he lets out a satisfied purr. "She's fucking wetter than rain."

"Of course she is," Ronak says cockily. "Look at her slurping on my cock like it's a straw full of fairy wine."

"She does like fairy wine," Sylred chirps in cheerfully.

He's not wrong.

To shut him up, I reach over and grab his balls in my hand and squeeze slightly. He makes a choked sound, sounding half aroused and half in pain. Evert laughs and smacks me hard across the ass cheek. I yelp and flinch up, but he just puts a hand between my wings and pushes my head back down. Ronak's cock hits the back of my throat, nearly making my eyes water, but because I have an excellent non-gag reflex, I swallow it down like a champ and keep going. I'm totally gonna brag to Belren later.

Ronak threads his hands through my pink hair, tangling and tugging with the perfect amount of pressure. "Just like that, little demon," he growls.

"Don't ignore your third mate," Evert chastises me, so I quickly grip Sylred's cock, smearing some of his cum over the head with my thumb. He makes a noise of satisfaction when I start stroking up and down his hot, smooth shaft. I work him in the same rhythm that I'm working Ronak with my mouth. When the spunk dries, I pop my mouth off of Ronak and move over to Sylred, stealing a surprised groan from him. It's messy as I move back and forth between them, strings of drool caught on my chin, but it only seems to excite them even more.

Evert is still moving way too slowly behind me, but every time I try to quicken the pace by slamming my hips against him, he just grips me tighter and slows me down again. A frustrated growl erupts from me when I realize that *still* none of them are playing with my clit.

Like he can read my mind, Sylred says, "I think our mate is getting impatient."

"Mmm," Evert says, running a hand up my ass crack before he starts teasing my nub. "What was it she told us back at our den? That she was ready for this ass to be taken?" Using the juices coming from my pussy, he slathers my back hole and dips a finger in. I yelp in surprise.

Sylred starts to laugh, but it ends in a groan when I play with his balls again. "I think she did say that."

"Careful what you wish for, little demon," Ronak says.

"Put your wings away," Ronak orders.

As soon as I do, Ronak moves out from under me. "I get her ass first," he declares as he forces Evert to change positions.

"Fucking asshole," Evert snarls.

"Exactly," Ronak retorts with a smirk.

Still on my hands and knees, Evert hooks his arms under mine and pulls me up over his chest so that I'm lying on top of him. He wastes no time in taking over my pussy again, pushing into me without warning.

My breath catches in my throat from the sudden invasion at this close angle. "*Fuck.*"

"You asked for it," Evert says against my mouth.

"Give it to me," I demand, out of my mind with lust and need. I need to be filled. To be claimed by all three of them. To orgasm again and again. If I don't get that, I'm liable to start frothing at the mouth and blow enough Lust in here that even I come apart at my dripping wet seams.

The guys all laugh.

Oh. I guess I said that out loud.

"Better give her what she wants, or we might have a feral cupid on our hands," Sylred says.

"Ronak, you sure you can handle her?" Evert asks as he rolls his hips deliciously.

"I don't know, can I handle you, little demon?" Ronak sucks on his finger again before pressing it against my back entrance. Dipping a finger inside, I cry out when he starts swirling it around. "Relax," he soothes.

"Here," Sylred says, coming forward. For the first time, my poor, aching clit finally gets some attention when he brings his hand to it and starts rubbing the spot. Evert doesn't seem to mind that Sylred's hand is touching me, even when his fingers brush against his slick cock. "Give us more of your cream," he coos in my ear, letting the dirty whisper tease my hair.

Being fucked by Evert and touched by Sylred at the same time, while Ronak is teasing my forbidden hole is all too much, and I *finally* orgasm, crying out like a woman possessed. My pussy clenches around Evert, hard enough that he curses and stills my rocking hips.

But apparently, it's the exact response that Sylred wanted, because he scoops up the cream that gushed out of me and uses it to help Ronak lube me up. Making sure his fingers and dick are covered, Ronak fists my hair so that he can get me at just the right angle.

Slowly, Ronak removes his finger and starts pushing into me.

Even with his cock covered in my slick, I suck in a sharp gasp of pain as his head slowly pushes into me. "I can't," I pant. "You're too big. You're gonna rip me for sure. Take it out," I tell him, panicking. "I keep telling you guys I have narrow channels!"

"Shh," Ronak rumbles. "You're too tense."

"I happen to like her fucking tense," Evert says beneath me, groaning at the vise-like grip my pussy has on his cock.

"I was just kidding about doing double penetration," I tell them breathlessly. "I can't handle it. I'm not cupid enough. I need to be trained back there first. I need to wear, like, a vibrating butt bullet for a week or something. Or maybe some beads. Do you have any anal beads?" I ask desperately.

I look up at them, but they just stare back at me. "No one has any anal beads?" I ask with exasperation.

"Sorry, that was in my other pants," Evert says dryly.

"Well, what about a slender dildo?" I ask seriously.

All three of them start laughing. The assholes. Oh—except the laughter kind of rumbles up me and makes it feel better.

Having an idea, I perk up. "Purr," I demand.

"Are you trying to give me orders?" Ronak asks with a hint of challenge.

"If you want to get your dick all the way inside of me, then purr, dammit!"

"I will, but only because I want to," he says, throwing my previous words back in my face.

In sync, Ronak and Evert start purring at the same time, and oh my gods...*yes*.

I sigh as I feel the vibrations travel up from their dicks to my insides. When Evert leans up, I think he's going to kiss me, but instead, he blows a breath of Lust right into my face.

"Gods!"

Just like that, I come around his cock *again*, and he chuckles in response.

The orgasm and their purring make me totally relax, and I feel my ass opening up for Ronak as he slides further in. Sylred comes up onto the bed to join us, his body poised above Evert's head, his dick ready and waiting for me.

"Fucking worst view ever," Evert deadpans.

I giggle from the look on his face as he decidedly looks away from Sylred's ball sack that hangs over his head, but my giggle is cut off when Sylred grabs my head and pulls my mouth back over his cock again.

At the same time, hands start invading me. Fingers dance over my clit, other fingers tug and pull at my nipples, while more grip my hips and tangle in my hair.

Eyes closed, back arched, purred vibrations running through me, three cocks pushing further and further into me, the four of us are moving perfectly in sync, and then Ronak slides all the way in.

"Fuck, *yes*," he snarls from behind.

My lips slip off of Sylred so that I can arch up and hiss an intake of air, feeling fuller than I've ever felt in my entire life.

"Oh gods. You're in," I say, wincing. "You're all the way in my cinnamon hole. You're freaking big. It kinda hurts. It feels weird. It feels *super* weird. Oh gods, don't move!"

Ronak and Evert freeze. We stay still like that for a while, my genfins giving me time to acclimate to Ronak's size, even though I can tell that staying still is killing them.

After who knows how long, I feel like I can breathe again. I shift around a little, now that I'm more used to the double cocks spearing me. Ronak's invasion still hurts a bit, but there's a throbbing that's begun that has nothing to do with pain. Tentatively, I start moving my hips, and my genfins continue to hold still and purr, letting me do this on my own time.

Getting bolder, I start to move up and down, and I can't help but look down and admire the erotic view. "Oh man. I'm doing it," I say breathlessly as I start moving faster. "I'm totally DP'ing the hell out of you guys right now." I fist pump a couple times before I can stop myself.

Evert chuckles, making his purr cut off. "Yeah, you are, Scratch. But do you think you're ready to get back to the TP'ing now, or have you forgotten you have three mates?"

Oh. Right.

Feeling uber enthusiastic now that I've successfully had my back door breached, I suck down on Sylred like a damn vacuum on an infomercial. I'm selling the shit out of it, too.

When the guys start moving again, I can feel Ronak's and Evert's cocks stroking up and down inside of me, sliding against the thin wall that separates them. It feels fucking amazing, and I'm not even embarrassed when a loud keening noise bubbles out of my mouth around Sylred's cock.

"Look how beautiful our mate is with all three of us inside her," Sylred grits out, his fingers tugging on my hair.

Ronak and Evert pick up the pace and start fucking me hard and fast, and every time they move, my mouth moves farther back on Sylred's dick until I'm choking on him and swallowing him down with each thrust.

"Shit," he curses, his dick tensing against my tongue. "I'm not gonna last."

My ears fill with their grunts and groans, as well as my own wild moans, and the entire thing is so erotic and perfect that I start leaking Lust all over the place. All three of them growl, and somehow, they grow even harder.

"Fucking. Lust," Evert grits out.

I don't even have the ability to feel smug about it, because a hand starts pressing and pinching at my clit again, and I come hard and fast.

"Fuck!" Evert growls.

"That's right," Ronak says behind me as he scrapes a nail up my curved spine. "Milk his cock, little demon."

And I do. My intense orgasm squeezes Evert to his own release, and he shouts out, making me suck down

Sylred with even more enthusiasm than before, and then they're both filling me with their seed. I lick and slurp on Sylred like he's the nectar of life, and only when I've had every last drop does Ronak wrench me up so that we're chest-to-back. With his hand fisted in my hair, he claims my mouth, not caring that I still taste like Sylred, and he pushes his hips deep into my ass as he comes, roaring.

The four of us collapse in a heap of sweaty limbs and wings. At one point, mine popped back out, but I have no idea when. I can't be held responsible during foursomes.

CHAPTER 30

*E*vert slaps my ass playfully where it's propped beside him. "Had enough orgasms, Scratch?" he teases.

"For now," I try to say primly. But really, how prim can you be when you have semen from three different mates caked to your skin? "But I'll let you know when I require more."

He laughs and kisses me on the top of my head. "So greedy."

"Are you sore?" Sylred asks sweetly.

"Yeah, but I like it," I answer honestly.

The guys groan. "Don't say that. You're just going to make us want to fuck you again," Ronak tells me.

"Sorry." I'm not sorry.

"We should go," Ronak says, the first one to get up. "I'm sick of being in this cell."

I take the opportunity to watch him and his gloriously tanned and muscled ass flex as he moves.

The other two genfins get up next, so with my elbow bent, I prop my head up on my hand to watch the show.

Evert and Sylred get dressed in their discarded pants, and I can't help the disappointed sigh that escapes me as their bodies get hidden away.

"Just gonna lie there and ogle us, Scratch?"

"Feral beast over there ruined my dress," I reply. When I stand up, I wince slightly at the soreness, but I take it like a champ because I'm badass.

Sylred picks up the dress that feral Ronak had been resting on earlier and tosses it over to me. I pull it over my head, and he helps me lace up the back around my wings. Besides being wrinkled, it's no worse for wear.

"We need to get back to the portal unless we want to get stuck here for a week," Sylred says as he finishes tying the laces up.

Fully dressed, Evert leaves the room, only to return with a pair of pants for Ronak.

I arch a brow. "You stole pants from someone?"

"I didn't steal. They offered."

I snort. "Sure they did. Right after you gave them your 'don't fuck with me glare,' I'm sure they offered it right up."

He smirks. "You know me so well."

"Is there any, umm, underwear in the alpha's little clothing pile over there?" I ask.

Evert laughs. "You think we brought him a pair of your used undies to sniff while you were gone?"

I blink up at him expectantly. "Well? Did you?"

He just laughs again, and Ronak rolls his eyes.

I didn't think the question was *that* outlandish, to be honest. "Well...there's a lot of umm...manjam coming out of me," I say, even as more cum drips down my legs. "This isn't hygienic. I need panties."

"Sorry, Scratch. Guess you're just gonna have to go bare."

He doesn't look sorry at all. In fact, he looks annoyingly smug.

"Here," Sylred says, taking the blanket from the bed so that I can clean myself off a bit. I kiss him on the cheek. "So polite."

He tucks my hair behind my ear and kisses me back. "Was I polite when I shoved my cock down your throat?"

My brows shoot up in surprise at his dirty talk and... yep. I'm horny again.

"Umm...Can we..."

Sylred laughs at me. "You're insatiable."

I shrug. "You guys are really good at the whole sex thing when you try."

All three of them whip around to look at me. "When we *try*?" Ronak asks incredulously.

"Yeah. When you try. Other times, you don't seem to really be on par. I'm sure it's not your fault. You can't be great *every* time," I say, keeping a straight face.

"I'll fucking show you *on par*," Evert growls.

Before he can pounce on me, Ronak puts a hand on his chest to stop him. "She's goading us, idiot. She knows damn well she's always satisfied. She just wants you to fuck her again, but our mate needs to learn patience."

I cross my arms in front of my chest. "I'm totally patient."

"Are not."

"Are too."

"Alright," Sylred says, stepping between us. "Emelle, no goading us into having more sex. We can't miss the portal, and it's due to come back for us soon."

"Fine," I relent as I start following them out of the cell

197

and to the doorway where the guard is waiting with the door open for us. "But I want more sex when we get back. And like, at least five more orgasms. Or I'm going to just have sex with myself. I'm *always* on par."

The guard makes a choking sound of surprise, and I see his nostrils flaring as he undoubtedly scents what we were just up to. His animal eyes flash for a half a second, but Ronak growls at him, and the guy immediately drops his eyes from me. "Apologies, Covey Fircrown. I'm glad to see you have recovered from your...condition."

Ronak's growl tapers off and he nods tersely. "Thank you. We will be leaving now."

The four of us make our way back out to the main part of the egg building.

"Your feathers are different," Ronak notes, looking at my black and white gilded feathers.

I spread my wings out a bit so he can get a better look. "Yeah. Funny story. It turns out I'm now a demon-angel-sandman-possibly other Veil Minor entities-cupid boss hybrid." I purse my lips in thought. "I gotta think of a better title."

Ronak looks at me incredulously. "Are...are you saying that you really are a demon?"

A stupidly smug and amused expression comes over the hard planes of his face. "Okay, first of all, wipe that look right off your face. Secondly...yes." When he opens his mouth to no doubt talk shit, I quickly cut him off. "But I wasn't a freaking demon when I landed on your damn island! That didn't happen until later." I pause. "At least I'm pretty sure it didn't. Like, eighty percent sure. I don't think it happened until I got the black feathers, and that was ages after," I explain.

The smug look doesn't leave his face. "I was right," he points out.

"Of course that's all you heard in that explanation."

Our conversation is interrupted when the elder from before spots us and comes marching over. "Ronak, you've recovered," he says, his expression belying his shock.

"I have," Ronak replies with a respectful nod. "My mate was able to tame my feral animal."

The elder looks at me with surprise and maybe even a reluctant admiration. "Well," he says as his furry wings adjust at his back. "To say I am relieved is an understatement. I'm glad to see you back to your full senses."

"Thank you, we're going to—"

Ronak doesn't get to finish his sentence, because in that moment, a huge boom goes off somewhere above us, and the next thing I know, the huge wooden egg building has cracked wide open.

CHAPTER 31

*D*aylight suddenly appears where it wasn't before, and huge wooden splinters start falling from the ceiling as it rips apart. Screaming ensues as dust and debris fall down, and Ronak tackles me to the ground, covering my body with his.

I hear shouting and more crashes all around us, and when I peek up between Ronak's limbs, I see a huge animal of some sort perched on the destroyed ceiling.

The thing is scaled and black, has at least two rows of razor-sharp teeth, and two huge emerald eyes that have no irises or pupils. When it opens its mouth to screech, something black and foul smelling emits. It shoots out of its mouth like black sparks, and wherever it lands, it burns and fills the air with the scent of sulfur.

"It's phoukas!" I hear Ronak shouting. "We need to get her out of here!"

I'm pulled to my feet, and both Evert and Sylred take one of my hands and then start pulling me toward the crumbled wall that once stood tall and seamless. Now, it's a heap of rubble and wooden splinters, and I can see genfins running and shouting outside.

I nearly trip over the debris at my feet, but Evert manages to keep me upright. When we get outside, I look around in horror at the destruction I see. Those phouka animals are *everywhere*. There has to be at least two dozen of them.

They're tearing through the town, burning things left and right with their weird spark-breath, while more scour the street, biting and attacking any genfins who get in their way. The only advantage the genfins have are their wings, but when I look up, I see a horde of the prince's high fae soldiers stationed in the air, holding bows and training them on the genfins. Any of them that try to take flight to escape the phoukas get shot down with dozens of arrows.

Ronak pulls us into a destroyed building that looks like it used to be some sort of café. Ripping up furniture, he props one up in front of us and stacks another on top, letting us crouch beneath it as we watch through the hole in the wall at the destruction and frenzy outside.

"We can't stay here!" Sylred yells over the noise. "Emelle, go invisible and get back to the rebel island."

I start to argue, but all three of them bear down on me. "Now, Emelle!" Ronak snarls.

"Fine, I'll go invisible, but I'm not leaving," I tell them firmly, leaving no room for argument.

With a breath, I pop into the Veil...and Ronak completely loses his shit.

Like a bomb going off, his whole body jolts, and his furious feral animal comes barreling out.

"Oh, shit!" Evert shouts, barely dodging Ronak's claw that comes swiping out to attack him.

I go visible again and pounce on Ronak's back, wrapping my arms around his neck. "Ronak!" I scream in his ear.

As soon as my skin is touching his, I feel his body jolt again, and Ronak stumbles forward, falling onto his knees. Panting, he looks over at me, his eyes bleeding back to black.

"Shit," Evert curses.

Ronak and I are both breathing heavily, staring at each other as realization hits.

"I can't go into the Veil," I say. "If I do, he goes feral again."

"Doesn't matter," Ronak says through gritted teeth, even though he's still panting. "Do it. It's the safest way for you."

Sylred draws a hand over his dirty face, and I see a cut on his forehead where something must have fallen on his head. "He's right, Emelle. If things get bad, you have to. Ronak can fight in his feral form, and as long as you're safe, there's a chance you can pull him back out of it. But we all need to know you're okay." Sylred turns back to the guys. "We need to get back to the meeting place for the portal and get out of here."

Ronak nods and I unwind my arms from around him as he gets shakily to his feet. The jolt from changing from his animal to himself has taken a toll on him, though he tries to hide it, and I know that he's still feeling the after-effects of being weakened by his iron cell for so long.

"I'll take point," Ronak says in a hard voice. "You two flank her. We have no weapons, so we'll have to do this half-animal." He looks at me. "You don't stop running. If we get separated, you keep going to the portal. If danger comes, you go into the Veil."

"But you'll—"

He cuts me off. "Doesn't matter. You go invisible. The prince wants you. He's punishing us for being your mates. He's pissed that he's never been able to capture any of us. Do *not* let him get you."

I want to argue, to insist that I stay with them, but the hardness in his eyes is never going to relent, and I know right now what he needs is for me to agree to his plan so that he can focus on getting the rest of his covey to safety.

"When you three get to the portal, keep Emelle safe. If the rebel base is compromised, go somewhere else and lie low."

When he moves to leave, I catch his arm. "Wait, what about you?" I demand.

He shakes his head. "I can't leave our people. I have to try and help defend them."

"Don't you dare," I hiss. "I'm not going without you."

Ronak looks back at me dispassionately and then glances over my shoulder at Evert. "That's an order. Now let's go."

He turns and starts walking out, and I scream at his back, only for Evert to tug me forward by the arm and Sylred to clamp a hand over my mouth.

The street is a mess.

Genfins are lying dead on the ground. The cobblestones are blackened and steaming, the domed buildings up and down the street are caved in and are nothing more than piles of rubble and that strange black smoke.

There is screaming and fighting and crying all around us, and when I see a little girl sobbing over three dead genfin bodies, I shove past Sylred to scoop her up. She screams and tries to wrench away, but I hold onto her and glare at Evert when he looks like he's about to argue.

"Come on," he snaps, pulling me forward again.

We keep to the edge of the street, using the ruined buildings to our advantage. All of the animals seem to be concentrated behind us at the egg building, but there are genfins fighting with high fae soldiers ahead of us with more phoukas threatening to tear them apart.

Sylred takes the little girl from me, tucking her against his chest. The thick smoke in the air is making it hard to breathe, but it also gives us the cover we wouldn't normally have otherwise. As she continues to scream and sob, I hear him immediately start to hum, filling the air with his strange sound power in order to soothe her.

But that cover works against us, too, because my eyes start burning through the strange smoke and ash that rains down on us. All I can see are shadows moving past us, and when we round a corner, a pair of phoukas spot us. A scream wrenches out of me when both of them launch at Ronak.

The things are as big as stallions, but their reptilian bodies make them look like some weird lizard horse with sparks coming out of its huffing mouth and smoking nostrils.

Ronak, shirtless, weakened, and still on shaky terms with his animal, doesn't hesitate to take them on. My strength-empowered mate steps in front of both beasts, blocking them from us. Lifting a leg, he aims a kick at the chest of the first one, his power making the thing go flying back and landing in a heap, dazed and even more pissed off than before.

But Ronak has already moved on to the second Phouka, grabbing the thing by its neck with his bare hands and snapping its spine.

He does all of this in the span of mere seconds, his

eyes flashing back and forth between gold and black, his muscular body shaking with adrenaline and tension. When we see more shadows surrounding us, this time it's two more beasts accompanied by a half a dozen high fae soldiers. The soldiers move as one, their movements so perfectly synchronized that it looks odd.

Ronak draws himself up in front of them, making himself look ten times scarier. "Go!" he shouts to us.

Sylred starts pulling me in the other direction, the child still in his arms. "Wait!" I say desperately, trying to get out of his grip. He doesn't let up, of course.

"That many of them will kill him!"

"And if anything happened to you, that would kill him, too!" Sylred shouts back at me.

When I look back, I see Ronak and Evert fighting off the horde, but they don't have weapons and they're vastly outnumbered. I know, with absolute certainty, that if I leave them now, they'll die.

And I won't let that happen.

CHAPTER 32

I won't leave Ronak and Evert to die. I *can't*.

"Take the girl to the portal!" I tell Sylred in a rush.

And then I go invisible.

Sylred shouts my name, but I'm already flying, racing toward the high fae that are trying to cut my genfins down.

When I get closer, I can see that Ronak has reverted to his feral state, just like I knew he would. I'm counting on his animal instincts to be as vicious as possible. Maybe with his animal loose, and me with my sneak attacks, we'll be able to get away.

I fly up behind a high fae perched on the roof of a shop, who is aiming his arrow right at Sylred. Sylred doesn't notice because he's struggling with the screaming girl in his arms. The fae has a full quiver of iron-tipped arrows over his back and a dagger at his belt. Putting my incorporeal hand above the hilt of the dagger, I go visible, grab the sword, and already have it stabbed through his back before he can let the arrow loose at Sylred.

The fae collapses against the roof, and I jerk the bow out of his arms while hiking the quiver over my shoulder and wing. Planting my feet on the domed roof, I nock an arrow and go for the high fae.

I was a cupid on Earth's realm for over sixty years. I am damn good with a bow. So when I let arrow after arrow loose, the wind doesn't mess me up. The moving shadows don't faze me. The smoke burns my eyes, but I just clear off the tears with my shoulder and keep shooting.

I take down three high fae before they even realize what's happening. Before they can retaliate, I launch into the sky, my wings taking me over to another roof, and I land again before any of the other archers can start aiming at me.

Ronak is battling it out with two high fae and a phouka below, but I can't see Evert anywhere. Ronak is a growling, snarling menace, but I can see blood dripping from his bare chest in multiple places, and I know even his feralness won't be able to sustain him for long.

Nocking three arrows at once, I let it fly at the phouka that's trying to spit sparks at my mate. The arrows hit the creature in the neck, and it shakes its head and releases a furious and agonized screech.

I nock another three around, aiming for its head this time, but before I can let them fly, a high fae soldier lands on top of me, pushing me off balance and sending the bow flying out of my hands.

My body goes sprawling onto the rounded roof, and I can't stop the momentum as I go rolling off the edge. I land in a heap on the ground, and just when I'm about to get my hands underneath me, the soldier is on me again, yanking me up by the hair. I scream in pain, only dazed for another second before I remember to go invisible again.

Because of my sudden absence, the high fae goes sprawling to the ground. When he gets up, I notice that his movements are oddly robotic, and when I take a moment to look at him, I notice that he looks strangely expressionless, too. Not like he's hyper-focused and shutting his emotions out, but almost like he's not even real.

But I can't linger on that, so I use his disorientation to my advantage. I go physical and grab the dagger at his belt. I have it stabbed into his back, pinning his wing against him before he can get up.

I fly up again, out of his reach, and spot Evert fighting three more high fae inside one of the ruined shops. He's fighting with only his claws and a broken table leg. He needs help. Just like Ronak, I can see that Evert is bleeding from several places, and even though he's snarling and fighting back with everything he has, he's tiring.

Flying through the smoke, searching desperately, I find a couple lifeless high fae in the rubble, fatal wounds torn through their bodies. I snatch up their swords and then fly back to Evert, dropping down beside him. He startles when I suddenly appear at his side, snarling when he sees it's me.

I pass him a sword, intending to keep the smaller one for myself, but he takes that one too and shoves me behind him. "What the bloody fuck are you doing here?"

"I'm not leaving you!" I snap.

Evert growls at me but then starts attacking the three high fae with new vigor, striking at the soldiers with a sword in each hand. He takes them out in seconds, before I even get the chance to go searching for another bow and arrow.

Heaving, he turns toward me, blood staining the blades of his swords. His face is mottled with rage. "Get the fuck out of here!"

Maybe before, I would've cowered at his super scary face, but I've dealt with genfin tempers enough to go toe to toe with them now. I glare back at him. "No."

He snarls at me and grabs me roughly by the shoulders like he wants to shake me. "You are a stubborn pain in my ass!"

"Well, too bad!"

He opens his mouth to say something back at me, but pained screams ring out through the air, cutting him off. We look at each other for a split second before running outside. I stumble to a stop when I see that the screams are coming from a high fae on the ground, a feral Ronak attacking him savagely. The fae's screams cut off when Ronak rushes forward and then viciously rips out the fae's throat with his teeth.

Spitting out blood and gore, Ronak spins in our direction, bloodied fangs and claws dripping onto the rubble.

"Ronak," I say, holding my hands up. "It's us."

But he doesn't hear me, and there are no black eyes to show me he's still there. His animal stalks forward and scoops me up, holding me protectively against his chest.

When Evert tries to come nearer, the alpha roars and gnashes his teeth.

"Fucking hell, Ronak!" Evert snaps.

"Evert!"

Our heads whip in the direction of Sylred's shout.

"The portal!"

Urging us forward, Sylred turns and starts leading the way.

Knowing I have to get Ronak to follow and that I'm

the only one who can do it, I turn invisible for just long enough so that I can get out of his hold. I won't let him stay here and fight alone. He may want to defend his people, but it's my job as his mate to defend him. When I reappear in front of him, I'm careful to stay out of his reach.

"Come on, Alpha," I coax him. He moves to grab me, but I jump back, out of reach. "You'll have to catch me."

He growls in response, but just like I'd hoped, he starts following me. Turning, I sprint toward Sylred, Evert covering our backs.

With every step, I can feel Ronak gaining on me, growling his displeasure at me for evading him.

"Here!" Sylred beckons, and I dart into the ruined building of what once was some sort of pub. The portal is already there, with other genfins rushing through it, some of them carrying the injured, but it's wavering—blinking in and out at the edges.

"Hurry! It's about to close! Go!" Sylred says.

Knowing that he and Evert won't go unless I do, and also because I need to get Ronak through, I rush forward alongside others, just as I feel Ronak's clawed hand clutching the back of my shirt.

We go falling through, landing in a heap on the ground.

$\mathcal{M}$y whole body feels like one giant bruise, and this landing didn't help. "Ugh."

Ronak's on top of me, and when I try to push him off, he snarls.

We're back at the giant tent on the rebel island, and I can see panicked genfins and rebel soldiers rushing all around as they try to cart off the injured.

"Alpha, let me up!" I snap.

He bites me on the back of the neck in response.

"Ouch!" I say, turning my head as I try to bat him away. "Evert! Sylred!"

"We're here," I hear Sylred say. "We'd help you up, but your feral mate is giving us the death glare."

I huff out a breath in annoyance and elbow Ronak in the gut. He lets out an "oof" of surprise, and I use the moment to roll out from under him and hop to my feet.

He jumps up to intercept me, so I reach up and bop him on the nose. "Bad boy," I tell him sternly.

Stunned, he stops his advance and stares at me. "That's better," I tell him. "Now heel."

His golden eyes continue to stare at me in bewilderment, but he doesn't try to tackle me again, so I take that as a win.

I beam at him and scratch him on the head. "Good boy."

He flicks his tail happily.

Evert and Sylred just gape at me.

I take a good look at all three of my genfins, and note every bleeding gash, mottled bruise, burn mark, and all the ash smeared across their skin.

"Are you guys okay?" I say, moving closer so I can inspect them better.

Evert waves me off and grabs my face instead. "We're fucking fine. Are *you* okay?" His blue eyes run up and down my body. "Why are you all bruised up? Who fucking touched you? I'll end them."

"I fell off a roof."

"I'll end the fucking roof, then."

I laugh at the perfectly serious look on his face and stand up on my tiptoes to give him a kiss. When the little girl starts crying again in Sylred's arms, I turn around and gently rub her on the back.

She can't be more than three and has pale blonde hair with a matching tail. "What's your name?" I ask her.

She sniffles and wipes her nose on Sylred's sleeve. He doesn't mind. "Tula."

"Tula, that's a pretty name." I smile at her.

"My daddies got hurt and stopped moving," she tells me, her bottom lip wobbling.

Sylred and I share a grim look, and I force myself not to cry. I feel her little heart breaking, like a window bursting open and letting in all the wind and stabbing ice. "I know, sweetheart," I tell her quietly as I rub her hair.

"Hey, would you like to come with me and meet a real-life princess?"

Tula's eyes widen and she stops crying enough to ask, "The princess?"

I nod. "Yep."

"Okay."

I move to turn to Evert, only to find my alpha right beside me, so close that when I try to straighten up, my back and arm run into his chest. "Oh. You're really close."

He starts to purr.

"Oh, for fuck's sake," Evert sighs.

Viessa and her covey come stalking over. "What the hell happened back there?" she asks.

"A full-scale attack from the prince. We knew he would strike soon, but we didn't expect it to be there," Sylred answers her.

"It's because of the cupid!" a voice calls out.

We all turn around at the voice and find a group of bloodied genfins forming a group where the portal had been.

"Me?" I ask.

"Yeah, you," the genfin male spits, looking like he wants to feed me to the phoukas. "The prince would've never launched an attack on our island if you hadn't mated to them," he says, pointing an accusatory finger at my guys.

The genfins around him start grumbling in agreement, and beside me, Ronak takes a step forward and snarls, placing his body protectively in front of me.

"Yeah! It's her that the prince wants! I say we just give her to him!" another genfin calls out.

"Why don't you just fucking try it," Evert growls, his voice deadly low.

"Let's all calm down," Sylred says, ever the peacemaker. "Our island was just attacked. We have no idea how many casualties there are. We need to regroup and then plan a course of action."

"I know what our course of action should be!" the genfin argues. "Kill the cupid."

My stomach drops all the way down to my feet, and I take an involuntary step back from the hate I see in the genfin's eyes.

"Threaten my mate one more time," Evert says. "I fucking dare you."

Picking up on Evert's fury, my anxiety, and the angry group of genfins, Ronak moves in front of me and lets out another warning growl.

We need to leave before things turn ugly. The last thing I want is for any of these genfins to have to do more fighting.

I reach out and tug on Evert's sleeve. "Let's just get out of here. We'll go talk to the princess."

"The princess is dead!" the other genfin interrupts. "Rumor is, she got involved with you, tried to help save you from the prince, and she was found out because of it. Seems to me that you're the one hurting us in this war."

"Yeah!" another genfin from the back pipes in. "Because of you, my home was attacked. My covey slaughtered."

"I'm sorry," I say weakly, tears welling up in my eyes.

"I say string her up and her mates, too. They betrayed their own people by bonding to her."

The blood drains from my face, and all three of my guys tense, their claws lengthening to ready for an attack.

"That's enough."

Everyone in the group turns at the procession that

files in through the flap. Front and center of her private guard is Princess Soora.

When everyone realizes who it is, they all fall to their knees.

"It's Princess Soora!"

"It's the princess!"

"That's impossible."

"It's really her!"

Voices mingle around the space, bouncing back and forth, until Princess Soora stops in front of us. She looks over at the rebels, dressed not in the finery of her usual silk gowns and tiara, but in the same fighting leathers that they all wear.

"Hear me clearly, and hear me now," she says, looking over everyone. "The cupid Emelle is not to blame for my death, because it did not happen. In fact, she is the one who saved me when the rest of the world had given up and thought me gone. She is also not to blame for today's horrific attack. Prince Elphar is to blame. He was the one to order it. If you misplace your blame now, then he has already won, because he has already divided us. If we have any chance at beating him, we cannot fall for his games, and make no mistake, there will be many. The prince enjoys toying with us. Don't let him win before we've even had a chance to fight back."

She eyes the rebels levelly, her face stern but her lavender eyes kind. "I give you my word that we will not let him get away with this. Meet with your leaders, bury your dead with honor, and then get ready to strike back. Or aren't you the revolutionaries I thought you were?"

The gathered genfins all answer with a chorus of ayes.

"The cupid is pivotal to our cause. Treat her with

215

respect, and she just might be able to help us win this thing." Princess Soora turns to me and says, "Come."

Stunned, it's all I can do to follow her as she and her guards lead the way back outside. On the road, there are multiple carriages lined up, with more of Princess Soora's guards unloading medical supplies for the injured.

"Do we have a count yet on how many injured there are?"

"The portal was opened and stayed open for fifteen minutes," the princess answers as she leads us to the largest carriage on the street. "We got out as many as we could, but the high fae was forced to close it. It was too many people coming through much too quickly, and she couldn't hold it. We're working to get another high fae with portal power as soon as possible so that we can send in reinforcements as well as a rescue and retrieval team, but it's not a common power. As it is, we don't have many high fae on our side. They enjoy the superiority that the prince has bestowed upon them." We all pile inside the carriage except Ronak, who eyes the horses, snapping his jaws at them.

I whistle and pat my leg. "Come on, Ro-Ro."

Turning to me, he gives a grunt but leaps inside the carriage with all the grace and supremacy of a jungle cat. Shoving Evert on his way to me, Ronak pushes his way forward and sits on his haunches between my legs. I pat him on the head again, earning a little purr as his tail flicks back and forth.

Princess Soora arches a purple brow. "He's in his animal state, but don't worry, he won't attack anyone. I don't think."

She just nods like this is perfectly acceptable. That's what I like about Soora. She may look like the perfectly poised and pampered princess, but she's actually a badass who doesn't get rattled by much.

Tula steals looks over at the monarch. "Oh, I almost forgot. Princess Soora, this is Tula. Tula, meet Princess Soora," I introduce them.

The blonde girl peeks out from Sylred's chest. "You're a real princess?" she asks Soora doubtfully.

The princess smiles. "I am. Apologies for not wearing my crown for our meeting."

"That's okay," Tula says. "I like your purple hair."

"Thank you."

Tula gives her a smile and then rests against Sylred once again, soon falling to sleep with the rocking of the carriage as we make our way back to the manor.

We're quiet for the rest of the way, all of us processing what just happened. My heart hurts for all of the genfins, and I dread to learn just how many were lost today. Evert puts his arm around my shoulders and tucks me in close, while Sylred sits on my other side and threads his fingers through mine. I'm grateful for all the touches, because it just reassures me that they're all here—that we made it out. But at the same time, it breaks my heart that so many didn't, including little Tula's fathers.

I keep playing over the hate I saw in those genfins' eyes as they blamed me for this attack, and sadness wells up inside of me. Are they right? Was this my fault?

I know what the guys will say if I voice this aloud, so I don't. But internally, the truth of the blame sinks into my bones and solidifies. Because those genfins were right. The prince *did* attack the genfin island because of me. He's a master game player, and he just made his first move.

"Did anyone notice anything weird about those soldiers?" I ask.

"Like what?" Sylred asks.

I keep thinking of the strange way they moved and their expressionless faces. "I don't know. They just seemed…off."

I can't put my finger on it, but nothing comes to mind, and no one else offers any sort of explanation, so the carriage goes quiet again. The prince made his move, and it was a quick and deadly one at that. The question is, what is he going to do next?

CHAPTER 34

When we get back to the manor, Zalit and Belren come out to greet us. "What happened?" Zalit asks, looking at all of our grim expressions.

"Prince Elphar made his first strike," Princess Soora answers.

Zalit presses his orange lips into a thin line. "I'll get the commanders gathered."

"That secret island," I blurt out. "Did you guys ever figure out what's on it?"

Zalit shakes his head. "We have no way of getting past his barrier. It's even stronger than Soora's barriers, and that's saying something, since she's one of the most talented in that type of glamour and barrier magic. But we know now that he's been keeping at least part of his army there. Our spies would've told us about any militia movement from the kingdom island otherwise. They wouldn't have been able to sneak attack the genfin island if they'd used those forces. We have too many eyes there."

"So we need to figure out what kind of force he has on

219

this secret island and whatever else he might be hiding there," I muse.

"The phoukas," Sylred says suddenly. "Those animals aren't trainable. He must've captured some and kept them hidden until today's attack when he let them loose on our island."

"Who knows what else he has there," Zalit says gravely.

I blow out a breath. "Okay, well, I guess it's time to find out."

Evert narrows his eyes. "Don't you even fucking think about it."

I throw up my hands. "Well, what do you want us to do?"

Evert takes three long strides forward until he's towering over me, a terrific scowl over his face. "Did you not learn your lesson after leaving the first time? Or do you need me to punish you again?" he says, his voice low and dangerous. "Do you need to be reminded what happens to our alpha every time you pull this shit?"

I shove his chest away, but I only manage to push myself backwards. Stupid strong genfin.

Keeping his feet planted in place, he gives a pointed look at Ronak, who is sticking right at my side, his animal eyes darting left and right as he watches the many guards around us. His tail flicks with agitation as he bares his teeth at anyone who gets too close.

"You gave me your word," Evert reminds me, and just like that, all of the defensiveness leaks out of me.

He's right. I did. I promised I wouldn't leave him again.

I blow out a breath and instead of trying to push him away, my hand instead fists his shirt. "You're right," I admit.

He opens his mouth to argue some more, only to

widen his eyes in surprise. "Wait. You're not gonna argue with me?"

I shake my head. "No. But we still need to find out what's on the prince's island. So we're gonna need...help."

Pink smoke puffs to life in front of me as Lex appears.

Ronak snarls at her, but I grab him by the tail like it's a leash, stopping him from launching at her. He makes a strangled sound as his snarl turns into a sort of whimpered groan.

"Ro-Ro, this is my good friend, Lex. No attacking her, okay?" I tell him.

The tail I'm holding goes stiff in my hand, and Evert gives me a smirk. "Keep doing that, and your fearless alpha is gonna come in his pants."

Oh.

I quickly drop his tail, but the alpha just wraps it around my waist and presses up against me so that his erection digs into my back. I do my best to ignore him as he starts nuzzling my hair, but I can hear Evert snickering under his breath.

The guards raise their swords at Lex, surrounding the princess protectively, but Belren flicks his wrists, sending all of their blades pointing up at the sky again. "She's not an enemy," Belren snaps. "Don't point your blades at her."

Lex looks at Belren, and I see a shy, small smile pull at the corners of her lips. Well, well, well. Maybe my go-getter cupid assistant is warming up to the idea of being seduced after all.

"It's alright," Princess Soora tells the guards. "Stand down."

Belren releases control, and the guards back down as instructed.

"Hello," Lex says, continuing to smile politely. I'm

pretty sure every guard softens under the sweet smile. Or the boobs. It could be the awesome boobs.

"Hey, Lex," I say. "I was wondering if you could help me with a mission?"

Belren storms over. "Absolutely not. You cannot send her to the prince's island alone."

A smile creeps over my face. Oh man, he has it hard for her. And… My eyes flick down to the front of his pants. Yep. That's hard, too.

"Aww. I think it's cute you have a crush on her," I tell him.

Through the hole in his mask, I see his lip pull back in a sneer. "The Horned Hook does not have *crushes*."

"Mm-hmm, sure," I say, brushing his answer off. He's a big old lying liar face, because I can sniff his crush a mile away, but I'll be the bigger person here and let it go. "Anyway, you have a point." I tap my lips in thought. "Lex, I know I'm able to pull you into this realm because you're my assistant, but what about other cupids?"

"Oh, yes." She nods and motions toward my hands. "That's part of your Head of Cupidity powers. You simply have to call the number…or name of the cupid you wish to summon. Those powers also enable you to create cupids from new recruits."

I look down at my mark with new respect. "Huh. Good to know. Thanks, Lex."

I shake my hand a bit to make it start glowing, and it immediately lights up like radioactive bubblegum.

Clearing my throat, I rub my hands together, and following my cupidly awesome instincts, I reach through the Veil and pluck a cupid right through space and time.

Another pink puff of smoke appears, and then there's

Sev in all of his pretty glory...with his pants around his ankles.

"Fooking shite on a clock! You've got the worst fooking timing to snatch me out!" He glares over at me, his dick still out, and I can't help but stare.

"Is that...pink glitter?"

Sev looks down at his dick like he isn't sure what I'm talking about. "Oh. That. It's my fooking spunk, innit? Must be a cupid thing."

I blink at it, unable to look away, until Evert stomps over and shoves a hand over my eyes. "Pull up your fucking pants," he snaps at Sev.

"Aye, keep your tail tucked," Sev mumbles, and I hear him start to pull up his clothes.

"Are you saying that your cum...comes out like pink glitter?" I ask, because I feel like I need to make sure. I shove Evert's hand off my eyes as Sev finishes tying up his pants. The evidence of his activity is still apparent on his hands, though. Huh. Who knew male cupid cum would be so pretty?

"Aye, that's what I'm sayin'," Sev confirms. "Shoulda seen her, too," he says with a wicked grin. "Had me paint her tits with it. You want me to paint you, boss?" he asks, giving me a wink.

"I will rip off your fucking head and feed it to the harpies," Evert growls.

"Easy, he's just kidding," I tell my pissed off mate. "Sev's harmless."

Evert shakes his head and mumbles something about "fucking cupids."

I smile at him. "You're so sexy when you get all possessive. I appreciate the reaction."

The anger immediately dissipates from his face, and he

flashes me his dimples. "Yeah? Why don't you come over here and show me just how much you appreciate it by giving me a reaction of your own? Preferably one that ends with you screaming my name into my ear."

I nod thoughtfully. "Yeah, we can totally do that. Later."

Seeing that Evert is no longer thinking murderous thoughts against my cupid, I turn back to Sev. Now that he's dressed, Sev takes a moment to look around. Seeing everyone circled around him, he claps and rubs his hands together, looking pleased as hell. "Is this an orgy invite, then? About fooking time!"

He saunters up to Evert with all the swagger in the realms. "I'll start with the angry one, and then..." Sev looks around like we're all inventory before settling his eyes on the princess. "And then get a taste of this pretty fooking purple flower. How are you, luv?"

The guards raise their swords again, but this time, Belren doesn't stop them.

I sigh. Evert looks pissed again, dammit. "Sev, you can't have sex with Evert *or* the princess. I called you here for official cupid business. Well, sorta."

He groans and shoves his hands into his pockets. "Fooking hell, boss. I've been right workin' off my arse since you left. It can't be all work and no play."

"Actually," Lex pipes in. "You have had exactly twelve sexual relations since being promoted." She tilts her head as she looks at his glittery palms. "Not including this incident."

"Don't be a fooking clipe!" he tells her. Whatever the hell that means.

I give him a pointed look. "Really, Sev? Twelve?"

He shrugs. "I'm making up for lost time, boss."

Well, I can't fault him for that. I open my mouth to tell them my plan, but stop when I notice their shirts. I hadn't noticed before because, well, the pink glitter cum and his exposed penis sort of stole the show. "What are you two wearing?"

Lex looks down at her pink shirt that says "Kiss Me, I'm Cupid" on the front.

"Sev has taken it upon himself to give some of us new uniforms. This was the least sexual choice," she tells me honestly.

I look over to Sev and see that he's wearing one that says "I blow & shoot for a living."

"Tryin' out some new uniforms, ain't I?" Sev says proudly.

"How very...creative of you."

"Bet your right rump it is." He nods in agreement.

"Don't talk about her rump," Evert snaps.

I reach down and curl my fingers through Evert's, mostly to keep him from lunging at Sev. "Could you back away from the princess, Sev? You're making the guards nervous," I tell him.

He looks behind him like he's just now noticing the swords pointed at him, and he runs a hand through his pink hair. "If you're gonna point your swords at me, you can at least get me a fooking drink first." He winks at them and draws a hand up one of the swords seductively. When the guard blanches, Sev's grin widens. "Aye, this one wants to skelp my arse, don't you? You right gantin'."

The guard just swallows and looks quickly away.

"Sev," I say, drawing his attention back to me. "Focus. I need you and Lex to do something for me, and it's really important."

He groans. "Fine. But I get to spend some time with these fae when I'm done, get it?"

I wave a hand. "Fine, fine. But no cupid tricks," I say, pointing at him. "You can't be Lusting fae left and right to get people into your pants."

He scoffs. "Like I even need to. I'm prettier than you are, luv."

He's not wrong.

"Alright, what the gobbin' shite do we need to do for your bossiness?"

I quickly relay the story about the prince, the war, and the secret island. When I'm done, Sev whistles. "You got yourself in a right load of shite with this realm, didn't you?"

"Yeah. Can you guys handle this?"

"Course we can," he says confidently. "Us two will find out what His Royal Shithead is up to, won't we, cupid sixty-nine?" he asks Lex. "Then maybe we'll do a little pre-orgy celebration, aye?"

Belren flicks his wrist, sending Sev careening toward a pair of guards, who barely manage to catch him.

"She's not participating in any orgies with you or otherwise," Belren tells him stonily.

Sev just brushes himself off and laughs. "These fooking fae are a trip, aye, boss? I can see why you like the place."

"Sev. Behave," I plead.

He waves me off. "Alright, alright. You ain't need to worry, boss."

"Lex?" I check with her.

"Of course, Madame Cupid Emelle. We can handle this."

"Thank you. Princess Soora will give you the coordinates

of where she believes this island is. Go into the Veil, do a little spying, and come right back. I'll call you back to visibility in...twelve hours."

"Then you throw us an orgy?" Sev supplies.

"No."

Sev curses under his breath and looks at me like I'm being unreasonable.

I turn to Lex. "Keep an eye on him, would you?"

Her left eye twitches, but she still manages a polite nod. "Of course."

"Okay. Good luck. Find out as much as you can."

Both cupids disappear in another pink cloud, and I'm left with a scowling Belren. "She's going to be fine," I assure him. "I wouldn't send them if I thought they'd be in any sort of danger. I promise."

He doesn't reply, just turns on his heel and stalks away. Yep. He's crushing so hard.

CHAPTER 35

"*J*ust look at all of this pink residue on the ground from the smoke," I hear an unimpressed voice huff out. "It's going to need to be scrubbed out."

I whirl around and beam at the short and stocky hearth hob fae who is now standing next to the princess. "Duru!" I exclaim, rushing forward. I wrap her into a huge hug, squeezing her excitedly.

She just stands there unmoving until I let her go, but she totally wanted to hug me back. I can tell.

"I missed you!" I tell her.

She frowns at me and starts dusting off what had been her pristine uniform, because I got a little grime on her.

She pulls out a cleaning cloth from her pocket and starts stain fighting that thing like a hearth hob on a mission.

"You led the hearth hob revolution, didn't you?" I ask her slyly. "The king is super pissy about not having any proper servants." I don't bring up how I know this or how he tried to get a happy ending to his bubble bath.

"Of course I did," she tells me as she puts the cloth away.

I blink down at her apron. "Wow. You made that stain your bitch."

She gives me an unimpressed look.

"The cupid said a bad word," I hear little Tula whisper to Sylred.

"She did," he agrees with a small smile.

Duru takes one look at the dirty and clinging genfin child and seems to understand what happened.

"Well, I have an entire cake baked fresh from the princess's kitchens. Could you come with me and try it to make sure it tastes good enough to serve to the princess for tea?" Duru asks, walking forward.

Tula only hesitates for a moment before nodding shyly. Sylred lets her down, and the little genfin girl clasps Duru by the hand. They go walking off to the inside of the manor, Duru jumping in to explain the importance of using lemons when polishing copper.

Princess Soora looks over all of us. My guys are still bleeding from several places, and I'm about ready to drop. Her eyes flicker to Ronak, who is still growling and grinding against me. Every time I try to bat him away, he just bites me on the neck, the asshole.

"Will your mate be alright?" she asks me.

I look over at him as he's trying to paw my dress off. Luckily, bodice ties seem to be too advanced for him in his current animalistic state, so he just does a lot of pushing and grunting to no avail.

"I hope so," I reply.

"There's a chance he won't come out of this," Evert tells me bluntly. "You brought him out of it once, but if you keep going into the Veil, there's gonna be a time where he stays animal."

I watch my alpha as he starts spinning around to chase his tail, and guilt saturates my insides. "Yeah, that wouldn't be good," I mumble.

"Go inside. Rest. I've already had adjoining rooms prepared for you," Princess Soora tells us.

We all file into the manor and part ways, with me leading up the stairs to my room. When one of the servants tries to show Evert that his room is down the hall, he gives her a snort and then stalks into my room instead.

"Sorry, two of my mates are assholes," I tell her.

She eyes Sylred warily. "Nope, he's the well-behaved one," I assure her.

"I'll be perfectly comfortable staying in my mate's room, though," Sylred replies with a kind smile.

"And what of..." She trails off with a pointed look to the left, and we follow her gaze to see Ronak, who undoes his pants, grabs his junk, and pees all over the carpet.

I pinch the bridge of my nose and shake my head. "Duru is gonna be so pissed," I say. Then I snort at my own joke.

I watch as Ronak gyrates his hips a bit, and I narrow my eyes. Is he... Yep. He's drawing a dick on the carpet with his urine. A piss dick pic. It's actually kind of impressive.

"Should I, umm, take him outside, my lady?" the servant asks nervously. Ronak chooses that moment to turn around full-frontal, flashing her with his impressive cooch cork.

"Ronak!" I snap. "Put your schmecky away; that is not polite!"

Sylred snorts out a laugh, but Ronak just stares at me with his dick still out.

The servant looks about equal parts ready to swoon and ready to flee.

An alpha's cock will do that to you, I suppose.

CHAPTER 36

I grab Ronak by the forearm and start pulling him in the room. I toss back a "sorry" to the servant and close the door to my room as soon as we're all inside. I can hear water splashing and go inside my bathroom to find Evert already in the giant tub.

"Come on, Scratch. Let's clean you up."

He doesn't have to tell me twice. I pull my wings inside my body and then tug my hair over my shoulders. Sylred comes up behind me and gets right to work untying my bodice. When he's done, I make my way across the bathroom to the tub. I can feel their eyes on me, sending a little thrill up my spine.

Ronak eyes the water with disgust, and then he gets distracted by the birds chirping outside the window. His golden eyes flash as he watches them, his tail flicking back and forth with cat-like interest.

Standing over the tub, I make sure to be extra seductive as I slowly dip my toes into the water before sliding all the way in. The warm water reaches just to my nipples, and I dip back, letting water soak my hair as I let out another breathy moan while running my hands up my sides.

"We hear you loud and clear, Scratch. You want our cocks. You can stop with the tease show."

Lifting my head back up, I toss Evert a nonchalant shrug. "Teasing? I don't know what you're talking about," I say innocently.

I grab the bar of soap on the edge of the tub and begin to lather myself up. I start with my shoulder, then move across my collarbone, and then pay extra attention to my breasts. I bring the soap up around my curves and nipples, watching as Evert's eyes follow my every movement. Yep. I'm super good at teasing.

Sylred steps into the tub and settles on the seat next to him so they both have a perfect view of my little tease show, as Evert called it.

When I have the perfect amount of bubbles on my breasts, I decide to kick things up a notch by sliding the bar of soap lower. I go down, down, down, all the way to my cupidy center.

Letting go of the soap, I spread my legs and let my fingers glide over my love lips. With my guys watching me like they're ready to pounce on me at any second, I feel like the sexiest person alive.

When my fingers dance over my nub, I let my head fall back with a breathy moan.

"Fucking hell," Evert groans from across the bath.

I keep going, rubbing it just the way I like, but before I can reach a climax, the water sloshes and Evert and Sylred are suddenly on either side of me, taking over.

Evert takes my hand from where I was touching myself and brings it to his groin. Looking him in the eye, I slowly wrap my fingers around his cock and start stroking him up and down. He hisses out a breath and covers my hand with his, urging me to squeeze harder and move faster.

"You're bossy," I tease. Turning to Sylred, I see that he's working his own cock in his hand, watching me with heavy-lidded eyes. I reach out and take him in my other hand, and as soon as I do, he leans forward to capture my mouth.

I feel Evert on the other side of me dip his fingers into the water and trail them up my thigh.

Desperate, I widen my legs even more, and I feel his scruffy jaw scrape against my cheek as he says, "Look at you, spreading your legs for me. What do you want us to do to you, Scratch? Tell me. I want to hear you say it."

Gods, I love it when he talks dirty to me.

"I want—" My words get cut off on a moan when he suddenly plunges two fingers inside of me, stretching me out.

He slides easily in and starts scissoring me, and my hands tighten around their cocks.

"She likes that," Sylred breathes, nipping at my neck.

"She must not like it enough, because she's still not doing what she's told," Evert replies.

Pressing a thumb to my clit, he works me over until I'm a moaning, writhing mess. And right as I'm reaching that perfect peak, he pulls his hand away.

My eyes pop open in a scowl. "You motherfucker."

"Now that's not very nice, was it, Syl?" Evert smirks.

Sylred hums under his breath. "Come here, Emelle."

He reaches over and picks me up by the waist, and then without warning, brings me down over his cock.

"Fuck!"

Fully seated inside of me, Sylred pushes my legs apart

so that I fully straddle him. "There, is that better?" he asks me.

"Yes!" I say as I start to move against him.

"Good. Now tell Evert what he wants to hear, and we'll take care of you," he promises.

He's still not moving inside of me, and even his fingers are staying on my hips instead of wandering to my aching breasts and swollen clit.

"I want you to fuck me in this tub and make me come," I tell him, a desperate twinge to my tone.

"Good girl," he croons, finally moving his hips up to go even deeper inside of me.

I hum, loving every movement.

Evert comes up behind me and fists my hair so that my back arches into him, my breasts thrusting out toward Sylred's face. "You washed those pretty tits so nicely for us, didn't you, Scratch?" Evert asks as he nibbles my ear.

"Yes."

He takes my hand and puts it back around his cock. "You look fucking gorgeous like this," he tells me. "Bouncing on Sylred's dick, your tits in his face, your hand gripping me." He curses as I squeeze him tighter and start working him fast.

"Just like that," he says, moving a hand to my clit.

With his touch, I start bucking on top of Sylred like crazy, desperate to finally reach the crescendo that's been building up inside of me. The faster I go, the harder Sylred breathes, and then my pussy clenches around him, and I cry out with my orgasm.

"Gods," Sylred grits out, gripping my ass as he fucks me harder, even as my walls squeeze around him. He comes with a growl, spurting into me with a surge of cum.

Spent with my own orgasm, I lose my grip around

Evert, but he just takes things into his own hands (literally), and after just a few more pumps, I feel his own release exploding over my back.

All three of us are panting, my face collapsed against Sylred's chest as Evert's face rests against my back. The water is considerably cooler than when I first got in, but I feel perfectly sated right now since my own skin is fevered from sex, so it doesn't bother me in the slightest.

When I open my eyes at a strange noise, I see my poor alpha whining and pacing around the tub like he's frantic to get to me but the water is his personal nemesis.

"Aww," I say, sitting up. I slide out from between Evert and Sylred, making them move back to their seats as I make my way over to the edge of the tub and hold a hand out. "It's okay."

Ronak comes over, sniffing my hand warily and whining again when he gets too close to the water.

"What is it with cats and water?"

"Now we know what to do when the asshole is pissing us off. Just toss him in a tub," Evert chuckles. Ronak curls back his lips and growls.

"Be nice," I chastise them both.

I look over at the floor beneath the window and notice that while we were…occupied, the alpha has dragged all of our clothes and piled them in the corner. He goes over there now and sits on top of the pile on his haunches, his tail flicking back and forth as he watches us.

I climb out of the tub and wrap myself in a soft white towel. I dry my hair and then wander into the bedroom where I collapse into bed.

Ronak follows me, bringing the pile of clothes with him clamped in his mouth. He even carries the guys' clothes, dirty and blood spackled, and dumps them on the mattress. "Uh-uh." I shake my head. "These are dirty, Ro-Ro."

When I try to toss them away, he nips my hand, making me flinch and drop them back down. "Hey!" I scowl at him.

Evert and Sylred wander in, both with towels slung low around their waists. The view is pretty scrumptious, and even though I just had some sexcapades, I can't help the flush of desire that runs through me. These guys have the best bodies. I could ogle them forever. Evert and Sylred get into bed on either side of me, sliding in close.

I try to toss the dirty clothes onto the floor again, but the alpha is too quick for me and nips my hand again. "Fine!" Ronak makes a cat-like chirping noise of victory.

With Evert and Sylred on either side of me, the alpha walks in a circle on top of the bed several times before curling up in a ball between my legs, and rests his head right on my coochie coo.

"That's not comfortable..." I try to shift, but he just head-butts me in the pelvis. "Ouch! You need to learn some manners."

He just nuzzles me.

I look over to see Evert lifting his hand away from Sylred's wounds, the skin knitting back together right before my eyes.

He moves to do the same for the wound on Ronak's chest, but the alpha snaps his teeth at him, making Evert flinch back.

"Listen, you fucking asshole, I'm trying to help you," Evert snaps.

"Ro," I coo, gaining his attention. "Let Stitch heal you, okay?"

He flicks his tail testily but allows Evert's hand to

touch his skin this time. As soon as Ronak's wound starts knitting back together, Evert lets go and settles back in bed. "You're welcome," he says snidely.

In thanks, Ronak kicks his leg out, hitting Evert squarely in the happy sacks.

"Motherfucker," he wheezes out, grabbing himself.

"It was an accident, I think," I tell him.

Ronak lays his head down with a rather smug look on his face. Evert just glares at him.

Sylred yawns. "What a day."

His hand snakes around my waist and pulls me in tight.

"Yeah," I agree. "Are you guys okay? Really? The attack on your people's island..."

"Was not your fault," Sylred interjects.

"But it sort of was."

"Scratch," Evert says. "Ignore those other genfins."

"He's right," Sylred says gently. "They'd just barely escaped an attack. They saw death and destruction. They were looking for a scapegoat."

"Yep. But I won't fucking let you take the fall for this shit," Evert tells me. "Now let's get some sleep. I'm fucking beat."

As soon as Evert mentions that he's tired, my palms go all tingly. "Why are your hands dirty?" he asks.

I pause and look down at my hands, which are in fact, dirty. With dust.

"Sandman powers," I mumble.

"Lemme see." Sylred and Evert each grab one of my dusted hands to look at.

Sylred drags a finger against my palm, removing some of the dust. He holds it up on the pads of his fingers, leaning in for a better look. "That's..." I watch as Sylred's eyes begin to droop, and then he flops backward onto the pillow, lids closed tight and out like a light.

"Umm...Syl?"

Aaaand he's already snoring. Okay then.

"What the fuck?" Evert asks.

"Yeah, so, funny thing...because I went back and forth in the Veil so much, I sort of have demon, angel, and sandman powers." I purse my lips in thought. "Possibly other powers, too. Minor Veil stuff. Did you know that karma is a literal bitch? I totally wish I could get some of those powers and really stick it to Prince Asshat. He has some serious bad karma owed to him, you know?"

"What the fuck does this sandman shit mean?" Evert holds my hand up to his face and sniffs it.

And then *he* promptly falls back onto the pillows and starts snoring. I pat him on his head with a sigh.

The alpha between my legs is asleep, too, without the aid of sandman or...sandlady powers, but I guess he's super good at catnaps in his current state.

I dust off the rest of the...dust from my hands by wiping it off on the blanket and then settle down on the pillows. The room is filled with the sound of my genfins snoring. "For the record, you guys totally would've fallen asleep quickly anyway." I tell the room. "Because I'm super good at sex. You were already worn out just from that. So. Just wanted to point that out."

Sylred mumbles in his sleep and turns over.

Over the covers, a calming purr comes from the alpha's chest when I bring my hand down and thread my fingers through his hair. Instead of falling asleep, I stay like that for a long time. Nestled between my three genfins, my mind flashes through everything that happened today. Being reunited with my genfins, finding

Ronak in his feral state, the sex, the prince's attack…I can't stop my mind from replaying it all.

So much went wrong today. And yet my mates and I made it out okay, and I'm entirely grateful for that. But many didn't. Like that little genfin girl's family. The thought of her tear-streaked face as she huddled over her dead fathers…it makes my heart hurt. And those genfins today were right. Sure, the prince launched the attack, but he chose to attack the genfins because of me. I can't let that stand. I won't.

Thoughts and plans swirl through my mind as the guys sleep around me. My genfins make me feel safe and adored like this, and I don't have to use my cupid powers to know that I've fallen hard.

The realization is both the most natural thing in the world—like I've simply loved them all along—and it's also the most surprising, profound thing ever.

I love my mates so much, and with that love comes a responsibility. A responsibility to protect them. And that means not letting the prince hurt them or their people again. That means fighting him. That means ending this once and for all.

I'm a cupid/angel/demon/sandlady/lady luck/boss bitch, and I'm gonna fuck the prince's shit up.

All is fair in love and war, bitches.

CHAPTER 37

When my eyes peel open the next morning, I find that Evert and Sylred are already gone, but Ronak is sitting on the floor beside the door, like he's guarding it.

Disappointment floods me when he perks up and looks over at me, because he's still in his animal state. Golden eyes watch me as I slip out of bed and grab a short silky robe from a hook on the door. My hair is a mess from getting into bed without brushing it, and I try to separate some of the pieces as I take a seat on the floor next to Ronak.

"Hey, Alpha," I tell him as I run my fingers over his tail. It curls around my waist and pulls me closer to him.

"I'm sorry I keep making you go animal. Is there any way you could let Ronak come back out here?"

The alpha just blinks at me with his head cocked to the side.

"Yeah, I didn't think so," I mumble under my breath.

The door opens, and the alpha immediately jumps to his feet, blocking me from whoever is entering.

"Easy, asshole," I hear Evert say. "It's us."

Ronak growls and then sits back down beside me.

Evert and Sylred come around and pass me a plate of food and a goblet with some pink fizzy drink inside.

"We figured you'd want to have breakfast in bed." Sylred eyes my position on the floor. "Or the floor."

"Thanks," I say, giving them a smile.

I start inhaling the toast with jam and eggs that they've brought me, swallowing down the entire goblet of sweet drink to polish it off. I pass Ronak the pieces of sausage, and he swallows them down happily.

When I'm done, I set the plate aside and eye Sylred and Evert where they sit on the chaise. "This is bad, yeah?" I ask, motioning to Ronak. "I mean, he probably should've turned back by now. Do you think I need to have sex with him again?"

Sylred shrugs. "I don't know. But like we said, there is a chance that he won't come out of it…"

I fight back the emotion that tries to flood my eyes. I look at my alpha. He's right here. Close enough to touch and hear and see, and yet Ronak feels so far away from me.

I put my hand on his cheek. "Ronak, can you hear me?"

I stare at his golden eyes, hoping for a sign, but the alpha just pushes my hand away and starts licking the plate. I sigh.

I start scratching my arm subconsciously, worrying my lip between my teeth.

"Scratch," Evert says, drawing my attention to him. "Ronak wanted you to go invisible to keep yourself safe. You did what you had to do."

"But look at him," I argue. "I can't do this. I can't go

invisible anymore. Not with knowing that he might go animal and never come back. It might already be too late."

We watch the alpha for a moment, and even though the guys try to hide their worries from me, I see it when they exchange a look. They think he might be stuck like this. And once again, it's my fault.

"Emelle," Sylred says gently. "The princess talked to us downstairs when we left to get you breakfast. She told us about Okot."

"I'm gonna kill the fucker," Evert bites out.

My multicolored eyes flash up to them. "You didn't know?"

Sylred braces his forearms on his knees and leans forward. "No. Ronak turned feral pretty quickly. We were never able to go look for Okot."

I look down at my lap and start picking at a loose thread in the material. I can feel the guys watching me, but I don't know what to say.

"Scratch. You can talk to us."

"You were right, okay?" I snap. "He betrayed me. He wasn't who I thought he was."

I catch the look that they exchange, and for some reason, it makes me unreasonably angry. I jump to my feet and stomp into the bathroom, slamming the door behind me. I clean myself up a bit and manage to tame my hair somewhat. When I come out, the guys are still in the same places that I left them. I head for the closet and pull out the first dress I see. It's gray and thick, not very fancy, but still delicate. I pull it over my head, but of course, I can't do up the ties at the back by myself. Doesn't mean I don't try. Stubbornly, I curl my hands behind my back and try to do them up alone, but it's nearly impossible.

"Here, let me."

I jump at Sylred's voice but try to cover it up as I shift from foot to foot. I feel his steady, warm fingers gently tugging at the ties, his fingers brushing over my bare skin. I relax a bit under his ministrations, and when he's done, he turns me around and pulls me into his chest. I rest my head against his shoulder and breathe him in.

"I'm so stupid," I confess thickly.

"No. You're not. Okot had us all fooled."

"Not Evert."

"Yes, even Evert. At least at first. This isn't your fault, Emelle. It's Okot's, and it's ours for not protecting you from him."

I look up at him. "How could he have done that? How could he have faked it?"

Sylred shakes his head, and a sympathetic look crosses his face. "I don't know. But you still have us."

"Sylred, you ready?" Evert calls out. "We need to get back to the cabin."

We walk back out and I eye him curiously as I fix the sleeves to my dress. "Back to the rebel cabin? Why?"

Evert avoids eye contact with me and starts heading toward the door. "You stay with our mate, asshole," he says to the alpha as he pulls open the door.

"Wait a minute," I interrupt, stepping up to the door before he can slip through. "Why do you need to go to the cabin? What's going on?"

Evert runs a hand through his black hair, looking a bit uncomfortable. "Nothing, Scratch. Just something I have to take care of." He looks over my head at Sylred. "Are you coming or what?"

I turn around to regard Sylred and find that he's on the verge of laughter.

Making up my mind, I step through the doorway and wait expectantly.

Evert blinks at me. "What are you doing?"

"I'm coming with you."

He shakes his head. "No, really, you don't want to come. It's nothing you need to bother with. You should stay here. Relax. You shouldn't leave your alpha here alone. He'll probably shit on the carpet."

I purse my lips and whistle. "Ro-Ro! Come here, boy!"

The alpha bounds out into the hallway and latches himself onto my side. I turn back to Evert triumphantly.

Looking more and more disgruntled, he looks to Sylred for help, but Sylred just shakes with silent laughter. "Really, Scratch. I'd prefer if you'd just stay here. I'm just gonna be…tidying."

I arch a brow, "Tidying?"

"Yeah. You know, since we're moving into the manor here. I should clean out our stuff in the cabin so someone else can move in. Tidying. Packing. Boring stuff. You don't want to come along. Really."

His tail gets all twitchy behind him, and I narrow my eyes. "I don't know what you're really doing, but I know damn well that you aren't *tidying*. So either tell me what's really going on or shut up and lead the way."

"But—"

"No," I cut him off.

Sylred grins like he's watching his favorite show. "I can't wait to see this."

"Fuck off," Evert snaps.

He turns on his heel and starts marching away, leaving Sylred and me to walk after him. Ronak trails behind, sniffing things and growling at any guards we pass. "No peeing inside the manor," I tell him sternly.

It's one of the many sentences I never thought I'd have to say to one of my mates.

CHAPTER 38

$\mathscr{E}$vert leads us into one of the princess's carriages, and we ride back to the rebel camp. I fill in the guys with everything that happened in the Veil and with Okot. When I tell Evert about how Okot had put his hands over my neck, he nearly breaks the carriage door when he slams his fist against it.

"I'll kill that fucking lamassu," he snarls.

My heart hurts to hear him say that, but it's not like I can defend Okot. I have no doubt that he would've choked me to death if I hadn't gotten away. But it still hurts. I still love him.

Sensing my distress, Sylred moves the conversation away and talks more about my powers. "So we know the soul-sucking comes from the demon powers," Sylred says.

"And I lit up that Arachno biotch," I add smugly.

"And that was an angel power?"

I nod. "I'm pretty sure. And I took you guys out in like three seconds flat with my sandlady powers."

"So what else is there?" Sylred asks as he puts his hand on my thigh and draws slow circles over me. Even through the fabric of my dress, I can feel the warmth of him.

From his spot on the floor, Ronak reaches up and bats Sylred's hand away with a warning growl. Sylred narrows his eyes at him but drops his hand back down in his own lap.

Ronak settles his head against my knees and purrs rather smugly.

"She's our mate too, you fucker," Evert says.

Before the two of them can get into a growl-off, I cut in. "To answer your question, Syl, there's the three Veil Majors—angels, demons, and cupids. As far as the Minors, I'm still learning, but I know for sure about the sandman, karma, lady luck, oh, and ghosts. But ghosts don't really have powers that I could get. I don't think. They just mumble a lot of nonsense and get easily distracted."

Sylred and Evert exchange an amused look over my head.

"She doesn't see it, does she?" Sylred asks.

Evert smirks. "Nope."

"What?" I demand.

Evert leans over and kisses me on top of the head. "Nothing, Scratch. Stop scratching your arm."

I look down at my hand and quickly drop it. The movement makes my mark light up.

"And that indicates your cupid boss powers?" Sylred asks, nodding at the arrow and heart that now looks like a glow-in-the-dark tattoo.

I sigh and place them in my lap. "Yeah."

"Lots of powers you're juggling these days," Evert says with a smirk.

"I have a very complicated life right now, Evert."

He just smirks at me, showing off that devastating dimple of his, and my insides immediately get all hot and bothered. "Hey, can we have some carriage sex real quick?" I ask.

Sylred makes a coughing noise on my other side, but Evert just laughs. "We could," he says with a nod, bringing his face up close to mine and throwing my hair over my shoulder. I feel his hot breath against my neck as he nips at the skin just below my ear.

"Carriage sex is gonna be a bit...cramped," he tells me, except he says it in this super low and husky voice and makes it sound like something utterly erotic.

"That's okay. I have a sex to-do list," I say breathlessly, my head tipping to the side to give him better access. "A fuck-it list. Get it?"

They don't laugh. I don't think they get it.

"Everyone should have a sex list," I say.

"Oh?" Evert asks curiously. I feel his lips grazing up my jaw. "And what's on this to-do list?"

"Oh, you know. Carriage sex. Sex on a roof. We already did sex in the tub. Sex while I'm eating. I'm super excited about that one," I tell him as he starts trailing a single finger down my chest until it hits the top of my bodice.

"Hmm. And what would we be feeding you that's any better than our cocks?" he asks.

His fingers dip down to my cleavage, and he continues to nibble his way up and down my neck, and gods, it's hard to concentrate. "Like...chocolate. And cookies. And something with syrup. Maybe even a nice fondue?"

I feel his chuckle against my chest, but I'm much too focused on the other hand of his that's started to trail up my thigh. Just a bit closer and...

The carriage lurches to a stop.

My eyes pop open and I look over to a cocky-as-hell-looking Evert, who's grinning over at me. "Guess the list is gonna have to wait. Unless you're okay with doing it right now while the rebels can hear you?"

I smack his arm. "Don't be such a tease."

He shrugs and opens the carriage door. Ronak bounds out, landing on all fours, and Sylred and I follow behind.

The carriage pulls away, and the four of us are left in the middle of the rebel camp on the dirt road. One of the training yards is behind us, and as soon as people see us, it seems like the entire place pauses to look at us. Whispers erupt in the air, fae are pointing, some people look friendly while others look...not so much.

"It's the cupid."

"That's the cupid and her mates."

"I heard she caused all those genfin deaths."

"You know the prince attacked them because of her."

"I heard she's the prince's spy."

"Nah, she's on our side."

"She's hotter in person."

"Ain't she s'pposed to have red wings? I bet it ain't even her!"

Sylred and I just sort of awkwardly smile and wave at the gathering crowd. I'm wondering if I'm gonna have to start a really big rebel orgy right here in the dirt road before they start mauling me, but Evert takes the head-on approach.

"Listen, you fuckers. You got something to say about my mate, you come say it to my fucking face," he says, his voice even but loud enough to carry.

Like he can understand what's going on, my alpha draws himself up beside Evert and I, highlighting his size, and snarls at the crowd. I'm pretty sure he even flexes his muscles to really get his point across. The fae seem to suddenly remember that he has strength power, because everyone takes an unconscious step back.

Except one guy.

The genfin from earlier. It seems like his night's sleep hasn't softened him at all to me, because he looks just as pissed off as he was before.

CHAPTER 39

The furious genfin stares me down, not at all cowed by my mates. "You might have the princess fooled, but not me. The rebels were always two steps ahead of the prince before. Now look at us. Hundreds of my people are dead, and we're like chickens with our heads cut off, no idea where he's going to strike at us next," the genfin spits. He points in my direction, his expression murderous. "I'll make you pay for this, cupid."

Ronak growls and all the blood drains from my face. Evert starts shouting curses and threats at him, but before a fight can break out, the genfin just turns around and stalks off. He shoves fae out of the way as he goes, leaving the rest of the crowd behind to stare at us.

"Well, this isn't awkward at all," I mumble.

Beside me, Evert is seething, his whole body tense and his hands clenched into fists as he stares daggers at the retreating genfin. "I'll fucking kill him."

"Come on," Sylred urges, but Evert just pushes him away.

"No. He just fucking threatened our mate. He doesn't get away with that!" Evert yells.

Sylred holds up two hands in surrender. "Hey, I'm on your side here. But we're out in the open, and if this crowd turns on us, we're outnumbered. Do you really want to do this right now? With Emelle right here?"

"Umm. I'm not helpless. I'm awesome with a bow. I could totally win in a fight," I insist. I tilt my head in thought. "Probably. Maybe. There's at least a fifty percent chance, if I take my attacker by surprise, anyway."

I guess my declaration doesn't comfort them with my defensive prowess, because Evert curses under his breath, and Sylred gives me a tight smile. "We need our fucking alpha," Evert snaps.

He shoots a glare at the growling genfin as if this is all his fault.

"Come on," Sylred says, grabbing me by the arm and leading us away.

I do my best to ignore all of the stares as we make our way down the road, but...yeah, I'm pretty sure half of these fae would like to chop off my head and mount it on their wall.

For the record, my head would look fantastic as an art piece. Not that I *want* to be an art piece, but...silver linings and all that.

We pass through the cluster of cabins until Evert stops in front of one. He hesitates at the door and runs a hand over the dark scruff on his jaw. "Okay, if you just stay here and—"

"Nope."

I walk forward and, before he can stop me, I sidestep around him and throw open the cabin door...and stop in my tracks.

I stare, wide-eyed, at the sight in front of me. Plik and Plak, the twin fae who pulled me out of the Veil when I was stuck, are in the middle of the cabin, tied down to a table. Not a chair since they're conjoined at the butt cheeks. They're also still naked. Their wrinkly penises are poking out like a baby bird trying to hatch out of its egg.

I turn to Evert. "Did...did you kidnap them for me?"

Warily, he nods.

I lunge at him.

He isn't expecting it, so he sort of fights me off for a second before he realizes that I'm hugging him. When he realizes I'm not actually attacking him, he stops trying to push me off and instead pulls me tighter against his chest and lifts me off my feet. I curl my arms around his neck and beam at him. "You kidnapped them for me," I nearly squeak with feels.

He grins and I poke his dimples. "I sure as fuck did," he says with pride.

"That was so sweet. I am so gonna suck your cock later," I tell him.

"I helped," Sylred quickly pipes in behind us.

Evert gives him a look. "You did not, you fucker. You kept trying to talk me out of it, telling me kidnapping was bad and shit."

"And that was super responsible of you," I tell Sylred. "You get a sexual service of your choice."

Sylred blushes and smiles at the same time. His pink hair looks so cute when he blushes.

"We should let them go now," I say.

Evert looks only slightly disappointed. "Fine."

I hop down out of Evert's arms and walk up to the conjoined twins. I notice the bucket and piles of food and water that have been left for them. At least it seems like he's been an attentive kidnapper.

I move to start undoing the bindings around them, but Evert comes over and pushes my hands out of the way. "I'll do it. I'd rather you not brush against their dicks."

"I wasn't gonna," I protest. "I was being super mindful of their dicks."

He gives me the side-eye. "Scratch. Don't be mindful of dicks that don't belong to your mates."

"Oh. Okay."

I remove the cloth that's stuffed into their mouths, and they both work their jaws a bit before talking. Of course, they speak in that disjointed way of theirs, trading off words between them as they go.

"Ah. It's the—Veil female. We informed your—idiotic mate here that—we could not—bring you back. But he—would not—listen. He was not—happy when we—failed to bring you—out of the Veil. But alas—you were not there. And now—here you are. Just as we—knew you would—you've come back."

Evert gets the rest of the bindings off of them and helps them to their feet. "Sorry, Plik," I tell the twin on the left.

"I'm Plak," he corrects.

"Oh, right. Sorry. Plak and Plik."

There's an awkward pause as they get steady on their feet and then cock their heads at Evert expectantly. They don't look angry. To be honest, they seem practically pleasant, considering they've been tied to a table and kept in this rebel cabin for gods knows how long.

Speaking of…

"How long have you kept them here?" I ask Evert.

He stuffs his hands in his pockets. "Not long."

I cock a brow. "How long?"

"I dunno. Just…a few days."

"Weeks," Sylred corrects cheerfully.

I grimace slightly and make eyes at Evert while also motioning my head toward the twins. He just stares at me, completely missing my signal. "What the fuck are you doing?"

"Apologize to them," I mouth.

"Fuck that. When you disappeared and we couldn't fucking feel your bond, I went to them. But these fuckers wouldn't get you back! It's their fault I kidnapped them. They wouldn't cooperate."

"Couldn't," Plik corrects.

Evert glares at him.

"We tried. But we—could immediately feel—that you were not—in the Veil. We informed your mate—that you were out of our reach. At which point—he knocked us out —and brought us here," Plik and Plak explain, sounding like it's all very exciting.

"Okay, well…sorry about the kidnapping," I tell them seriously. "I apologize on my mate's behalf. Is there anything we can do?"

Without skipping a beat, they say, "We'd like—sexual intercourse."

I blink at them. "Ummm…what?"

"You had better not be propositioning my fucking mate," Evert growls, looking like he's ready to throttle them.

Plik and Plak scratch the tops of their scraggly-haired heads, right between their antlers. "Not with your mate," Plak explains. "But we understand—that your cupid—can induce sexual fervor. As restitution for our kidnapping—

we require—a full sexual encounter—so that we may sow our oats. It has been—some time."

The twins look at me expectantly. "Oh. Umm, sure?"

They nod at the same time. "Wonderful. We shall wait —here for you to bring—us a willing—participant."

"Oh. Umm…right now?"

Plik and Plak nod again. "Yes. Unless you'd rather—us settle the debt—by putting in a—formal complaint—to the crown for—kidnapping?"

I shake my head adamantly. "Nope. No. Definitely don't need to do that. Sex it is. I'll just…go find someone? For the kidnapping restitution. Like you said. Right now."

"Excellent. We will wait exactly ten minutes."

Geez. No pressure.

"Do you have any preferences?"

They shake their heads. "We are—not picky," they say, and then they both start…primping. And by primping, I mean that they start tugging on their penises and brushing down their chest hair with their hands.

"Okay, I'll just go find someone who can deal with…" I wave a hand in the twins' direction. "All of this."

"We will—be ready."

I give them a tight smile. "Great."

I turn around and make a *what the fuck am I supposed to do right now* face at Sylred.

"I'll help you," he quickly says.

I point at Evert. "You're helping me too. Come on."

The things I have to do in this realm just get crazier and crazier.

CHAPTER 40

We go back outside, and I waste no time walking through the rebels, eyeing anyone who doesn't look like they want to stab me through the face.

"Wanna have sex with some conjoined twins?" I ask a group of fae as they walk by.

They just stare at me. Geez, hard sell. I keep walking. "How about you?" I ask a couple of water sprites. "Sex? Twins? That's gotta be like a fantasy in this realm, too, right?"

"Pretty sure Plik and Plak don't fit that particular fantasy," Evert says with a chuckle.

"This is your fault, mister, so no jokes. We have to fix this or they're gonna go to the king. They've been kept here on the super-secret rebel island for who knows how long. We can't let them go to him. We have to get them some sex, or we're in big trouble."

Evert scoffs and throws his arm around my shoulder like this is no big deal. "Oh, come on. I wouldn't actually let them leave here to do that. But we can try to help them out. Besides, it's just sex. Fae are horny motherfuckers. It'll be an easy sell."

"Evert. They have hairy balls. And pig noses. And conjoined butt cheeks! This is not going to be an easy sell!" I say somewhat hysterically.

I continue propositioning fae as we walk along the path, but no one bites. When we get to the outdoor eating area, Evert leaves my side and strolls over to an occupied table. He steps up onto the bench and then the table, not caring when his boots come down on plates of food, and fae sitting there glare up at him.

He puts his hands around his mouth and hollers, "Oy! Listen up, you rebel fucks! We got a set of horny conjoined twins in cabin number fifty. First couple of fae who make it there get to experience their very own cupid Lust-Breath!" he says, looking around the crowd. "And trust me, that shit is powerful. You'll come harder than a fucking geyser. All you gotta do is sex it up with the weird twin fuckers. Who's in?"

To my utter surprise, a dozen fae, male and female alike, hop up from their tables and start running toward the cabin.

"Huh."

Evert jumps down from the table and strolls back toward us, looking arrogant as hell. And yeah, sexy. Super sexy. I kind of want to punch him. After I climb onto his cock.

He grins down at me, hands in pockets. "Well?"

"Well, what?"

"Come on, Scratch, you owe me."

I scoff. "I do not. I totally could've done that."

He arches a black brow. "Mm-hmm," he says, unconvinced.

259

"I could have!" I protest. "I'm a cupid. *The* cupid. I'm the Head of Cupidity. The badass cupid boss. I could've totally gotten takers on the sex thing. I was just…letting you take the reins to teach you a lesson about correcting your own mistakes."

"Sure you were."

When we get back to the cabin, there's a line of fourteen fae waiting outside the door.

"You and Ronak stay here," I tell Sylred before making my way to the crowd.

"Alright," I announce to the line of fae, marching up to them, all business-like. "I'll let each of you inside, and you can decide who wants to…umm, participate."

I open the door and let them file in, and Plik and Plak look over them expectantly. Right away, nine turn around and walk out. The rest of them seem game.

"Okay…who wants to—" They all raise their hands before I can finish my sentence. "Oh. Okay…Plik? Plak?"

"Multiple sexual—partners is perfectly—acceptable," they say together.

"Okay then."

"When do we get the Lust stuff?" a fae with two mouths asks. I try to ignore the way that Plik is eyeing him. I want to be far, far away when this particular physical activity gets started.

"Right now," I tell them.

Starting with Plik and Plak, I inhale deeply and then blow out a stream of pink breath, letting the Lust loose. Beside me, Evert does the same. In just a few breaths, the entire cabin is saturated with it. Plik's and Plak's penises promptly rise to attention.

Evert claps a hand over my eyes. I hear clothing being discarded. "Time to go, Scratch."

He leads me out of the cabin, and once we're outside, he slams the door behind us. Moaning starts sounding through the walls. Yikes. Thin walls.

I see a pair of fae rushing forward. "Did we miss the Lust orgy?"

Evert and I exchange a look and then shrug. "No harm in two more, I guess," I say and then breathe Lust into their faces while Evert holds the door open for them.

"Enjoy!" he calls to their backs before closing the door again.

"Now let's get the fuck out of here before I have to hear anything else and be scarred for life."

We make our way back to Sylred and Ronak, who are standing on the other side of the road.

"All set?" Sylred asks.

"Yeah, I think we're good."

"Hey, it's you." I turn at the voice and find a familiar fae walking toward us. The metal spikes in his eyebrows give him away as the fae I talked to when I first got to the rebel camp and was looking for my guys.

"Oh, hey."

He eyes me. "Is it true you're conducting a fornication function in your cabin?"

"Yeah, I guess."

"Are you joining in?" he asks quickly.

Evert takes a step forward with a snarl, but I put my hand on his chest and quickly shake my head. "Nope, no fornicating function for me. I have mates."

"Oh," he says, looking disappointed. "Well, which cabin is the orgy?" he asks eagerly, and I point the way. He bounds off without another word.

"Wow. Word about orgies really spreads quickly here," I muse.

"How'd you know that guy?" Evert asks immediately.

"Oh, he was showing me to the copulation room."

Evert stops in his tracks. "Why the *fuck* was he showing you the copulation room?"

I wave my hand at him. "Not like that. He thought I was here to have sex. He was just being helpful. Offered to show me the way."

Evert stares at me. "Let me get this straight. He was bringing you to the copulation room because he was being *helpful*?" he asks incredulously.

I nod. "Exactly."

Evert closes his eyes and rubs a finger across his brows. "Sylred."

My pink-haired genfin steps forward and takes my hand in his. "Emelle, let's not talk about you copulating with other fae, okay?"

"I wasn't gonna copulate him," I protest.

"I know," he says, patting me on the hand. "Let's drop it, okay? Before Evert's head explodes."

"Fine. I would've liked to see the copulating room, though."

"No fucking way," Evert snaps.

Touchy, touchy.

He grumbles under his breath all the way back to the manor. Males. They're so unreasonable sometimes.

CHAPTER 41

As soon as we get back to the manor, I realize that I'm late in calling back Lex and Sev. They can't enter the physical realm without me calling them, so as soon as we get settled in our room and have the princess, Belren, and Zalit in attendance, I do just that.

"Lex? Sev?"

Pink smoke puffs into existence, and Sev and Lex are there waiting.

"Took you fooking long enough, aye?" Sev says.

"Sorry. I had sex and then fell asleep and then had to start an orgy. Time got away from me," I explain.

Evert shakes his head at me, but Lex just nods in understanding. She gets it. Sev starts complaining about starting an orgy without him. "Next time I start an orgy, I promise to include you," I tell him.

He finally nods. "Right fooking shite, you will."

I motion for them to sit, and Sev grabs the tray of food and starts chowing down on everything on it.

"So? What did you find?" I ask.

Lex pulls out her pink notepad. "Well, the island is

indeed heavily protected. There are aerial guards and ground guards. Approximately one hundred of each, as far as I could tell.

I exchange a look with the princess. The fact that they have two hundred guards alone is incredibly distressing.

"What's on the island?" Princess Soora asks.

Sev continues to chow down on food as Lex flips through her pages of notes. "Well, I have an estimated count of...nine thousand, nine hundred and...nineteen soldiers on the island."

Shock goes through the room, and I blink at her, my mouth going dry. "What?"

She starts to repeat the number, and Zalit cuts her off. "He has nearly ten thousand soldiers on this island?" he asks incredulously.

"Yes," Lex answers simply.

"And they're organized?" Sylred asks.

Lex cocks her head in thought. "Well, would them being in full uniform, following scheduled drills, and going through intense synchronized training be considered organized?" she asks.

Belren nods. "Yep. That about covers organized."

"Fooking weird right little pricks, they were," Sev says around a mouthful of food as he lounges on the chair.

"What do you mean?" I ask.

He shrugs and takes another bite of fruit. "Don't know how to explain it. But they were fooking...off, get it?"

I look to Lex for more explanation, and she purses her lips in thought. "He's right. There did seem to be something...very regimented about them."

Evert rolls his eyes. "Probably because they're a military *regiment*," he says dryly.

"Perhaps," Lex says.

"No, explain it more," I insist.

Lex shifts in her seat to get further away from Sev since he's propped his boots up on the table in front of her. "Well…they didn't have any love."

My brows lower. "What?"

"You know, as cupids, we can sense love and desire. Heartbreak, flirtatiousness, longing. But there was none of that. Most of them seemed focused, some of them agitated. But their emotions were limited. It made my cupid powers feel strange," she says, looking off to the side in memory as she tries to explain. "It was almost as if they were children. Or…"

"Or fooking robots," Sev puts in, a piece of apple flying out of his mouth as he chews and talks.

Princess Soora leans forward slightly. "All of them seemed this way?"

Sev and Lex both nod.

"What does that mean?" I ask.

Soora shakes her head. "I'm not sure…"

Our group goes quiet in thought, the only sounds are Ronak purring slightly in his sleep where he's sprawled out on his back on the floor at my feet, and Sev chewing more food.

"These soldiers, what type of fae were they?" Zalit asks.

"Oh, all sorts."

His orange brows rise in surprise. "All sorts?"

She nods. "Mm-hmm. Just from my short reading on the fae realm, I recognized high fae, sprites, some genfins, hearth hobs, pixies, oh, and a large amount of alven fae."

Princess Soora shakes her head. "Wait a moment, that cannot be. Those fae are all extremely loyal to the rebel cause. Primarily the alvens. They're the ones that began

265

the resistance. The prince has never had any followers except for high fae in the past. Other breeds of fae detest the prince for his ill treatment of them. Why would they be following him now? It doesn't make any sense."

"And how did he get such high numbers so suddenly?" Belren asks.

"How many soldiers do we have?" I ask.

A worried look crosses Princess Soora's face. "Zalit?"

He clasps his hands together and leans forward, balancing his forearms on his thighs. "At my last count from our commanders and after taking the genfin attack, we have roughly two thousand."

My eyes widen, and I exchange a look with my guys. "That's it?"

Zalit nods. "We have the public's support, but the prince is powerful. Not all fae are willing to move against him."

"Two against ten are not good odds."

"There was something else…" Lex says carefully.

All eyes go back to her, and she blushes slightly under the attention.

"What is it?" I prompt.

She shifts in her chair, and Belren takes extra notice when her skirt rides up slightly on one side. "Well, there were…crops."

"Crops?"

Lex nods.

"Crops of what?"

"They looked like…tea leaves?" she says with uncertainty.

"Okay…"

Failing to see the significance, I look at Soora, but she seems just as lost as I am. "Alright. What about these crops

266

concerns you?" she asks gently. See? The princess is regal as shit.

"There were a lot of them," Lex quickly says.

Sev snorts under his breath, finally setting the tray of food down. "I tried to tell her, didn't I? That crop shite don't matter. Probably been there before the soldiers set up shop."

But Lex shakes her head. "I don't believe so. Those crops are regularly maintained by soldiers. There is new growth as well as old. If they simply took over the island to serve as base, they wouldn't have cared about the crops. They would have built up their camp right on top of them, but that isn't the case. They make sure that the crops are guarded at all times."

Well, that…is strange.

"And one more thing," Lex goes on. "I saw the king there."

Princess Soora sits up straighter. "What was he doing?"

"Walking through the crops."

"Just walking through them?"

Lex nods. "As far as I could tell."

Baffled, I run a hand through my tangled hair. I have no idea what all of this means, but regardless, we are vastly outnumbered. Ten thousand trained soldiers? Yeah, that's *really* bad.

CHAPTER 42

Our little gathering quickly disperses after Lex and Sev dropped the information bomb. I send them back to Cupidville, and the princess and her posse are holing up, strategizing. I'm alone with my guys, and we're just sitting around quietly, all of us lost in thought.

My alpha is spread out on the rug, his tail wrapped around my ankles, and I'm leaning against Sylred's shoulder where we're resting on the chaise, while Evert is on my other side, his arm tucked behind my head.

When a knock sounds at the door, Ronak immediately jumps to his feet and stalks over to it. He reaches his hand out and starts batting at the handle over and over again.

Evert snorts and shoves him away. "Our alpha, bested by a fucking knob."

Ronak hisses at him.

When Evert throws open the door, I look up to see a dozen sunflowers standing up at attention from a familiar earth sprite's head.

"Mossie!"

I run forward, hip-checking Evert out of the way to

greet her. My friend is in all her green vined glory, her bright green eyes locking on me instantly, and the sunflowers growing out of her scalp turn to face me.

"Emelle," she beams. She shoves the silver tray laden with tea cups in Evert's arms and envelops me in a hug. He rolls his eyes at her and sets it down on the table.

When we pull back, she keeps hold of my arms and gives me a once-over as if to check that I'm okay. "Girl. I knew that pink didn't look right," she says, mentioning my previously dyed self. "You look much better like this."

"Thanks. Your flowers look nicely pruned."

Mossie runs a hand over the vines cascading down her back and gives her sunflowers a pat. "Thank you. I did just tend to them. I also added some new mulch to my scalp," she says proudly.

"Well, whatever you're doing, it's working," I assure her. "How did things go with Blix?" I don't mention my run-in with him when we broke out all the prisoners in the tower because, well, that might get awkward.

She waves a dismissive hand. "Oh, that *water sprite*," she says with disdain. "We're over. I've moved on."

"Oh. Who's the lucky fae?"

She shrugs a shoulder and makes her way further into the room. "His name is Dune. He's an arid earth sprite," she tells me, as if I should be super impressed by that.

"Oh. Awesome."

She nods and sits down on the chaise where I join her. "Mm-hmm. He grows cacti out of his head. He's very refined."

"Huh. That sounds…sharp."

"Exactly. But he doesn't want to make things exclu-sive," she says with a slight pout. "Anyway, you pretended to be a servant! And a noble! But all along, you've been a cupid. How did you not tell me?"

"Sorry. It was top secret stuff."

"Apology accepted. You're forgiven. Now," she says, breezing past the conversation, still holding my hands. "Down to business. How many fae can you get to fall in love with me?"

"Uh, what?"

"How many?" she asks, her green eyes expectant.

"Oh, umm, there's not really, like, a limit. I just—"

"Good!" she says, dropping my hands so that she can clap. She reaches into the bodice of her dress and pulls out a piece of paper from between her green boobs and hands it over to me. I open it and a little soil falls out onto my lap. It also smells like roses.

"What's this?" I ask.

"That's my list of fae. There's no particular order. You can make any one of them fall in love with me first. Dune is going to get *so* jealous. That'll teach him not to want exclusivity with me."

I look at her long list of names and cringe. "Mossie…"

But her attention is already elsewhere. Particularly on my genfins. "So, these are your mates, huh? They're superhot." Her eyes land on Ronak where he's sniffing the ficus in the corner of the room. "That one is naked."

"Yeah…he won't keep any clothes on right now. He just shreds them."

"Hmm. Is he about to pee on that?" she asks, eyeing how he's still sniffing intently at the potted plant.

I laugh nervously and run a hand through my hair. "What? No. Of course not."

As soon as she turns her back on him, I wave my hands around wildly in his direction to get his attention. He looks up at me lazily. "Do. Not. Pee," I mouth to him sternly.

He keeps his golden eyes locked onto me. Then he grabs his dilly whacker and...pees all over the bloody ficus.

I scrunch my nose. Unbelievable.

"As soon as I heard the rumors about the cupid, I just *knew* it was you," Mossie says as she starts serving the tea she brought up. "I heard some of the hearth hobs talking about defecting, so I knew I needed to leave with them. Luckily, one of them let me tag along; otherwise, I'd still be stuck at the palace. I much prefer working here with the princess than that grimy old king. I'm so glad the princess wasn't actually beheaded. She has such a nice head."

Ignoring the pee puddle behind me, I sit back down on the chaise as she serves me some tea. "She does have a nice head," I agree. "And I'm glad you're here, too."

"Well, there's your tea. One of the servants insisted I bring it up to you. I guess you had a rough time at the rebel camp?"

"You could say that..."

Mossie passes tea cups to me and the guys and then straightens up. "I'd better get back down. Just call if you need me. Oh, and let me know when you're ready to start on my love list!" With a happy wave, she turns and breezes out of the room, leaving me with a love list in one hand and a teacup in the other.

Evert and Sylred blink at the door and then look at me. "Friend of yours?" Evert drawls.

"Yeah, that was Mossie. I tried to hook her up with a water sprite after she snuck me into the prison tower entrance. She liked his butt. The water sprite's butt, I mean. I guess it didn't work out. We also got drunk. We both like fairy wine. We drank *a lot* of wine."

Evert grins and I watch as Sylred starts cleaning Ronak's mess with some towels.

I take a sip of the tea, and flavor explodes on my tongue. "Mmm," I hum appreciatively. I then down the entire cup, not even caring that it burns off half my taste buds. Some things are just worth it.

Evert cocks a black brow as I try to fan off my tongue. "Good?"

I drop my hand and set the cup down. "Delicious. I'm sleepy."

"Let's get you to bed then."

Seeing the look in his eye, I shake my head. "Uh-uh. I really am sleepy. No sexy times."

He laughs. "Sure."

I cross my arms. "I'm serious. My puss pearl is clammed up for the night. My tuna pot pie is already put away in the Tupperware. This fun hatch is closed for business, Evert."

He gives me a cocky look. "As if you could resist me."

I scoff. "I can totally resist you. Look at me resisting you right now. I'm resisting the hell out of you, and I'm not even trying."

To drive my point home, I yank off my dress and toss it at his face before sidestepping around his reaching arms. I hurry to the closet and shut myself inside. I stifle a giggle as he curses on the other side of the door, and I slip on some panties. After pulling my wings into my back, I put on a white night dress. When I'm decent again, I saunter out, totally nailing this resisting stuff, even when I see that Evert has stripped down to only a loose pair of pants hanging low on his waist.

"Nice nightie," he says with a smirk, his blue eyes hot on my exposed skin.

"Thanks," I say, trying not to ogle the yummy lines going from his abdomen to his nether region. I fail in that endeavor.

"How's that resisting going?"

I hear the humor in his voice, and I force my eyes back up. "What?"

A lethal smile spreads across his face, and now he's flashing his dimples at me, too. Realms have mercy on my poor little horny soul.

He starts to slowly prowl toward me. It's a sexy prowl, too. "I said, are you done resisting me yet?"

"Yes. No. I mean..." Flustered, I shake my head to try to clear it. "Can you put a shirt on? Your V is distracting me."

He laughs. "My what?"

I point at the offending muscles. "Your V. That shape from your abs to your naughty bits. It's delicious and I can't concentrate when you're just flashing it around all willy-nilly."

Heat fills his blue eyes, and he crooks a finger at me. "Come here."

I shake my head and race to the other side of the bed. "Nope. Nuh-uh. Sleeping." I hurry under the covers and pull them nearly up to my chin.

Sylred returns from wherever he disposed of the soiled cloth that he used to clean up Ronak's pee, and he starts stripping for bed. Ronak's already naked, so now I have three muscled and seriously hot genfins closing in on me. Why did I turn down sex? I can't even remember now.

Evert slides into bed on one side, Sylred on the other,

and Ronak once again lies down at my legs, his head lying right on top of my pelvis.

Evert rests a hand on my hip as he lies beside me, and even through the silky fabric of my nightgown, I can feel the heat coming from his palm. Sylred's legs are tangled with mine, and Ronak starts purring, and the vibration shoots right to my core.

Like he knows I'm already breaking, Evert starts trailing his hand up my side, his finger barely grazing over some side boob action. I shoot up into a sitting position, my face flushed. "Okay! I get it! I suck at resisting! Give me sex."

He starts laughing. *Laughing!* What a jerk.

"What's funny?" I demand, crossing my arms in front of me.

He props his hands behind his head and leans back. "You couldn't even last five minutes."

"What did I miss?" Sylred asks, looking between us. "I always miss stuff when I'm cleaning up piss."

"Scratch can't get enough of us," Evert explains with a smirk.

"You're flashing your naked torsos at me!" I say hotly.

Evert's dimples come out in full effect, and Sylred's eyes crinkle with his own smile. "Our naked torsos?" he teases.

"Yes!" I feel all jittery from that tea, and it's now sitting in my stomach, sloshing around. "You guys are laughing at me."

"No one is laughing," Sylred points out.

I point at their smiling faces. "The laughs are there. Right there. I can see them behind your quivering lips."

"Don't say quivering lips," Evert drawls.

"I'll say quivering lips as much as I like, thank you very

much. And you think I can't go without sex? I totally can. I mean it this time. I'm going to sleep. We've just had our first fight, and I can't be bothered with you or your naked torsos."

I slump back on the pillows, ignoring their chuckles completely by stuffing the pillow over my face. I fall asleep feeling horny and grumpy as hell.

Freaking genfins.

CHAPTER 43

I blink open my eyes at the daylight streaming across my face, and I groan. Feeling like total shit, I sit up, only to clutch my stomach, feeling a tinge of pain.

All night, I kept tossing and turning, pain radiating from my gut. I don't know if it's the stress or if I'm getting sick—I didn't even know cupids could get sick. But instead of feeling better this morning, I feel worse.

The guys are all out of bed, so I'm alone on the large mattress, but I can hear someone in the bathroom running water. Hopefully, someone left to go let Ronak out. Sylred tried to train him to use the toilet. Let's just say he ended up with a clawed arm and piss all over his boots. So now, the guys just take turns bringing him outside.

Needing a drink of water, I sit up and fling the covers off of me, only to freeze in horror.

"Oh my gods!" I screech.

I don't even blink. I just keep staring at my lap like maybe I'm hallucinating and it will go away. Blood.

There's so much blood. I check myself for a wound, thinking maybe someone snuck in this morning and stabbed me, but I find no wound. When another pain wracks my body, it makes me whimper and curl into myself.

I must've made enough noise to alert him, because Sylred suddenly comes barreling out of the bathroom, looking around for the threat, and then he's at my side in a flash.

"What is it? What's wrong?" he asks, his voice tight with concern.

"I've been poisoned!" I cry, my eyes wild with panic. "That tea. I think it was the tea, Syl. Maybe someone tricked Mossie into bringing it up. I bet it was that super pissed genfin guy. *I'll make you pay,*' that's what he said, remember? He basically warned us that he was gonna kill me!" I whimper again as another wave of pain crashes over me. "Oh gods, it hurts. I'm bleeding out. I have internal injuries. The poison is stripping out my insides. I'm dying, Syl!"

My panicked babbling cuts off with my dismayed sob.

Sylred is frozen, probably from the shock of watching me bleed out. I look up at him, my face watery. A strange expression crosses his face, and then he clears his throat and says, "Umm, Emelle? Sweetheart? I think you're just...menstruating."

"Don't say words with more than two syllables right now, Sylred," I snap. "I'm freaking *dying*! You should be running to the healer or something. This poison is making my internal organs bleed out of me! Look!" I screech, showing him the very obvious bloodstains on my nightdress and blankets.

"Emelle," he says gently. "You're not dying, I promise.

You're just experiencing your first period. It makes you bleed and have cramps. You're going to be okay."

I shake my head adamantly. He's not taking this seriously. He's gonna feel *so* guilty after I keel over from blood loss. "No. There are invisible knives stabbing my gut. I can feel it. I'm definitely dying. Look at all the blood, Syl! That's not normal!"

He bites his bottom lip, like he's actually trying to hold in a laugh. I nearly crack him over the head. As if sensing my fury, he digs into his pocket and pulls out an offering. "Here."

I perk up. "The whole box?" I ask, looking at the chocolates warily.

He never lets me have the whole box. He always feeds me one by one; otherwise, he says I'll turn into a gluttonous vulture and devour the whole thing in seconds. He's not wrong.

"Yep. The whole box," he says, sounding way too friendly. "It'll make it all better."

I sniff. "Until I die, you mean."

This time, he lets the smile break through. "You're still not dying. It's just your period."

I look at him dubiously. "That can't be right. Surely females don't deal with this? I mean, I saw the occasional tampon-toting woman, and I heard about a million complaints about periods while I worked on Earth, but this...this seems a bit extreme. I think something is wrong. Are you sure I haven't been poisoned? Like really, *really* sure?"

"I'm sure," he says, his brown eyes lit up with amusement. "I had a cup of that tea myself, and I'm fine."

"Maybe just my cup was poisoned," I point out.

"No."

"You're not just trying to keep me calm because I'm on my literal deathbed right now, are you?" I ask, eyeing him suspiciously.

He full on beams. "Nope."

Opening the box of chocolates, I start shoving them into my mouth. "Well, this sucks. I mean, people always said periods sucked, but I just thought they were being dramatic. But no. This is legitimately the worst. It feels like I'm being juiced like a lemon. Except instead of lemonade leaking out, it's freaking period blood!"

Sylred grimaces a bit, but otherwise stays wisely silent.

"If you're wrong and I really have been poisoned and am bleeding out, you're gonna feel so bad," I tell him.

He laughs. "I'm not wrong."

"How do you know? This can't possibly be natural."

He taps his nose, and I blanch. "Oh my gods, you can *smell* me bleeding from my vagina?"

He chuckles and rubs the back of his neck. "It's nothing to be embarrassed about."

"Don't smell me," I order him.

"I kinda can't help it."

I glare at him. Looking contrite, he slowly raises his hand and makes a show of plugging his nose.

I nod. "Better."

Another cramp stabs my insides, and I flop back onto the bed with a groan. "How can females bleed this much without dying? We're freaking warriors, Syl."

When he doesn't reply, I pick up my head from the pillow to look at him. He quickly nods. "Oh. Yeah. Warriors."

Nodding in satisfaction, I drop back down and eat

another chocolate. Oddly, it does help. "Keep these comin', genfin," I tell him.

"I've got it handled," he says. "I'll take care of you."

And he does. Because my sweet genfin always takes care of me. Even when I'm being a feisty, raging, hormonal beast.

CHAPTER 44

Sylred leaves to call one of the servants to clean the bedding, and when he gets back, he helps me into a bath. I wash off the blood and let the hot water soothe my cramping belly, and then Mossie comes up and wraps my muffin mound up like a mummy. I have so many layers of cloth stuffed into my underwear that I'm pretty sure it has the liquid contained better than the Hoover Dam.

For the rest of the day, Sylred feeds me, rubs my feet, and tells me stories about what they did while I was gone. Despite my grumpy mood, he makes me feel better. Evert is gone until evening, but when he returns, he takes one sniff and gleans my situation. With Ronak in tow, he carefully makes his way over to me.

I watch him like a hawk. "Hmm. There he is. My mate," I say in a falsely chipper tone. "The one out gallivanting around all day. While I was just here. Seeping out blood." His steps stop as my glare takes over my face. "Did you know the fae realm doesn't have tampons yet? It's not a thing here, Evert. Which means my vagina has been

281

mummified instead. *Mummified*," I say again, just to really drive my point home. "And you've been gone. Probably enjoying yourself. Talking. Walking around with a lovely breeze against your groin. Smiling at people and making females fantasize about licking your dimples and having your scruff scrape against their non-bloody thighs."

Gods, even I know I'm being a bitch. It's like all my sweetness and reason has drained out along with all of the blood, but I can't stop it.

Evert approaches me like one might approach a savage lioness. "Hey, Scratch."

I cock a brow. "Hey? I'm sitting here with my womb trying to squeeze itself out of my body, and you just saunter in and say *hey*?"

Evert exchanges a look with Sylred, but they both seem equally unsure how to handle me. He scratches the black scruff on his chin. "For the record, I only smile at you," Evert finally says. "So, you're the only one who gets to fantasize about licking my dimples. You know how I am—I tell everyone else to fuck off. Besides, I think the dimple-licking is just a *you* thing. It's a bit weird, if you ask me. Hot, but weird."

I just blink at him, trying to figure out if I wanna punch him or not. I think no, but who really knows? When you're on your period, you kinda always want to punch someone.

He blows out a breath. "So... Bloody elephant in the room—you got your period. I guess that answers that question."

"What question?"

Sylred takes over. "Well, we'd wondered whether or not you're...uh, able to breed. This is a good sign, actually."

282

I narrow my eyes at him, making his cheeks turn pink from the ferocity of my glare. "Oh, I see. So you were all talking about me. Behind my back. Keeping secrets. Not including me in important breeding discussions." Tears well in my eyes, and Sylred gets a panicked look on his face. "I didn't even know you guys wanted kids right away. And what if I didn't get my period? What if I can't breed? You guys don't talk to me enough!" I start ugly crying. Again, I can't stop it.

Frazzled, in pain, and now freaking out, my emotions are going haywire, and the tears gush out like I'm freaking Niagara Falls.

Evert, not knowing how to handle a weepy mate, just sort of stands there and pats me on the back. He keeps saying, "There, there, buddy," like I'm a coworker who just lost the chance at a promotion.

Sylred, more in touch with his emotional side, slides in next to me on the bed and wraps his arms around me. "Sweetheart, we don't keep things from you. We were just discussing the likelihood of us having offspring. It's already difficult for genfins to conceive, and the chances of doing it outside our own breed…"

"I know!" I hiccup. "I told you guys! I told you not to go through with our mating ceremony if you weren't sure. I didn't want to condemn you to living a life without kids. But now it's too late, because we *are* mates, and I freaking love you! I've always wanted to fall in love and now I have, but I'm bleeding, and you're talking about breeding, and I'm *so hungry!*"

I've crossed over into totally psycho status. My hormones are bouncing around more than…sports balls that bounce around a lot. I actually don't know a lot about Earth sports, to be honest. I tried to go to a few games, but I never made it past the locker rooms. Which I'm fine with, since I'm sure the balls in there were far more impressive anyway.

Gently, Sylred pulls my hands away from my face. "Breathe. Come on. One, two, three..."

Following his directions, I calm my frenzied, hiccupped gasps and start breathing in and out. After several times of him leading me, he gives me a smile and wipes the tears from my face using the pads of his thumbs. "There. That's better," he says, kissing the corner of my eye. "Now. Let's back up just a bit."

A rasping grunt sounds from behind me. "Yeah, I'd like to get to the part where she just said she loved us."

My head snaps up at the voice, and my mouth drops open in shock.

"Ronak!"

There at the foot of the bed is my naked mate, his black eyes looking back at me.

I launch myself at him and he catches me, enveloping me completely with his arms and wings. Pressing my face against his chest, I let myself bask in his warmth, my relief immense. "You're you again," I say into his skin.

He pulls me away and grasps my chin, making me look up at him. "I'm back," he confirms. "My animal really didn't want to give up its hold. I'd almost lost hope, but then you were crying, and he didn't like that at all. He finally let me resurface."

"I won't go into the Veil again," I promise. "Not until I can figure out how to do it without you going animal. I was so worried that you wouldn't come back this time."

"I'm here," he says, leaning forward to nip at my bottom lip. When my mouth parts, he dips his tongue inside and licks at my tongue, making a moan slip out of

284

me. "Gods, I missed you, little demon. It was fucking torture watching behind the scenes, unable to get out and be with you."

"You're here now."

"I am." He nods. "And I was here when you just told us you loved us. Was that true, or were you just doing the thing where you ramble?" he asks, his eyes intense as he studies me.

"I don't ramble."

"You definitely ramble," Evert pipes up. "But let's get back to the question."

Ronak drops his wings so that we can see the guys, but continues to keep his arms wrapped around me. I fidget on my spot on the bed as all three of them watch me intently. I pinch the comforter between my fingers, avoiding eye contact. I can't believe I just blurted it out like that. I'm such a rambling idiot.

"Scratch. Talk to us."

I sigh and flick my eyes up to look at them. "Fine! Yes, I love you. I'm freaking insanely in love with you all. All I've wanted since forever was to be in love, and now I am, and it's…"

"It's what?" Sylred gently prods.

I meet his eyes. "It's better than I ever imagined. But it's scary, too."

"Look at me," Ronak orders, and my stomach has a little thrill at his authoritative voice. "You don't ever have to be scared. Not with us. We're your mates."

"Exactly," Evert agrees. "And we fucking love you more than life itself."

My heart does a flip and my mouth parts in surprise at the vehemency of his declaration.

I look to the other guys in confirmation, and they look

steadily back at me, Ronak with a nod and Sylred with a smile.

"You...you love me?"

Evert snorts. "Yeah, we fucking love you. Sylred's hair turned pink. Ronak has fucking cupid wings. I have Lust leaking out of me every time I fucking sneeze. If that doesn't show our connection to you, I don't know what will."

I wipe my nose on my sleeve, and I know that this is it. This feeling right here. This is what I've been chasing for my entire cupid existence. I love them, and they love me right back.

And you know what? It really *is* the best thing in all the realms.

CHAPTER 45

he princess and her advisors, including the commanders for the rebel force, argue for days. They debate about our next move for so long, in fact, that my period comes and goes.

Mossie also comes and goes. A lot. Mostly to add more names to her love list. She just added a seelie fae named Peekabu, I shit you not.

We're sitting in the formal dining room, eating what has to be a twelve-course dinner. I'm sandwiched between Evert and Ronak, while Sylred sits across from me, and I have all three of their tails wrapped around some part of me. If it's possible, they've been even more touchy-feely since I emotionally declared my love for them. Sylred has his tail wrapped around my ankle, Ronak has my waist, and Evert keeps wrapping his tail around my arm, even though I keep shrugging it off so that I can eat. Not that it stops him.

When he does it again, I sigh. "Evert, if you keep doing that, you're going to make me spill." I set my goblet down before his tail can make me dump its contents all over my dress. "Can't you anaconda some other part of me?"

He gives me a wicked grin and leans in close so that his mouth is against my ear. "Scratch, I'll bend you over this table and give you my anaconda right here."

I roll my eyes. "I'm pretty sure the princess wouldn't be too pleased with that at her dinner table."

Evert just shrugs and leans back, putting his arm over the back of my chair. As soon as I reach for my fork, his tail wraps around my arm again, making me drop it against the plate.

"I give up," I say with a huff.

"Good. Let's go back to our room and you can tell me more about where you want my anaconda."

I try not to encourage him, I really do. But sometimes the laugh just slips right past me.

"I'm so glad you've returned to us, Ronak," I hear Princess Soora say from the head of the table.

Ronak finishes chewing his bite and nods. "Thank you, princess."

"I'm told you and your covey have been very instrumental in helping train some of our rebellion force. We are indebted to you."

Ronak shakes his head. "The only debt that needs to be paid is by King Beluar and Prince Elphar themselves. They are the ones bringing death and tyranny to the realm, and they will answer for it," he says, his voice hard. I know that the attack on his island sits heavy with him.

The princess opens her mouth to reply, but she never gets the chance.

A huge sound cracks through the air, and the entire ground starts shaking violently. The princess tries to get to her feet, but when another blast sounds from somewhere,

I see her stumble back into her seat, and her hands clutch her head.

The room is still shaking, and Ronak yanks me under the dinner table, while he and the other guys start yelling for everyone else to do the same. Covering my head with my arms, I look over at Princess Soora's little sisters under the table, their faces pinched with panic. "What's happening?"

Just when the shaking stops, another boom resounds, and the ground trembles again. I see the princess's legs wobble, and then her knees buckle and she's lying prostrate on the floor.

Despite the rolling and shaking of the ground, I crawl over to her, missing the broken plates and smashed food where it litters the ground. People are yelling, and I'm pretty sure this manor is about to fall on top of us if the shaking doesn't stop.

The princess's face is shockingly pale with barely a hint of her usual purple complexion. I watch, alarmed, as a trail of blood begins to fall from her nose and ear.

"What is it? What's wrong?" I ask her.

When there's another boom, she winces and clutches her head. "The...barrier. It's...breaking," she pants out.

"What?"

But she can't answer, because in the next heartbeat, she passes out cold.

"Shit, shit, shit."

Hands pull her away from me, and I see her brother Zalit cradle her in his arms. He turns his orange eyes on me. "We need to get out of here before the place collapses!"

I nod and Zalit yells at his sisters and father to bring out their wings and get ready to fly out. At the yelling of

289

my name, I scramble back, passing servants who are also taking refuge under the table. When another huge boom hits, I fall against the floor, yelping when I hear pieces of the ceiling crash against the table above me.

Sylred gets to me first, latching his hand on my arm and yanking me toward him.

"Ronak is holding up the ceiling," he says, shouting in my ear so I can hear him. "We need to get out of here now!"

I nod in understanding, and I can hear Evert telling everyone else to do the same. I watch all of the fae bring their wings out and zoom out from under the table. "What about you? You don't have wings!"

"Ronak's strong enough to take us. Don't worry. We'll be right behind you," Sylred assures me.

"Come on, Veil female," I hear Belren tell me, his silver wings already out on display. "This place can't take much more."

With a nod, I crawl out from under the table. As soon as I'm on my feet, I leap in the air and fan my wings out wide.

Ronak is a good thirty feet above me, and he is indeed holding up the ceiling from falling on us all. His muscles are straining with the weight of the massive stone ceiling, and his wings are flapping vigorously to keep him up.

I watch as the last of Soora's family and the servants zoom out through the broken windows, leaving the five of us behind.

"Come on!" Belren says, tugging on my arm.

I fly behind him through the window, and when I'm safely through, I see Ronak let go of the huge chunk of ceiling. As soon as he does, the rest of the ceiling and walls begin to crumble and cave in. With my heart in my throat, I watch as he swoops down, where Evert and Sylred are already waiting, their forearms raised above their heads.

Ronak latches onto them, one in each hand, and then uses his momentum to fly all three of them up and out through crumbling ceiling. Then the entire manor collapses.

CHAPTER 46

I follow Belren around the manor to meet up with my genfins, and all five of us land in the garden where Zalit is carrying an unconscious Soora. The ground is still shaking, and the manor lies in a heap of rubble behind us.

All of our faces tilt upward, watching the attack being launched at the barrier over the entire island. There are royal soldiers *everywhere*. I can't even see the blue of the sky, because hovering bodies of soldiers are surrounding us from the other side of the failing barrier that the princess erected. Judging from the blood now pouring from her ears and both nostrils, she's losing the fight.

"The barrier is about to fall!" I yell.

Grim faces watch as the once invisible barrier now crackles and sparks, fissures of purple trailing down it as it weakens.

"Watch her," Zalit says, passing the princess to Belren. "I've got to go organize our forces."

"Don't go!" his little sister pleads, tears trailing down her face.

Zalit kisses her on the forehead and says something low in her ear and then launches into the sky. Their father tries to comfort them, but the girls are inconsolable and terrified.

Another attack of power beats against the barrier, making all of us stumble on the ground.

"What do we do?" I ask the guys. "Can we try to get a portal out?"

Belren shakes his head. "The portal wouldn't be able to take that many of us at once, and besides, the prince will be expecting that. He'll have his own fae ready to latch onto our portal and infiltrate it. It would only let them get to us faster."

"They need to hide," Ronak says, looking at Soora's family.

Soora's father nods. "I have a place."

"Good. Go now before it's too late."

Belren passes Soora to her father, and the four of them disappear through the garden, flying as quickly as they can. I hear the girls crying even after they're out of sight. I can only hope that they get to their hiding spot before the barrier is breached.

The soldiers above us are eerily in sync as they launch their assault at the barrier. Blasts of power are propelled against it, and my heart pounds about a mile a minute. We're like fish in a bowl, trapped and waiting for them to hook us.

When the next attack comes, the last of the barrier hisses and pops, and then a deafening crack fills the air. I watch in horror as the last of the barrier falls away, pieces of it shattering like an electrified mirror, leaving us completely exposed.

"We need weapons," Ronak says.

Wasting no time, Ronak grabs the guys again, and we fly toward the rebel camp as thousands of the prince's soldiers begin their descent.

The ground looks oddly shadowed, the sun totally blocked out, and I fly faster than I've ever flown before as I follow Ronak to the weaponry room at the rebel camp.

By the time we reach it, the prince's militia are halfway to the ground. They aren't making a single sound. No battle cries, no shouts of encouragement or even sneers of intimidation. They're spookily quiet as they fly toward us, weapons raised, and that quietness sets my teeth on edge.

The rebels are a flurry of activity. Commanders are shouting orders, formations are trying to be organized, the weapons room is being ransacked, and some of the buildings have caved in due to the earthquakes caused by the barrier breaking.

Ronak bursts into the weapons room and starts strapping blades onto himself as the others do the same. As soon as he's suited up, I feel him tear a slit into my skirt at the side so that I can move easier. Then Evert slips a thick leather shirt over my head, with chainmail attached to it. Ronak surprises me by fitting a bow and two quivers full of arrows over my shoulder. He presses the bow into my shaking hands and holds firm as he looks into my eyes.

"Aim and shoot. No hesitation."

I swallow thickly and nod. "No hesitation."

"Same orders apply. You don't get captured, you don't get killed. You see a blade coming at you, you go into the Veil. Understood?"

"But you'll—"

"I don't give a flying fuck if I go feral and never come back," he cuts me off, his black eyes intense. "My first priority as alpha is, and always will be, my mate and my covey. You go into the Veil and you stay alive. That's an order."

I wish I could smooth my hand across his beard and furrowed brow and let his strong arms protect me from the world, but I can't. The world just won't let us be, and I already knew it would come to this. I promised myself that I would take down the prince once and for all—or die trying. So that's what I'm going to do. And yeah, I'm just a cupid with no battle training, but I'm not helpless, and I won't hide. Not anymore.

"I'll do what I have to," I say cryptically.

Ronak nods once, and just as Belren and my guys finish gearing up, we hear ten thousand pairs of feet land on the island, like they did it all at the same time. Then the fighting begins. Shouting rings out, metal hits metal, and power clashes against power.

"Stay together!" Ronak orders us.

Evert looks fierce as he flanks me, Sylred clutches his sword with determination, and I nock an arrow, just trying not to show them how much my hands are trembling.

When we race out of the weapons room, we see the mayhem unleashed outside. The ten thousand soldiers to our two is now grievously obvious. Our rebels are fighting with everything they have, but they're not nearly as organized as the prince's military, and there are simply too many of Prince Elphar's soldiers.

Evert, Ronak, and Belren immediately start cutting fae down, while Sylred steers me to a pile of rubble that was once a cabin. The roof is still in one piece, and I scramble up it, while Sylred covers my back. I perch on the top and cover my guys, launching arrows as fast as I can nock them. I don't let a single soldier advance, and the bodies start piling up around Ronak and Evert, arrows sticking out of their bodies like living pin cushions. I don't think about it. I can't. If I start worrying over the fact that I'm actually taking lives, I don't know if I can keep going. And I *have* to keep going, because otherwise, they'll kill us. So I shut that part down in my mind and force myself to keep shooting.

With both eyes open, I aim and loose the arrows with perfect accuracy. My arms start to burn, and my fingers slice open from the wire, but I don't stop or slow. There's no room for error, not with being so outnumbered. I hear Sylred fighting behind me, protecting my back, and I keep going. But I can see the futility of the fight. I see it, and yet I try to ignore it.

Noticing more fae advancing toward Ronak, Evert, and Belren, I reach back for another arrow, only to find that I've exhausted both of my quivers, and I only have a single arrow left.

"Shit! I'm out, Syl!"

I look over my shoulder, only to find that he's fighting off three fae and struggling. There are piles of dead bodies littered all over the ground in every direction that I can see, and I can already tell that our rebel force has been nearly annihilated. Rebel after rebel is cut down, but all I can hear is my pounding heart as my chest rises and falls with adrenaline and fear. Blood saturates the ground, and there's so much heartbreak in the air that I can't breathe properly.

More soldiers drop from the sky and close in on us. With icy cold realization, I realize that there's too many.

We're going to lose.

When I hear Sylred cry out in pain, my mate bond pulses inside of me. Whirling around, I ignore the soldiers who are now marching toward me and grip the arrow in my hand, ready to use it to attack anyone who dares to hurt Sylred. He's on his knees, his sword gone, and I watch, horrified, as a blade is pressed to his throat.

My vision goes red.

I begin to lunge for him when I'm stopped by a clear, booming voice.

"Stop!"

As if on cue, the prince's soldiers cease fighting, and I look around wildly to see that the rest of the rebels in my vicinity have been overpowered. Ronak is being held down by some sort of giant fae with stone-like skin, his strength power not even enough to break out of the giant's hold. Sylred is on his knees with a blade to his throat, while Evert, Belren, and all the rest of the rebels are in the same position.

"Hold."

I whirl around at the voice, my chest heaving and still clutching onto the arrow in my bloody hand.

Sauntering toward me, out of the plumes of dust and smoke, is Prince Elphar.

CHAPTER 47

*P*rince Elphar's blue skin is unmarred, his clothes pristine, his handsome face pleased. Flanking him is his right-hand advisor, Chaucel, and on the other side is the guard, Gammon. The two of them oversaw my beating when I was captured. My eyes automatically flick down to Gammon's arm, to the place where his hand should be. But there's only a stump from where Okot cut it off. Sick satisfaction washes over me at the sight.

Like my mind conjured him up, suddenly Okot is there, and all of that satisfaction whooshes out of me.

The four of them stand twenty feet away from me, their eyes watching me, and me alone. The prince has a playing card in his hand, and he flicks it between his graceful fingers as he toys with it, like he doesn't have a care in the world—like he isn't standing amidst hundreds of dead bodies, nearly walking right on top of them.

His soldiers wait, their faces expressionless, their bodies relaxed, even as they hold back the rebels. Just like when I saw them on the genfin island, I'm struck with how very odd they look. When I send my cupid senses out, I confirm Lex's declaration. I feel nothing from any of the soldiers. No love, no longing, no worry over loved ones, no heartbreak, no desire...nothing.

"There she is," Prince Elphar says, and my eyes snap back to focus on him. "The famous *cupid*." He spits the last word like it's a curse.

I don't dare blink or look away from him, not even when I hear Ronak struggling again to get away.

"You have a choice to make," the prince tells me.

"Yeah? What's that?" I ask, my hands itching to grab my bow. If I could just get it...

"Your pathetic rebels are beaten. The fight is over." He raises his hands and turns around, gloating over his victory, and I follow his gaze, seeing the rest of the rebels held at sword point, their lives a breath away from being ended. "I can see you don't want to give up," Prince Elphar says, facing me once again. "I admire that fight, I do. So here's your choice," he says, taking another predatory step closer to me. "You can try to nock that arrow that you're gripping in your hand. You can try to shoot me faster than Chaucel here can throw up a shield. It would be a gamble, but oh, what a gamble! Imagine if you won," he exclaims, looking positively giddy at the thought. "But be warned, if you miss, I will give the order and kill every single other rebel on this island. Including your genfin mates. They will all die. Because of you."

I swallow hard, trying not to show the fear in my expression, even though I can feel the blood draining from my face. "And the other choice?" I ask, glad when my voice sounds steady.

"Choice number two is much less entertaining," he

explains. "You simply surrender. We take you, and we let the rest of the rebels live. The choice is yours."

"No!"

My eyes dart to Ronak, where he strains against the giant. Evert and Sylred are trying to fight off their captors too, but it's no use. They're already wrapped in iron chains.

"Don't you dare," Ronak growls at me, his eyes locked on me.

I turn back to the prince, only to get caught on Okot's eyes. Just like the rest of the prince's soldiers, there's just...nothing there. No expression whatsoever. The emptiness of it makes me shudder.

"What are you doing? I'm your brother!" I hear a fae shouting, and I look over to find a rebel struggling under the hold of a soldier. It's clear by their similar appearance that they're related. "You've fought against the prince all your bloody life! How could you side with him?"

The soldier doesn't even look at him. Doesn't react whatsoever. Just continues to hold the blade at his brother's throat.

My eyes move past them to the genfin from before. The one who blamed me for the attack on his island—the one who threatened me. He stares stonily back at me, and I can see the challenge in his eyes, like he's already expecting me not to surrender to the prince to spare their lives.

"Well?" Prince Elphar says, regaining my attention. "What will it be? Shall I give the order to end everyone so that you can try your little arrow trick? Will you be that selfish to try? Or are you going to use what little intelligence you have and come with me now?"

The arrow in my hand suddenly feels heavier than any

weight in all the worlds, and I sag under the heavy burden of choice. It would be so gratifying to send it flying at the prince's face, but I can't. This is a game I can't win, and we both know it.

The prince's eyes dance with amusement when he sees the defeat in my expression.

I don't look back at my guys. I can't. Not even when they start screaming my name. Not even when Chaucel opens a portal. Not even as the prince reaches forward and grabs hold of my arm.

I just let the arrow drop, and I fall into the portal.

CHAPTER 48

We land on the prince's secret island.

I know this because of Lex's descriptions of the crops. I spot them immediately off to the left, and she was right, they are obviously very well kept up. There are also still a few hundred soldiers on this island from what I can see, which just shows how much of a force he really has. He didn't even have to send all of his soldiers to completely devastate our forces.

The prince's soldiers are standing in formation, perfectly lined up and staring straight ahead. Not one head turns toward us when we appear, and I don't see a single fae fidget or hear a noise coming from them. They even seem to breathe at the same time. My brow furrows as I watch them.

Something is very, very wrong.

Movement catches my eye, and I turn to see King Beluar walking back from the crops. He's being helped by two fae on either side of him, his weight leaning against them. Further down, there's a line of soldiers waiting for a drink. I think it's water at first and watch as the soldiers come up one by one to drink a ladle full of liquid. But when I see a wheelbarrow of leaves and steaming water being brought over and dumped into the huge barrel for a refill, I realize that it's not water—it's tea. And it's the same tea leaves from the crops.

"Go on, lamassu," I hear, and my attention moves over to see Okot being herded away by Gammon.

When Gammon touches him, Okot growls, and it's the first expression I've seen on his face today. Okot slams a fist into Gammon's face, making the guard go flying back. Chaucel erects a barrier between them before Okot can charge again, and he slams his fist against it, furious and wanting to get at him.

"Enough," the prince says. "Lamassu, stand down."

Immediately, Okot's body jerks and his fists drop to his sides. The anger bleeds out of his face, and he's left impassive once again.

I look from Okot to the Beluar Blade he's clutching, to the blank-faced soldiers, to the king, to the crops, to the tea, and it all clicks into place. I cover my mouth with my hand, my eyes widening in shock. "Oh my gods."

I know what the king and the prince have done. And with the numbing realization, my head spins until it lands on one thought. *Okot.*

Before I can voice my realization, the portal, still open, suddenly flashes. The next thing I know, my guys and Belren are being escorted through. They're all in iron chains, and Ronak's body is flung over the back of a horse, unmoving.

"Ronak!" I try to get to them, but my own guards have a firm hold on me.

"He's fine!" Sylred calls back to me. "Just knocked out."

Sylred's face is puffy and bloody, and Evert is sporting

similar injuries. "Scratch. Disappear," Evert orders, but the prince just laughs.

"You disappear, and they're dead. Why do you think I brought them with us?" Prince Elphar says, his icy blue eyes trained on me. "They're here to give you proper incentive."

"Don't hurt them," I say, my voice somewhere between a warning and a plea.

"That will be entirely up to you."

Gods, I hate him.

"Elphar!"

Everyone turns to look at the princess's voice as she comes storming out of the portal. She still has bloodstains beneath her nose and dripped onto the bodice of her dress.

"Ah. My wife," the prince says with a smirk as he saunters toward her.

My brows crinkle in confusion as he walks up to her and places a kiss on her cheek. He pulls back and pats her head like one might pat a dog. "Very well done, wife. Your acting skills are remarkable." He taps the dried blood above her lip. "Terribly sorry about the barrier. It had to be done, you know."

She curls her purple hands into fists. "You attacked my home island. That was not agreed upon. You put my family in danger! You said you wouldn't kill unless necessary!"

Prince Elphar just shrugs, her anger not fazing him at all. "It was the move I wanted to make on the board. You know I love a good surprise. It's good to keep the other players on their toes."

She shakes her head, furious tears apparent on her face.

Belren looks between them, shaking his head in disbelief. "No…this… It's not possible. You can't have… Soora?"

She glances at him, her face immediately filling with guilt. "He has Benicia," she replies, as if that will make up for her betrayal.

Belren's face goes hard. "How long since you've double-crossed us?"

"Belren—"

His entire body tenses with fury. "How. Long?" he grits out between clenched teeth.

"Four weeks. The night he captured me, he gave me a choice. Tell him the rebellion's plans, or he'd kill Benicia," she confesses, and I watch as a single tear falls down her lavender cheek.

"You deceived us all," he says, his voice belying the shock he's feeling. "You've signed our death warrant."

"I had to!" she argues, looking up at him for the first time. "I couldn't let him kill her."

I crush the heel of my palms against my eyes. This can't be happening.

"My sister would *hate* you for making that choice," Belren bites back. "She lived and bled and breathed for this rebellion—to fight this monster who just uses fae, playing with us like game pieces and tossing us away when he's bored."

"You'd rather I have let her die?" she challenges. "Your own sister?"

"I'd rather you have acted with honor!" he yells back at her, straining against the guards. "I'd rather you have told me. I could have helped, Soora. I've always helped you, even when you left my sister so you could marry the fucking prince."

Soora flinches. "I did that to help the rebellion."

"That's what you told yourself. But I think you wanted the status. You broke her heart when you left her. No wonder she ran away."

Prince Elphar grins. "Yes. And I caught her. I've had her ever since. She's terribly entertaining company."

Belren practically smolders with rage. "I will kill you if you've hurt her."

The prince's grin never wavers. "I'd love to see the attempt."

I'm pretty sure he's serious. He's that much of a psycho.

Prince Elphar watches Belren with a smug expression on his face. "The great Horned Hook," he says in a mocking tone. "The one who can find and take *anything* in the realm." He lets out a barking laugh. "Isn't that what they say about you? People will believe anything these days. You couldn't even find your own sister. That must really wound your ego."

Belren seethes and moves his hands, but whatever telekinesis powers he's trying to use don't work under the chains of iron shackled to him.

Prince Elphar runs a finger down Soora's cheek. "I see your imprisonment was successful in luring the cupid. It seems you were more useful than I believed."

Gods, I really wish I hadn't bragged so much about rescuing her now.

The prince claps his hands, making me flinch at the noise. "I think it's time for tea," he says enthusiastically. Yep. He really is a psychopath.

A dead-eyed servant brings over a tea tray and stands in front of the prince.

"Let's bring Benicia out, shall we?" the prince says jovially.

Gammon nods and walks away, only to come back seconds later with a female fae I've never seen before but who looks familiar. She has silver-toned skin and delicate wings at her back. Her hair is white and short in a pixie-cut style, and she has large gray eyes. And as if those weren't enough similarities, then the two horns coming out at her hairline and curving back behind her ears would be revelation enough.

"Benicia!" Belren tries to lunge forward, but the soldier behind him holds him back by the chains.

The female glides up and takes up the space beside the prince, never once looking in Belren's direction, no matter how many times he calls her name.

"You said you wouldn't do that to her," Soora says quietly to the prince, her lavender eyes locked onto Benicia.

Prince Elphar shrugs. "She was being unreasonable."

"Benicia," Belren says again, but his sister still doesn't look at him.

The prince toys with her short hair. "She doesn't answer to you. She only answers to me."

"What did you do to her?"

Ignoring her, he turns to the servant. He looks her figure up and down, noting her beautiful face, and grips the female's chin, forcing her to look at him. Her head turns and she looks up at him vacantly. "Mmm. I don't think I've had a taste of you, yet," he says, giving her another lascivious look. She doesn't react at all. When he hooks a finger into the top of her dress and pulls it down so that he can steal a look at her cleavage and cop a feel, fury takes over my mouth.

"Stop!"

Prince Elphar looks over at me, his icy eyes gleaming.

307

"What did you say?" He voices it as a question, but I can hear the threat.

"Leave her alone," I tell him.

While keeping his eyes locked on me, he reaches up, grips her dress with both hands, and rips. The fabric falls to the ground in a heap, and then she's left there, completely exposed.

Still watching me, he starts fondling her breasts. The sight makes me shake with rage.

"Stop it!" I scream.

He just grins cruelly. "You don't give the orders, cupid. I do." Leaning into the servant's still-vacant face, he speaks directly into her ear after giving it a lecherous lick. "The cupid needs her tea. Serve her."

"No!" I blurt out. "I won't drink it."

The prince's eyes flash. "Now, now, cupid. Don't be rude."

Ignoring him, I look to the others to explain what I've figured out. "The crops that they're growing here are tea leaves. The king is using his power to infuse his will into the crops and then the prince forces the fae to drink it. That's why everyone seems so robotic. They're not themselves. Their minds are being controlled."

Shocked faces look back at me, and I meet their eyes, desperate to make them understand. "Nobody drink it," I warn them.

The prince sighs. "There's nothing I hate more than when a player tries to ruin the game."

"You can't control an entire realm," I tell him.

He motions to the soldiers at our backs. "I can, and I will."

"But the king is sick. I've seen it. He won't last much longer."

Instead of getting angry, the prince simply nods his head in agreement. "Which is why you're here."

My brow furrows. "What?"

He sighs at me like I'm a simpleton. "You're right. My father has just about reached the end of his usefulness. His life was a sacrifice I was willing to make. But that's where you come in. You're a cupid, yes? So you will make all of my subjects love me. Every single one, or I'll kill them all," he says simply, like he's mentioning that it might rain.

I stare at him, completely bewildered. I can't possibly have heard him right. When he doesn't say anything else, I shake my head. "It doesn't work that way. I can't *make* anyone love you. There has to be an inclination already there."

"Then I suggest you'd better get to work on making sure they're properly *inclined*. Because once my father dries up and dies off, my people had better be ready to bow down to me with reverence in all things, or I will purge them all."

I shake my head, at a loss. What a narcissistic sociopath. Surely this can't be happening? His ego can't possibly be that big that he expects me to make everyone in the entire realm love him? But I can see by the look on his face that he's perfectly serious, and I'm in trouble.

"I'll even help you, cupid. You'd do better if you didn't think so much. It's not one of your skills," he taunts. "But don't worry. You'll be the only one partaking in my mind-control tea, as you called it. I prefer for your mates to watch."

He looks behind me, and before I can react, I feel the soldier at my back step up to me, clamping my arms tight against the wings at my back. The servant strides forward and forces the cup against my lips while the guard grabs my jaw. I shake my head left and right to try to prevent what's about to happen, but the soldier keeps his punishing grip, holding my head still, and squeezes until I open my mouth in a cry of pain. I hear Evert and Sylred yelling and fighting as I continue to struggle, but it's no use. The servant places the cup against my lips and dumps the mind-controlling liquid down my throat.

CHAPTER 49

The liquid hits my system even as I choke on it, sputtering and coughing as it trickles down my throat.

Everyone watches me, totally horrified. Except for, you know, the bad guys.

Eyes wide, I wait for the tea to take effect on me.

I wait, and I wait, and I wait.

But nothing happens.

Oh shit! It doesn't work on me! I really want to give the prince the finger and brag about my awesome cupid shield or whatever it is that makes some magic useless against me, but I realize that would be a dumb move. Instead, I quickly school my features and force my body to relax. I put on that same blank expression that all of his soldiers are wearing.

"The cupid looks better when she doesn't have a thought in her head, doesn't she, dear?" Prince Elphar asks his wife.

Soora looks miserable, but I don't feel the least bit

sorry for her. She betrayed me, Belren, Duru, Okot, the rebellion...everyone.

"You will follow my every command," Prince Elphar says to me. "Your loyalty belongs to me now."

"I'll fucking kill you," Evert threatens the prince, thrashing against his iron chains and the guards holding him back.

The prince ignores him and looks at me calculatingly, so I quickly nod. Crap. Do mind-controlled people nod? I don't know.

I guess he's satisfied with my response, though, because he goes on. "The first thing you will do is use your cupid powers on my soldiers here. I want each and every one of them to love and respect me. Once you're done with that, you can move on to every fae on every last island."

Gods, did this guy not get hugged enough as a kid, or what?

The prince turns to address his men. "Take them all to a cell. Except the unconscious one. He can be locked up with her while she works. Keep a sword trained on him at all times."

I clench my teeth together but keep the empty look on my face as Sylred, Evert, and Belren are dragged away. Evert manages to kick one of them in the shin, but the guy barely flinches. When two soldiers move to pick up Ronak, I see him crack open one eye to look at me before feigning unconsciousness again. Hope surges through me.

Elphar speaks to Gammon. "Start lining up fae to bring to her. Bring the ones whose tea administration is due to wear off soon."

Gammon nods and marches off to follow his bidding. The prince looks to Okot. "Lamassu, show your mate to her new room. Remember, she is your enemy. You are loyal to me. If the genfin tries anything, take him out."

Okot nods and stands up from the table to make his way over to me.

I grit my teeth. It takes everything in me not to tell the prince to fuck off. He took my mate from me. He reduced Okot to this shell of a fae, angry and empty inside. I hate him for it, and I'm going to make sure he pays.

Okot stomps over to me and then takes my arm to start leading me away. Ronak and I are dumped into an empty building across from the pavilion. It smells of leather and sweat. Ronak is shackled to a hook on the wall, while I'm left standing in the middle of the room, and I do my best impression of a mannequin. It's surprisingly easy to stand there and look like no thoughts are going through my head.

Okot goes to the door, facing out, and my eyes dart to Ronak, who once again peels his eyes open. Making sure no one else is looking, I shoot him a wink. Surprise crosses his face, and it's then replaced with a look of pride before he pretends to be unconscious again. Now that he knows I'm not mind-controlled, and I know that he's aware of what's going on, I let my mind race with the plan that I'm formulating. It's a long shot, and it depends on outside sources, but if it works, we may just make it out of this alive. Maybe. Probably. Fuck, I really hope so.

I watch as soldiers line up at the doorway in front of Okot. Unlike the blank stares and mechanical movements of the others, these soldiers are clearly distressed. Some of them are jerking awkwardly, and some of them keep pulling at their hair or ears, or hitting their heads, like they're trying to silence the voice that is controlling them. Others are yelling or blinking around in confusion, but many seem angry and agitated—just like Okot was when I found him pacing his room. It's obvious that the tea is wearing off of them.

While Okot is occupied, I quickly call Lex. She appears immediately, and before she can even say hello, I'm already ripping her bow and arrow off her back. "I need these," I whisper, quickly strapping them on my own body.

"Okay."

"Quick, back to the Veil. It's not safe," I whisper-shout, shooing her away.

With a nod, she disappears, and not a second too soon, because as soon as the twitchy soldiers are lined up, the prince strolls past them and comes inside to join me.

Two guards behind him carry a throne-like chair and settle it in the room for him to sit on before taking their places to stand watch over Ronak. The prince sits down with a flourish, looking like quite the asshole when he starts to drum his fingers impatiently. He flicks his icy eyes up to me. "For your sake, cupid, you'd better hope you can succeed in this endeavor, or things are about to get very, very bloody."

Gulp.

I turn and watch as Okot brings the first fae forward. She must be a stone fae of some kind, because she has geodes and gems growing out of her scalp.

She looks around wildly, clearly distressed. Okot stops her in front of the prince, and I take up my spot behind her.

"What's happening? Where...where am I?"

The prince just stares dispassionately back at her. I nock a Love Arrow in my bow. I don't want to shoot her, but if I don't, then I have no doubt that the prince will kill

Ronak right here, right now. It's made pretty obvious based on the sword being pointed at him.

Remembering how the fire fae Ferno reacted when I shot him, I aim for a non-lethal part of her body and let it fly. It hits her on the arm, and I cringe on impact.

She jerks in a hiss of pain. But I rush forward and make sure she stays facing the prince. A plume of pink seeps out of the Love Arrow along with her blood. I wish I could go into the Veil and do this properly so the arrow wouldn't actually wound her, but the prince would never let me, and besides, I can't risk Ronak going feral and never coming back. I got lucky these past two times. I'm not willing to chance it again.

The female stumbles a bit as she clutches her arm, the Love Arrow still sticking out of her. I stand at her side, not really sure what to do. Should I pull the arrow out? Should I let it ruminate? With Ferno, his loving adoration seemed to kick in almost immediately.

She jerks her arm away from me when I touch her. She looks down at the arrow numbly, seeming more confused than ever.

"Well?" the prince says, watching intently. "Did it work?"

Shit. How should I react? Should I say something? Should I fall at his feet in prostration? I don't know how mind-controlled people should act. I wish there was, like, a manual for this sort of thing. I end up just nodding with my mouth gaping open like a suffocating fish.

I come around to face the female, and she scrapes her hand across the geodes on her head, scratching certain crevices. "Erm... Do you love the prince?" I ask dumbly in the most mechanical voice I can.

She tilts her head at me. "I...arm...hurts."

315

Right. Maybe I should be answering in monosyllabic one-words? Looking back at the prince, I turn my head stiffly left and right, not moving my neck. My shoulders are practically up to my ears. I don't know why. It just seems like the thing to do when mind-controlled.

I wish the fae could somehow fake love, but she's not even capable of sentences, so I'm forced to confirm what he already surmised so that he doesn't get suspicious. "Not. Working. Prince."

There. That answer seemed like legit mind-puppet stuff. Maybe the prince will realize this is a stupid plan that in no way is going to work.

"Send in another," the prince barks.

Dammit.

The fae female is dragged away, the arrow still stuck in her arm, and another fae is brought forward. This time it's a broad-shouldered male with a face on each side of his head. He keeps knocking his fist against the face in the back, agitated with whatever is going through his befuddled mind. Or is it minds—plural? Does he have two? His skull *is* slightly large.

"Do it," the prince orders impatiently when I continue to stand there.

Whoops. I really should try not to get distracted when my arch nemesis is around. I nock another arrow and hit this fae in the same spot on the back of the arm. The guy doesn't even flinch. There's no reaction whatsoever. It's like he doesn't even realize I just hit him. And there's definitely no love coming from him.

When the prince looks at me for confirmation, I shake my head, still without moving my neck. Admittedly, it's weird. I just sort of turn my entire torso left and right.

The prince looks at me like I'm the biggest idiot he's ever had the misfortune to deal with.

"Another," he says.

I shoot Love Arrows four more times, all with the same result. No love. Not even an inkling of *like*. There's just…nothing. I even try to blow some Lust a few times. If they want to jump his bones, that might buy me some time, but nope. That doesn't work either.

By now, there's a puddle of blood collected on the wooden floor from where all the poor saps keep getting shot.

"Are you completely useless?" the prince asks me when the sixth person gets dragged away.

He slowly stands, and I automatically take a step back from him on accident. If he catches the non mind-controlled movement, he doesn't say anything.

As he stalks toward me, I can feel his magic simmering under his skin right beside his irrational fury. He's powerful and unhinged. It's not a good combo. I wouldn't order it off the menu.

Out of the corner of my eye, I see Ronak lift his head up, watching the prince's every movement, just waiting to spring into action if he hurts me. I can't let Ronak intervene. They'll kill him in a heartbeat.

The prince gets in my face, intimidating me with the magic that now crackles around him like lightning. "You have *one* use to me, cupid," he says, raising a finger in case I didn't know what number one looked like. He's such a douchecrown. "Make them love me as a prince should be loved, or I'll rip out your heart and feed it to your lamassu mate. If they don't love and respect me, then I will kill every last one of them, and the blood will be on your hands."

I blink back the terror I'm feeling, trying to keep my face neutral. "Apologies, prince."

Just when I think he's about to melt my face off with his scary raw magic, a huge boom sounds outside, and the prince's attention is wrenched away. He whirls on his heel and heads for the door, pushing Okot and the other soldiers aside. I follow behind, hearing a roar of commotion.

What I see makes my heart nearly jump out of my throat. Genfins.

Hundreds of genfins and more still coming.

CHAPTER 50

Somehow, the genfins have infiltrated the portal that Chaucel left open. It's not just trained rebels, either. These are everyday genfins, male and female, young and old, warriors and shopkeepers. I even see the genfin elders flying in, screaming with a battle cry. None of them are holding back. They're crashing into Prince Elphar's forces with vicious retribution for the attack that was launched on their own island.

They're using the element of surprise to their advantage and attacking from the sky. Swords, bows, spears, magic, they're cutting through the confused and empty soldiers on the ground with brutal abandon.

The prince begins shouting orders, making his soldiers scramble into formation, but without being able to hear his direct orders, many of them are just standing there blankly while the genfins attack them.

Part of me is like, *Hell yeah! Get those mothersucker prince soldiers!* But the other part is like, *Oh no, they're being mind-controlled, it's not their fault!*

Ronak is at my back in an instant, already having

knocked out the two guards who were standing sentry over him. Pride surges through him as he watches his people attack, fighting to get retribution for when the prince attacked their island.

"I need to go help," he says.

At the sound of his voice, Okot turns. When he notices Ronak is up, he immediately goes on the offensive. Ronak managed to rip the shackles off the wall, but they're still attached to his wrists, so he's at a disadvantage. Not to mention, I can tell his strength is waning from the iron contact, and whoever hit him over the head left a nasty wound that is caked with blood that's easily visible through his closely shaved hair.

Okot swings an arm at him, and Ronak uses his chains to wrap it around his arm and twist. That's all I'm able to keep track of, because after that, they're a mess of thrown punches, elbows, knees, hands, and headbutts. Butt heads? Whatever. The point is, they're fighting the eff out of each other.

"Stop!"

My heart is tearing in two at watching my two mates go at it. Ronak's claws are out, Okot is charging at him like a bull, and I don't know what the fuck to do.

"Ronak, don't hurt him!" I yell, then wince as he gets thrown across the room and into the wall. "But don't let yourself get hurt, either!" I reprimand.

He curses something before dodging another blow and then kicking Okot's massive legs out from under him, making him fall.

"We need to break the mind control."

"Well, duh! But I don't freaking know how! The Love Arrows don't work!"

Ronak throws his fist into Okot's gut, making a

whoosh of air escape him, and he clutches his middle with a grimace.

"Well, you'd better figure something out! I can't keep evading him!"

Ronak uses his wings to fly above the bull man in question, which only seems to infuriate Okot more.

Figure something out. Right.

Determination settles in my bones. It's like someone suddenly pours a full cup of the stuff directly into my head and doesn't stop until I'm full-up.

I march forward, determined to face-off with Okot on my own. "I got this," I say confidently to Ronak.

Okot's head swings in my direction. He narrows his murderous gaze on me, and then he charges.

Oh, shit.

"I don't got this!" I squeal.

With an annoyed huff, Ronak flies down, wraps a strong arm around my middle and hauls me up. Okot can't stop in time, so he goes barreling into the wall, busting a hole right through it. Ronak and I fly out after him.

The outside is a mess of battles taking place—and so loud I nearly want to close my ears. Battle cries, agonized shouts, magic being hurtled every which way, and swords clashing sound in the air.

Ronak drops me on my feet and distracts Okot again. He continues to take punches and evade the lamassu, but he's getting tired, and I know he can't just keep fending Okot off forever.

"We need a plan!" I yell at Ronak, who is once again grappling with my lamassu mate. "He's like a machine! He might as well be freaking sleepwalking!"

I stop, my own words sinking into me like a lightning

bolt of inspiration, leaving me slightly jolted. "Oh my freaking gods, that's it!"

Ronak doesn't reply, because, you know, he's too busy fighting off the three-hundred-pound lamassu.

"Don't worry! I got this!" I shout over to Ronak.

"That's what you said before!"

Gods, he just doesn't let anything go.

"Yeah, but for reals this time!"

"Whatever you're going to do, fucking do it!" he says.

"Don't take that tone with me, Not-First!"

He takes a huge blow to the face and goes flying backward. Ouch. Did I just karma him?

He gets up, shaking his head to clear the confusion from the blow. "Can you do whatever it is you said you were going to do?" he asks with exasperation.

Right. I'd better get to it.

I jump up into the air and fly toward Okot. Right when I'm directly above him, I drop onto his back and wrap my limbs around him. Startled, he wobbles backward until straightening himself up, and then the poor guy starts spinning and flailing around, trying to get to me.

With my elbows locked against his neck for leverage, I bring my hands together and rub. "Please let this work."

Dust gathers on my palms, and I waste no time. I shove my hands against Okot's face. The second it makes contact and he breathes the dust in, his eyes roll to the back of his head and his knees buckle.

He crashes to the ground, kicking up dust, and I stay on top of him, my chest heaving with hurried breath. I wait to see if he'll wake, but if the snoring is any indication, he's out hard.

Ronak comes over, and I quickly bury my hands in the

folds of my dress so that I don't inadvertently knock him out, too.

I don't even get to relax for a moment, though, because the battle happening all around us has only intensified, and the genfins no longer have the upper hand.

Genfins are being shot out of the sky where they fly, cut down on the ground, and being burnt, suffocated, drowned, and hit with different forms of magic. It's a bloodbath.

I can see in his face that watching his people die is killing Ronak inside. I don't even stop him when he shoves me back inside the ruined building to hide before he flies toward the fight. That's just who he is. He'll always fight.

But me? I'm going to make sure that this time, we don't lose.

CHAPTER 51

As soon as I'm inside the building, I get to work. "Lex."

When she appears, she starts to hand over her new bow and arrow, but I shake my head. I quickly relay my plan, and as soon as she hears it, she nods. "That might just work, Madame Cupid. Good thinking."

"Here goes nothing." I blow out a breath, praying that this will work.

"Raziel? Jerkahf?" I call. Nothing happens. "Oh. Right." I clear my throat. "For *heaven's* sake, can you both get the *hell* down here?"

To my delight, white and black puffs of smoke appear, and then, there the angel and demon are, in all their pissed-off glory.

Raziel glows with irritated righteousness. He whirls around, pinning me with a furious glare. "I told you before, cupid, *do not* summon us!"

His eyes start to glow white. Whoa. For an angel, he really seems to have an anger problem. I thought he'd be more, you know, angelic.

"Wait!" I say, throwing my hands up in front of me. "No more walking toward me all menacing-like. It's rude," I tell him pertly. He actually does stop, so that's something.

Jerkahf is dusting off his suit, making bits of ash and charcoal fall onto the floor. "Why did you call us here, cupid?" he asks.

"I need your help," I confess, motioning outside where the fighting is happening.

Raziel barely spares a glance, but Jerkahf walks closer to the hole in the wall to peer out. "Oh, I love a good massacre," he says cheerfully.

I glare at him. "That massacre happening is what I need your help to stop."

The demon shakes his head. "Angels and demons do not interfere in the battles of the living."

"True. Unless the living are breaking the Laws of Life," I say with a flourish. They stare at me. "Boom." I pretend to do a mic drop to really drive the magnitude home.

Raziel's beautifully sculpted brow creases. "Breaking the Laws of Life?"

I nod emphatically. "Yep. Prince Harming out there performed mind-control magic to create that horde of soldiers that's currently winning."

Raziel looks outside and then back to me with a shrug. His angel wings look super good when he shrugs. "So?"

Gods, he's pretty, but he sure is slow. "*So*, he took away their free will. He's broken the number one Law of Life." Lex passes over said book of laws, and I hold it up triumphantly. "And according to the Veil Lawbook, you angels and demons are obligated to intervene when that happens. So there."

Raziel and Jerkahf stare at me. I watch the emotions

flit over Raziel's face. First it's surprise, then anger, then a begrudging look that's just conniving enough that I suspect he's trying to think of a way out of it. So I throw the rulebook at him. Literally.

I take the book in question and chuck it at Raziel's face. It's heavy, though, so I only manage to throw it as high as his stomach. It grazes off his middle and lands with a thump on the floor. His eyes go from the book and back up to my face. "Don't throw books at me."

"Sorry. I got a little carried away," I confess. "But will you help?"

Raziel sighs like it's some huge inconvenience. "Fine."

Jerkahf looks far more amused. He rubs his hands together, making fireballs appear in his palms. "Fuck, yeah. I could do with a bit of killing. Torturing immortal souls gets pretty old after a few thousand years. I haven't had a good killing in ages."

I crinkle my nose in distaste. "Yeah...umm. How terribly boring for you."

He nods nostalgically. "Yeah."

"You can't kill them, though," I tell him. I swear, his face falls like I just told him his demonic kitten ran away.

"Why not?" he asks petulantly.

"They're mind-controlled, Jerkahf," I say with exasperation. "No killing. They need to be, like, incapacitated. I'll try to put some to sleep, too. Just go stop them from killing each other! Hurry up!"

Jerkahf takes a second to pout, and Raziel looks like he'd rather be anywhere else. The angel sighs. It's a long, dramatic, long-suffering sound. But then he snaps his fingers, and a dozen more angels appear. They're all loin-clothed, shiny, and prettier than sculptures crafted by the best artists, but they also look deadly and fierce.

"Umm...there are thousands of soldiers out there," I point out helpfully. "I'm pretty sure you're gonna need more than twelve angels."

Raziel looks at me with unconcealed distaste. "Twelve angels can defeat hundreds of thousands of these puny fae soldiers."

Wow. Cocky much?

Raziel turns his back on me, wasting no time commanding his dozen shiny cherubs, and then they're off, flying into the fray.

Jerkahf points a smoking finger in my face. "I get to hit them *very* hard," he says resentfully.

"Fine, fine. Just go!"

He claps his hands together, and the flames of hell rise up in a circle around him, making me squeal and jump back, tugging Lex with me. The room fills with demons, and the smell of sulfur is so strong that I have to plug my nose.

Lex wrinkles her nose. "That is a terrible smell."

"I know. They're real sensitive about it though, so don't say anything."

Jerkahf sends me a glare, letting me know that he heard, but then he leads his demons outside to join the fight, too. "Remember! No killing!" I call behind them. I hear multiple sets of grumbled complaints.

"Come on!" I say, tugging Lex behind me.

Running outside, my heart leaps with hope when I see the angels and demons making short work of the prince's forces. There may not be very many of the Veil Major entities, but they're freaking powerful. But then, I suppose when you hold the powers of hell and heaven, you would be.

The demons round up huge groups of soldiers with

flaming circles of fire, and then make quick work of knocking them all over the heads. While grinning. It's a bit gratuitous and...evil? But what can you really expect from demons? The angels are also wasting no time in taking down the fae left and right. The angels come popping up, teleporting to different spots and taking the fae by surprise. Some of them are wielding swords of holyfire that flicker in white flames, and I watch as Raziel blasts hundreds of the fae soldiers with the white light of the heavens, temporarily blinding them in an instant.

Huh. Impressive.

Not that I'll tell him that. He is one pompous seraph.

Now that I see them in action, I'm actually realizing how much I should not have ever poked and prodded them. They're super scary.

My eyes dart around, but I know we should move so we're not so out in the open. "Lex, I need to find my genfins."

"Send me back to the Veil," she says stoically. "I'll search for them and return to you."

Nodding, I push her back to the Veil and then run back over to Okot. He's still sleeping, but his eyes are moving rapidly behind his lids.

I press my palms against his cheeks. "Okot, please snap out of it," I plead. "Fight the mind control. Please. I need you back."

He doesn't stir, and it breaks my heart just a little. There's a raging battle going on, everything is coming to a head, and I could really use my strong, gentle giant of a bull man to wake up and be my mate again.

Just like I did when I went invisible, I crawl up next to him and lie down in the crook of his body. I bury my head into his neck and, even still asleep, his head turns at the movement.

The battle rages around us. Smoke, shouts, explosions of power, ringing of swords—all of it is a cacophony of conflict that rings in my ears and makes my body tremble with fear.

"I need you," I admit, holding him tight.

I breathe him in, my eyes closing with the spiced scent. Just smelling him again eases my dread. I can't explain it exactly, but it ties me to him somehow—it grounds me in a way I don't understand. I smell him, and all I feel is—I'm home.

"Please, Okot," I say again, feeling his hot breath as I press my neck against his nose. "Please."

And then, at the next rise of his chest, his breathing changes.

Instead of the slow, steady breath of sleep, I feel and hear him take a huge inhale. His breath catches on it, and he makes a low noise that I feel in his chest more than I actually hear.

Before I can react, his hands suddenly shoot up to my head and back, pinning me in place. He rolls, and suddenly I'm beneath him and his body is poised over me, his face buried into the crook of my neck.

His nose presses against my skin, right beneath my ear, and the long, slow inhalation he takes in makes his entire body shudder.

Then I hear two of the best words ever spoken in any language.

"My beloved."

CHAPTER 52

Those two words are a jolt to my system. They echo in my head over and over again. *My beloved, my beloved, my beloved.*

I thought I'd never hear those words again.

I suddenly explode into movement. I turn my head, shoving my pink hair aside, and blink up to see Okot looking back down at me. His eyes aren't pure black and full of hate anymore. Now, I can see the bright red rims pulsing with life once again, and it makes my own eyes fill.

"Okot!"

I wrap my arms around him and pull him down against me, my heart breaking and bursting all at once. I feel every kind of emotion there is to feel. His lips come against mine, soft but resolute in his desire for me. When he cradles his hand around my neck and runs his thumb against my collarbone, I nearly swoon. *There he is,* I think to myself. *My mate is back.*

I think we both realize I'm crying at the same time, because he pulls back and holds my face in his huge palms. "I…was…dreaming of you," he says slowly, his black brow slightly furrowed with confusion as he studies every inch of my face. "But the dream felt just out of reach, and trying to wake up felt even further."

"The king and prince have been poisoning you with mind-control tea," I quickly explain, and his expression darkens.

"I…remember. Bits and pieces. Did I…hurt you?"

My mouth opens but then quickly shuts. "Umm…"

His hands immediately drop from touching me, and he gets to his feet. I scramble up after him, but when I reach for him, he takes a step back. "I hurt you."

The look on his face and the way he says it sends a dagger straight through my heart. "Okot, no. Don't do this. Don't. It wasn't your fault."

His red, pulsing eyes drop down to my neck. It's like he can see his hands wrapped around it again from when he was choking me. "I laid hands on you. Hurt you. Made you cry."

I shake my head adamantly and try to move toward him again, but for every step I move forward, he takes one step back. "It wasn't you. You were being controlled."

"Your genfins should have killed me. I have brought shame upon our mate bond. I do not deserve to be in your covey."

I can see it. I can see the tortured look in his face. I can see that he wants to leave. He totally believes that he's unworthy of me. He's so disgusted with himself that he can barely look at me.

Now, maybe if this were happening in a different time, maybe if there wasn't a raging battle going on around us, or maybe if I didn't have some demonesque traits running through my body, I would react differently.

331

But right now? I get freaking pissed. I even start to smoke a little.

I march forward and jab a steaming finger into his chest. "Now you listen here, you big-headed bull. You are *not* leaving my covey. You are my mate. So you choked me a bit. So what? Some people like that kind of thing," I point out. "I'm *fine*. You are going to stay right here, sniff me, and call me your beloved until the end of time, or so help me, Okot, I will go full on demonesque on your ass and trap you in a ring of fire until you see reason."

His clothes singe a bit from where my finger is jabbing him, and when I notice him grimace slightly, I quickly drop my hand. "Sorry. Demon powers have a crazy kick to them. Now, pull on your big girl panties and ovary it up. We're mates, and we have a war to win."

He blinks at me and runs a hand through his gorgeous bright red mohawk. "I…have no idea what that means."

"It means kiss me right now because I missed the freaking heck out of you."

He stares at me. There are only inches between us, but it feels like so much more. I hold my breath, waiting to see what he'll do. If he rejects me right now, it might kill me a little. I meant what I said about not letting him go, but I so badly want him to choose to forgive himself and stay. I just want things to go back to the way they were before the prince messed everything up.

I see the hesitation in his face. Okot may look huge and mean, but he's actually incredibly kind and loyal and honorable. So I know the fact that he laid hands on me is despicable to him. I see him warring with himself about whether or not he deserves to stay with me. His fists clench at his sides, like he wants to touch me but is denying himself.

A huge booming noise sounds, causing me to fall into him. He catches me easily, keeping me steady on my feet, and we look at the huge blast of power that exploded into a contingent of genfins.

He keeps a protective hold around my waist. "I must get you out of here."

I shake my head. "We can't leave."

Before he can argue, I call to Lex. She appears, looking somewhat bedraggled. "They're heading your way," she says breathlessly. "Belren was able to get the chains off himself and then broke out the others."

Another boom sounds, and a group of genfins and the prince's soldiers land nearly on top of us as they drop from the sky. Okot pulls Lex and me out of the way just in time, and a dead genfin lands at my feet.

But just when the soldiers are about to kill more of them, Jerkahf drops down and cuts off the prince's soldiers with a huge wall of fire. One of them tries to extinguish it with water magic, but it barely makes a spit of protest. I guess hellfire is strong stuff.

The fae soldiers pull up short, and then Jerkahf knocks them out one by one. His entire body is smoking and sparking, and his eyes are glowing with the fires of the underworld. He looks freaking scary.

When the last one is out cold on the hard, dirty ground, I arch a brow at him. "A little much, don't you think?"

"I told you I get to hit them hard," he says with an unapologetic shrug before taking off into the sky again.

I can see from my vantage point that the battle is all but over. The angels and demons are rounding the last of the mind-controlled soldiers up, the genfins are counting their dead, and I see Prince Elphar himself being restrained by two angels. The sight makes me smile in victory.

Ronak, Evert, Sylred, and Belren come walking up to us, and I breathe out a sigh of relief.

But it's too soon.

Because the prince suddenly blasts out a massive ball of raw, vicious power. It's so powerful that a sonic boom comes with it, blasting away the angels at his side and making everyone else in a twenty-foot radius go flying back.

"Cupid!"

The prince's furious voice cuts through the distance and makes the hair rise on the back of my neck. He doesn't even sound like a person. The fury in his tone and in his icy eyes is so strong that he's glowing with it. The world shakes with his wrath, and he has eyes only for me.

The blast sends me and Lex stumbling to the ground, and her hands clutch my arms. We struggle to get up, our limbs and wings and hair tangled. Lex finally manages to stand, and I untangle my legs as my face is smashed against the dirt ground. Lex dusts herself off, her wings out and her hair torn loose from her ponytail. She moves to offer a hand down to help me up, but I spot the prince behind her. I see him focus on Lex's pink hair and red wings with narrowed eyes. Power collects in his palm, and then he throws.

Time slows.

I see the power hurtling toward Lex, her back still facing the prince. I try to get up and reach for her to pull her away, but I know I won't get to her in time. I open my mouth to send her back to the Veil, but all I get out is her name, and then it hits.

The raw power hits with a blinding light and heat so

intense that, for a moment, I'm sure it must be scorching us all alive. I feel her body fall on top of mine, and the ringing in my ears makes me dizzy with disorientation.

With rising horror, I push at her until I can sit up, but when I'm able to see, my heart stops.

Lex is...alive.

She's sitting up, looking back, and I follow her horrified gaze to see the prone form lying on the ground.

"Oh my gods. Belren."

CHAPTER 53

*M*y mates are at my side in an instant, pulling me and Lex to our feet, but my eyes stay locked on the Horned Hook.

"He...he jumped in front of me."

I turn at the sound of Lex's wobbly voice. She's shaking from head to toe, her eyes wide with shock.

I move to take her hand, but she rushes forward and falls beside Belren. Whatever she finds makes her cover her face with her hands and start to cry.

My eyes move up and lock onto the prince. He realizes his mistake at aiming for the wrong cupid and hitting the wrong person entirely, and his eyes move to meet mine.

There's a moment there where we're just staring at each other as if no one else in the realm exists. It's just him and me. The hater and the lover. The prince and the cupid. We both know that this is it. One of us won't be walking away this time.

We move toward each other.

He collects magic in his hands.

I draw out a Love Arrow and have it nocked faster

than I blink. If I ever needed some luck powers, now would be the time. Just as I think it, my eyes tingle with power.

Come on, lady luck stuff, don't fail me now.

We both aim.

And then we let loose.

Time is slow and yet fast. I watch as his power comes hurtling for me, but my focus is on my own weapon. My eyes continue to tingle, until I can barely keep them open from the burn that takes over. But I keep my gaze locked on my arrow, and then I see it go straight through his heart.

I only get a heartbeat of satisfaction as I watch it pierce his flesh, black smoke and blood exploding on impact as it hits him full force.

But then his magic hits *me* full force, and I go careening backwards.

And then, everything goes black.

CHAPTER 54

OKOT

I watch as my mate stalks toward the prince with a look of determination on her face. Her pink hair is flying around wildly, and her red wings are spread majestically behind her. In this moment, she doesn't look like the sweet, fun female she is. No, in this moment, she looks like someone ready to exact vengeance.

She reaches behind her and palms an arrow and her bow, lining them up without ever faltering a step as she continues forward. She looks like a beautiful goddess—an angel of love and retribution. She looks so otherworldly that it makes my heart ache.

But panic takes over the awe when I see the prince collect his raw, offensive magic in his hands. I've seen him place a single finger of magic on someone and suck the life right out of them. Hitting her with that much magic... it will kill her.

I'm moving before I can blink, and I notice the genfins moving, too. We're all rushing forward, ready to defend her with our life. Ready to die for her.

But we're too far away, and she's too quick.

The moment she lets the arrow loose, the prince hurls his power at her. I watch, filled with horror, as the power slams into her. Her arrow pierces him at the same time, and both of their bodies go flying back before landing in a heap on the hard-packed dirt.

My heart thumps with so much fear that I cannot breathe.

My beloved is not moving.

I'm almost to her when I see the guard, Gammon, out of the corner of my eye. He's coming up behind the genfins, aiming to catch them unaware.

I already let my mate down. I let myself get captured on the princess's mission and allowed myself to be open to mind-control manipulations. That's something that I have to live with for the rest of my life. Every time I blink my eyes, a new recollection comes of when I was a mere puppet being pulled on taut strings. The memory of my hands wrapped around her throat as I squeezed the breath out of my mate…I am haunted by it.

I won't let her get hurt again, or anyone else in our covey. And this guard, Gammon? He already laid hands on my mate once. I made sure he paid for that, with the stub of an arm he now has. He never saw me that night I cut it from him, but he knows it was me. I made sure of that. I told him if he ever laid a finger on my mate again, I wouldn't just take a hand. I'd take his life.

The bastard made sure to make my life a living hell while I was under the prince's control. He's a coward, which is made even more clear when he raises his sword to run the blond genfin through the back. I see red and unleash my bull.

My lamassu form ripples beneath my skin. In an

339

instant, I change into my animal, and then I'm nearly two tons of solid mass, huge horns, and a massive wingspan.

Gammon turns his head when he catches movement out of the corner of his eye, but I'm too fast. His face pales, and he doesn't even have time to swing his sword against me before I'm charging at him head-on.

My bull horns catch him in the middle, impaling him with satisfying force. I toss my head back, sending his body flying. I run at his collapsed form on the ground, snorting my breath in his face as blood oozes from his chest and abdomen. My bull breathes at him, roaring and gnashing his teeth.

Gammon chokes on the blood flooding his insides, making a wet, gurgling sound. My horns drip with his blood, landing in droplets on his face. With one last crackled breath, he dies, and my bull snorts in satisfaction.

"Somebody get the fucking lamassu over here!"

I swing my head around and see the three genfins are poised over our mate. She's still not moving. Shame and fear ripple through me, and I shift back into my normal form in an instant. The prince's body is unmoving as well, a perfectly aimed arrow sticking out of his heart, and a puddle of blood beneath him.

I run to her, kneeling beside her with the others. Tears fill my eyes, and I rest my forehead against hers.

"My beloved," I choke out.

But she can't hear me.

The genfins are growling, their animals whining, their hands touching, as if we can rouse her, but nothing works. When I place my hand over the spot where her heart is, I don't feel it beating.

I've always felt her. Even when she was in the Veil,

even before our mating bond was solidified, I had a sense of her. Her presence has always been ingrained inside of me. I don't understand it, and perhaps I never will, but there's no doubt in my mind that she was meant for me.

I won't fail her again.

She managed to bring me back, so I, alongside her genfins, will do the same for her. If ever there was a moment where she needed us, it's now. She needs her mates to anchor her and pull her back home. So that's what we'll do. No matter how long it takes.

$\mathcal{I}$ remember when I first came to the afterlife.

I floated. For a long time. Just like I'm doing now.

There was a lot of nothing. A lot of waiting for nothing. A lot of *being* nothing. I have no way of knowing how long I waited in that nothing, because then there was just suddenly *something*.

Something that pulled me.

I'd forgotten about that until right now. Now that I'm stuck in the nothing again, I remember. Because that same pull is here again.

I'm drawn through the ether until I'm surrounded by four solid shadows. I can't see bodies or faces—just looming shapes around me. But inside those shadows are floating threads, and those threads, I realize, are trying to reach for me.

The threads wind and blow and float around, and all the while, I can feel them calling to me. When I look down at my own shadowed form, I see a similar knotted thread straining to reach back. It's blackened and wilted-looking, but it's there.

I know that if my thread can just touch them, everything will be alright. I don't know how or why, but it's the only sure thought I have.

It takes great effort to reach for them. It takes every ounce of strength and willpower that I have. They reach for me, too, pulsing with life in shades of white, and the closer I get, the more my own thread begins to glow again, too.

The moment the threads touch, I'm yanked out of the nothing.

CHAPTER 56

$\mathcal{M}$y eyes blink open and I see four shadowed figures above me. Is something glowing? I blink again, letting my eyes adjust, and my vision clears enough to see my four mates staring down at me.

There's a collective sigh that escapes each of their mouths, and then Evert is cupping my face, looking stern. "Don't you ever fucking do that again."

He sounds angry, but I can see the fear in his eyes.

I move to sit up, and Sylred and Okot help me manage it. I look around, seeing that I'm in an unfamiliar room. The bed is large and trimmed with white and gold embellishments. The stone floor is polished, but the painted walls are somewhat tarnished with age. There's an open window to my right, and I can hear birds singing to the dawn.

Okot sees the question in my eyes and says, "You're in my home," he explains. "You've been here for three days."

"The bonds," I say, my throat scratchy from disuse. "They pulled me back to you. I felt it."

Sylred nods. "Remember what Plik and Plak said? Your life is tied to ours. You don't die without us."

I nod slowly, trying to catch up. My mind whirls with memories, and when I start remembering the battle, my eyes shoot up to Ronak.

"Belren?"

The guys exchange a look, and then slowly, Ronak shakes his head. "He was dead on impact."

"No." My hand covers my mouth in shock. I can't believe he jumped in front of Lex and took the prince's blast.

"I'm sorry."

"Where is she?" I ask.

"She's here," Sylred answers, knowing I'm asking about Lex. "I'll go get her."

He disappears out of the room, and even though I'm afraid of the answer to my next question, I have to ask it.

"The prince. Did I..."

"You did," Evert says with pride. "You killed that asshole with a Love Arrow straight through his fucking heart. Poetic justice, if you ask me."

Ronak adds, "Genfins burned his body and dumped his charred corpse off the edge of the island. A ritual of disgrace for his acts against faekind."

I run a hand through my hair, but even though I've been flung around and then stuck in a bed for three days, my fingers don't get caught on any tangles. I have a feeling my sweet Okot tended to me while I was out.

"The prince is finally dead. But what about the king?"

"Dead, too. They found him in the crops. He drained himself by using too much magic."

I'm glad they're dead, but I don't feel any real sense of relief. Instead, I just feel tired.

"And the princess?"

"She's gone," Ronak answers with an angry shake of his head. "There are scouts looking for her, but she's nowhere to be found. The hearth hobs left with her, and we're almost positive she took the female, Benicia, with her." Ronak runs a hand over his beard. "That bastard Chaucel is unaccounted for, too."

Part of me is furious with the princess for betraying us. And yet, another part is sympathetic to her, because I felt how much she loved that female fae, and who knows what I would have done in her shoes? If the prince had my mates, I might have betrayed the rebellion, too. You'll do a lot of things for the ones you love. Even bad things. Good people are capable of bad choices, just like bad people are capable of good. There is no certainty when it comes to individuals.

"Who's running the kingdom?" I ask.

"Well, there were no other crowned heirs. A few high fae nobles have attempted to take the throne, but the rebellion shot them down. There's to be a vote held soon."

Well, that's good. Hopefully, the next monarchs will be less...psychotic.

"Has the mind control worn off yet for the rest of the soldiers?"

"It's getting there. More and more come out of the fog every day. Until it's completely worn off, we have people watching them."

"A lot of fae died."

It's not a question, because I don't have to ask. I know that there was a lot of death. A lot of unnecessary death. If the prince hadn't been such a needy sociopath, none of this would have happened.

When Sylred returns with Lex in tow, the guys gracefully

346

bow out, giving me privacy. She's dressed in the most modest fae clothing I've ever seen. The neckline to her dress goes all the way up to her throat, and the bottom flares out from the waist and ends in some frills at her ankles. Her hair is sleek and straight as usual, swung up in a perfect ponytail. She has all the elements of her usual perfect, cupid self.

Except for her eyes.

I take in the puffiness around them that tells me about her tears. I see the dark circles under her eyes and know that she hasn't slept. I notice the bloodshot lines reaching for her irises like they're trying to leech the color out.

The brave face she puts on for me breaks my heart. Without warning, I stand and then pull her into a hug. She freezes for a moment, and I wonder if this is the first time she's ever been touched.

"Lex?" I ask, pulling away. I don't want to push her, but I wish she would talk to me so I can know what she's feeling.

She barely meets my eyes before dropping her gaze to the floor. "He jumped in front of me," she says, her tone full of confusion. "I don't know why he did that."

I shake my head. "He surprised me a lot," I admit. "He tried to come across as this super mysterious thief who was only out for himself, but he wasn't really."

"He died," she says flatly. "For me. I don't understand."

I give her a small smile. "Sometimes we don't understand why people do the things that they do. But he *did* do it, and so all that I can do to honor his decision is be grateful to him for his sacrifice." I reach down and grab her hand, squeezing it in mine. "And I am grateful, Lex. I'm so glad you're okay."

She gives me a watery smile and then backs away,

disentangling my hand from hers. "If you want some more time off..."

She shakes her head quickly. "No. Please. Send me back to the Veil. I have so much work to do. I'm behind on Love Matches, my Arrow surplus, don't even get me started on the Flirt-Touch deficit. I also am severely neglecting my Cupid of the Month goals, not to mention I'm not sure Sev should be left to his own devices for much longer..."

She's all business now, putting on the professional cupidity mask. I want to insist she take more time to process, but I can see that she needs this. She needs to stay busy, so I nod.

"Okay. Do you want to go tonight or—"

"Now," she cuts me off quickly. Realizing her jumpiness, she takes a breath and smooths down her dress before clearing her throat. "Now, please, Madame Cupid."

With a nod, I push her back into the Veil, and then I'm left alone with pink smoke to keep me company, hoping that I've done the right thing.

CHAPTER 57

It's been a week since the prince was defeated, and we're back on the genfin island, working on repairs. Well, my mates are actually working on repairs. I'm sitting in the street with my back against the building, watching as all four of them hammer, saw, lift, and install materials as they rebuild the town. And they're shirtless. All four of them.

Sweat glistens off their skin, and I have no shame as I sip on my fairy wine from a straw and watch them.

"How does he have that many muscles?" Mossie asks beside me.

Without pulling my eyes away from my mates as they work, I ask, "Which one?"

She tilts her head in thought and steals a sip from my bottle before passing it back. "Well, all of them have impressive muscles. But the big mohawk guy and mister Strength over there have muscles on their muscles."

I sigh appreciatively and take another long suck from the straw. "Yeah."

She's currently taking a break, while I've been

grounded. Just because I made one roof cave in, they all freaked out and told me to sit out here where I can't get hurt and wait until they're done.

Mossie, along with many other fae, volunteered to come here to help clean up the wreckage from the prince's attack. It's slow work, but with all of the different fae breeds working together, the genfin island will be put back together again. The dead have all been honored and buried, and the people are trying to move on, though it will take time.

Mossie takes one more drink and then stands. "Alright, you continue to ogle your mates, while I go clean."

"Let me help," I say, jumping to my feet.

She holds out her hands to stop me like she's fending off a monster. "No! No. You stay right here."

"Oh, come on, I only knocked over one bucket!" I protest.

She pets the flower petals on her head before tossing the vines over her shoulders. "Yeah, but 'knocked over' is an understatement. You actually tripped over the bucket, sending soapy water all over the floor, and then when that poor fae tried to catch you, you slipped and smacked him in the face with a handful of your weird sandman dust. Then when *he* fell, passed out cold and muttering about sex dreams, you tried to catch *him* and ended up face-first in the crotch of a genfin elder. Whose robes you then accidentally lit on fire with your demonesque fire-touch, as you called it."

I glare at her. "Yeah, I was there. I don't need the recap."

She giggles. "I'll see you at the feast. Oh, and before I forget, I have two new names for you to add to my love list."

I shake my head at her, suppressing a small smile. At the rate she's going, she'll have a harem of a hundred different fae. "Things with your arid earth sprite not going well?" I ask.

"I'm quite sure I'm nearly making him almost jealous," she says matter-of-factly.

"Oh. Good."

She nods and gives me a wave. "See you later!"

I'm left alone to enjoy the view of my mates again, and when Evert bends down to grab a piece of wood for the wall, my head tilts with the motion, giving me a delectable view of his toned ass.

"Seriously hit the mate lottery," I mumble to myself as I take another sip of wine.

"You did."

My head turns up in surprise at the voice, and I see Viessa, the genfin female, settle in beside me. We sit there for a moment in total awkward silence. I shift nervously beside her and take another sip of wine because I don't know what else to do with myself. We both continue to watch the guys work, which is also uncomfortable as hell. Is she watching how Ronak's biceps flex as he lifts that huge piece of stone? Is she appreciating Evert's rear end or Sylred's tanned skin? I don't know whether I should ask her what the heck she's doing.

Besides my four guys rebuilding the shop across the way, I recognize her mates working on the street, refilling the holes blasted into the dirt and laying down cobblestones on top.

After another moment of tense silence, Viessa holds a hand out for the wine. "May I?"

"Umm, sure."

I pass the bottle over and she takes a long, long, *long* sip.

I raise my brows but don't say anything as she passes it back.

I steal sideways looks at her. She's beautiful and strong looking, and I can see why the guys thought about making her their mate. I don't like it one bit. I also don't like the wafts of longing I'm still feeling from her.

"I'd like to ask a favor from you," she says, surprising me.

I turn to look at her. "Okay," I say tentatively.

She meets my eyes for the first time, and I see the heartache there. "I'd like...I mean, I'd appreciate it if you would possibly think about granting me the honor of one of your Love Arrows."

My brow furrows in confusion. "What?"

Shame crosses over her face as she tilts her head toward her mates. "They're good genfins. Strong. Caring. Loyal. I'm lucky to have them."

She says it in a matter-of-fact tone, but there's pain there, too. When she turns back to face me again, her eyes shine with unshed tears.

"But I don't love them. I've tried. I can't," she says with a pitiful shrug. "And they deserve better. I want to love them so much," she says, surprising me with her vehemency. "But..."

Her eyes drift back to my genfins, and I understand.

"But you still love my mates," I guess.

She nods. "I don't want to love them anymore. And female to female, just know, I would never try to come between you. I can see how much they adore you and how much you adore them. That's what I want. I want that kind of love in my own covey. I know you don't owe me anything. You might even hate me. But please," she says, her voice pleading now. "If you can find it in your heart to help me…"

"I'll help you," I tell her with a determined nod. "But you have to have a fondness already there. You have to *want* to love them," I warn her.

She nods emphatically. "I do. I swear on my life I do. Please," she says, gripping my hand. "Please help me love them the way that they deserve."

I don't even hesitate. "Of course."

A look of relief crosses her face. "Thank you."

"Close your eyes."

Immediately, she does as I ask, and her lids flutter closed.

I lift the Love Arrow from my back and take her hand. Using the sharp tip of the arrow, I pierce her fingertip.

"Now go to them," I say quietly.

Still with her eyes closed, I help her to her feet and guide her toward her covey. As soon her mates see her, all three of them smile and move to greet her. In seconds, she's enveloped in their presence, and I whisper in her ear. "Open your eyes."

She does, and I slip away, trailing Flirt-Touches across her back as I go.

I wait on the other side of the road, watching.

She beams up at them, each of them touching some part of her, and when her genfin tail lifts and starts tangling in the tails of her mates, I feel it.

It's newly born, and it's fragile, but it's there.

She meets my eye and beams, mouthing a thank you before the four of them walk away. And the smile on my own face doesn't fade for the rest of the day. Because I think I might have just made the most significant Love Match of my entire cupid life.

CHAPTER 58

"*Y*ou're in a good mood," Sylred notes as we eat at the feast later that night.

Everyone is gathered in the town square, the huge egg building behind us with a new roof installed on it. There's a bonfire with roasts turning over it, and people are talking and enjoying themselves in quiet gaiety.

"Why wouldn't I be in a good mood?" I ask as I take another bite of the tender meat. "I have all four of my mates here, the prince can't terrorize us anymore, and I'm eating food. Plus, the other genfins aren't threatening to kill me anymore."

It's true. Even that one *really* mad genfin. I saw him earlier, and he gave me a grudging nod. It was basically like an enthusiastic fist bump of solidarity. We're totally cool now. I guess being the cupid who killed the crazy-ass prince has its perks.

I'm sitting between Ronak's legs on the grass while Evert is on my left and Okot on my right. Sylred is sitting directly in front of me, our legs tangled together. All four of them are touching me in some small way, except for Ronak, whose very *not small* erection is digging into my back.

Okot is careful with me—quieter, more restrained. I know he still feels guilty for attacking me, and it's going to take time to work past it.

As I'm finishing up the last of my food, a familiar fire fae comes bounding forward. His smoking scalp curls into the air above him, and sparks of fire spit out of his fingertips. I tense and sit up at his approach. I try to shake my head and wave him away, but the dummy just keeps coming.

Feeling the rigidness of my body, Ronak leans forward, pulling me against him with a super possessive hold. The four of my mates stare at the fire fae where he stops in front of me.

"Who the fuck are you?" Evert snaps.

"Ferno," he answers, keeping his flaming eyes locked on me.

He's wearing a dopey look on his face, and he's clutching a bouquet of... "Is that beavertail cactus?" I ask.

He nods proudly and holds it out. I blink at him and look down at the hand that clutches them. The thorns are digging into his palms, making him bleed in several places, but he doesn't even seem to notice.

"The thorns reminded me of the way your arrow pierced me so sweetly," he says with a sigh. "And the pink blossom reminded me of your hair and how it would look fanned out over my chest after an intense lovemaking session."

I groan and bury my head in my hands.

"What. The. Actual. Fuck," Evert growls.

"Okay, okay. I can explain," I say, looking over at my guys.

"You'd better do it fucking quick, Scratch."

"It's silly, really. You're totally gonna laugh," I say nervously. "I accidentally Love-Arrowed him and made him fall in love with me."

They don't laugh. Tough crowd.

Ronak sighs. "Will it wear off?"

"Umm…maybe?"

"Fucking hell," Evert curses. "You are in *so* much trouble right now."

"It was an accident! He was trying to attack me. The Love Arrow was all I had."

All four of them growl at the knowledge that Ferno was trying to hurt me. Ferno, still clutching the cactus, continues to grin at me lovingly.

I sigh. "I'll see if I can match him up with someone else."

"You'd better do that soon," Sylred says gently. "Before your other mates end up killing the poor sap."

"I will," I promise.

"Screw off, Flame Fuck," Evert growls. "Our mate will deal with you later."

Ferno just blinks.

"Go on," I tell him. "Take care of those stickers in your hand, and don't pick up cacti anymore. I'll…umm…find you later," I say, cringing at how happy that makes him look.

When he bounds away, I give my mates a sheepish smile. "Those Love Arrows really have some oomph in them, you know?"

Evert points a finger in my face. "No more stabbing

fae with Love Arrows and accidentally making them fall in love with you."

You would think I wouldn't have to hesitate before promising him that, but...you just never know in this damn realm.

CHAPTER 59

*L*eft alone once again, I relax back on my mates, watching the crackling bonfire under the dark cover of night and enjoying the sounds of the other fae's voices rising in the air.

When I yawn, Sylred smiles and takes my now empty plate to set it aside. "I think we should get our mate to bed."

I instantly perk up. "You mean like bed-bed, or are you four finally going to let me play with your penises again?"

I feel a puff of breath on my neck as Ronak sighs. "Don't say play with our penises. It sounds weird."

"You know what sounds weird to me? How every night, you guys keep falling asleep on me without giving me the D!"

Evert looks at me sardonically. "That's because you keep *making* us go to sleep with your dust shit."

"I don't do it on purpose, and that's not the point," I argue.

"What is the point, then?" he challenges.

"The point is, my pink canoe is not floating up enough cum creeks."

All three of my genfins groan. Okot just looks puzzled.

"What is she saying?" he asks.

Evert rolls his eyes. "Fucking lamassu."

I smile and wriggle against Ronak's length, earning a lustful noise in return.

"Stop that," he reprimands.

I smile innocently. "Stop what, Not-First?"

He sighs. "That nickname is going to follow me forever, isn't it?"

"Yep."

When I shift against his hardening erection again, Ronak's hands grip my waist, trying to hold me in place. "If you keep doing that, I will lift up your skirts and sit you over my cock right here, right now."

My eyes widen in excitement. "Oh, exhibitionism! That's on my sex list!"

Evert chuckles beside me. "We really do need to get a copy of this sex list."

"I agree," Sylred pipes in. His tail trails further and further up my leg, and even though it's hidden from view by the skirts of my dress, it feels like everyone can see.

Not that anyone is really paying us any attention. They're all enjoying themselves, talking and eating and drinking. We're in our own quiet corner, further back from the fire and the crowd.

When Sylred's tail flicks against my panties, I inhale sharply, and my center goes red-hot. Of course, that's when I wriggle my bottom against Ronak again, my core seeking the friction it so desperately wants.

Ronak's fingers dig into my hips. "You do that one more time…"

I turn my neck to look at him. And then I hop into Sylred's lap instead.

Ronak blinks at the spot where I'd just been, and then looks over to where I now straddle Sylred. "What just happened?"

"This is happening," I say, and with my arms wrapped around Sylred's neck, I start grinding on his already hard erection.

"What the fuck? If you're gonna hop ship for a different dick, come over and rub that sweet pussy on me, Scratch. I'll take care of that itch for you," Evert says.

But I shake my head, keeping my eyes trained on my sweet, brown-eyed genfin. "Tonight, I'm going to take care of you, Syl. Because you always take care of me."

I see his throat bob as I start to slowly rock on top of him, and I trail a hand down, down, down. When I get to his lap, I dip my fingers into his pocket and pull out the small box he always has stashed there.

His brown eyes flick down at it, but he doesn't say a word as I open it and stick a piece of chocolate in my mouth. With my hands, I reach down and unhook his pants, setting him free.

I can feel Ronak and Evert move on either side of me, but I keep my eyes locked on him. And then I slowly slide down.

The chocolate is warm and melted on my tongue when I dart it out to the head of his cock. Then I open wide and suck him inside, and he groans.

"Fucking hell. She's making his cock her own personal chocolate bar. I don't know whether to be impressed or jealous," Evert says.

"Jealous. Definitely jealous," Sylred says, his voice strained with a groan.

I smile. Well, I mean, I would smile if my mouth weren't currently full of chocolate-covered cock. Which, by the way, is delicious. I totally recommend it.

I lick and suck like a champ, moving my mouth up and down his chocolatey shaft, enjoying every second of it.

Taking him in as far as I can go, I let his cock hit the back of my throat and then swallow, while also reaching down to fondle his balls at the same time. The noise of surprised pleasure that he makes, along with the way that his dick seems to grow even harder, is like I've just earned a gold sticker in sex.

"Gods, Emelle. That mouth of yours is *perfect*."

He reaches forward, but instead of holding my head down on him, he lifts me up. Bunching up my skirt, he moves my panties aside and impales me onto his cock.

"Oh gods, we're doing it," I say excitedly as I begin to bounce up and down on his delicious length. "We're doing it outside while all these fae are around!"

Sylred smiles, gripping my hips as he moves me in the way that he wants. "Like exhibitionism, do you?"

I place my hands on his shoulders to get more leverage. When he thrusts up into me, hitting me right at that perfect spot, my head falls back on a moan. "Mm-hmm. So far, it's really working out great."

"Bloody fucking hell," I hear Evert curse. "Look at her go."

He's right, I am impressive right now. I'm bouncing up and down on Sylred so fast, my boobs bouncing in his face and threatening to topple out of my dress. The guys must notice too, because their hands are suddenly all over me, but not one of them actually pulls the fabric down. Just in case someone were to look over, my genfins don't want anyone to get an eyeful of me. They're totally protecting my virtue right now, even as I fuck Sylred in the middle of a public bonfire. It's sweet.

Ronak leans forward and scrapes his beard against the sensitive parts of my neck. "If anyone sees you fucking him right now, I'll have to take you home and teach you a lesson," he growls.

Coals over hellfire, that's hot. "Fuck. Yes, teach me lessons. Lots of lessons. All the lessons in the world," I pant.

The guys chuckle.

I look over my shoulder at Okot, and I see that he's still standing protectively over us, ever my gentle giant. I wish he'd join in, but I know that he's still working through his own things. And while I'll give him time, what I won't do is give him space.

"Okot," I say, and my lamassu immediately turns to face me. I stop bouncing and change my movements to a slow, erotic grind. Okot's eyes become hooded as he takes in the way Sylred's hips move against mine, and the hands flicking at the stiff peak of my nipples through my dress.

"Kiss me," I tell him, my voice husky with want. But he hesitates. "Please. I need you," I admit. And I don't just mean now. I don't just mean physically. I can tell by the look in his eye that he understands exactly what I do mean.

My lamassu mate is before me in an instant, kneeling behind Sylred. He tenderly takes hold of my neck in an almost reverent way and then pulls me in.

The kiss is gentle and worshipping, and I suckle on his tongue and lean against Sylred's chest to get even closer to them. With me on Sylred's lap, Ronak and Evert teasing and stroking my breasts and clit, and Okot's tongue dancing with mine, everything is so

362

perfect that I come with a dazzling orgasm that makes me see stars.

Sylred follows me into the pleasurable oblivion, and I don't come back down for a long while, my face pressed against Sylred's shoulder. When I'm able to move again, I lean up and smile. "How was that?" I ask.

Sylred tucks a piece of my hair behind my ear. "Perfect."

"I'll say," Evert drawls. "Lucky bastard."

"He deserves it," I say, still looking at Sylred. "He's always taking care of me."

Sylred places a kiss on my nose. "I'll take care of you forever."

"I know you will, genfin. Which is why I'll be enjoying many more chocococks in the future."

"She already has a name for it," Evert says dryly.

"Of course she does," Ronak says before getting to his feet and scooping me up in his arms. "Let's go home, little demon."

I wrap my arms around his neck and nod.

"Sure. I look messy, and things are about to get real awkwardly wet," I reply, indicating my lower half.

"You don't look messy," Evert says from beside Ronak as we begin making our way toward our den. "You look good any time, any way. Naked, clothed, dripping with our cum...you're fucking stunning."

"Aww, that was really dirty and lovely."

He nods in affirmation and then elbows Okot. "You hear that? She said I'm *dirty and lovely*," Evert goads. "I'm totally getting my cock sucked next."

At first, I think Okot will ignore him since he's been quieter since our reunion, but then he shrugs and says, "Brag all you want, genfin, but just remember, I mated with her first. And...I have the largest dick," he says, surprising the hell out of me with his sudden playful banter.

Evert chokes out a surprised laugh. He looks at Okot and then claps him on the back. "Fucking lamassu."

Hope surges into me. Yep. I think my mates are going to be just fine.

CHAPTER 60

When we make it back to the den, I clean myself up in the tub and get into bed, where Evert and Ronak pounce on me. Laughing, I make them lie back so that I can kneel between them on the bed. With them flat on their backs, I pull their cocks free and begin to stroke...only to realize that sandlady dust covers my palms.

"Crap!"

It's too late. Their eyes close, their heads flop to the side, and with cocks still stiff and pointing skyward, they fall deeply asleep.

From the other side of Evert, Sylred laughs. "Really? Again?"

I shake my head at my hands like I'm conveying how disappointed I am in their actions. "I was just trying to give a couple handies. This stupid dust is such a cock-blocker."

Sylred lies back, the smile still playing around his lips and making the crinkles around his eyes form. "Maybe you should start wearing gloves to bed."

"I don't need... Actually, that's a good idea."

"Mm-hmm."

Bending his elbow, he tucks his arm under his head and closes his eyes.

"You're just gonna go to sleep?" I ask, still kneeling beside Erection One and Erection Two. "What about them?"

"Their dicks will go down eventually."

I sigh and look at the poor, unused erections. I really gotta get a handle on this sleep dust stuff. I reach down and pull up the sheet to awkwardly cover them. The sheet pokes up and stretches between them like a sporting net.

"Such a waste," I mumble to myself. "I promise I'll try to be better," I say to the passed-out genfins and their erections. It sounds weird to make promises to penises, but they've earned it since this is the fourth time I've done this to them.

Taking me by surprise, Sylred suddenly sits up and pulls me forward with a grip on my chin. He plants a sweet kiss on my lips.

"You are perfect," he says.

I smile and wave off the compliment, but he uses his hold to force me to look at him. "I mean it, Emelle," he says, and the sound of my name rolling off his tongue makes my breath catch. "Ronak and Evert aren't good with words, but I thought you should know. You are everything to us. And your lamassu, too."

I swallow hard, not letting the happy tears that formed fall. "You four are everything to me," I whisper, my heart fluttering when he rubs his thumb across my bottom lip.

With one last sweet kiss, he releases me and lies back down, throwing an arm over his eyes. He falls asleep shortly after, while I'm still hearing the echo of his words, wondering how the hell I got so lucky.

Realizing that Okot has still not come inside, I slip out of bed, careful not to wake Sylred, and pad across the bedroom. I find my lamassu outside in the garden, sitting on the bench and watching the stars. Just like I knew he would be.

I sit down beside him, my skin chilled against the cool night air. He automatically raises his arm and tucks me into his side, enveloping me in his warmth as I burrow closer to him.

We watch the night sky for a while in silence, just like we've done every night this week. But this time, Okot actually starts to talk.

"I felt you before I even knew you existed."

Startled, I turn my face to look at him. The hard planes of his face are softened in the moonlight, and his nose piercing glints silver.

"What do you mean?"

"Lamassus have a very strong bond to their mates, arguably the strongest mate bonds of all fae. So it's not uncommon for us to have a sense of our mates even before we meet them."

Listening to the low timbre of his voice makes me want to curl up inside of his words and live there forever.

"But I felt your bond always, and it was strong. Stronger than what was normal, even for lamassus," he explains, looking down at me.

"What did it feel like?" I ask, my voice caught in a whisper.

He brings his hand up to his chest and taps two fingers against him. "Like a heartbeat." He drums his fingers against his skin in the same cadence as his heart. I can't look away, and I'm hanging on his every word.

"Then I was sent to you. The moment you opened the door, that heartbeat of a bond that had always beat right alongside my own heart suddenly snapped. I smelled your scent, and the air around you was…home. The tapping of the bond settled and then matched with the beating of your heart, and I knew that this bond was something more. Something far deeper than any other of my kind has ever experienced."

He gathers me in his arms and pulls me onto his lap, cradling me against him so that his heart is pressed to my ear. I close my damp eyes and listen to the soft drum of his heart, and it's the sweetest lullaby I've ever heard.

"When I called you my beloved from that first moment I met you, it was because I meant it. You are the most beloved thing to me that has ever existed, and I am in constant awe that you crossed realms and Veils to get to me."

I pick up my head at his reverential words and let my forehead rest against his. His hands tremble slightly as he circles my waist, and the love he feels for me is so strong in this moment that it makes my own body tremble with the force of it.

"I'd cross a thousand realms and go through a thousand more Veils for you, Okot."

I mean every word.

"Can you ever forgive me?"

Leaning back, I look into his eyes and slowly shake my head. His expression falls with shame, but I hold steady. "No. Because there's nothing to forgive. And you and I? We're gonna move on from that now, lamassu. No more holding back. No more hating yourself. No more shame. It. Wasn't. You," I say firmly, my hands gripping his shirt.

"My heart is yours, my beloved. It always has been."

A smile spreads across my face. "Good. Because you've been carrying mine all along."

He kisses me tenderly, our heartbeats drumming as one. "Let's go to bed."

He carries me inside and we climb into the giant bed together, me settling in the middle. As soon as I do, all four of my mates seek me out, even in their sleep, and their limbs tangle around me.

And as I'm here, surrounded by them and their touches, I realize that this is it. This is my perfect love, made up of all five of us, and its worth is inestimable.

I will love them with my entire heart, body, and soul, for as long as I live...and even after that.

Because love? It really *is* the greatest thing you can ever have.

Trust me. I'm a cupid.

The End

EPILOGUE

BELREN

There's nothing.

There is a grimy whiteness all around that is neither light nor shadowed, cool nor warm. There is no land or water or air. I have no body. No sense of touch. No recollection of what came before or if anything is coming after.

But there is one thing in the nothing.

One single, solitary thing that I remember.

Her.

Red wings, serious face, pink hair pulled back tight.

I have no idea who she was. But I remember her in this nothingness.

I don't know how long I'm stuck in this strange existence. Maybe seconds. Maybe decades. Maybe I'm not here at all, and this is all a dream. But then suddenly, the nothingness shifts. And then I feel a pull.

I'm yanked out of this ether of nothing, and the next thing I know, I blink into being.

Confused and shaking, I look down, realizing that I *can* look, and see a body. *My* body. I raise my silver hands in front of my face and then carefully touch my cheeks. Except I don't feel a thing.

My fingers go through me, and I pull them back to study them again and realize that they're slightly see-through.

"What…"

My voice sounds hoarse and loud and not familiar at all.

Who am I?

Where am I?

"Next!"

My head snaps up, and I blink at the sight before me. I'm in a large room, and there are lots of other…translucent bodies around me.

All shapes, sizes, colors, sexes, and I can't be sure if I recognize any of them or not, because I don't even recognize myself.

"Next!" the voice calls out again, sounding irritated.

I look ahead again, only to realize that I'm actually standing in line. Based on the winged female sitting at the desk and glaring at me, I'd say that I'm next and I'm wasting her time.

I step forward, discovering that this translucent body doesn't actually step. It takes some finagling, but I manage to float forward until I'm standing before her.

"You're here to be processed."

I blanch. "What? What does that mean?"

She points to the brochures that are presented on her desk. One of them has an angel on it with the slogan, "Were you good in life? Well, now you can be great!"

My eyes dart to the next brochure over, and I see a

picture of a black-winged demon with the words, "Like it sizzling hot? Come down under for a good time!" When I lean in closer, I read the fine print that says "*Some torturing may apply" underneath.

I frown and look back up at the female. "What is this?"

Sighing, she gives me a look that says she's been asked to explain this far too many times for her liking. And, judging by the length of the line behind me, I suppose she has.

"Welcome to the afterlife," she drawls. "Time to pick your new job."

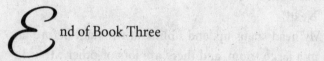

*E*nd of Book Three

Want more of Raven Kennedy?

Check out the phenomenal and addictive Plated Prisoner Series.

A fantasy retelling of the notorious King Midas myth, with a dark and magical twist . . .

And the final epic chapter in the series . . .

GOLD coming December 2023

He just wanted a decent book to read ...

Not too much to ask, is it? It was in 1935 when Allen Lane, Managing Director of Bodley Head Publishers, stood on a platform at Exeter railway station looking for something good to read on his journey back to London. His choice was limited to popular magazines and poor-quality paperbacks – the same choice faced every day by the vast majority of readers, few of whom could afford hardbacks. Lane's disappointment and subsequent anger at the range of books generally available led him to found a company – and change the world.

'We believed in the existence in this country of a vast reading public for intelligent books at a low price, and staked everything on it'
Sir Allen Lane, 1902–1970, founder of Penguin Books

The quality paperback had arrived – and not just in bookshops. Lane was adamant that his Penguins should appear in chain stores and tobacconists, and should cost no more than a packet of cigarettes.

Reading habits (and cigarette prices) have changed since 1935, but Penguin still believes in publishing the best books for everybody to enjoy. We still believe that good design costs no more than bad design, and we still believe that quality books published passionately and responsibly make the world a better place.

So wherever you see the little bird – whether it's on a piece of prize-winning literary fiction or a celebrity autobiography, political tour de force or historical masterpiece, a serial-killer thriller, reference book, world classic or a piece of pure escapism – you can bet that it represents the very best that the genre has to offer.

Whatever you like to read – trust Penguin.